TRIALS OF BLOOD

THE COMPLETE SERIES

REBECCA ROYCE

Flame

Ebook 978-1-960447-01-2

Print 978-1-960447-04-3

Hardback 978-1-960447-05-0

Copyright @ 2023 by Rebecca Royce

Cover art by Artscandre

Content Editing: Virginia Nelson

Copy Editing: Jennifer Jones at Bookends Editing

Final Proof Editing: Viv Jackson

Formatting: Ripley Proserpina

ISBN 978-1-960447-08-1

Published by Rebecca Royce

www.rebeccaroyce.com

❀ Created with Vellum

SERVANT

For Vanessa. Taken from us too soon. Gone but never forgotten.

FOREWORD

Dearest Reader,

This book has a cliffhanger. It is the first of three books. At the end of the third book, you'll get a happy ending, I promise. I ask you to trust me to get Maci to her Happily Ever After.

Because this book starts when she is 16, there is lots of longing but no sex. It is what we call a slow burn in book one, but by book two, you'll get to the love scenes. I promise.

These characters woke me from sleep demanding their story be told. They interrupted my writing schedule and altered the writing outcome for this entire year. I had no choice but to tell you their love story. I hope you love them as I do, but if this doesn't seem like the kind of read you're interested in, please feel free to return the book. I completely understand.

This is a Reverse Harem, Paranormal Romance with certain scenes (mostly toward the end of book 1 and onward into books 2 and 3) that might trigger some readers. You have been warned.

All my best
  RR

THE BEGINNING
AGES 16-18

1

MACI

I t was impossible to study when Rowan Kennedy was in the room. Not because he was gorgeous—*arguably he was, but I had no time for such fleeting fantasies with finals next week*—but because I wasn't certain that he wasn't about to set something on fire. The last thing I needed was to be the one to put out such a mess in the middle of the library the week before I'd have to take the hardest tests of my life so far. Junior year just sucked.

I had half an hour left before I had to go to work, where I'd spend the next four hours loading and unloading boxes at the grocery store. I was lucky to get that job, considering my mother had lost hers there in such a huge way. That was true at almost every place in a ten-mile radius. I was pretty sure the manager took pity on me.

I lifted my eyes to watch Rowan and his group laughing way too loudly at the table across from me. It was always the five of them together. Rowan seemed to be their leader, but I didn't really know for sure. They never bothered me and I didn't mess with them, which meant, other than knowing their names, that they were a grade ahead of me in school, and they looked ridiculously cute in the way rich people seemed to be, I'd never interacted with them at all.

Rowan Kennedy. Ace Monroe. Caesar Douglass. Griffin Gaines. Tanner Eastwick.

From day one, they'd been each other's best friends and completely uninterested in the rest of the world, at least according to the gossips I could sometimes hear in low voices in the bathroom.

Not that I wanted the guys' attention. I really didn't. In one and a half years, I'd leave this town that time forgot—as I liked to think of it—and get the hell out of Kenton, Idaho. I planned to head anywhere else I could go. Someplace with actual working cellular data that didn't require me to stand on top of our trailer to get a signal.

Even then, it only worked sometimes.

Lately, though, the five richest guys in town had started causing problems—big problems, like setting things on fire. Publicly and in front of people who should probably have put them in jail for doing so. Only nothing ever seemed to happen to them. Maybe they got away with it because Ace's father was the mayor? If I set fire to something, like Rowan had, or trashed cars up and down main street in broad daylight, the way Caesar had, I would've been arrested.

The police chief never held back before arresting anyone from my trailer park, particularly my mother. I chewed on my lip as I thought about her. She might even be in jail right then, for all I knew.

Griffin threw a book at Tanner's head, who then jumped to his feet like he was going to pound on him.

"Stop." I spoke the word before I could overthink it, or I would've never addressed them at all. Part of them leaving me alone, so I never had to bother with them, meant I actually had to follow through—I never spoke to them or brought attention to myself.

But I'd just broken my own unspoken rule. I swallowed. *Whoops.*

Five sets of eyes regarded me all at once, Rowan and Ace having to turn around to do so.

Oh well. In for a penny, in for a pound. "Sorry. Look, this is the library." *Thank you, Captain Obvious.* Internally, I winced. "And we have finals next week. I know that you guys are pretty much done with school. Graduating in a few weeks." Griffin was the valedictorian, if I wasn't mistaken. "But I have to get this done, so whatever you're going to do, could you take it outside? Please? Like, destroy something outside, because I have a very limited amount of time to actually learn what I need to know for this test. Please?"

According to all of the YA books I'd read, this would be the part where one of them would suddenly become my bully. They'd decide they needed to pick on me, and we would fall into a destructive pattern that would leave me ultimately destroyed. At least until I rose up to become some sort of spy or something.

Maybe I'd read too much fiction because that wasn't what happened next.

Rowan nodded. "My apologies. You're right."

I swallowed. *Well, that is unexpected. What am I supposed to say now?* "Okay."

"You're Maci Green, right?" Griffin rose from his seat. "You're in my math class, which makes you two years ahead in math."

He took the seat across from me, pulling the chair back with a squeak. Griffin towered over his friends by a few inches. Long, lean, and fit, he had huge green eyes to go with the blond hair he pulled up in a bun on top of his head. In addition to being his class valedictorian, he was also captain of the track team. I never had time for extracurriculars, not in addition to my work schedule. I envied him his time and the way that he felt perfectly confident answering questions in class. Sometimes, he even argued with the teacher because the way they were teaching was wrong.

As though he didn't care at all if he might be considered rude.

"That's me." I looked down at my book. "Sorry to have interrupted. I just..."

He held up his hand. "You were right. Rowan apologized. We're all sorry. I've always wanted to talk to you. But for reasons, I didn't. Now that you've talked to us, I've decided to start doing it."

From their table, Ace groaned and got up to join us. "If you've never talked to Griffin before, then you don't know he's an arrogant ass. Give him two seconds, and he's going to tell you about how he's the *valedictorian*."

What was funny about how Ace said it was that the other three all said it with him, like they were reciting it together because they'd heard it so much. I tried and failed not to grin at that, which must have been the right move because Ace grinned back at me.

He was also tall—well, it wasn't hard to be taller than me at my tiny five feet—but I'd have put him at six feet, at least. He had dark hair and darker eyes. He took a seat next to Griffin. "You wanted to study, but now you have our attention. We have to talk to you because if a pretty girl gives you attention, as a male member of our species, we are obligated to at least spend a few minutes talking to her."

Griffin rolled his eyes. "I might be an arrogant ass, but you're a ridiculous flirt." He put out his hand. "I'm Griffin; that's Ace."

Thoughts of my studies rapidly fled. I'd never had so much attention all at once before. One by one, they sat down at my table, surrounding me, with Rowan taking the last seat to my left and Tanner to my right. Caesar sat on the very end of the table.

Griffin pointed at all of them. "Rowan. Caesar. Tanner."

I nodded. "I know who you all are. I mean...everyone does."

Rowan leaned toward me. "Do they? Why? We're completely normal. Nothing to remark on or write home about."

"Um, you've been setting things on fire."

Caesar shoved at his shoulder. "Yes, you have."

"Like you haven't been..." He waved his hand. "Good point, we need to be more discreet." He closed his eyes for a second. "Even when it's hard." Having stated that, he lifted his lids. "Are we bothering you, Maci? You can tell us to leave." He put his arm across the back of my chair. "We'd probably even go."

Tanner shook his head. "Speak for yourself. I'm going to stay here and get to know Maci. Pretty name."

"My mother thought she was naming me after the department store. She always thought they had the prettiest shoes, but she didn't know how to spell it. So...that's me."

Caesar lifted an eyebrow. "Great story, actually."

I couldn't believe I'd just told it. I never explained my mother's thinking in naming me. "Listen, I have to... I have to study, then I have to go to work, but I really like talking to you." Since my best friend Stacy's mother had committed suicide and she'd gone to live with her grandmother in Iowa, I really didn't have friends to talk to in a real or fun way. There was the way that I spoke to my teachers, the way that I addressed my superiors at work, and then there was the little I communicated with my mother.

But my peers didn't talk to me.

Unfortunately, I was just one of the lost trailer kids in town. We didn't do much or go places and weren't thought of by most people. Even within that community, they hated my mother and left me alone.

Always alone.

"Where do you work?" Rowan hadn't moved his arm or indicated in any way that he was going to do as I asked and leave me to study. Even though Griffin had been the one to walk over first, I still got the impression they all took their cues from Rowan. Maybe it was the way each of them looked at him every so often, as though they needed to check for his approval.

Maybe Griffin wouldn't have come over if he hadn't already known somehow it was okay with Rowan. I didn't always get the social cues of large groups—what was said, what wasn't, and how everyone either understood the rules or didn't. One-on-one, I did just fine, but I spent so little time in groups, I didn't have practice with this type of thing.

"Hedge's," I answered him, naming the local grocery store. He'd know what I meant. There wasn't another grocery store for fifty miles, so even the rich people got their food from Hedge's unless they wanted to drive for an hour every time they ran out of milk.

"I've never seen you there," Tanner said.

Ace nodded. "Right. Me neither, and I go every Wednesday."

They do their own grocery shopping? I didn't know why that surprised me, since I did mine as well. I guessed I thought most parents did the shopping rather than the kids.

Or their housekeepers or something? Or even have their groceries delivered?

"I'm in the back. I load and unload." Studying was probably not going to happen. I'd done this to myself by addressing them. Even if they were just doing this because I was a temporary interest to them for a few minutes, I didn't mind the attention. I was usually so diligent, so this was downright strange behavior from me.

Ace shook his head. "You're five foot nothing. How in the hell do they have you loading and unloading anything?"

Before I could answer, Griffin groaned. "You can't say that to her. That's not polite."

"Who cares about polite? It's true. I'm horrified they have her lifting. I mean, how do you get the boxes up high?"

I lifted an eyebrow. "It's called a ladder."

They all laughed this time, even Ace, who shook his head at the same time. He looked like he'd like to say more, but Rowan shook his head too, so Ace stopped. *Aha. I'm right. They follow his lead, but why?*

"So should we all study until she has to go?" Rowan rose and walked over to the table where they had been sitting and came back with everyone's books. He passed Griffin a bag, from which Griffin pulled out a laptop. It was always crazy to me that people had their own. I had to use the ones at the library, but at least I had a phone. An old one, but it worked.

All of us started to look down at things we had to study. Or at least I pretended to. How was I supposed to concentrate when they were all there with me? Rowan smelled great, Ace kept drawing my attention just by the way that he read, and Griffin typed lightly on his computer, which was actually a comforting sound. I was pretty sure Tanner wasn't really reading his book but was instead looking at me from under his lids, while Caesar wrote frantically into a notebook.

Suddenly, all of it stopped.

They went terribly still, and Rowan eventually sighed quietly.

"My father is here, isn't he?" he asked Tanner, who was looking away from us, toward the entrance to the library.

"Yes." He crossed his hands in front of him. "And I'm not sure for how long. He might have been there for a while, we just didn't notice him."

Rowan nodded. "He's not alone, right?"

"Ace's dad is behind him." Tanner practically groaned.

How had Rowan known without looking? I shifted in my seat a little, and sure enough, there was his father. Edwin Kennedy owned most of the town, including the trailer park where I lived. He was a businessman of some kind, tall, pale, big-eyed, and scary. Behind him stood Ace's father, Vincent Monroe. He was some sort of academic, a professor or something. It was amazing how little I knew about these people when it came down to it.

He also had the same pale look as Edwin.

All five guys jumped to their feet practically in unison, grabbing their stuff and moving toward the waiting men. But the two men weren't looking at my temporary companions. No, they seemed to only have eyes for me. I shivered and dropped my gaze from them. I'd never wanted to *not* make eye contact with people so much in my life.

Caesar met my gaze for one second, a worried look crossing his face before he steeled his expression and followed the rest of them out of the library. They walked in a straight line, backs stiff, with Ace's father and then Rowan's father finally exiting after them. My mouth fell open. That had been a strange interaction. What had just happened?

Were they not allowed to be in the library? Or was the problem because they'd been sitting with me? Maybe it had nothing to do with me at all, some sort of internal rich boy issues that I didn't need to know anything about.

My phone dinged, reminding me that I had to go to work. I silenced it and collected my stuff. It had been the strangest day.

In a good way. Kind of.

I'D PUT away the third box of toilet paper when I collided with Ace. It took me a second to realize he stood there, even as he grabbed my arms to keep me upright.

"Hey." He smiled. "Had to see for myself how you take those boxes up the ladder without killing yourself."

I blinked, our earlier conversation coming back to me. I shook my head, pulled out of his hands to grab a box, and did just what he wanted to see, even skipping the bottom rung on my way down just to show him that I could.

He raised a dark eyebrow. "Okay. Point taken."

I mock curtsied. "See? I can go up and down ladders carrying boxes."

Ace leaned against the wall, watching me. "Why don't they let you work as a cashier or stocking the shelves out there on the main floor or, I don't know, the bakery? You could wear one of those hats!" "Hats?" I had no idea what he was talking about.

He sort of pantomimed over his head. "You know, the white hats."

It took me a second to follow what he was saying. "Oh, a chef's hat or something? No, I mean, have you ever seen anyone in the bakery wearing that? It's more like plastic sanitary things that hold their hair back. Besides, I can't have those jobs."

"The chef's hat would be cool." Ace walked past me and sat down on the rung of the ladder I'd skipped. "Why can't you have one of those jobs?"

I sighed. "Because my mother is really bad at keeping jobs and she tends to make things really difficult for me when I need to find one. They don't mind me working here as long as I stay in the back."

His laugh surprised me, and then he shook his head. "Like the dirty little secret they keep in the back where no one has to see it? I am actually familiar with that feeling."

I almost scoffed, but the truth was I had no idea about his life. None. Maybe they did keep him locked in the back of the house or something. "I'm not complaining. It's a job. I keep the lights on, eat some food, and in a year, I'll be where you are—waiting to leave here."

"I'm not going anywhere." A muscle ticked in his jaw. "I'm sorry about earlier. It was rude of us to just go like that. First, we disrupted your studying, then we ran off. I wanted to say I was sorry about that."

I opened and closed my mouth. My supervisor might be coming to check on me any second. "That's okay. It was fun to talk to you. I...I don't talk to a lot of people, and you could have been mean to me but you weren't."

He blinked. "If you knew who I am, who I *really* am, you wouldn't want me to be nice to you."

"Why not?"

Just then, the door opened. My supervisor, Trey, entered the room. He was a nice man, forty-ish, married, and I was pretty sure I'd caught my mother giving him a blow job in the back of our trailer before he'd taken off running too fast for me to be sure it was him. He remained nice to me and had never done anything to make me uncomfortable, but I really hoped he wasn't expecting that I, in turn, would be down for getting on my knees and servicing him, because I absolutely wasn't.

"Trey." I smiled. "Sorry, I..."

Turning around, I didn't see Ace anywhere. It was like he'd vanished. The window was open, as it sometimes was because it got so warm, but I hadn't been the one to wrench it open this time. I smiled. That was how he must have gotten in—through the same window he'd used to leave.

Okay. Ace was rather good at sneaking around.

"Nothing to be sorry about. Looks like you got most of it done. You can take off for the night." He smiled. "Get home safe."

"Ah, thanks." Had that much time passed already? Sometimes nights dragged and sometimes they went fast. This was one of the latter. I would go home, eat something, get some sleep, and do it all again tomorrow.

But it was almost summer, so I could work more, which meant saving for my eventual out plan. I grabbed my coat, not that I'd needed it, since it was seventy degrees outside, but sometimes I froze if they overdid it with the AC.

I walked out into the night. The moon hung full in the sky, but it didn't hold my attention.

Not when Ace leaned against my car.

"You got out of there fast."

He grinned. "I'm sneaky. Snuck out of my house tonight, for example. It's what I do."

Well, that was obvious. He'd gone through the window like an expert. "Why did you guys have to jet out of the library like that? Did you do something wrong? Your father showed up, and you ran."

"Oh, I wondered if you were sure who we were talking about?"

That was a deflection if ever I'd heard one. Question for a question, but we'd just met, and I was prying.

I decided to act like I didn't notice. "Everyone knows who your father is, and Rowan's father. I would have recognized the other dads, too. You guys are the rich folks in town. I'm on the opposite end of the spectrum. Between you and me, there is a world of difference with most other people falling in the middle. I guess your dad is sort of a celebrity just for being who he is."

Ace rocked back on his feet. "Well...that is more unfortunate than you'll ever know. If there ever were people that others shouldn't know, it's my dad and his friends. Sometimes he notices what I do, and sometimes he doesn't. This is one of those times that he's noticing, and not for good reasons. When they show up places, we just leave. It's easier on everyone." He patted my car. "Goodnight, Maci. Be careful getting home. Look over your shoulder when you walk to your door. Extra caution, always. You never know what's out in the darkness."

I stepped toward him. "That's very sweet, but I don't think anyone wants to hurt me. There are better people to rob."

"If only it was just that you might get robbed."

I supposed he had a point. Terrible things could happen. A whole bunch of fucking scary things. "Goodnight, Ace. Today has been...different."

"For me, too. I'm not sure what's going on, but I'm very glad to have met you today. Drive safe."

Did he like me? That was the question I asked myself as I drove away. I mean...guys paid attention when they liked you. No, it wasn't possible. He was vague and a little off, but then again, so was I, when it came down to it. Ace was gorgeous. I wasn't ugly, but maybe not pretty enough to have caught his eye that way.

I had dark hair and dark eyes. When I looked in the mirror, I didn't see anything special. My breasts were mid-sized, maybe a little large for my size, and my hips matched them. A little rounder than was fashionable, but I was obviously strong and certainly not offensive to look at. *Could* he like me? Was that why he showed up at my work?

It was dangerous to get my hopes up, but there it was. My hopes. Going up. I locked my car after I pulled into the driveway. It was really my mom's car, but she was missing, so she didn't need it anyway. I looked over my shoulder to see if anyone was there as I made it to my front door. Shaking my head, I let my anxiety go. We didn't have a crime problem, other than my mom and people like her doing a string of petty crimes that put them in and out of jail.

Nothing serious, mostly minor drug offenses. It was a transient town. People came and went a lot. We didn't see or hear from them again.

An envelope was taped to the door with my name on it. I grabbed it, not recognizing the handwriting, unlocked my door, and entered the trailer. It was hot, so before I could look at whatever it was in the envelope, I turned on the AC unit in the window. It would be a few minutes before it did any good.

A note fell out of the envelope when I opened it.

Question for you...

Molly is in charge of a group of miners. There has been a cave-in. Four people, including Molly, survive, but one miner, Jen, is injured. She needs medical help. It will be 36 hours until anyone can reach them. Molly knows they have enough oxygen for 3 people to survive 36 hours, but not enough for 4 people to survive that long. Should Molly kill Jen to save the others?

What do you think?

Sorry for the weird way we had to leave today. Tell me your answer in math class. —GG

I blinked. He'd left me an ethical dilemma, a famous one. The cave-in dilemma. Huh. I grinned. Why had Griffin done this? The same questions I had about Ace struck me about Griffin. They couldn't *both* like me. Maybe this was a friend thing.

Had I somehow stumbled into making some friends today?

I grabbed a pen to answer him.

2

I considered the words I wrote to Griffin many times before I even tried to get into bed. Even then, I couldn't sleep for thinking about it. The tale of the miners was famous, intended to make you consider whether the needs of the many outweighed the means of the few. Most people knew the quote from *Star Trek*, the old movie with Spock in it. I'd watched them at night when I couldn't sleep and imagined a world that could be like that instead of the one where I lived.

Was it better to kill the sick person and leave the air for those likely to survive, or was it never okay to play god and they should just let the cards fall as they would? If everyone died, everyone died—it wasn't ever one person's job to make decisions like that.

I rolled onto my stomach. Or perhaps there was a third option? I looked at what I'd written to him.

Hi GG,

Cool initials, by the way. I guess I should be feeling lucky you didn't send me the trolley question. I hoped he'd know what that meant, but if he was leaving egalitarian questions on people's doorsteps, I was pretty sure he did. Besides, he was valedictorian—as he must really like to tell people, since his friends teased him about it—and he was clearly very bright. He probably knew the one about the trolley smashing into five people or killing everyone on board. *You must be trying to figure out who I am based on how I answer this question.*

And much as I obsessed, I came up with way too many scenarios as to how you would judge me, so I can't let myself go there in my own head. Bet you're sorry you sent me that question now, aren't you?

Okay, my answer is that there is a third answer. We only need three people to have enough oxygen. The leader could end her own life, thereby leaving enough air for the sick and the other two people to survive. That is the leader's job, right? Sometimes, you have to sacrifice yourself for others. I would, therefore, say that is how I would answer it. If I were Molly, I'd end myself before I ended anyone else, because I couldn't watch people suffocate to death.

That's just too awful.

Hope math class is going well for you.

MG

My phone dinged, and I grabbed it to look at it. Was Mom finally telling me where she'd been? It was a number I didn't recognize.

Just wishing you a good night's sleep. Hope you have your ringer off so that if you're already out, you're not woken by this. —Rowan.

He had my number?

How did he have my number?

Not that it mattered. He was Rowan Kennedy—if he wanted my number, it was probably pretty easy for him to get it.

Texting him back was tricky. I had to play it cool. *Just got in bed now. Looks like we're both night owls. Sleep well.*

I sent it before I could overthink it and saved him in my contacts.

I closed my eyes, but it was a long time before sleep came. My mother was often drugged up or drunk, but at least she was an adult in the vicinity. When I was alone, every creak I heard or noise outside was someone coming to murder me.

Someday, when I was a grownup, I would know what it was like to sleep soundly. In a big house, with an alarm system and a big dog that would tear off the faces of anyone who came near me while I rested.

And a husband who loved me so much, he'd go downstairs with a baseball bat ready to do battle with all the noises I heard.

That was someday. This was now, and right now, it kind of sucked to be alone in my trailer.

Even if it was a far better day than the one I'd anticipated.

By the time I got to school, I was doing math in my head, but not the fun math, like I did in class. It was the kind where I was trying to figure out why I didn't have enough money to pay for my cell phone. What had I spent it on that I couldn't remember that had eaten up the last ten dollars I needed? I sighed. Sometimes, I could be downright spacey, and I wasn't supposed to have to do this anyway. Teenagers had adults to handle these kinds of problems, or at least they were supposed to.

Even if my mother arrived home that night, it wouldn't be with hundreds of dollars to pay for things so that I could eat a full dinner. I knew that much.

"Hey." Tanner caught my attention as he ran up to my car. He passed me a hot cup of coffee and smiled. "Got this for you."

I blinked. "You did? Why? I mean, thank you."

Oh, sweet heavenly coffee, how I loved it. I never got to have any, but I loved it. Other girls craved chocolate. For me, it was this.

"You're welcome. You had a long night yesterday. I thought you could use it. I sure did. I wasn't sure you drank coffee, because I never see you walking around with any, but I took a chance."

He had no idea what he'd just done for my entire day. "I want to hug you, and I'm not a hugger. Thank you. A million thank yous."

Maybe that was the right response, because Tanner's whole face lit up into a grin to match my own. "I'm... You're welcome. So you do drink it, then?"

"I hardly ever get to, because I don't have the funds, but I love it. Thank you."

His face fell. "Really? I...I would have gotten you better coffee. This was very basic. I could've done better than this."

I touched his arm as I took a sip of the bliss he'd brought me. "No, this is perfect. Seriously. Thank you. It's perfect." We started walking together toward the front of the building, and something he'd said dawned on me. Maybe it was the coffee finally waking up my brain, because I remembered I'd given the ten dollars to a homeless man on the street. That was where it had gone, back at the beginning of the month. I'd thought Mom was getting paid from her job at the gas station, so I'd be okay with bills. He'd been so hungry. I was too, but he'd been worse off. It had then and still did seem like the right thing to do.

"You noticed I never have coffee?" I hoped he got the underlying question, which was me checking on the fact he'd noticed me at all.

Tanner was long, lean, and gorgeous. He looked like he could truly be on the cover of a magazine. He could sell... Well, I didn't know what he could sell, but his cheekbones alone would make people haul out their money for products they didn't need.

"Of course. You're a pretty girl. I'd have to be dead not to notice you."

My cheeks heated up. I must have been absolutely red. He grinned at me. "Well, I just made you blush. That's sort of awesome." He swung around to look at me as we finally entered the building. "I don't talk to people. Not much. I can't. Long story, but it doesn't mean I don't notice you. I do. I really do." He spun around, then faced me again. Tanner seemed to have lots of energy in a really good way. It was amazing he needed coffee at all. "Which way is your class?"

I groaned. I had English first period. It was an AP class and I loved English most years, but this year, the teacher hated me. I had no idea why, but she seemed to relish torturing and embarrassing me every morning, first thing. "That way."

My class was on this floor. I'd have to run up two stories for math, but for the moment, I was close to where I needed to go.

"Then why are you talking to me, if you don't talk to anyone?" His words had struck me right in my gut and lodged there where I imagined they'd stay for a while. No one talked to me, but he didn't talk to others. There was something sort of synchronous about it.

"You talked to me first. Well, the whole table, but it counts. So that made it way easier to talk back."

I stopped walking. "Hold on—so what you're telling me is you don't talk to people unless they talk to you, so therefore, you don't talk to people, generally."

He nodded, a piece of his light brown hair falling in his face. Tanner pushed it away. "That's it exactly."

"Then you *have* to talk to a lot of people. People must talk to you all day. You must be inundated with conversation."

Several groups of people passed us, and an ache struck my heel. That was happening more and more to me lately. I needed a new pair of shoes. The heels on my sneakers were just completely worn out. I felt like I might as well have not been wearing shoes at all sometimes.

"You might be surprised. You know what this place is like, right? You only talk to your friends and sort of stare at other people. Everyone has these groups, and they pretty much don't venture out of them. They stare at us. Maybe they have a sense they should stay away? An instinct. I don't know. But no, most people leave us be." He nodded toward me. "Except you. You spoke to me. Well, us. It counted."

We started walking again. "Is this like an unwritten rule you guys just follow?"

"It's what our fathers want from us, not to talk to others, but of course, we have to answer if spoken to." He rolled his eyes. "This you? Junior English?"

We had gotten to my room. He was right. "What does your mother say? I only have a mother and she's never around, so I don't know what it's like to have a dad. But maybe she could intervene or something? That seems kind of rough."

He shook his head. "I don't have a mother anymore. None of my friends do. Bunch of motherless boys running around, setting things on fire, pissing off girls in libraries. See you later, Maci with an I because your mother couldn't spell it."

The good mood that talking to him caused followed me all the way to my seat. Two minutes into class, it fled. My good mood took a big giant leap right out the window.

"Well, well, well, Maci Green," Mrs. Reemus said to me from the front of the class. "Is that a new hole in your sleeve? We should have read *Oliver Twist*. You would fit right in with those poor orphans. Except they didn't have parents and you do, so what does that say about you? That they don't even want to dress you properly?"

I stared down at the long sleeve T-shirt I'd shoved on that morning. She was right. There was a hole in the top of the sleeve. I hadn't even noticed it. A small hole, but there it was. There were some things a teacher could do to insult a student that would make others laugh, and then there were some things that were so awful, even high schoolers didn't laugh, as though even we understood that it had gone too far.

As I was never very important in the cliques—Tanner was right, people did tend to stick to themselves—it didn't surprise me that no one laughed. I was already too low to be of much interest to anyone. Picking on me didn't fix anything for anyone else. My group was just me, myself, and I. The teacher had made fun of me, and it made the others so uncomfortable, they didn't even laugh.

I sank down in my seat and prayed that my stomach

didn't grumble. The coffee was going to be my breakfast and lunch today. I couldn't give this woman any more ammunition against me. So far, she hadn't been able to mess with my grades, but the big essay for the end of the year was coming. She'd be able to grade it without there having been a right or wrong answer she had to abide by.

Mrs. Reemus would be able to do as she liked with my grade. Clearly, she was a miserable person and my existence pissed her off. Despite my good grades, I wasn't college-bound. I had no money, not even for the applications, and my only motivation was to get out of town. I'd worry about things like further education later.

I just needed her not to fail me. I couldn't go to summer school, because I had to really work this summer to earn money for my escape. Besides, I heard she sometimes taught this class in summer school. If so, she could fail me again and outright prevent me from graduating at all.

Looking down at my hands, I said nothing. Just like I always did.

And I died a little bit inside. Just like I always did.

By the time I got to math, I'd finished my coffee and felt more exhausted than I had been before I had any. That class was like a war.

"Hey," Caesar said, walking up next to me. "I thought that was you." He smiled, and then his face fell. "You okay?"

"What?" I rubbed my eyes. One of the good things about being completely ignored and left alone was I never had to explain to anyone how I felt. Or maybe I just told myself it was one of the good things. I didn't really know any difference. "Hi. Where are you all coming from?"

He blinked and then took my hand, squeezing it. "Something happened to you. What is it?"

"Nothing new." I wiped at my eyes, which were dry. I wasn't a crier. Not a hugger. Nothing that came to being physical or asking for attention. What was the point of any of that? I just wanted to make sure I didn't give any indication that I wasn't okay when I entered my next class. As Frost said, the only way out was through. I had to keep going. Then I could disappear and reappear someplace else that wasn't here.

He opened and closed his eyes. "Shit. I don't know... Rowan is better at this, but if you tell me to beat someone up, I can do it."

I pointed to the class across the hall. "We can't beat up teachers. Don't worry about me, but it is sweet of you to offer."

He eyed the room I'd indicated. "There?"

I waved my hand in the air and gave him my best *I'm okay* smile. "Thank you for caring. It's really nice. I mean, you're all being really, incredibly nice. Thank you for that. It's just...nothing." I pointed at my next class. "Can't be late. You can't be, either."

"I can be whatever I want. If I don't go, it doesn't even matter. You have no idea how little it matters." He squeezed my hand. "Can't get you out of my head. Seems they can't either, from what you're saying. I don't know what that means, but I'm not going to worry about it because you are like a dose of light, Maci."

No one had ever said such a nice thing to me before. I wasn't a dose of light. I was a pile of something that most people forgot about the second they met me.

Most of the class was already seated, including Griffin, when I got inside. He looked up when I entered, and despite my frozen feelings, I remembered I had something for him —the note I'd stayed up writing. I put it down on his desk, which made him grin at me, but his smile quickly fell as I walked past him.

Damn. I must not have been doing such a great job with my fake smile. I sat down in my chair at the back of the room and settled. Math was always my best subject. It was right or it was wrong. I didn't have to think too hard about it to figure it out.

Griffin sat down in the desk next to mine that was usually empty, the chair squeaking when he pulled it back. "Great answer." He smiled. "I mean really. I didn't see it coming. I'm impressed. What's more, I think that you mean it, and I love it."

I looked up from my open textbook. "I...I thought about it a long time."

"I love that. I stay up at night thinking about those kinds of questions." He shook his head. "So what's wrong? I saw you talking to Caesar. Did he upset you? Because I know he can be a dick, but he's actually..."

I interrupted him. "Caesar is great. I think he was offering to beat up my teacher. Of course he can't do that, but it was a first for me."

"Why do we need to beat up your teacher?" Our math teacher had started class, so Griffin lowered his voice. "And I doubt he was going to beat him up. He'd probably find someone to do something else entirely, but I digress. What is the problem?"

"Mr. Gaines," Mrs. Hollow, our math teacher, spoke from the front of the class. "Is this desk change permanent or are you just going to bother Ms. Green for today?"

He smiled at her, but there was no mirth in his eyes. "Permanent."

She nodded, a funny look on her face, before she started instruction.

He lowered his voice. "Maci..."

I let out a breath. "I don't know what to do with all of you. People don't pay me this much attention. Are you guys up to something? Why are you doing this? Is it some kind of game? Why bother with this?"

He winked at me. "Let's just say that you got our attention. It's hard to do. Most people are terribly boring. The same things over and over again. We didn't see you coming, you surprised us, and now we've all decided that we like you. That's also unique. We never like the same people. So you've made five new friends." He scribbled on his paper, answering a question I hadn't even heard the teacher ask. "What happened to you with your teacher?"

I had *five* new friends. "Doesn't matter. Friends, huh? I don't currently have any. My only friend left, like everyone around here does. They go, and they're never heard from again."

"Yes. They do. They leave. They vanish. Or they can never leave at all." He winked at me. "So come on, friend. Let's do math. Rowan will get your secrets out. He's good at it."

Why would they want to? "You don't even know me."

"Well, you're never going to really know me, so we'll have that kind of friendship—one where we have each other's back and we both think the other one is awfully good-looking, but we can't and don't ever do anything about it. We'll watch movies, laugh, and always have things that we keep from the other one. You'll probably feel that way about all of us, so that is the friendship we'll have."

I opened and closed my mouth. What was I supposed to say about that? "Okay. Sounds good."

He nodded. "Great."

AFTER MATH CLASS, things sort of slowed down. My day regulated. Lunchtime came around, and I grabbed my books to go sit in the library. On the days when I didn't have enough cash to buy food or bring anything from home, it was easier to not be around everyone else eating. I found my place in the corner and picked up my books. I had the essay to write and needed to study for a test. In all my other classes, I was pretty confident I'd do well on the tests.

My stomach grumbled, but I ignored the pang. Reading. That was what I needed to do. And...

Rowan flopped down in the chair next to me. "You spend so much time in the library. It's very commendable, but it's lunchtime and you're not in the cafeteria. Study later. Eat now."

I sighed. "Griffin says you're now all my friends. It's a strange thing. I mean, I didn't know friendships worked like this."

His smile was huge. "That's how it works with us, apparently. I haven't made a new friend ever. So you're it. Come on. Lunch."

This was about to be awkward. "I don't have any lunch."

"Hence the cafeteria." He rose. "That's where one buys food."

I shook my head. "I don't have any money today. My mother hasn't been around in a bit. I never know when she's coming back, but she's broke anyway. I have to pay all the bills. It adds up. Some days, there isn't lunch." I shrugged. "Better to just stay here. And I get it if it just got weird and we can't be friends now."

Rowan sat back down. "I can buy your lunch. Trust me, it's not a problem. I don't have many things in my life, but money is something I have in abundance. You've got to have lunch. It's a long day without food."

"Thank you, but I'm not comfortable with that." My mother took from everyone and anyone. She practically defined the word grifter. It was humiliating. I worked. I would always find a way to pay for myself. "So we can be the kind of friends that Griffin described, but who also can't really go out and do anything because I can't afford it." I winced. "I just made it awkward."

He shook his head. "You didn't. Okay. Stay here. I'll be back."

I nodded. Griffin had been right—Rowan did seem to be able to naturally get me to talk without doing very much. How did he get me to tell him about my issues? I sighed, looking back at my book.

Moments later, all five of them arrived. They took all the seats around me at the table. It was like the night before. We were even all back in our same seats.

They all had their food with them. *Really?* They'd brought their food with them where, among other things, I came to escape it? *What the ever-loving hell?*

But then they selected half of their food, each one of them placing part of their own lunch in front of me.

When I would have objected, Rowan raised a hand to stop me. "I didn't buy you any lunch. It was lunch I already had. Same for them, so please eat. I'd never let a friend go hungry, I don't think. At least now I wouldn't. Who knows what the future holds? Please."

I'd never had anyone do for me what they'd all just done. These five guys who'd declared we were friends like that sort of thing could just happen.

I was lonely. Hungry. And starved for just what they were offering.

I never could have turned any of it down, even if I knew in my heart that it was off. And I did. I was many things, but I wasn't stupid. I went in with my eyes wide open.

3

The rest of my day was markedly better because I had a full stomach. I didn't know if my new friends made their lunches themselves or if they had staff to do it. Or if their pale, rich fathers got up to make sure their children were fed. All I knew was I'd just had the best half a turkey and cheese sandwich I'd ever eaten.

I was so full, I could practically have fallen asleep if I'd let myself. Only I didn't. I forced myself to concentrate. To drive forward, just like I always did. I kept my head down and didn't see them the rest of the day, not even in the library after school, where I performed my ritual of studying for the hours before I had to go to work. I chewed on my lower lip—a bad habit that I needed to break, considering my bottom lip was perpetually sore because I did that so often—and learned physics as best as I could.

Science was always my least favorite class. Well, physics was. I liked chemistry.

I could just quit school and hit the road. The thought hit me the same way it always did—all of a sudden and hard enough to knock my thoughts right off the track. I sighed. I wanted a high school diploma. I was only sixteen years old. If I left, I'd be homeless. I had nowhere to go. Mom's family was gone, long dead, and she'd blown through the small inheritance she'd gotten from them by purchasing our trailer—and thank goodness she'd done that—before buying more drugs and alcohol. At the very least, I had a roof over my head. I wasn't homeless; I wasn't on the streets.

I had to stay the course. Work this summer to save everything I could. When I wasn't in school, I had more hours to earn. I took a deep breath. I needed to stay the course. Even if it was just in my head, a high school diploma was something I could earn, something I could know I had done. It would be a tangible sign of my having survived this.

I steeled my shoulders. I could do this. I had to somehow stay the course, stay focused, and not run from town like my life depended on it. I wasn't in danger. Things were hard, but I was okay. I lifted my head and stared into the stacks. For just a second, goose bumps broke out all over my arms and then seemed to flee my skin just as fast.

What was that? I shuddered. Sometimes, I could downright spook myself. There was nothing in the stacks, nothing that should make me nervous, except maybe some old dusty books. I collected my stuff. This was ridiculous. I wasn't going to get any work done.

Maybe it was going to be the kind of day where I didn't really accomplish anything. Work was pretty mundane, all of the excitement of Ace being there the day before gone. Some nights dragged, and it was proving to be one of them.

But when I came outside, Tanner sat on the hood of his car, raising his eyebrows when he saw me approach. "Hey there."

I shook my head. "Hey, what are you doing here?"

"Well, I thought I could pick you up. We'll leave your car

here, and then I'll take you to meet the guys at a place where we sometimes hang out on the outskirts of town. Like maybe you could use some fun, and we can have dinner or whatever on the way over there."

He threw in that last bit like it was an afterthought, when my sense that was always on alert about people pitying me recognized it as the truth. Tanner wanted to feed me. "I had a granola bar a few hours ago. I swear, I'm not starving."

Tanner put out his hand, and before I could overthink it, I linked my fingers with his. "I'd be starving if that was all that I ate. Besides, it was hours ago, so surely you can eat again. We're teenagers. Didn't you hear, we're supposed to have endless pits for stomachs?"

I laughed, despite the feeling that having to take charity always caused in me. "I thanked you for that coffee, right?"

"You did." His smile fell. "I know we just met, but I feel like I've known you a long time. That's never happened to me before. Does it happen to you?"

"No." But I did feel that way...and also, I didn't. "Somehow, it's like I've known you, but you're also brand spanking new and exciting. That makes me nervous, like you're all about to pull the rug out from under me and I'll regret not being more cautious."

He took my other hand. "That's not who we are. I mean...we're fucked-up. We have secrets. Big ones. You don't want to know them. And there might come a time you'll wish you didn't know us because we're just so screwed up, but it won't be because we did anything to hurt you. That's not the kind of humans we are."

That was a funny way to put it. I almost pointed that out —they all said they had secrets, and there was only so many times I could hear them mention it before I'd have to ask what they meant. Only I didn't want this to end tonight. Reality was a cold, harsh master, and if I pushed this too far, I wouldn't get to go have fun. It would end.

"Okay, I believe you. So...dinner and fun? It's late. What is there to do this late at night? We're not exactly in a city, where things are open."

He grinned. "Come along, Maci. There is a lot going on. I love that you don't know about it. How are you this person? How are you sheltered from the shit around here?"

"The thing about being who I am is people don't really invite me to do things. So even though I live where I live, and my mother is sometimes a junkie" —I winced as I said the word. I almost never said it aloud. Thinking it was one thing, saying it to Tanner felt like more of a betrayal somehow— "I don't have people to do things with. I'm just busy. Maybe that doesn't make sense. Like I'm so low, I'm untouchable."

He squeezed my hands. "I'm touching you. Screw everyone in this town. They're either total lunatics or morons. I can never decide which one. You know what? Never mind. Come on. Let's get out of here." He nodded toward my car. "We'll come back for it."

I let him lead me away because that was what I wanted to do. What he was describing was a night I'd never had. Sure, I used to watch movies at my best friend's house, but I'd never been out to dinner, not even once. And I didn't know what people did to have fun. Why shouldn't I have one night like this? Why shouldn't I take a break?

That thought jarred me. I really couldn't. I had to be at school in the morning and go to work the next day. "How late will we be out? I have all the obvious things tomorrow. Class. Work. I can't... I'm not great when I'm exhausted." I was always a little tired. That was the status quo for me, but there was a line. If I crossed it, I fell apart. Wow. I was sixteen. I sounded so old to myself. Was I aging backward? Like would I actually have energy and fun when I was sixty, since I was so constantly tired at sixteen?

"Do you work every day? We had school today, but we're off tomorrow for some teacher thing."

I laughed, throwing my head back. "Can you believe I had no idea what day it was?"

"I can because I just saw you do it." His smile was huge as he pulled the car out of the parking lot. I knew nothing about cars, but his was obviously new. It just started—like, it wasn't a game to see if it would—and it smelled clean and fresh without any kind of air freshener anywhere. "Do you work tomorrow?"

"No, unfortunately. They won't let me work all seven days. I do work some Sundays. When I do, then I'm off Monday. Then I do the rest of the week until Saturday. Or I don't work Sundays and it all shits. It's complicated." Sometimes, I couldn't even keep it straight.

He frowned, his eyebrows sloping down when he did. "Remind me to never complain about how busy I feel ever again."

"We all have our own version of busy. What do you do that makes you feel that way?" I didn't want him to think of me as being too much, as too stressed, and not enough fun. I read all the memes talking about not feeling that way, about self-empowerment, but I wasn't exactly how that worked when I felt like too much even in my own head. Maybe I really was just that.

He side-eyed me. "I play baseball and soccer. I do it basically to pacify my father, who wants us to look like model citizens so we don't get looked at too much. Like, if you fit in just enough, then no one notices that you really don't."

I shook my head. "The same father who only wants you to talk to people if they talk to you first."

"The same one." He nodded and pulled onto what constituted the busiest street in town. It wasn't a highway, but it did take us from one end of town to the other. If you actually left town—from what I heard, since I'd never done it—you could get on the highway from this road. My dream was to board a bus and just go. See the streets change to places I'd never been before. I was going to make it happen.

"You don't seem really odd to me. None of you do." It warranted my pointing it out since he'd brought it up. I could stay out of their private business unless they dragged me into it. He kind of had.

He grinned. "See? Then it's working."

"Where are we going? I don't know what's open this late. Is *anything* open this late?"

Tanner took my hand, holding it over the gear shift. He didn't look at me when he spoke, but I'd swear every bit of his attention was on me right then, which meant it was good we were the only car on the street.

"Lots of things are open on the other side of school, closer to where I live. Do you like sushi?"

There was one sushi place in town. I'd heard about it when it opened, but I'd never been. Asking me if I liked sushi was like asking me if I enjoyed riding unicorns. Yes, in my dreams, I enjoyed such things. "I've never had it."

"Are you adventurous? Like, you'd give it a try?" He squeezed my hand.

Was his question a test? Or was I just looking too deep into what he said? "I think that people love sushi, right? I don't know why I wouldn't want to try it. I mean...I'll have no idea what to order. You'd have to do it for me."

He nodded. "Sushi it is, then. If you hate it, I'll take you for a cheeseburger."

"So which do you like better? Soccer or baseball?" I wanted to know him. Just feeling like I did wasn't enough. I had to actually learn some things about Tanner, or it was just a feeling that would fade because there was nothing real to hold it up.

He sighed. "I guess baseball, but the truth is that I'd rather not play sports. When I'm doing them, I spend most of the time counting down how much longer before I can go home and play my guitar." With a little bit of a shrug, he tried to cover the fact that he winced when he said that. "Not that I have any intentions of being a rock star or anything. That's not a possibility, but I do love to play. Even if it's pointless, it is just one of those things, I guess."

"Will you play for me?" I'd love to hear him. Besides, I wasn't sure why Tanner couldn't be a rock star. If he was talented, he could pull it off. He was certainly good-looking enough. Like a rock star already, with his long brown hair, green eyes, and lean physique. I could see him selling albums. Girls going crazy whenever they saw his image.

"If that's something you'd like, I will. Not in the restaurant, but afterward, when we meet up with everyone else. If there aren't too many others around."

I let go of his hand to touch the end of his hair, just to see if it was as soft as it seemed. Realizing how completely inappropriate that was, I dropped my hand. "Sorry. I can be weird too. I just wanted to feel it. And...and..." I forced myself to catch my breath. What was the worst that was going to happen? Was he going to shove me out of his car for touching his hair? "I thought it might be soft. Sorry."

We rolled to a slow stop at the stoplight, and he leaned over closer to me. "Touch my hair. I'd love it."

Really? With a shake to my hand, I let myself feel his soft brown locks, running my hand through his hair once. "Thanks. Weird moment over." His hair was truly just as silky as it looked. Yes, he could be a rock star. That was for sure. "I'll try to refrain from any more, and I promise if I can't, I can at least limit it to four times a night. How about that?"

"Really?" He took the chance to reach over and touch my hair. "I may get stuck with ten. I tend to hit ten a night, so you'll beat me."

The light changed, and I stared out the window. This side of town was really hopping. Everything was lit up and people wandered all around. "Would you believe I grew up here and I've never been to this place? We might as well have left my total understanding of our town behind."

My mother probably frequented the area when she was actually around. People doing exciting things. Laughing. Drinking. Probably just enjoying the heck out of life. But I'd been alone, and no one had ever brought me. Not even my mother, who used to drag me with her occasionally to a closer bar.

Why hadn't she? I chewed on my lip and then abruptly stopped. "That's Mrs. Reemus."

"Your English teacher." Tanner visibly gripped the steering wheel tighter, his hands white in the knuckles. "Yes, she tends to hang out down here. I imagine she's about to have a very memorable night."

I could ignore a lot of the strange things he said because of the whole secrets issue, but that, I wasn't going to let go. I had a line. Apparently. As this was all new to me, I just had to figure it out. "What does that mean?"

"It means that she has, for a long time, been very interested in getting involved with my extended family. Tonight, she's going to get what she thinks she wants. It might be a case of be careful what you wish for. Griffin opened some doors for her. He gave her just enough rope, she might be able to hang herself with it. Or not. Maybe she's smarter than she thinks."

We pulled into a parking lot and stopped. I wanted to look around and see the building, really drink the view in, but the goose bumps on my arms insisted I listen to my gut. "Is she getting this chance to really screw up her life because of me? Whatever is about to happen to her, is it because of me?"

My heart raced, and I wasn't sure I could actually eat the sushi we'd planned to order. My thoughts were so muddled.

He took my hand back in his. "She's getting this opportunity to destroy her own life because of her own actions. She's the kind of woman who would take out her anger, because her husband was unfaithful with your mother, on a sixteen-year-old girl who she is responsible for during the time she is in her classroom. She humiliated you. And you haven't done a thing to her. I'd like to think that we'd do this for anyone. I don't know if we would. I do know you're our friend, and we all have the same feeling—that you're going to be very important to us. I know she doesn't get to do that with no consequences."

Tears flooded my eyes. "I should have known that was why." I tried really hard to suck back my tears. Some of them still found a way to travel down my cheeks. "She...my mother. She can't help it. I mean...she's a good person. I know she is. But she's lost, and I'm always being judged because she's lost." I closed my eyes to stop the tears. "I should be used to it by now."

His lips brushed my cheek, caressing the escaping tears. "No, you shouldn't. Look at me. Please."

I forced my lids open to stare at him in the light coming off the street. "Sorry about the crying."

"I know you're the kind of person who doesn't like people to see you cry, so I'll promise you that I'll never tell a soul about it, but you have no reason to feel that way. What she's been doing to you deserves the tears. A real quality person would have found a way to not be your teacher if she couldn't take the conflict of interest. Or she would have sucked it up and treated you like her student. Any number of fucking things. All that's going to happen tonight is that she'll get what she wants. Time with some of my...cousins, who she's been trying to get the attention of for some time. She may not end up liking them very much. Or maybe she will. In any case, it's on her. It's on Griffin. It's on me, even. It has nothing to do with you if she ends up unhappy, okay?" He cupped my cheeks. "No more tears over that terrible woman."

I swallowed. "Okay."

"I might kiss you tonight. If you let me. Not just your cheek. And my friends might too. I know that's weird, but it's fine if you want to kiss all of us. We don't have... I guess I'll just say that for a lot of reasons, that boundary of one-on-one which exists in society doesn't apply to us. If you want to kiss all of us, kiss us. If you don't want to, don't. It's okay."

That series of statements pushed all thoughts of Mrs. Reemus and what she'd gotten herself into from my mind. He unhooked his seatbelt, and I did the same, exiting the car at the same time. He hurried around and took my hand. "I'm not my mother."

"I know that." When he would have led me inside, I didn't move. "Maci?"

"I won't go around kissing all of you or whatever because I'm some sort of person who can't control herself or can't respect herself. Or whatever. So if this is just a thing you guys do and you think I'll be game because I'm like her, then you should probably just take me back to my car." My heart raced as I said the words. Even as I said them, I couldn't believe I'd spoken the words, but at least I now knew I was the kind of person who would.

He widened his eyes. "That's not what I meant at all. Shit. I should have... Rowan is just better at this stuff. No, what I meant is..." He took a long breath. "Imagine if you knew that you had a use-by date."

"Like milk going bad?"

He nodded, his breaths coming in and out fast. "Exactly like that. Would you care about rules? Probably not, right? So what I was saying was, if you have any interest toward being physical with me, with Caesar, with all of us, that is something I know we'd all like. If you don't, that's good too. Okay? It's only what you want. I don't want you to be held back because you think there are any lines. There aren't, not like that. I don't think you're your mother. Before yesterday, I didn't know who she was. I meet a lot of women like your mom. I don't know that I've ever specifically met her. But you? You're just this amazing girl who for some reason is giving me the time of day, even though I keep having to say stupid cryptic shit that makes no sense. I'd be rid of me. I'll take you home if you want. For sure."

I don't know why I hugged him, exactly. Only, he looked so sad. Tanner really needed a hug in that moment. "Are you sick? Is that why you have a use-by date or whatever? I hate that description."

"No." He hugged me back. "But my family has expectations, I guess is the best way to say it. The rest of the guys too. The day those expectations come to fruition, my life will no longer be my own."

We stayed like that, with him just holding me in his arms. Cicada song practically drowned out the sounds of crowds laughing in the distance. Those same cicadas, arisen only days earlier, would be dead soon. We weren't even cognizant of their existence until almost the end of their lives. Their song was so loud, as though they knew they had little time to get it out before they couldn't. Their song was so loud, I wouldn't forget the noise for a long time after they were gone.

He smelled like cinnamon, a warm and safe scent.

Finally, I pulled back. I never knew what to do with other people's expectations. No one thought I'd amount to anything. Sometimes not even me, and I knew I was smart. Life just sucked sometimes. "I might be a little sensitive about my mom too. And people's expectations."

"I get it. I do." He squeezed me one more time. "Sushi?"

"Yes, please."

I let him lead me inside a restaurant I'd never expected to see. Tanner's explanation made sense. Maybe he was in the mafia or something. I was okay with not asking. I'd drawn a line, and he seemed to get it.

The restaurant was mostly empty. There was one couple in the corner of the room. They laughed quietly together, but we were seated well away from them. The hostess smiled at Tanner, but her eyes seemed wary. That was a weird thing to notice, but this night had been filled with weird. Ten, he'd told me. So I was on two and he was maybe on...five?

4

I loved everything he ordered, even though I didn't have a clue what most of it was. Tuna, I understood. And the salmon. Other than that, it was all mysterious fish and mysterious rolls that tasted like heaven in my stomach. Oh, and the green tea. I was full a lot faster than him, so I leaned back in my chair to admire him while he ate. I didn't even feel weird about it, because he'd been watching me the whole time I'd been eating too.

"That was so good. Thank you. I mean...just, wow."

He reached across the table. "You're so welcome. I've never liked food more. Seriously. I think it was the company that made it so good."

Maybe all the food in my stomach had gone to my head, but happiness felt like it seeped into my cells. "This was my first sushi, and if I kiss you, it would be my first kiss. So...I probably won't kiss you. Not because I don't want to, but because I don't know exactly how to go about doing that." I set down my green tea. "And there is some truth, I guess."

He leaned closer. "Do I have your permission to kiss you? If the moment calls for it?"

My cheeks had to be the color of a bright red tomato. Still, I'd opened this door. It was my turn to answer him. "You do, in the right situation. Yes."

He took a sip, biting on the edge of the straw that stuck out of his diet cola. "Awesome."

"Good, you two ate." Rowan slid into the chair next to me, and I almost knocked over my tea, I was so surprised by his arrival. Where had he come from?

"Hi." I laughed. Had I been that caught up in talking about kissing with Tanner? Well, yes, it seemed I absolutely had been. I was so ridiculously predictable.

Tanner shifted in his seat, leaning back. "Thought we were meeting you at Wanda's."

"Wanda's?" I looked between them.

"I got tired of waiting." Rowan gave me a sideways grin. "If you weren't here, I would have tried all the other restaurants until I found you. But I see she was a yes for sushi." He turned to me. "It's good here, right?"

Rowan had the bluest eyes I'd ever seen. It would be as easy to get lost in his as it was in Tanner's. "First time. Nothing to compare it with. I do love food, though. I mean, this was, like, five birthdays for me." I turned to Tanner. "Thank you for this, seriously."

"You have no idea how much it was my absolute pleasure."

Rowan squeezed my shoulder. "You guys done?"

"Yes." Tanner signaled for the waitress, who had given us a wide berth after leaving our food with us, and she rushed over.

"It's on the house."

Tanner scrunched up his face. "What?"

Rowan muttered under his breath. "Fuck."

"It's on the house. Tell your fathers that we did that,

okay? That my father said you always eat here for free. Okay?" The woman had to be forty years old, graying, and she walked with a limp, but right then, I would swear she would run a marathon to get away from us. Sprint to Alaska, if she had to.

Tanner sat forward. "No, I'm going to pay."

"Tanner." Rowan rose. "Nothing to do. Trust me. I know. I get it. I hate it too. I thought that we were all past this, but sometimes, it rears its head. We can go spend at Wanda's. They love to take our cash."

He put out his hand. "Come on. You'll come with me. Tanner will cool off in the car and meet us over there."

My dinner date rose slowly. "I'm fine. I'll take her."

"I think you need a break first." Rowan shook his head. "Come on, Maci. Let's go."

I rose but didn't move. I didn't know what was happening, why they hadn't gotten to pay, or why it made Tanner so upset. It had to be one of those things I couldn't know, or they would've explained it. Still, he was back to hurting, just like in the parking lot. I hated it. I'd always been able to feel other people's pain acutely. It was one of the reasons my mother was such a constant drain on me. Maybe I was just naturally sensitive, or maybe I spoke to so few people that the ones I did found a way to dig into my soul and stay there deeply.

I didn't know. It didn't matter right then. The situation really upset him. Before I could overthink it or get scared, I kissed him. It was a light press of my lips to his, but when he caught his breath, I deepened the pressure. Tanner lifted his hand, and using the back of my hair, pulled me even closer. For a good minute, we kissed, standing right there.

I pulled back. "How'd I do?"

He breathed hard. "So fucking good."

I smiled at him. "Guess I was wrong about what I would and wouldn't do."

He cupped my cheek. "Well, if we'd had two more seconds alone, I would have admitted I've never kissed anyone, either. So I guess we both just had our first kiss. Right here. In this restaurant."

With an audience. My cheeks heated up. What seemed spontaneous sort of seemed more voyeuristic than anything else. I turned slowly. Although I expected Rowan to be annoyed at the whole thing, he leaned against a table with the smallest of smirks on his face. "Ready?"

I guessed I was. "I'll see you at...Wanda's?" It took a second for me to remember the name. Maybe my head was muddled from very publicly kissing Tanner.

He nodded. "Wouldn't miss it. I'll go...calm down, even though the last thing I'm feeling right now is angry. Maybe it's more about Rowan getting Maci time. That's fine. I'll see you in about ten minutes, as long as you're fine with that."

Was I? This obviously felt like a date, which was why I'd kissed him. But it wasn't, not really. They—through Tanner —had been very clear about that. We were friends who occasionally kissed, I guessed. And now, one of the other friends wanted me to go with him instead of Tanner. Rowan, with his blue eyes and long blond hair. The one with the faraway look in his eyes, like he wanted to be somewhere else, always. Only, as he looked at me, I didn't see it. Rowan really did want to be right where he was.

He put out his hand, and I linked our fingers together. They always asked that way. An offer...and I had to meet it with my own acceptance. If I didn't link us, it didn't happen. I forced my thoughts back to the present.

Rowan was quiet as we left the restaurant, and I tried not to notice the way that a group of grownups standing outside vaping went completely silent when we passed. One of them actually took a step back.

We were teenagers. What did they think was going to happen to them when we walked by? Yeah. I was more and more on the mafia train. They were from some sort of families that were threatening or something. I had to dwell on this for a while.

Rowan had an SUV, and like Tanner's car, when I got in it, I knew right away it was a newer model car. The smell gave it away before I even noticed all the gadgets that made it seem more like a game machine than a car. My car turned on sometimes, drove forward, and in reverse. This one might sprout wings and go to the moon, if he asked it to try.

He hadn't moved the car, but instead seemed to be regarding me. "Are you okay?"

I tried to figure out the best answer to give him. "I told Tanner I am bound to do about four things a night that are weird. If I'm acting off, you can just add it to the tally."

"Just four? I'm much more than that."

Rolling my eyes seemed the right thing to do. "I doubt that very much. You don't seem like the weird type to me."

He put the car on and backed out of the space. "See? Looks can be deceiving. I do plenty of weird things. Like, I know you know about the fire incident."

"Everyone knew about that. I don't hear a lot of gossip, but that was even repeated to me in the library. It's a big deal when the king of the school sets things on fire."

He side-eyed me and then smirked. "What makes me the king of the school? I don't even talk to anyone, other than the guys and now you. I keep to myself. I'm not the king of anything, not even my own life."

That was an interesting diversion technique. He completely didn't answer my question. But I wanted to know why he wasn't the king of his own life. "Rowan, why *did* you set that dumpster ablaze, all the other small things you lit up, and why aren't you the king of your own life?"

Run on sentence for the win to get both my questions asked. He groaned. "You don't let things go, even if you're quiet about it. I see that now. And I brought it up, anyway. That'll teach me to think I can get away with anything. Um, I set that stuff on fire because I was half out of my mind. I don't really know why that was, except it happens to me sometimes. Like, I'm suddenly just filled with rage. It's a family trait, unfortunately. I'm not dangerous to you or anything. I swear it. I just...had to light that dumpster up right at that moment."

I stared at him. Well, at least he was honest. I liked honesty—loved it, even. I went dark sometimes. Maybe we all did. Or whatever. I barely had time to think about that kind of stuff most of the time. "Are you feeling like you want to spark something up right now?"

He shook his head. "Absolutely not. In fact, I've been feeling really calm the last few days."

"I have to be crazy to sit here listening to you and not demand you pull over and let me out. I mean...you've just said that you feel the need to burn things."

Rowan winced and nodded. "I wouldn't blame you if you wanted that. I will, if you want, but we're almost there. You can always have one of the other guys bring you home after we get there, if I make you nervous."

"The thing is, you don't make me nervous, and I think that may speak more to there being something wrong with me than something wrong with you. And...no, I don't want to go home, because I've never had a night like this and I want to have just one." I looked out the window. "Even if I end up being one of those heroines in the novels that everyone is screaming at to get out of the car or whatever."

He laughed. "Maci, look at me for a second."

I did because the truth was, I preferred to look at Rowan more than anything else I could stare at right then. "Looking."

"You can have more than one night like this. I promise you that. We were all so excited you were coming. Very excited. I obviously couldn't sit and wait any longer. I know that's weird. But, so long as there is breath in my body, I am not now, nor will I ever, be a bully. I promise you that. You're not on some journey that's going to leave you broken."

I believed him. That was the funny thing about it. Maybe I was stupid, but I did. As he parked the car, I decided to just go for it. For one night, I wasn't alone in a trailer. If it was too weird or went in any way badly, I'd never do it again.

Wanda's was an older-looking building. Or at least it appeared that way. Sometimes, that was a motif that people applied to newer things. I didn't really know why people did that. If I ever had money, I wasn't going to let anything look old or worn, but whatever made people happy made them happy. I thought Wanda's really was old.

Maybe it was the way that the paint peeled around the bricks. As we approached the door, with Rowan's hand on the small of my back, Griffin came outside. He blinked when he saw us. "Was just coming to find all of you. Tanner's not answering his cell. I thought maybe you were still in sushi heaven. I could get behind a little spicy tuna right now."

Rowan laughed. "Tanner is driving. If he's not texting, that's a good thing. He got a little put out that his meal was comped." Griffin winced. "But we are here. I think I've only moderately freaked out Maci."

I picked up my fingers to indicate with my pointer finger and thumb that it was a small amount. "I'm weird, so it works for me. Still, stop saying things I can't ask about. Okay?"

Griffin took my hand. "She's as smart as I am, Rowan, so she'd know good-weird from bad-weird. Just don't push her into restraining her curiosity too much. Come on in. Wanda's is fun. This is where we are most of the time when we're anywhere."

I looked over my shoulder at Rowan. "I'm surprised it's withstood so long. You don't want to burn it down?"

"So far, I'm good. No burning tonight." He winked at me.

Griffin shook his head. "Fuck, I hope not. I like this place and I don't feel like trashing it, so we're all good it would seem."

"Do you trash things?" Was that what he sometimes felt compelled to do? Did I have anything I absolutely did when things inside just felt like they were too much? I really didn't. I was too busy trying to eat. What would I do if I ever had the time?

He shrugged. "I can neither confirm nor deny that with an answer. I suppose you'll have to wonder."

Inside, the air conditioning hit me, and I shivered. Why was it so cold inside? Griffin dropped my hand and put his arm around me. "It's warmer once we get farther inside. The owner, Wanda, is going through what she calls *the change*. She talks about it constantly. Anyway, she gets hot and then we all freeze. But where we're going to hang out, it's not this cold."

I looked around. This was a real bar. I'd never been inside one, other than trying to drag my mother home. It was crowded, with groups of people talking in low voices. Some of them drank, some of them absolutely didn't. It was strange. Why were so many people completely drinkless in a bar? They didn't seem to be really doing anything at all. I recognized some of them—a few had been seniors when I'd been a freshman.

I hadn't seen them in a while. A whole group of them. What were their names? The thought soon pushed out of my head as we entered a backroom, leaving whoever was in the other room behind us. Sitting on some couches, lounging around like they owned the place, were Ace and Caesar. Ace pounded on his phone, but he jumped to his feet when he saw us. Caesar was slower, but his smile was just as broad at our approach.

"I told you I'd find them." Griffin let me go and headed to the couch closest to us before he threw himself down on it.

Rowan sat next to him. "On the way here. Tanner's cooling off. Be here soon."

"That's fine." Ace hugged me. "Tanner gets here when he gets here. You brought Maci. That's the key for tonight. Glad you made it."

"I didn't even know these places existed. It's cozy in here. How early did you have to get here to secure this backroom?"

Caesar yawned and patted the seat next to him. Ace and I walked over toward him and sat, me in between them. I'd just been hugged. My body buzzed. I was hardly ever hugged, hardly ever touched. It was like every cell in my skin had sat up and paid attention. I took a deep breath. *Wow*. They just did that like it was the most normal thing in the world.

"Welcome. We're not doing anything particularly exciting in here tonight. Not that we ever do. But it's different than sitting in our house and it allows us to be present. That's what we're supposed to be doing. It's so much better with you here."

I grinned. Had I ever smiled so much in one night? "Well, it's the most excitement I've maybe ever had. At least of the good kind. So you just hang out in a bar? They let you in a bar? I usually have to beg to get in to find my mother, back when I used to do that."

Rowan nodded before he rose to make his way over to the television on the wall. He pushed a button and turned it to a football game. I had no idea who the teams were. That was okay. I'd watch whatever just to hang out here for a while.

"We don't tend to get kicked out of too many places. Besides, my father has some financial interest in this place. So, yeah, we get in. Whoever is sitting in here moves when we arrive."

It was like a different world from mine. In that second, Tanner strolled in, his guitar case strapped to his back. "It's busy tonight. Too busy. The whole gang is in town." He shut the door to the backroom behind him, essentially shutting us in. "Wanda is going to bring us some drinks."

"Oh." This was probably important. "I don't drink. Obvious reasons. Or maybe not. My mother has a substance abuse problem. I think it's just better if I don't."

I'd actually had plenty of alcohol in my life. My mother started to give me some when I was about ten years old. Maybe earlier, but I didn't remember it. Around my twelfth birthday I'd stopped taking it. There was nothing funny about her getting me drunk, that much I'd understood by then. I remembered the feeling, but that story was too much for me to share. Some secrets I would keep to myself...probably for always.

"We don't drink. Better if we're always in our best headspace. I mean, maybe that's obvious too." Rowan winked at me. Man, his blue eyes were so gorgeous. Like really, really gorgeous. "I burn things when I'm not drunk."

Caesar groaned. "No. None of that. That was a bad one. Just soda, probably. Tanner sometimes orders seltzers that taste like fruit. Yuck." He made a gagging noise. "No thank you. Just no."

"For that alone, I am going to go order one and wrestle you to the ground until you drink the whole thing." Tanner took off his guitar case and set it down, while next to me, Caesar jerked up.

"Number one, you couldn't take me down to make me drink that shit. Second, are you going to play tonight? Been too long."

Tanner stretched out on the couch, placing his feet on the coffee table in front of him. "Maci asked."

"Thanks for asking, Maci." Ace squeezed my hand. "He had stopped playing. None us were exactly sure why, but it's great to have him playing again."

"I..." I cleared my throat. "I can't take credit for him playing, just for wanting to hear him."

Ace sighed. "He doesn't play for us anymore."

"Here." Griffin pulled out a board game from under the table. "We haven't done this in a long while. Let's play. That is, if you want to, Maci."

I'd never seen that game before. My board game repertoire had to do with whatever they played with us in school when we were very young. I hadn't even seen one in more years than I could remember. My mother sometimes played cards, but it was mostly so she could giggle her way through taking off her clothes with whatever bozo she'd brought home for the night, the week, whatever.

He passed me the game, and I looked at the back of the

box to read the directions. Scanning the words, I read fast. Basically, we were going to each get cards that would create a character. Then we had to argue why our character could beat the character of the person sitting next to us on the left. In the end, everyone would vote.

It was different than rolling dice and connecting four or whatever. I passed Griffin back the box. "Sure. Looks like fun."

That must have been what he was hoping for, because his smile was huge. Ace whistled through his teeth. "Ooph. The valedictorian must think that you're a worthy opponent. Like someone else and his music, he doesn't play with us anymore."

"Maybe we've all been a little bit bored." Caesar lounged lazily next to me. His eyes were barely slits.

I touched his knee. "You okay?"

"I don't sleep very much. Sometimes it catches up to me. I'll be struck with adrenaline any minute, and then I'll be more fun."

I wasn't concerned with how fun he was or wasn't. "Maybe you should go home and get some sleep."

"That's where I'm the least tired. My father is away for a long time, and I have a hard time sleeping when he's gone. I don't sleep that well when he's there, either, but it's worse when I know he's absolutely not around to control the surroundings, so to speak." He shrugged. "It's fine. By tomorrow morning, I'll seem relatively normal. I guess I really don't need that much."

We all needed a certain amount of rest, that much I knew. We could go long periods of time without it, but eventually, it caught up in tricky, nasty ways. I knew it from personal experience. "Take a nap now. The couches are comfortable." More comfortable than my bed, if I were being honest.

"No." He sat up and rubbed his eyes. "First of all, you're here with us, and that's a treat. Second, I don't sleep in public places. That's called being vulnerable, and I am never that, if I can avoid it. Only certain people get to see me while I'm not alert, and there are too many people out there in the bar area whom I would never let see me like that."

The door slid open, and the woman who must have been Wanda came inside carrying a tray with a bunch of sodas. "Sorry it took a few minutes, boys. Big crowd out there tonight. A lot of hopefuls."

Rowan shook his head. "Not that. Not in here. Not tonight. We're cutting that off right now. I promised her not to say too many things she couldn't ask about. That goes for all of us, including you, Wanda."

She set down the tray and laughed. "Oh, honey, start asking questions and fast. I know they're cute, but these five are trouble. Good trouble, for now."

Tanner jumped to his feet. "Thanks for the soda." He ran a hand through his hair. "We'll pay you in a bit."

"Yes, you will." She waved her hand by her face. "How can you stand how hot it is in here?"

"Games." Griffin held up the box. "Let's play now."

5

"Does everyone in the whole bar know what I don't know?" I had to ask. This was all getting to be too much. "Are you in the mob?"

"The mob?" Ace's eyebrows shot up. "I like that one. And no, they don't. They absolutely don't. Wanda doesn't really know what she thinks she knows." He sighed. "Don't leave. Let's play."

I guessed it wasn't the mob. Fine. If I were too stupid to live, like one of those heroines that I screamed at to run away, then so be it. Tomorrow, I would figure things out.

The door swung open again, this time with a bang. Four of the guys who had been sitting outside not drinking—the ones I thought I recognized—stood in the doorway. They were tall, all of them, and strong. That much was clear. They were also incredibly pale. When was the last time they'd been in the sun?

Whoever they were, the guys really didn't like them. The tension in the room increased tenfold. Caesar was wide awake now.

"What do you want?" Rowan grabbed the board game

from Griffin and opened the box. He started piling the cards out on the table. Although he'd spoken to the newcomers, he hadn't looked at them. The others were, but not Rowan, like he couldn't bother to raise his gaze.

"Hello to you too, cousin." The man in front walked a few more steps inside the room. "We saw you come in with a girl. Thought we'd make sure that you were behaving yourselves. Can't have you five getting into trouble, now, can we? Since we're all going to be listening to you soon."

Caesar put his arm around me. It was an odd feeling. Ace and Caesar both held me. Still, it seemed important when he'd done that, and I had enough self-preservation from years of the men my mother brought home to know when I was in danger. I just stayed still and silent.

"Not so soon," Griffin answered. "Or did you lose the ability to count?" He held up his hands. "We have uninformed company, so unless you have something generic to say, go do whatever you were going to do tonight and leave us alone."

He took another step inside, although his two companions didn't move. "We could inform her."

"Do it and see what happens to you." This time, it was Tanner who spoke. "Whatever you think, you're nothing to them. Nothing. And we may still be who we are, but we matter. You don't. Make me unhappy and see what happens, I dare you."

Ace rose. "Come on, we're leaving." He extended his hand, obviously toward me, and I took it. He squeezed our fingers together. "Leave her alone. Don't look at her or even think about her. She's nothing to do with this."

The others rose, and so did I. With a gentle tug, Ace pulled me from the room and back out into the bar.

"We knew you in school." Obviously not listening,

Rowan's cousin stared at me. "Your mother can't keep her legs closed. Are you a slut like her? Is that what you're doing here? Going to give these virgins some blow jobs? Let them lick your pussy? How much do women in your family charge for your services?"

"Hey," Rowan practically roared. "I think he told you not to even look at her. That means keep your mouth shut."

"I don't listen to you. Yet. If I ever will."

What was about to happen? Rowan was tall and fit. I would even bet on him in any regular fight, but there was something about the three guys who inserted themselves into our evening that screamed of aggression. Something about them that wasn't quite right. My heart raced, and if I thought that he couldn't simply reach out and grab me if I tried, I might have run. As it was, I wouldn't leave these guys. Not that I could do much in a fight, but numbers were numbers.

I knew how to throw a punch and land a kick. That was about it, but it was something.

"No, but you listen to me."

It was like all the air in the room went away. Rowan's father seemed to appear out of the darkness of a back hallway. He walked toward us, wearing his standard black, his long blond hair falling to his shoulders. He had the same long, lean face of his son and yet none of Rowan's beauty. His eyes were dark, so brown they almost seemed black.

The cousin stepped back. "Sir, I apologize."

"You will. Go to my house. Now. All three of you."

As if on cue, all three of the aggressive men dropped their heads and exited the room. Their movements were almost beautiful in a way I couldn't explain. Like they could transfix with the way they walked. I blinked.

"Rowan, take this girl home, then go home for the night. All of you. Now."

They didn't answer, but perhaps their assent was implied, because he disappeared into the back of the bar just as fast as he'd appeared. Ace let out an audible breath, but it was the only noise I heard in the room.

Caesar shook his head. "Should have known taking her out in public was going to cause a problem."

"No, we shouldn't. This is our place." Griffin stared at the hallway where Rowan's father had vanished. "No one cared about it but us. Why now? Why are they circling?"

Tanner stormed toward the front door. "You know why. Come on. We have to get her car. And all the fathers will know by now that we're expected back home. No dawdling."

Rowan met my gaze. "I'm sorry, Maci. Have to cut this short. We'll do this again another time."

I had a feeling we absolutely would not.

THE DRIVE to my car was quiet. Rowan was behind the wheel and had insisted I sit up front with him, which put Griffin and Tanner in the back. Caesar and Ace had gone home in Ace's car, watching us drive away like they wished they were in the car with us. Or maybe I projected. Maybe I just wished they were all with me.

So I could make sure they were all okay. I didn't know exactly what had happened back there, but I knew they weren't okay. That they were all shaken and silent. Seeing Rowan's father bothered them more than being threatened by Rowan's cousin and his friends who hadn't spoken.

I thought about the man. Rowan looked like him. Blond hair, long face. But the resemblance ended there. Next to me, the guy I was just starting to know had sun-kissed skin and streaks in his hair, a bright gaze and happiness surrounding him every second that he wasn't being battered by some secret that I was sure had something to do with his father. They were all afraid of him.

Going on instinct alone, I took the hand he rested on top of the stick shift and squeezed. "Are you okay?" I looked over my shoulder into the backseat. "Are you all okay? I don't know what's happening with you, but I certainly know how it is to have a shitty parent."

Tanner met my gaze. "You're so nice. We've just given you a terrible evening, and you're checking on us. Why are you so kind? Shouldn't you be pissed off and raving?"

Griffin shook his head. "I think Maci is more likely to silently stew. But maybe we can get her to open up to us if we can have an evening that ends differently than this one, if she doesn't decide we're more trouble than we're worth."

"I wouldn't decide that. I have a parent that troubles me too." That was the politest way I could find to say it. "Whatever is happening, as long as you're okay, that's what matters."

Griffin blinked rapidly. "We're okay."

The silence descended again. Arriving at my car, I undid my seatbelt, but Rowan stopped me when I would've opened the door. With his hand on my arm, he shook his head. "No. Tanner will drive your car home. Stay here with me. It's late."

I supposed it was, but I was used to being up late. Arguing with him was an option, and I was sure I could get my own car and leave. But despite the silence, I liked their company. Who knew what his father was going to say tonight? Maybe they wouldn't be allowed to see me again.

Then there would be no more moments where I felt like I basked in their attention.

Maybe they'd move on to give this feeling to someone else. Internally, I sighed. The truth was I knew this couldn't be my reality. It never was. I'd be back to being alone in my trailer soon enough, left wondering if I'd imagined tonight.

Tanner held out his hand, and I handed him my keys. His smile was huge. "I'll take good care of your car. See you in a minute."

He jumped out of Rowan's car and rushed toward mine. In the dim light from the closed grocery store, my car looked lonely in the all but empty lot. We watched him walk to the driver's side door, and I winced as Tanner had to pull it three times to open it. If my poverty weren't already obvious —and I was sure it had to have been because I hadn't had any lunch that day—it would be now. I kept the car clean, but it wasn't like theirs.

"Maybe I should drive it," I said aloud.

Griffin answered, "He'll be fine. It's okay, Maci." He leaned forward and placed his hand on my side. "Whatever it is, don't worry."

The trouble was I was bound to worry. It really was my natural state.

WE ARRIVED AT MY TRAILER, the darkness of the night increasing until the blinding yellow of the fluorescents coming from the park around us blared at me like the light purposely wanted to give me a headache. I winced. *Wow. I must be really tired.*

But as we approached, a truth struck me beyond the nasty lights hitting my eyes. My trailer blared as bright as any of the others, and there were three cars in the driveway that I didn't recognize.

I forced myself to swallow as the truth hit me. "My mom is home."

That was good news. I preferred when she was. Otherwise, every noise was a potential threat I'd have to handle alone. However, that didn't include the times she brought guests home. They were almost always men, and not all of them kept their focus on her. Sometimes, they turned their attention to me. So far, I'd managed to avoid anything terrible happening just because I'd been smart and lucky. Mom was always too out of it or desperate for drug money to care what they did to me in those moments.

I swallowed. "Well, looks like I have some people over tonight. Thanks for bringing me home."

Griffin sat forward in his seat, the noise stretching the leather enough that I could hear him move. "Who would she have in there?"

"I don't know." But I could guess the type. It was always the same kind of person. "Thanks, guys. I am so grateful. I'll see you on Monday, I guess."

"Hey." Rowan stopped me again. "Let me walk you in. We all will. Just to check things."

I knew what he would find, and after the night this had turned out to be, I wasn't sure I could handle them seeing my mother with a needle in her arm or sucking someone's dick so that she could do just that. Some things were for my eyes only.

I shook my head. "Thanks. That's sweet, but I need to say no, okay?"

I gave him a chance to answer. It had to be okay. This was one of those situations. We were going to be friends who had secrets. This one was mine. Maybe he understood, because he didn't say anything as I rushed from the car. Tanner waited outside of mine, and I took the keys from him with a smile. "I had so much fun getting sushi. Got to go now."

"Maci?" I could hear his unasked question. He hadn't been in the car to hear me put off Rowan, but nothing had changed in the seconds since then. This part was mine and mine alone.

"See you Monday."

He ran a hand through his hair and walked toward Rowan's vehicle. "Be safe."

"You too."

I took a deep breath and pretended that they weren't all staring at me from behind as I entered the trailer that had been my home for most of my life. I swallowed, stepping into the smell of smoke—mostly pot, I thought, but cigarettes too—and incense that my mother always thought covered up the rest of what was going on.

Over the years, I'd developed a real hatred for that scent, so much so that it was almost a psychosomatic allergy. I had to actually convince myself I could breathe when I smelled it.

Loud music blared through the room, something hard rock, and a piece of red silk covered the light, bathing the room in the color, so much so that it looked like I'd walked into the center of a volcano. Mama was, as expected, not alone. Two men sat with her. But I couldn't focus, not really, on any of them. Not when all I could see was the mess everywhere. Forgetting the drugs—I was right, she was back on heroin, if the needles were any indication—everything was strewn everywhere. When she left again, I was going to have to clean all of it up.

I hated that part.

For the most part, I kept my life really fucking clean. Everything had a place. My mother was barely back hours, and our home was already a mess.

"Baby!" My mom jumped to her feet. "You're home. I thought maybe you had taken my car and run away finally, and who could blame you? I always forget just how much I hate it here until I come back."

I tried to smile at her. She was more than her addiction, more than what she did to herself. She was the woman who had taught me to love rom-coms. Who had known the names of every star in the sky. She knew how to cook everything without ever having to look at a recipe. The first thing she did every year was renew her library card on January second.

Trying to remember those things kept me sane with her, sometimes. Other times, nothing worked, and I just had to bathe in the fact that I both loved and hated her in equal measure and that there was nothing in the world I could do about any of it. Maybe that made me a bad person.

"I'm here." I smiled at her. "At least until graduation. We've talked about this. Sorry I wasn't here to greet you. I was out with friends."

"Friends?" She laughed hard. "You don't have friends. Baby, this is my new husband. We've been in Vegas, getting *married*. Would you believe he's lived five miles away this whole time?" The way she stressed the m-word made it seem she thought I wouldn't understand what she was saying. "This is Kyle." He rose for the introduction, and she wrapped her arms around him, patting his big round belly when she did so. "Baby, this is your new daddy."

Oh, he was absolutely not that. I didn't have a father. I'd never known him, but this man was not going to take on the role. My mother had gone to Vegas so many times to get married, I'd lost track of them. As far as I knew, she never got divorced, either. My mother might be the biggest polygamist in the state, as far as I knew. No, Kyle was not going to be my daddy. He probably wouldn't even be her husband for very long.

I put out my hand. "Nice to meet you."

His track marks complement hers.

Maybe it was because I was so distracted by introductions, but I didn't expect to be grabbed from behind by the other man in the room. "You were right. She's gorgeous."

I yelped and struggled as I was hauled into the arms of the smelly man with my mother and her newest fling.

"You and me, we're going to have such a good time. Your mama told me all about you, Maci. From now on, you belong to me."

My mother clapped her hands. "Isn't it wonderful? We're going to be like a big old-fashioned family."

When his hand moved to grab my breast, I screamed, even knowing it was fruitless. Screaming. Crying. They did nothing. Ever.

But this time, it actually did. The door swung open, and my friends ran inside. All three of them. Why hadn't they left? Relief warred with humiliation as I continued to struggle to get out of the hold of the man who smelled like a dead rat.

"Put her down." Rowan enunciated every word. "Now."

Kyle reared back. "Fuck. I mean, fuck. Jerry, put her down. That's Rowan Kennedy."

"What? He's just a kid. Why should I...?"

Kyle visibly shook. "Put her the fuck down. Now. You're not from around here. Trust me. Down. Now."

I was dropped and would've hit the floor if Tanner hadn't caught me. "Got you, Maci. You're okay."

Rowan stood stoic and still. "Tanner, Griffin, take her into her room and pack a bag. Enough for several days. She's obviously not staying here. Now, these men and I are going to have a conversation."

Griffin stepped forward. "Which one is yours, sweetheart?"

Almost in a daze, because I couldn't believe it was happening, I showed them my tiny bedroom in the back of the trailer. Tanner closed the door, setting me down, so I sat on the bed, and abruptly, the music that had been blaring ceased.

"Do you have a bag?" Griffin cupped my cheek.

"Um." I rubbed my eyes. "Yes, something...an old back-pack. In the closet."

"Great." He walked from me, grabbed the bag, and made his way over to my dresser. I should have been embarrassed. Griffin was going through my drawers, but my heart beat too fast in my ears for me to think of much else besides the fact that my mother was going to give me to that man.

I leaned over, putting my head on my knees, and tried to breathe. The bed dipped as Tanner sat next to me. "Do you ever wonder...like really wonder...what the fuck is the matter with the people we know?"

Lifting my head, I gave him a wobbly grin. "Like every day."

"Me too." He rubbed my back, an easy circular motion. "I'm just glad we decided to be nosy right when we did."

What would have happened if they hadn't? I caught my breath. Maybe it would have been the night my luck ran out. My chest tightened. *Shit.* I covered my eyes with my hands. Something had to help this moment, something.

Tanner drew my head to his shoulder. "You're okay. You are."

"I think I've got enough stuff for you to be good for three days." Griffin knelt in front of me. "Let's get out of here."

I hadn't really agreed to leave, but I was certainly not going to argue. I didn't even know where they were taking me, but I'd throw myself into this, because it couldn't be worse than what was going to happen if I stayed.

All three grownups stood by the couch, watching us with wide eyes. My mother's hands shook, and casually, like he'd done nothing at all, Rowan waited by the door. "Good. Come on. I don't expect to have any more trouble from any of you. That's the deal. Anything else happens that I don't like, and you won't get the same deal."

My mother and her horrible friends nodded fast. I could just leave. Get out, go.

But I stopped and stared at her. "How could you do that? How?"

She didn't have an answer, and neither did I.

THE COLDER AIR hitting me finally jarred me out of my stunned stupor. "She was going to *give* me to him."

We walked toward the car but stopped as Griffin's arms came around me. "You got away. It's okay."

I shuddered in his embrace. Who were these guys who kept offering up so much affection when I'd done nothing to deserve it? "I'm not usually a hugger."

"Neither are we," he whispered in my ear. "Maybe you have some sort of theory as to why you bring this out in us?"

I really didn't, but I was piled back into Rowan's car before I even thought to ask them the obvious question. "Where are we going?"

"Caesar's. His father is away for another few weeks, most likely. Tanner, could you—?"

"Already on it, text has been sent," he interrupted Rowan. "Good idea. You may solve two problems at once."

"That's what I thought too. Really, he'll like having you, Maci. Caesar can never sleep, and he ends up wandering the halls, overthinking things. I'll feel better having you there. Is that okay? I realize I'm sort of ordering you around. That's what I do. People listen to me. It's just how it's always been. I problem solve..."

I touched his arm to stop his justifications. "I'm grateful, if Caesar doesn't mind."

"He doesn't," Tanner supplied. "He's glad you're coming."

"Here." Griffin reached toward me. "Give me your phone. I'm going to put all of us into it so you can reach us at any time."

Tanner touched my shoulder. "I'm texting Ace. He needs to know what went on too."

Rowan nodded. "Good call." We were all quiet for a long minute until Rowan spoke again. "Did you see how they reacted to me? That wouldn't have happened a year ago. Every month, it changes. And those are people who don't really know what's going on. Sorry, Maci. That was rude."

I closed my eyes. "Well, you all just saw my secret. That is how I live. That is what happens to me. And..." A thought dawned on me, and my eyes flew open. "Fuck. Sorry, I left my money. Sometimes, she finds it and takes it from me. That is my bailout bag. Even though I sometimes can't afford to eat, I always put some aside so I can leave the evening of graduation next year."

"We'll go get it." Griffin handed me back my phone.

"Tomorrow morning, before I take you to work. And yes, I'm doing that. We'll stop and get your money."

"Thank you." I wasn't sure my thanks were sufficient for what they were doing for me. I stared down at my phone, just as a message came in. The name lit up, Ace.

That will never happen to you again.

I wished I could believe him, but even as we drove farther away from where I'd spent my life, I knew better than that. Things were just getting started.

6

We pulled up to Caesar's driveway, and I caught my breath. I knew they were rich, but the sheer size of the mansion made my stomach drop. It was amazing this kind of wealth existed so close to me and I just never saw it. Like I'd lived in a cocoon where I really hadn't understood the outside world.

Rowan parked, and Tanner leaned forward. "You okay?"

"Sure. You?" I turned to look at him. "Are you all okay? You were supposed to get back fast, but you're still with me."

Rowan shrugged. "My father has no sense of time anymore. As long as I show up before dawn, it'll be fine. Come on."

Just then, the front door opened, light spilling out onto the already well-lit yard, as Caesar stepped outside. Wearing only long black pajama pants, he held a water bottle in his left hand. Although his feet were bare, he walked toward us like he wasn't the least bit concerned about tearing them up.

I'd barely gotten my seatbelt off before he had me out of the car and pressed up against him in a hug. "If I had been there, I might have killed him."

I hugged him back. "I told the others, I'm not a hugger, but I really like it tonight."

"I'm not hugely affectionate. It's all you, Maci. I've got her. She's safe here. Pop the trunk, Rowan. I need her bag."

"Not in the trunk." Griffin rolled down the window and passed him my backpack. "Here."

My cheeks heated up, and I stared at Griff through the window he'd opened. "I totally let you go through my drawers."

He winked at me. "Did you? I can hardly remember."

"Good answer." Tanner took the front seat I'd vacated at the same time as Rowan got out of the car. He walked over to me with a fast gait and embraced me. He whispered in my ear, "This will feel like nothing someday. Something that happened to you, but like it all happened in a different existence. When you're far away from here, living out your dreams. You'll remember it, but that's all it will be." He kissed my cheek. "Sleep well, Maci."

Caesar took my hand and drew me toward him as I watched Rowan drive away. *My rescuers. What would have happened to me if they hadn't come?* I tried to swallow past the lump in my throat. Crying wouldn't help. It never fucking did.

"Is this okay?" I managed to say the words. "Or did they force you to put me up for the night?"

"No one forces me to do anything." He squeezed my hand. "I'm glad for the company. Come on."

I followed him into the house, and he closed the door behind us. With a strong turn, he locked the door as soon as it was closed. I didn't know much about locking mechanisms, but his seemed old. Like it might be iron, and not installed recently.

"No one is here but us. Still, I think that it would be best if you stayed in my room. I don't expect my father home any day soon, but just in case, I don't want you surprising him or vice versa. So stay in my room."

I supposed that made sense. It would be bad to run into a strange man in the dark. Sometimes, it was hard to do that in the day too. The lights had been on in my trailer.

"Thanks for doing this. I really don't want to put you out."

"Maci..." He said my name on a sigh. "You're not a burden. You're this really interesting person that has completely stolen our attention and made us all suddenly want to hold you. I can't explain it, and I find I'm good with the uncertainty of it. Come on."

He put his arm around me again, and we walked the hallways of his huge, cold house in silence. It wasn't that the temperature was chilly. No, it was the atmosphere. There was nothing that spoke of anyone actually living in the ginormous space. No paintings. Nothing. Even my trailer had some posters on the wall my mother liked and a picture of the two of us with lollipops when I was eight years old.

There was nothing here but dark, outdated furniture with torn cushions lining the hallways and the sounds of our footsteps as we crossed the hallways. Eventually, we found our way to his room. I was pretty sure I wouldn't find my way there again if I had to without help.

Caesar's room couldn't have been more different than the rest of the mansion. It was bright, well lit. The bed was made, his blue comforter and white pillows neatly presented like he'd taken time to make the bed. On the walls, he'd taped up pencil sketches of all kinds of things. I lost my interest in anything else and walked over to examine them.

People who could draw amazed me. I didn't have an

artistic bone in my body. *Horses. Landscapes. The ocean. People.* Most of the faces he'd drawn I recognized from the hallways at school, but some were strangers.

"Maci..." His voice trailed off. "I..."

He didn't finish because I came to the one that stopped me short. It was me. I looked to the side in the depiction, toward something away from view.

"That's me." I turned to look at him. "You did this recently?"

"Yesterday." He walked to me. "I hope that's not weird. I...I didn't think you'd ever see it, and I didn't remember until just now that it was here."

I grinned at him. How was I to explain...? I'd never thought myself important enough to ever be captured in a drawing like that. "It's beautiful. Much prettier than me. But thank you. I...I'm touched you took the time."

He took it off the wall and stared at it for a second. "I actually don't think I did you justice." Caesar crossed to the desk in the corner of the room and opened a drawer. "I keep the ones I do of my friends in here. You'll be in there too, but I may try again, to get you right."

"I can't draw. Not at all. Thank you."

Caesar waved his hand. "Don't think of it again. I...I mean, that should have been more embarrassing than it was. I actually liked you looking at what I drew."

"Do you want to be an artist? I think you're really talented." I stepped toward him. "I think...I think people would like to see what you do."

His smile fell. "It doesn't really matter what I want, actually. There is a future lined up for me that I'm not getting away from. I suspect I won't have time for drawing. Anyway, thank you. I really like that you feel that way."

I wasn't sure what to say. It sounded like he shared a

future with Tanner, who couldn't be a rock star. I didn't have much, but at least my dreams were my own and not taken from me by an outlined future. Or maybe they were? Poverty had the tendency to keep people right where they were born in life.

"Is there some place I could shower?"

His eyebrows shot up. "Yes, of course. There. Yes, go rinse away the day. Good idea. Um, so I made an air mattress on the floor."

I looked down. Yes, that would do nicely. Better than anything else I could have hoped for. In truth, it was the size of my regular bed.

"Great. Thank you." I turned and headed toward the bathroom. I had to find my equilibrium and get the feel of that man's hands off my body. Was it possible to have someone's grip implanted on you cellularly, so that you never stopped feeling it? I shuddered and pushed the thought out of my mind. *This has just been a long day. Rowan is right— someday, it will just be a memory.* All things eventually became memories, if we were lucky enough to live through them.

I was getting way too philosophical. The shower was huge, with three showerheads, and it took me a good minute to figure out how to work it. Considering how old the rest of the house seemed, the shower seemed downright modern. They'd clearly updated the bathrooms at some point.

Quickly, I took off my clothes and stepped under the spray. We hadn't thought to grab any of my own products, so I hoped Caesar didn't mind me using his. I wasn't going to impose on him too much. Tonight was one thing, but I'd have to go back tomorrow. There was only so much time I could spend living in his house with him, considering he really just started talking to me. Whatever this affection thing we had for each other was, it was bound to go away sooner rather than later.

Nice, sweet things had a tendency to die in my presence. I let the hot water push at me until I couldn't think about anything but the steam and how my body sort of tingled when I touched it with his soap. I took a deep smell of the body wash as I applied it. I'd seen the brand on the shelves —even put it there myself, stocking after hours when no one was there in the store—but never smelled it before. It was a woodsy scent. Perfect for Caesar and probably strange on me, but it would do for the moment.

I couldn't spend all night in the shower, so I hurried to get through a modified routine and came out, grabbing one of the towels stacked neatly on a shelf. So far, he was neat, like me. Things had a place, and that was where they got put.

Toweling off, I took a look at myself in the mirror. My hair was a mess and I didn't have my brush, which meant it would air dry and curl, and not in a good way. I regularly blew my hair straight. It was all I did, really, since I had no time for makeup. I loved how other women could make their curls behave. Mine seemed to laugh at me when I tried. Tomorrow, I would buy some hair elastics at work and braid it as fast as I could.

The thought reminded me that I had to set my alarm and figure out how I was getting to work, since I'd left my car at home. Ace said he'd bring me. I grabbed my phone and sent him a text.

Are you sure it's not a problem to bring me to work tomorrow? I have to be there at eleven.

A text came back fast. *None. I'll be at C's by 10.*

Ace was sweet. *Thank you. I owe you all major favors.*

No, you don't, Maci. See you then.

I looked at a clock. It was almost one in the morning. Where had all the time gone? Had I really been home so long? I shook my head. Tonight was weird, and that was saying a lot. With that as my last obsession, I hoped, I pulled my night clothes out of my backpack. Griffin had picked out royal blue boxer shorts and a white tank top. I smiled. I actually didn't wear these two items together.

Usually, if I wore the shorts, it was with a really big flannel shirt over them. Or the tank top with a big pair of men's pajama pants. He sort of mixed and matched, considering they had been folded together. It was such a guy thing to do—to make my pjs more visually appealing.

After I hung my towel up on the back of the door on a hook, I came out. The TV played low on the wall across from the bed, some black and white movie I didn't recognize, and Caesar lay on the air mattress on the floor.

I blinked. "Why are you down there?"

He sat up, staring at me for a long moment before he answered. "I'm sleeping here."

No, he absolutely was not. "You're not on the floor. I am. This is your bed." I pointed to his bed like he might not know what it was and then dropped my hand because of course he knew which bed was his.

He leaned up on his elbows. "Of course you're not sleeping on the floor."

"It's a mattress, not the floor. I'll be fine." I walked toward him. "Your feet are practically hanging off the edge. Come on. Get on your bed."

Caesar scowled at me for a second. "Absolutely not. I'm not putting you on the floor when that bed will make you much more comfortable. When I heard you were coming, I even changed the sheets. I do that every other week anyway."

I'd been right—he was neat like me, not that it mattered right then.

"If you won't trade with me, then I guess we're both going to have to sleep on your big bed. It's a king; we can both fit."

I said the words and then digested what I'd said. I'd never shared a bed with anyone. Despite the warm feelings we were all having, I barely knew him. Was it just over the top weird that I suggested it?

"Sure." He got off the mattress. "That's a good idea. We'll do that."

I let out a breath I'd held.

"Which side do you sleep on?" I'd be really glad when this conversation was over. Super-duper glad.

He pointed to the left. "That okay?"

I nodded. "For sure. It's your bed. You pick. You're doing me a huge favor and—"

"Maci," he said as he climbed in, interrupting me. "I like your company. I'm almost always alone at night, and I have been for years. My dad comes and goes, but even when he's here, he's not here. I'm not sure I would want his attention if I got it." He patted next to him, and I climbed in.

We shuffled the pillows around and climbed under the covers together. He was warm—even spaced out, I could feel him—and his mattress was heavy. I liked the sensation. It was a little bit like being in a cocoon. He rolled over and hit a light switch that bathed the room in darkness except for the television and the light that shone through the edge of the curtains on his windows from the well-lit yard.

"TV on or off?" His voice was low, a little bit strained. What must it feel like to be endlessly, constantly tired? I was pretty worn out myself, but I did get some sleep some of the time.

"Off."

He grabbed his phone and hit a button that shut off the TV. "Oh, plug in your phone next to the bed. I have chargers on both sides in case I need to charge my tablet. And set your alarm. I'll be up because I don't sleep, but just in case. Ace texted he's picking you up at ten."

"Right. That is so nice of him. I should have thought to bring my car. Although, it's my mom's car, technically, so she could take it away if she wanted."

He rolled over onto his side to look at me. "I could have brought you to work. Ace wants to, but just so you know, I would have done it. And I think you thought about all the things you could manage in that moment. Whenever I'm scared, I can barely function, if you want to know the truth. My brain goes into survival mode, and I can make poor decisions. You did great."

It was hard to picture him scared. He was so much bigger than me and shirtless, so I'd gotten a good look at how buff he was. There were few people who could take him on, or at least that's how it felt looking at him. He'd told me he didn't like the noises being alone at night, so it would seem even strong, tough people could get hit with things that bothered them, too.

"Thank you." I adjusted my pillow and then rolled on my side to face him. "What do you usually do when you're up at night?"

He reached over and put his hand in my hair, running through it gently. "Draw. Obsess. Draw some more. Fall asleep for an hour. Jolt awake. Watch television. Around five, I work out. Get ready for school or the day. Last night, I thought a lot about you. Now you're here." He smiled. The little bit of light through the shades let me see him. "I hate thinking of you alone by yourself. Anyone could have come through the door to hurt you."

I could have pointed out the same could be said about him. "Well...I'm not alone now. Thank you for that."

"What can I make you for breakfast? What do you like?"

Food? I was still stuffed from dinner. It was an unusual occurrence for me, and I loved the sensation. "I am a food fan. I eat...everything. But you don't have to feed me. I can..."

"Maci." He lifted his eyebrows. "I'm going to feed you breakfast."

He stroked my hair, and I loved it. Maybe he'd like the same done to him? If he touched me, that was pretty much guaranteed to be permission that I could touch him. I reached toward him and did to him what he was doing to me.

"You have to at least let me contribute to the food. I get a discount at work."

He leaned into my hand. "Let's drop it. You're not winning this one with me."

"Fine." I was going to find a way to pay him back for his kindness. I'd work it out. "Thank you. I eat anything. Whatever you're making for yourself."

He nodded. "Okay. That's fine. What is your absolute favorite place you've ever been? I like to picture places in my head and picture people there. It's weird, I know, but I think you've been calling yourself that, so I guess I'll fit right in."

My favorite place? I took a moment to answer him. "I guess my favorite place I've ever been was the sushi restaurant tonight. I haven't been a lot of places. So...yeah, that."

He groaned. "And Tanner got to bring you. Lucky bastard. I'm going to take you someplace cool too."

I shook my head. "This could be a favorite place too."

"Then I'll picture you here."

We didn't talk after that, just lay in the dark, our hands running through each other's hair like we'd done this a million times. It was just so strangely natural, and I was less and less concerned with the oddity of the whole thing. His hand suddenly stopped, and I looked over at him. His eyes were closed. I lifted my eyebrows. Caesar had just fallen asleep.

It was sweet, really. The guy who never slept had knocked out right next to me like it was the most natural thing in the world. Maybe it was because my own eyes drifted closed, so without giving it another thought, I fell asleep next to him.

He jostled me awake sometime later. I lifted my eyelids. Caesar was still asleep, just pulling me against his body so that I was pressed entirely against his chest. It startled me, but not enough to object to the motion. Actually, being close to him was even warmer, like getting to sleep in a really close hug.

Caesar exhaled audibly and grumbled. "Where were you for so long? I missed you."

That must have been some dream he was having. I closed my eyes again.

My alarm blaring woke both of us the next morning. I blinked, struggling to come back to consciousness as Caesar reached over me to stop the noise on my phone.

His voice was low, scratchy. "Is it nine? Really? I slept all fucking night."

So had I. It took a second for me to rouse enough to realize how we were lying together. I was still pressed against his chest, but I clung to his shirt like it was a lifeline. He had swung one leg over me, and my head was officially on his arm.

He was also hard. For the first time in my life, I wasn't terrified of that thought. Mom's guys got erect all the time around me, and I hated seeing it, like something bad was about to happen. Here, warm in bed with Caesar, it was an entirely different feeling. My nipples hardened, and I ignored that occurrence. He smelled clean and male. I closed my eyes and just held on to him.

"Five minutes." I whispered. "And I can let go if this is strange."

"Don't." He kissed my neck, breathing me in as he did. "I love this. I don't know how we ended up like this, but it's my best wake up ever."

I smiled against his chest. "You pulled me to you in the middle of the night."

"Should I apologize?"

I shook my head. "Best sleep ever."

"Maci..." His voice trailed off, so I lifted my head to make eye contact with him, which did mean I had to shift a bit and let go.

"Caesar?" He'd said my name, so I responded with the same.

"You're so fucking beautiful. You know that, right? So beautiful."

I shook my head. "I'm not. You're the beautiful one. Have you looked at yourself?"

He leaned in and kissed me square on the lips. I sighed against him. Yes, I'd wanted that. Needed it, even. "Trust me, you're the beautiful one, Maci. Those eyes have slayed me for years. Thank you for finally talking to us."

I leaned up on my elbow. "How many years?" Just then, a noise sounded in the hall. I sat up, grabbing the blanket and pulling it to my neck. "Your dad?"

"Not at this hour. I bet it's Ace. Boy couldn't wait an

hour." Caesar tugged me back down just as Ace came in carrying a coffee holder.

"Morning, you two. That looks so comfy. Thought you might all like some of this after the not-sleeping that went on all night. But...I'm thinking maybe you did sleep, which is even better."

Caesar put out his hand, and Ace placed a cup in it. "Thank you. Yes, all night. Give me a second to get up, then we'll let Maci have a few minutes alone to get ready. Good morning, Ace. I'm almost sluggish."

He dislodged himself from me, more gracefully than I would have done, and in a quick move, headed to the bathroom.

I smiled at Ace and took his offering of coffee. "Good morning."

"I'd love you at my house, Maci. But my father is there right now. I'm so glad you look okay today."

I felt okay. Better than I should have, considering the situation. I sipped my coffee. "This is awesome. Thank you."

He squeezed my foot at the end of the bed. "You are so welcome."

7

They waited in the kitchen for me. It took me ten minutes to find it. I was pretty sure there were thirty rooms in this crazy huge house. If I hadn't heard their voices, I might have never found it. I could see the headlines now... *"Girl Lost in Big Mansion, Never Seen Again."* I smiled at my own stupid thoughts.

"You're doing it wrong." Ace sighed. "Seriously, *that's* how you make scrambled eggs?"

"This is how everyone makes scrambled eggs." Caesar sighed. "If you make them differently, you're doing it wrong."

I grinned. "Hi."

They both turned to regard me and smiled almost simultaneously. "Hi," they said together.

"Eggs look good." I approached slowly, and my stomach grumbled. I guessed I was hungry. I almost never noticed anymore.

"Told you." Caesar grinned, winking at Ace. "Come. Sit down. Ace, you want some?"

"Of your poorly made eggs? Absolutely not. I ate some

very good ones before I left my house—over easy. I would love to make you some sometime, Maci." Still, he sat next to me at the counter when I sat down.

I took his hand in mine, admiring the way his hand looked so much bigger holding mine. He stroked his thumb over my palm. "I don't think I've ever had eggs over easy."

"Well, we need to correct that." He kissed my cheek. I grinned at him. Affection seemed so easy for Ace. Like his eggs. "I'll make them for you tomorrow morning."

I swallowed my anxiety before I took a bite of my eggs. "I don't know if I can put Caesar out two nights in a row."

Caesar sat on my other side. "It wasn't putting me out. I loved it. You're welcome to stay here whenever you want. In fact, I hope you will. Feel free to move in." He spooned some eggs into his mouth. "Except on the rare occasions that my father is here. Then stay away, Maci. Please stay *far* away."

"Isn't your father the mayor?" The way Caesar spoke about his dad went in direct contrast to the way I pictured the mayor.

"That's what they tell me."

"Hey," Ace said, taking my attention. I knew I was being misdirected, and that was fine by me. I'd pretend I hadn't been, and I wouldn't ask. "Do you want to watch a movie tonight?"

That sounded like an amazing idea. "I do if you do. I mean...is that okay? I know there were problems yesterday."

"We'll do it here." Caesar smiled. "The trouble is going out in public and only recently, so we'll watch a movie here. Unless you had big plans, Ace, to take her to the theater, in which case I can shut up and let you."

He shook his head. "We'll all watch a movie here. Get everyone and do it together. It'll be fun. We haven't done that in a long while."

The eggs were warm in my mouth, and I closed my eyes to savor the taste. *Wow*. I lifted my lids. "These are fantastic."

They stared at me, both of them, and I had no idea what either of them were thinking in that moment. I set down my fork. "Did I do something weird? Weird number one for the day, and I don't even know what it is."

"No." Caesar pushed a strand of my hair behind my ear. "You didn't. I'm so glad you like the eggs. I'll make them for you every morning. After you try Ace's really bad ones, that is."

Ace laughed, throwing back his head. "Okay, maybe you cook better than me. Fine, I concede. I didn't have your teacher. I'll take you out to eat after work, Maci? Then we'll come back here and watch the movie."

"Sounds good." I continued to eat my eggs, and they dug into their own. I still wasn't sure what to make of them having stared at me, but maybe it was that I'd looked so odd in that moment and they just didn't want to be rude about it. I wished I'd spent more time studying people and less time trying to figure out how to get away from them.

I thought I had time to figure these things out, but now these guys had entered my life who were my friends but also *not* normal friends. So were they more? Were they less? Was I ever going to understand what exactly had happened?

Why I liked it so much?

I finished, and Caesar grabbed my plate. "Hey, who taught you to cook? The one that was better than Ace's."

"We have helpers. We've had them since we were little, people responsible for us for a long time. Sort of nannies, but not really. Just watchers, kind of. Mine was a kind lady named Roseanna who liked to cook. She didn't talk much, but she liked to be in the kitchen, so I hung out in the kitchen with her." He shrugged. "Picked up some things."

Interesting. "Why did you need them? After your mothers left, couldn't your fathers, I don't know, raise you, for the most part? They had one child each. Or hire nannies?"

He shook his head. "They aren't really paternal. I suppose they thought those helpers were as good as nannies. I guess it was good enough. And I learned how to cook scrambled eggs." He winked at me. "Are you guys going straight to work? It's early to be leaving."

I shook my head. "I realized last night I left my money, all my savings, in the trailer. I can't leave it there. My mother has stolen from me before, so Ace is going to bring me there to get it first."

Caesar frowned and then turned to Ace. "Do you think you'll run into any problems?"

"Maybe. If you want to come along, two of us are certainly better than one. Just in case they don't know my name as well as they know Rowan's, since apparently just seeing him made a grown man all but piss himself and sober up fast."

Caesar nodded. "Give me two seconds to get dressed, and I'll meet you guys over there. I'll run some errands before I come back home. Don't go in without me."

"We'll wait. Or knowing you, you'll beat us there since you drive like a lunatic." Ace reached out his hand, and I took it. I supposed I could object. It was my problem and my place, after all. I agreed to go with Ace, not with Caesar, but I sort of liked that they would both be there. It was more distant, but I could still feel that creepy man's hands on me.

Two of them were better than one in this situation.

"So, in this part of the story, you won't tell me why... Rowan is scarier than you two?" I winked at Ace and smiled at Caesar. "That's what you're saying?"

Ace choked and then laughed. "Actually, no. But I suppose people think that he is. I'm probably the scariest of the whole bunch of us."

Caesar nodded. "I'd disagree, but I think he probably is deep down. He looks like such a sweetheart and acts like such a good guy, but if you take away the veneer, Ace is psychotic. Am I kidding? Wow. I just don't know, but you're getting in the car with him."

I laughed as Ace squeezed my hand. "Not to you, Maci. I'm as sweet as a newborn kitten with you."

My mother had brought a kitten home once. "They bite."

"Yes, they do." He kissed my cheek. "But not you. Never you."

Maybe I'd have to revisit the *Ace is the sweetest* idea I had earlier.

He hadn't been wrong. After playing with his song list in the car—he liked a surprising amount of nineties metal—and giggling most of the time, we only beat Caesar to my trailer by a minute. How they all knew exactly where it was fell beyond my knowledge. I could ask and probably get an answer to that one, however, it seemed highly likely I was getting used to not being told things. I wasn't sure what that said about me. I decided right then not to consider that issue until I was alone and had some time to dwell. In any case, Caesar showed up thirty seconds after we arrived.

"Told you." Ace pointed at Caesar's car with his thumb. "Maniac."

"Good to know." I winked at him, and he winked back. My cheeks heated up. Flirting was fun. It just was, and I loved it.

I headed toward my home. My mom's car, the one I always used, was still there, and the other one that had been there the night before. I stopped and turned to my friends. "They're probably out cold. I'd like to keep them that way. They won't wake early, but don't actively try, okay?"

Ace nodded. "No banging pots and pans. Got it."

"This is your mom. That's why she gets any respect at all," Caesar added. "But yes, we'll do as you want when it comes to your mom."

"Otherwise, you'd do to her whatever you did to Mrs. Reemus?" I shot that out as I headed to the door.

Ace laughed. "That was Griffin, but point taken."

"Like you wouldn't have done exactly the same thing," Caesar answered him. "I was going to. He just did it first."

"No, that's not actually what I would have done," Ace replied.

I didn't get to hear what else they said as I quickly entered my trailer. I took a deep breath. It stunk of the party they must have continued after I left. The living room was empty. Disgusting, like it had been trampled by a group of barn animals, but empty of anyone who might see me. My mother's door was open enough, I could hear snores coming from inside. Loud ones.

If I weren't mistaken, snores from at least two different people. Maybe even three. Perhaps they were all in there together. She'd certainly wanted me to participate. I shuddered, and a strong set of arms came around me from behind.

Ace whispered in my ear, "It's okay. You're not alone. Just go get your money, and we'll leave. No need to stay while she has them here."

"This is a nice location." Caesar looked around. "Pretty views of the woods. Developers keep trying to knock those down, but believe it or not, my father, the mayor, has turned out to be something of an environmentalist. The woods are staying. Anyway, pretty view."

I stepped out of Ace's arms, wishing I was back in them immediately. "My mother forbade me from ever going in the woods. They're right there, and I've never been. Funny, that's the only thing she ever told me not to do."

"Seems kind of random." Ace shrugged. "But what do I know?"

I walked to my room and stopped abruptly. My mother had torn my sleeping space apart. Literally smashed my lamps and destroyed my pillows. I forced myself to swallow. That wasn't the biggest problem. I didn't mind that my clothes were on the floor, or even that if the stains were any indication, they'd fucked in my bed. Well, actually, that bothered me a whole shit ton, but not as much as the fact that she had found the false bottom to my drawer and that the money that had been in an envelope there was entirely gone.

How had she known? It had looked nearly flawless to me, and my mother wasn't observant. Still, the how didn't matter. The point was she had my money.

"It's gone. She has it." Or had it. This was my mother— she might have already spent all of it. "The money I had saved to pay bills and get out of here. It's gone. All of it." I'd gone without eating to save that money. I closed my eyes. I wasn't even sure who I'd spoken to. Neither one of the guys might have heard me.

I disobeyed my own order and swung open her door, loudly. My mother startled on the bed. "Maci? Come back to apologize?"

"Where is it?" I stood in the doorway, my hands fisted almost of their own accord because I'd certainly not consciously done it, and I screamed at her. The two men on the bed strewn over each other roused, all of them staring at me. "Where is the money, Mom?"

She scowled at me. "After the way your friends treated us last night, I decided I was entitled to recompense." She slurred that last word, like she didn't know how to say it. "And we made ourselves very happy."

I caught my breath. This had been my fear. "Mom, that was two thousand dollars. You can't have spent two thousand dollars last night. You can't have done that. That's for the lights, Mom. That's for food. That's for us to live, Mom." I wouldn't talk about my escape plan. That was none of her business. "How could you do that?"

Downright shouting, I lunged forward, only to be stopped by Ace wrapping his arms around my waist and hauling me backward. "Not worth it. And I don't trust them not to accuse you of something awful if you do make contact with them. They're not worth jail time. They're just not."

I didn't fight him. He was right. But with my heart racing like I'd just run ten miles, I didn't know how I was going to get through it if I didn't slug someone.

"Take her outside," Caesar said softly. "I'm going to have words with her mother."

A second later, he set me down outside. I paced around. "All of it. She took *all* of it."

"I know." He grasped my shoulders. "I'm not trying to manhandle you, by the way. I respect your ability to make decisions. I—"

"Ace," I interrupted him. "I'm not upset with you. Thank you for stopping me from committing assault. I can't..." My voice trailed off.

He cupped my cheek. "You can't what?"

I burst into tears. It had been such an incredibly long time since I'd cried, I couldn't even remember the last time

I'd done it. What did it solve? Nothing. And no one cared when I cried. I'd learned to just shut up and deal. There was no choice.

But I was sobbing, and there was nothing I could do about it. Ace pulled me against his chest and pressed my head against him so that I literally sobbed into his body. I couldn't stop. I didn't even know how I would attempt it.

Blubbering, I tried to explain. "I went without food to save that. I...I paid the electricity. I..."

I was done. Whatever I was going to say after that, I couldn't get the words out. He rocked me gently. His voice was low. "You shouldn't have to do those things. There should be a very limited expectation of the people who are responsible for us, that they will do their best to keep the lights on. No one is going to turn them off on you. No one is going to make you homeless. No one is going to harm you, and when you want to go next year, you'll go. I promise you that."

I cried harder. Those weren't things he could legitimately say to me and make happen. I had to breathe. I had to try.

"I've got you. For just a minute, believe that I've got you." He continued his rocking. "I never make promises I can't keep. Fuck this. Seriously. I know she's your mom, but this is monstrous, and trust me, I know about monsters."

The sound of footsteps approaching us told me Caesar was there. "I have two hundred dollars of your money. Trust Ace, Maci. He never lies. If he told you this was going to be okay, then it will. And I'm making the same promise. You're safe. You're not going to be homeless."

I pulled back. Were they kidding? "You guys lie all the time." I wiped my eyes. It did no good. "You just dodge and refuse to elaborate and that's fine, but you can't tell me you don't lie. Everyone lies, literally everyone, even if it's just lying to ourselves. We all lie all the time."

Ace nodded, slowly. "You're right—everyone lies. I guess I do even more than most. Every day. I hate that idea, but what amazes me is that I don't think you mind it that much. I don't know why. I wonder if you even do? I wonder if it matters? All of that is not important, because we're being honest with each other right this second. Brilliantly, horribly, truthful. And what I'm saying to you is that I will not allow your life to fall apart because of this."

Caesar held out my two hundred dollars, so I took it, pocketing the money. "Thanks." Guilt spread over me. These guys were helping me, and I'd just launched at them, calling them liars. "Guys, I'm so sorry. That was uncalled for. I..."

Ace pulled me into a hug. "You were right. What you said was right. You don't ever have to apologize for being right. The things I don't tell you...I can't tell you. If I could, I'd share in a heartbeat."

"I wouldn't." Caesar's voice was low. "Because they fucking suck. Come on. You're not going to work today. Call in sick. Or text in sick. Whatever you do."

That made no sense. "I can't earn *less* now. If anything, I'm going to have to somehow work more." I closed my eyes. "Or I'm never getting out of here."

"Yes, you are," Ace whispered in my ear. "I promise."

WORK WAS LONG. The guys hadn't argued with me the rest of the way there, and I'd managed to get through minute by minute without breaking down in tears again. Every second was an effort, but it was hardly the first time I'd worked on what amounted to autopilot. One step after another. Minute by minute. I tried to focus on the next right thing.

"Hand it to me." I jumped as Rowan spoke to me, leaning against the wall. He stepped toward me. "Come on. I'll help. I can carry the box for you. Take a break. Sit down."

I shook my head. "It's my job. You don't have to carry anything for me."

"I know I don't have to, but I offered. I want to. You had a very long morning, and that's my fault. We should have gone back last night."

I shook my head. "I don't think I was in any condition then either. This isn't on you."

He put out his arms. "Hand me the box."

"Rowan, this is my job. And now it looks like I'll be keeping it a lot longer than I thought I would be. Like a year longer. So thank you for wanting to help, but I'm going to do it." I kept my box.

He walked toward me. "I solve everyone's problems. You won't let me solve yours?"

"No, but thank you. I was pretty mean to Ace and Caesar. They didn't deserve it. I'm surprised you want anything to do with me."

A noise outside startled me, and I almost dropped the box. It must have been a car backfiring. Rowan walked to the window to stare outside. It was open again, the same way Ace had gotten in. "That's old man Peterson. His car really needs a tune-up. I'm going to fix it for him later this week." He turned back around. "See? Other people's problems, I fix them. And whatever you said to Ace and Caesar, they felt you were particularly on point. They don't like lying. Neither do I." He was really close to me right then. "I wonder if you could handle the truth. I would really love to tell you."

I swallowed. "It's that bad that you can't be sure I can handle it? What kind of trouble are you in?"

He cupped my cheeks. "So much trouble."

The door swung open to the storage room, and my manager stood there. He stared at Rowan for a second and then at me. When he spoke, his voice was shaky. "There's someone here to see you, Maci."

There was? I didn't believe the guys would come through the front door to speak to my manager. Ace and Rowan had both snuck in. "Who?"

"Fuck," Rowan whispered as a man walked in behind my manager. I blinked. Was that Rowan's father?

I swallowed. "Sir, we were just talking. I swear I'm not a bad influence on your son."

"Oh," he glided toward me, "that I believe. I think you are going to be just what I need for my son and the others." He put out his hand, bending toward me when he did. "Put down that box and come with me. We can do this the easy way or the hard way." He looked over his shoulder to my manager. "Go, now."

Like he was a puppet on a string being directed, my boss scurried away.

"Father, I'm not sure what you are hoping to achieve here. I've told you, Maci is a friend. An unknowing person. We've done nothing we shouldn't..."

His father held up his hand. "Look at me in the eyes, Maci."

I lifted my head, not sure I could have said no if I wanted to. He stared at me for a long moment. "You're right. She's just a human girl. I had to be sure. Come with me."

"Father." Rowan sounded like he spoke through gritted teeth, but I couldn't look at him.

His father took my wrist, and before I could even

consider why, he bit me. Hard. I yelped and tried to yank back, checking out of my stupor finally, but he had me in a hold like I couldn't believe. As I shrieked, he sucked the blood from my wrist.

The whole thing lasted seconds, but Rowan bellowed, grabbing his father's arm, tugging to no avail. "Stop it. Come on. Not her. Stop."

The man—*is he a man?*—sucking on me stopped. He lifted his head, my blood dripping down his chin. With a lick of his tongue, my wrist stopped bleeding, and he stepped away.

"Now, Maci."

I hurried to catch up to him, not even sure why I would do that. I didn't want to go with him. This man who sucked my blood, who... Was he a vampire?

"Rowan?" My voice shook. I didn't even know what I was asking him.

"Don't fight it." He sounded defeated. "For at least the next hour or so, you won't be able to resist doing what he wants. It will be easier if you just go. Maci." He ran to walk with me. "Try to forgive me. I told you this was bad."

"Vampire?"

We made it out to the parking lot in the streaming sun, into the afternoon glare.

"Yes."

His father opened a door to his super expensive car, and I got in.

8

This was really happening. I was in the car with Rowan's father, who was a vampire. He'd bit me. I stared at the wound. It was small and closed. I probably wouldn't even see it tomorrow.

"It's his saliva." Rowan stared at me, looking where I did, straight at my wrist. "It has properties to heal the wound fast, but it's also what makes people addicted."

I gasped. This was news to me. "What?" The last thing I wanted was to be addicted to anything.

He put his hand on my arm. "It's okay. You've only been bitten once. You're not addicted, but you're probably feeling a little bit...a little bit like you're feeling no pain. Not good, per se, but not bad. Numb, right? Like what happened this morning matters less to you now."

Rowan was absolutely right. I couldn't even get startled about that. Even the idea of being addicted, which moments earlier had made me gasp, faded to unimportance. "Yes. I see what you mean."

"I know you do. Now, imagine you're a person who needs

to feel this way all the time. Just not to feel it, whatever it is that you don't want to feel, so you seek out the bite again and again until you absolutely can't live without it. I think I've heard it takes about ten times."

His father eyed him in the rearview mirror. "Don't be ridiculous. Most humans can't withstand five bites before they're ours. But they're ours before that too. We don't let people who know about us come and go. Everyone is carefully watched, as you know."

That begged the next question. "So you're a vampire. All five of you are? I guess, since you can walk in the daylight, there is no way to tell."

This was so bizarre. The whole situation seemed unreal, and yet it was absolutely happening. Vampires were somehow real, and I was in the car with two of them.

"No, I'm not yet a vampire." He took my hand and squeezed it. "Feel me? I'm warm. If you touched my father, he'd be cold."

Okay, I amended my thought. *One vampire. I am in the car with* one *vampire.*

Hold on. "What? Not *yet* a vampire?"

"I'll explain all of it. I promise I will. I told you, I hate lying. Here's how it works—when I was born—"

His father cut him off. "You will, but not yet. I have things to say first. And, Maci..." He said my name like it tasted bad. "Only elder vampires can day walk. It takes hundreds of years. The younger vampires are not able to do it. You are going to want to listen very carefully and do just as I say. If anything happens to Rowan, it will be on your head."

"What?" Rowan and I spoke at the same time. *What does that even mean?*

My friend, who had been carrying a much bigger lie than I ever imagined, sat forward. "I don't know what you're pulling here, but—"

"Quiet."

We both sat back in our seats. His father, a vampire who had bitten me on the wrist, drove the car. Maybe being drugged by his saliva kept me from throwing myself out the window.

Rowan stroked his hand down my face and whispered the words, "I'm sorry. So sorry."

I believed him. The question was how sorry was he going to be, and just how much trouble was I in for ever having said something to Rowan and the others in the library that day?

I wasn't able to do anything but follow Rowan's father into his house and up the stairs to what turned out to be Rowan's very big bedroom. I hurried to keep up. Rowan put himself between his father and me. He remained silent, his back stiff, but he abruptly came to a stop when we reached his bedroom. I could immediately see why. On their knees, on the floor facing us, were the other four guys.

Closest to me was Tanner. He actually jolted when he saw me. Next to him was Ace, and on his other side, Caesar. Griffin was the farthest away.

Tanner closed his eyes like they hurt him. "No."

"It's bad," Rowan spoke to him as he crossed the room to get on his knees next to Griffin. I couldn't be sure, but it seemed they had been in this order before. Rowan knew right where to go.

All of the other fathers were there too, or at least that

was who I assumed they were. They seemed to be lined up facing their individual sons. Rowan's father crossed the room and stood right in front of where Rowan knelt.

"Boys," he spoke, and all eyes in the room landed on him. "I got your message. We all got it, but I have news for you—saying no isn't an option. When I tell you how something is going to be, that is how it's going to be."

Tanner quietly reached over and took my hand in his. He squeezed our fingers together. It was a sweet gesture. He was warm. Rowan said they were warm. That was what made them human. Had his father been cold when he'd bitten me? I really didn't know. I'd been too terrified to take note of the temperature of his skin.

Rowan's bedroom was huge, bigger than Caesar's, and unlike his friend, he didn't have drawings on the walls. Instead, he'd hung framed prints of various cities all over the world. Had he visited these places or just wanted to someday?

It didn't matter right then, and I needed to focus. It must have been the saliva running through me, messing with my head. *Really, could it be any more gross to think about? Ugh.*

"August is not so far off, Father." When Rowan spoke, it was to the floor. "Not so unreasonable. We have done everything you asked of us. We are asking for one summer, that is it."

"It is unreasonable because I said it is." His father practically snarled. "The others will be rising any day. You will take your place on the night of your graduation."

I blinked. *What does that mean?* Tanner squeezed my hand harder. He wanted me to keep quiet. I had no intention of speaking right then.

"So, you want us to take our place next week." Rowan looked pained, his face scrunched up. "It's a lot to digest. I know you have next to no memories of this time for your-selves, but you have to know how unfair it is, what you're asking. And now to bring in a girl? A person with no ties to our life, who would have gone without ever discovering any of our secrets? To bite her. To..."

This time, it was Ace's father who spoke. "There is a poetic justice to it. So much more than you'll ever under-stand." He smiled, but there was no mirth. "You'll graduate from one life to the next. You're eighteen. It's time. If we're right about what happens next, there is real...irony, because you all got caught up with a human woman. By this time next year, I imagine you'll understand why."

"She is here so that you will behave. So you'll stop pestering us with your complaints, with your demands. So you will do what you were born to do. Next week. Without fail. Because if you displease any of us again, even a little bit, we will make things much harder for her. Right now," he stared at me for the first time, "she's been bitten once. That means, for a little while longer, she will feel the blankness—the nothing, as my son who is too poetic for his own good, referred to it in the car. She will feel compelled to do as I tell her, but that will fade shortly. Unless she is rabidly unlucky, and maybe she is, she won't be addicted from our one encounter." He smiled. It was a sick, twisted expression that turned my stomach. There was no happiness in him, none at all. Besides, I was feeling sensations just fine. Yes, the saliva induced yuckiness of nothing—I liked Rowan's description—must be fading. "But she could be addicted if we kept biting her. And we will. Over and over again until you comply. You've known her mere days, and I don't know why you all took to her the way that you did. It seems sense-less, but I am happy to use it now. You can keep her well or you can make her just like her mother."

I caught my breath. That really was my biggest fear. Or I could be worse than my mother, that was always a possibility. My mother still looked good. She wasn't homeless. She had all her teeth. The way I imagined things, they could be much, much worse than being my mother. Not that I wanted to test that theory. Not at all.

He shook his head. "I visited with her mother an hour ago."

"What?" Now I had to speak. "What did you do to her?"

"Maci." Griffin met my gaze. "Quiet. Trust me. That is the smart move here. Be as silent as you can be."

Doesn't he understand? "Griffin, my mother—"

Rowan's father interrupted me. "Is alive and very wealthy now. Not as wealthy as she could have been, but wealthier than she was. About twenty thousand dollars wealthier."

Tanner's father rolled his eyes. "Humans."

"What did you want for that money?" I wanted to scream. Not doing so was taking real effort. *Huge* effort.

"You. And she handed you over, so now you are mine, Maci. No one will be looking for you. Not at home. Not at school. The police will turn away if someone says your name. From now on, you are part of our collection of people. Congratulations. You are now our servant, as so many have been before you. The question is...do you want to live through the experience?"

Caesar lifted his head. "Say yes. Trust me. Say yes."

That wasn't hard. I absolutely wanted to live through the experience, and hopefully lots of future ones too. "Yes."

"Good." He nodded. "The training starts now. The four of you who don't live here will go get your things and return. You live here now for the remainder of your time. You do too, Maci. You are always here. That is how this works, or she gets bit. Again and again."

With that, he stormed from the room. The other grownup vampires followed him, all of them moving with an alien gliding stride unlike normal human walking. I wasn't sure I could ever move my feet that way, like they didn't quite touch the floor. I'd noticed it at the bar. Caesar's father stopped and turned to face us. "The war is coming. We have years left, not decades. I see it more and more. The Betrayer is everywhere. There is no time to waste. You *will* do what you were born to do."

Tanner was on his feet as soon as they left, and he pulled me into a hug. "I'm sorry. I'm so sorry. This wasn't supposed to happen."

I wanted to hug him back, but I couldn't. It was as though I couldn't make my arms move. I'd been bitten by a vampire. These guys were all the children of them, who were...what? I didn't understand what was happening.

"Maci, you have to let us explain," he whispered in my ear. "Believe me, this was the last thing we wanted."

"I do. I believe you never wanted me to know about this." I stepped back. "But I think you'd better start explaining some things, because now I'm in it. With a bite on my wrist and a lot of fucking questions, including the fact that my mother has twice tried to give me away over the last two days, and this time, apparently she fucking did it." By the end of my words, I was downright screaming at them. At all of them.

I made it through most days without getting too worked up about anything, but lately, it was like I was loaded with emotions I had nothing to do about except yell or cry.

"Guys," Rowan answered. "This is too much. I know. We knew this day would come. It's not fair that it's now, not even a little bit, but there is nothing to do. Not one fucking thing. So go home and get your shit. We're in this together. We always have been. And I'll explain it to Maci. All of it. Every little bit."

They were all so quiet, I would swear I could've heard a pin drop. Eventually, Griffin nodded. He walked toward me. "We'll make this okay for you, Maci." He accompanied his statement by placing a warm hand on my back. "Go with Rowan. Then you'll understand. Well, as much as we do. We'll talk when we get back."

"Caesar, bring her stuff from your house," Rowan finished.

"I...I shouldn't be yelling or crying. I need to have better responses to terrible things. I'm sorry."

Ace kissed my cheek. "It's okay. We've all yelled and cried over this. Trust me on this, I want to scream right now, and I've known about all this since I was old enough to know. I can't believe he dragged you into this. I absolutely should have seen it coming. We all should have, but we didn't. This is on us."

Caesar and Tanner both smiled at me—sad attempts, but attempts nonetheless—on their way out the door.

"I know something terrible is happening to you, to all of you. I'm sorry if I just made it all about me." I shouldn't have done that. They needed to know. "I'm just so confused and..."

Ace placed his hand on my wrist. "It's okay. We're not any worse off than we've always been. Your life just went haywire. Forgive us, if you can. Please?"

With that spoken, my sushi date left with the guy I'd slept next to the night before. Griffin, the valedictorian, followed them, and Ace, who had promised me dinner tonight, went last, finally leaving me with the guy who had just watched me get bitten.

All of this was just too much. "Rowan?"

He sank down on the floor. "Come sit with me? I promise I have no descending fangs. Nothing I can do can hurt you, nor would I if I could."

I did need to sit. I might even fall over if I didn't. I sank down next to him. "Your room is nice."

"Thanks. I spend a lot of time in here alone, so...I do tend to try to make it stuff I want to look at."

I pointed at the picture of Tokyo. "Been there?"

"Oh no. I've never been anywhere. This is it for me, and probably all there will be. You see, I was born to be a vampire. Well, sort of. I was born a human. My mother was human when she had me. My father a vampire. The logistics of how that can happen are pretty simple. Vampires can have sex just like humans. Female vampires, of which there are not a lot of them, can't have kids. But vampires can breed with human females."

I couldn't imagine it. "Really? I mean...a non-vampire woman signs up to participate?"

He laughed. "A lot of them, actually. Remember that addiction thing? Yeah... so some women want the bite. They want it bad. Your teacher, Mrs. Reemus, begged for it for years, even though she's married. Anyway, most of the time, the women who participate in the breeding, they want to be vampires. That's the deal—they breed, and then they're made vampires."

"Oh, I see. That's why you're not a vampire now. You have to be made into one." I'd seen that in movies.

"No, actually. Sorry, it's a mess of complications." He sighed. "Female vampires are made. Male vampires are born. Sort of. Or reborn? We're born human. We grow up.

Then we die and are reborn vampires." He rose. "I just made you sit, but come with me. I'll show you."

Show me? I followed him from the room and outside onto his lawn. His backyard was huge, and there were small cabins everywhere leading down a hill past where I could see. The property had to be immense. The afternoon had gotten later, and it was almost that moment when night breathed in to take over. I stopped walking. "Are we safe out here? It's almost dark."

"You're safe. You're with me—they wouldn't dare touch me—and Dad marked you today. For now, you can walk safely unmolested by vampires. That might not always be true, but today it is." He pointed left. "We're going that way."

One of the cabins turned out to be our destination. Outside, two very tall men side-eyed us when we approached. They were pale, and I bet if I touched them, they'd be cold. I was new to this, but it was a pretty good guess that they were also vampires.

"Dad said to show her. Let us in." Rowan wasn't afraid of the men, and they stood aside to let us inside. I shivered as they stared at me. Did they want to bite me, suck my blood, and addict me to the need for them?

I wasn't great with bodily fluids to begin with.

This was going to take a lot of getting used to.

"Don't take too long in there. They're going to emerge soon. Probably tomorrow or the next day, but if one of them is early, you don't want to get caught."

Rowan nodded. "Fair enough."

Inside the large room, five coffins were laid out around the edges and one in the center. Scratching noises, like there were rats somewhere, caught my ears, and I winced. First blood and saliva, now vermin.

"Inside those coffins are five people who used to be alive.

Like me, they were born, and like I will do next week," he choked on the words, "they were sealed inside of those boxes where they died. They stayed that way for most of this year. Now they have been reborn as vampires. When they manage to break themselves out of the boxes, they will be among the vampires living here. We've gotten pretty good at telling when that will happen, so we think tomorrow or soon after. They'll be new vampires. Crazy. Blood sucking. Rabid. They will have no control and will be locked away in another cabin, where they will be brought people to feed on until they are under control. That takes as long as it takes. Most of their victims will die. Those that don't might become servants." He walked over and touched the coffin in the middle. "This will be where mine is put. A position of honor. Because my father is the big dick in charge. Sorry, the leader of our clan."

My mouth fell open and coldness seeped into my veins. "Rowan."

"I know. It's just about as bad as you can picture, right?" He shook his head. "That is what they want us to do graduation night. We requested they wait till August. I mean, how fucking dare we?" He stalked to the wall and pounded his fist against it. "So, for recompense, they took you and... well, you were there. You know what happened."

I ran over to him, wrapping my arms around his waist. "Rowan, no. You can't do that. You can't climb in there, and what? Starve to death?"

"Suffocate." He shook his head. "Takes about five hours. More, if you panic. They drug us into submission, so there is no panic, but sometimes it can even take just a little bit longer than the five hours."

I pressed my head into his shoulder, and he hugged me tightly. "We'll run away. Right now. The six of us. We'll just go. Fuck graduation. We will run to the sunniest spot on the planet and hide."

"I am so crazy about you, and you just said the best thing." He laughed, but it was more of a groan. "There is nowhere we can go where they won't find us, and then they'll make it even more painful. We will have shamed them with disgrace. If I thought it would work, I'd run forever."

I could hardly think. "Rowan, I have so many questions."

"Let's walk. More to show you, and like the guard said, we don't want to be here when they wake up."

I let him take my arm, and I leaned against him, walking slowly together. "This just can't be."

"Yet it is." He shrugged like it didn't matter, but boy did it, and I could see how he covered his emotions in that single movement. "What are your questions?"

"You're only eighteen. Will you be eighteen forever?"

"No, we'll age slowly. My father is several hundred years old. You wouldn't know it. Looks about fifty, right?"

Maybe that was the stupidest one I could ask. "So is this what your dad does, then? He just breeds young men to go die and make new vampires? Over and over?"

"I love how your brain works. No, we are the first, and that is where it gets even more complicated. The five of us, as it turns out, are really complicated."

Once again, we went inside a cabin. Everywhere I looked, there were really old books. "Would you believe vampires have prophecies?"

"Well, seeing as there are vampires, I guess I can believe that they have prophecies. I mean, I don't know a thing about prophecies."

He gestured toward the books. "In there is a prophecy

that says that five great vampires who died would be reborn. They think that's us."

I pointed at him. "You? And the others? You're reincarnated great vampires?"

"Well, right now, I'm an eighteen-year-old high school student, but apparently when I wake up, I will have that vampire's soul. No one really explained it to me, just that is what is going to happen. Why we're so fucking important." He looked away. "So important we can't wait until August. You see, there is a war, and it's been going on a long time. Our clan and someone else's. They need us to be part of the fight."

I threw my arms around him again. "How long will you be dead before you wake up?"

"Could be between nine months and a year. They say the longer you take, the stronger you'll be. I don't know if that is true, because the ones that go down together also seem to wake up together. So...how does that work? I don't know."

I took his cheeks in my hands the way he had taken mine. "Rowan, the point is that you will wake up. You *will* wake up. You won't be dead."

"No, *I* will be dead. Everything you know about me? Gone. I'll be dead. My body will be here, changed significantly. I'll be drinking blood. And I will be a monster. My dad? He's not as bad as I could be. He's had centuries to calm down. I will be a living nightmare to anyone who runs into me for years. Yes, I'll be dead." His voice hitched. "We dragged you into this nightmare with us, but, Maci, I am so glad to have known you. So glad you are in my life, even if just for a week. You made us all so happy. Thank you. And I'm sorry."

I kissed his lips. "Rowan, don't apologize again. We're

going to fix this. I'm here now, and we're going to brainstorm."

He kissed me back, hard, possessive, loving. "Don't hope for that. We have to make you safe. We have to figure this out. And then we have to die. But in the meantime, maybe we could have fun this week. Maybe that's possible."

9

We walked in silence, arms around each other, through the darkness that had started to fall around us. He would point things out to me in a quiet voice. "That's where the servants live."

I turned to look. "I don't think it means cleaners and cooks, right?"

"Well, they do that, but no, it mostly means blood servants."

I almost asked him if they would be who he would feed from in his blood frenzy—if they were who he would kill—but I fortunately fought the impulse. Rowan really didn't need any more pain. Most of the servants wore all black. Was that a uniform? They were all women. But then there were also some gorgeously dressed women strolling the pavement. They didn't look like they were rushing anywhere. One of them stopped to hug another one, throwing her head back in joy.

"Who are they?"

He sighed. "Paramours. Sometimes, a vampire will

attach to a particular feeding source and decide she belongs to him alone. They become the paramour."

"Usually that would imply sex." I watched the women a moment longer. I wasn't wrong. Those women were in much better physical condition than the others. Being a paramour had its perks, it would seem.

"It still does. I mean, gross to think about, because it involves my dad, but vampires still have sex. Hence, the siring bit. But make no mistake, it *always* has to do with the blood, from what I understand. There is no part of life, or afterlife, for the vampire that doesn't involve blood."

I winced. It really was gross to think about. I wasn't sure it was a vampire problem as much as a *parents having sex* problem. No one wanted to picture that. Not at all. I'd unfortunately caught my mother on more than one occasion, but I worked hard to repress those memories. I didn't let myself think about it. At all.

"So you've got blood servants. Paramours. Vampires. And you. All living here." I wanted to make sure I had it right.

He nodded. "And now you. And the other guys, who lived in their own houses, which were on the outskirts of here. We have to be close by. Everyone who is in this clan. There is a war going on. For hundreds and hundreds of years. There is a guy, they call him the Betrayer, and I don't know that much about him, except he apparently did just that for a long time —betrayed. Our vamps fight his vamps. It's a big giant mess. We lose a lot of vampires to it, which is why there is a constant need to make new ones, to have new troops."

I scratched my head. "I thought male vampires were born."

"The upper crust are, but some males are made like

females are made. However, they're low rung. They never get to live in a place like this. They fight for them, if they live through that, they hang on the outside. They're considered very low." He squeezed my hand. "Understand that's now how I currently feel. That's how it is for them. I guess I'll feel that way when I'm one of them."

I tugged on his shirt, turning him toward me. "The bottom line here is that you are going to wake up. You are going to be alive again. If we can't stop this—"

"We can't," he interrupted. "I don't want you to get your hopes up about that. There isn't any stopping it. If I run away, they will find me, kill me, and put me in that coffin to rise again. I am never going to let that happen. All five of us. It's a done deal. Period." He shook his head. "And the thing that rises won't be me. Whatever it is that makes me, me, that'll be gone. I'll be one of them. My cousin—our fathers were cousins—who went after me at the bar the other night, he was quiet and gentle when he was alive. Used to paint pictures of horses in his free time. Now he just wants to feed, to kill, and to kick my ass because of some sort of alpha vampire thing I really don't understand that means he's going to be compelled to listen to me when I rise from the dead. Who the fuck knows who I'm going to be? Am I going to be worse than my father? Am I—"

I kissed him. Some part of my soul cried out to do so, and I listened to the instinct. He needed my lips on his in that moment, and I needed to answer the call. It was primal and desperate. Two people in an impossible situation not of our own making. One of us not going to survive this.

When we pulled apart, we both breathed heavily. He cupped my cheek. My lips were sore from the brief embrace. I hadn't realized we'd clung to each other so tightly, but we had.

"I should have left you alone. When you asked us to be quiet, I should have said sure and we could've left."

I shook my head. "Whatever happens now, I'm really glad you didn't."

"You say that because you don't yet know" —he kissed the end of my nose— "just how bad this will get. I won't blame you when you hate me." He blinked. "I may not even care, because I'll be something else. So I'm here to tell you that I'm sorry. Even if I don't seem that way then, I am. I'm sorry."

He hugged me, and I let him. There was so much to digest and a million questions to answer. But one had bugged me from the beginning before I even knew about this craziness. "Where are your mothers?"

"They're vampires. It was part of the deal. Birth us and be made five years later."

"And once they're vampires, they don't care about you anymore?" I closed my eyes. We couldn't make that excuse for my mother. She was solidly human and flawed like all the rest of us.

He sighed. "Something happens to the women, almost an amnesia. They don't really remember their lives the way men seem to. It seems easier to ship them off, according to my father, than keep them here with people trying to get them to remember. Plus, no, they wouldn't be safe to their human children for a long time. So they go somewhere else, but I'm not clear on where. They rise from the dead in another location, and they leave."

That didn't make sense. "Are you sure they're not killing them and just pretending that's what they're doing?"

"I am, actually. Tanner has seen the rising. His father supervises it and does the shipping off. Our mothers are just gone." He sighed. "Let's get back. I don't want a lot of eyes on us. We're always being watched, but I don't need extra observation. It creeps me out how they watch me. Like they're all waiting, counting the days until I'm dead."

I looked around. "I don't see anyone looking."

"That's right, you wouldn't. But some day, you'll feel it because you'll have learned to tell. The longer you spend here, the more you'll feel it."

I swallowed. "Rowan, how long will I have to stay here?"

"Forever." Griffin's voice answered me. He stepped toward us, where he must have been waiting near Rowan's house. "He might try to sugarcoat this a bit, but now that you're in the know—and really, his dad put you incredibly in the know—they'll never let you leave. That house with the servants? My guess is this time next year, you'll be living there."

"Griffin, fuck." Rowan ran a hand through his hair. "You could be a little gentler about things."

He shook his head. "Do you want more lies and easy words? Or do you want the truth, Maci? The hard truth sometimes is what's called for."

I didn't want any more lies. Rowan stepped away from me, his gaze on the house. Ten of the servants rushed out the front door. I blinked. What had they been doing in there? "I better go look and see what they just did. One time, my father had them repaint all the walls while I was in school. No idea what that was."

Griffin ran a hand through his dark hair. "Look, I don't want to be harsh with you. That's not, like...what I want to do."

"I actually appreciated the truth. I...I can't live here forever in that house, running around doing the deeds of vampires. This can't be my life."

Rowan shot Griffin a look before he headed toward his

house. For his part, Griffin walked to me, putting his hands on my shoulders. "We can't stop what happens to us, but maybe I can work out how to save you. I have a plan. Trust me for a little while. I don't want you to live in that house either."

"But maybe you will when you're a vampire? You will want me to live there?"

He blinked. "When I'm a vampire, I'll probably just want to kill you and drink your blood. I probably won't care where you live, so let's go with I care now."

I laughed, despite the fact that none of this was at all funny. But darker was suddenly becoming ridiculously amusing. "All right, we'll go with that."

"When I look at you, you are the prettiest person I've ever seen. Like, the most beautiful ever. And I want to take care of you. Hold you. Make you laugh." He visibly swallowed. "But when I look at you, it's like I've already hurt you. I've already let you down. I feel that way every time I look at you. Why is that?"

I didn't have an answer. "No clue. I think that is more about you than it is about me."

He smirked at me. "Fair enough."

"Why did you bother with all the things you've done? The valedictorian? The captain of the track team? Why did you do all of that if you knew there would be no future? Seems like a ton of effort."

He took my hand in his and drew me to him. "We all want our life to count for something, right? We all want that. We want to know that what we did here mattered. For most people, they know they have time for that. They get to be grownups, at least. I mean, no one is guaranteed any particular amount of time, but people have an expectation of a certain bit of it. Mine ends next week. I knew that it would go fast. I wanted what I did here to matter during that time. Like all those trophies, they have my name on them. I'll give a speech someone will remember." He sighed. "That's why I did it. That's why I worked so hard at it."

I touched his hand. "I think that's beautiful."

"Stupid and beautiful? Or dumb and...?"

I shook my head. "Just beautiful."

"Well...I feel like playing basketball. You want to?"

That was one of the most abrupt jumps I'd ever heard in my life. "Really?"

He took my hand, pulling me with him. "Yes. There's a ball in Rowan's garage and a net on the other side of the house that they put up to distract us when we were young. Do you want to play?"

"I've never played. I mean...ever." That wasn't one of the things we did in gym. Mostly, we spent all our time on football and baseball. "So I don't think I can play. I mean, I've seen it. I know how it's done. But I've never, what's it called? Dribbled or anything."

He lifted his eyebrows. "Then it is beyond time that we do something about that. Let's end the day better than it has gone so far. You can at least say that you played basketball once. Maybe, when I'm gone—and you are an expert at it—you'll remember me."

"Griffin." My voice was low because I could hardly speak. "I'm never going to forget you. I can promise you that."

He winked at me. "Good."

I followed him to the garage, which Griffin knew the code to get into, even though it was Rowan's house, and grabbed a basketball out of a bin in the corner. I caught my breath. There were ten cars in the garage. I hadn't even realized that was what it was from the outside, since the doors had been made to blend in. It just looked like part of the house. When we'd come earlier, he'd parked in the driveway.

Maybe, when you got to live as long as these guys did, you just acquired wealth? Well, some did. There were probably ancient vampires living in abject poverty for eternity too.

Griffin grabbed the ball. "Come on."

I followed him back out, and he locked up behind us. With a shrug, he reentered the code. "It would be a stupid person to rob a vampire, but there are dumbasses everywhere. They're big on locking up."

"Maybe it's a vampire thing. Like, a natural thing."

He shrugged. "Maybe."

I followed after him, and he turned around to walk backward while he talked to me. "You look really pretty in the setting sun."

Griffin made me blush. I shook my head. "You're very flattering and handsome in the almost darkness yourself."

"I wish you had spoken to me years ago. Even asked me for help with math."

I winked at him. "That would assume I needed your help in math. I'm the one way ahead, right? I think maybe you should have asked *me* for help in math. Surely, needing a tutor might have allowed you to break the no talking rule, right?"

Griffin laughed. "Who knows? Probably not. And that's right. You'd never need my help in math. So I guess we're stuck with just these few weeks. Hey, when is your birthday?"

I stopped moving. That was too on-point to be random. "When did you know?"

"That your birthday is tomorrow? About an hour ago.

This is me. I figure things out. Seventeen." He rushed over to stand right in front of me. "So we need to do something after school tomorrow to celebrate your birthday. What would you like to do?"

It had been a long time since anyone celebrated my birthday. When I was young, we did some things to celebrate, mostly clowns in big public places with a lot of video games. But it had been years since that place closed down, and eventually, Mom gave up celebrating my birthday. Maybe she'd forgotten it altogether.

"Nothing." I shrugged. "I don't really celebrate. I mean, if you said happy birthday, that would be good enough."

He shook his head. "All right, so I'll come up with my own plans for you. Get everyone else involved. That'll be great. Did you know that the five of us were all born within one week? I mean...the vamp dads really planned things well, didn't they?"

"So much can go askew with pregnancies. Early deliveries. Late deliveries. How could they possibly have known how it would go?" We got to the basketball court. "What if something had gone wrong?"

He grinned at me. "If something had gone wrong, that would have meant we weren't really the five. That we weren't carrying the souls. Or whatever. It happened. It just makes them believe they were right."

That was interesting. Still, it begged the question I had to ask him. "Do you believe that's who you are? The guy in the prophecy?"

He dribbled the ball on the court. "How would I know? I mean...conceivably, if I'm carrying around the soul of a dead vampire who is going to wake up and be in my body, how would I know the difference? Seriously? It's like asking a person who is left-handed, hey, what's that like? How would they know?"

I scrunched up my nose. This was like the scenario he'd handed me the first night. It was almost like Griffin was challenging me again, trying to see how I'd consider a problem. The newest strange thing was that I didn't mind it at all. It should have felt annoying and maybe even a little violating that he threw these things at me. Instead, it was as though being around Griffin woke me up a little bit in a way that I wasn't usually. I had to consider what I said with him sometimes, and I sort of liked it.

My hands tingled. "I don't know that what you say is exactly true. Left-handed people are frequently forced to write with their right hands. Or at least they used to be. There are absolutely left-handed people who might be able to tell us what it is like to be right-handed and vice versa."

He stopped dribbling the ball. "Just because they were forced to be right-handed doesn't mean they ever stopped being left-handed. They were just left-handed people being forced to use their right hand."

"Maybe. Or maybe they thought they were right-handed because they weren't told differently. And then one day they were given the chance to use their left hand, realized they were left-handed, and it changed everything for them. So they were right-handed. And then they were left-handed. But both were true for different periods of time."

He tilted his head. "So what you're saying is both existences are true because they were both true for a period of time. Okay. I'll accept that. But then the argument remains. I can't compare until I've had both experiences. And then I'm afraid I won't care. Things like that aren't interesting to a vampire. So the original vampire question remains. Do I think I'm carrying the soul of a dead vampire? Sure, why not? It's certainly more interesting than not carrying one."

I groaned. "I think it's pretty interesting both ways. All right, so you dribbled this thing." I attempted to do what he'd done. I bounced it, and it came back. Okay, that was simple enough. But then I attempted again. The basketball seemed like it had a mind of its own. It simply didn't want to stay where I wanted it to go.

Griffin cleared his throat. "It's supposed to be fun, but you're staring at it like you want to do the ball harm."

"I'm finding it frustrating." I stopped dribbling. "And we shoot, right? The ball has to go into the hoop."

He nodded. "If you're not dribbling, you have to pass or shoot. Move too much without dribbling, and the other team gets the ball. So shoot." He nodded toward it. "Let's see if you can."

How hard could it be? I aimed, and...the ball went nowhere near the basket, just under it, as it fell behind and not through the hoop. Okay. So, it was a lot harder than I'd thought it would be.

"I'm really quite good at throwing a baseball." I smiled. "This might not be my game."

"Miss once and done?" He raised an eyebrow at me as he retrieved the ball. It took him a second to return to where he was farther away from the hoop than me. In an easy moment, he'd made a basket with the ball. "I did this for hours. Days. I'd stand here and just shoot the ball until I made it. Until I almost never missed. Even then, sometimes I missed. The others got tired of playing with me. I think Ace called me obsessive. I needed to know that I could do it. That I could make a basket more than I missed."

I walked over to him. "Is this part of making it count? Of knowing you were here?"

"This is part of me having to be the best at everything." His grin, this time, was sardonic, some of his cocky was gone. "Maybe the vampire in me was a real egomaniac. Maybe we'll blame him."

I put my arms around his waist. "Maybe you're just a really smart, talented, athletic, good-looking, eighteen-year-old guy. I think you're all egomaniacs, a little bit."

"I fucking love talking to you." He picked me up, and I squealed at the unexpected momentum. He bent us both over. "Pick up the ball." As I was in his embrace and bent over, I really didn't have a choice but to comply. Once I had it in my hands, he swung us both up until we were right next to the hoop. "Dunk. I've got you. Put the ball in."

I dropped into the net with a whoosh. Maybe it was the sound, but I couldn't help my grin. "She shoots. She scores."

"And the crowd goes wild." He let me down, bringing me toward the ground so that I slid against his body. My nipples hardened at the contact, and I caught my breath. "Maybe I brought you here to make sure you'd remember me correctly—as a little fucked-up."

"Griffin..." I touched his cheek. "We're all a little fucked-up. And I don't even have the excuse that I've been on a death march toward vampirism since birth."

His mouth stroked against mine. "I like that description. I like how you think. I like everything about you. I thought I was good with this happening. It was inevitable. But now? I want to fight it. I want more time."

"Fight it." I kissed him again, and his body hardened against mine, his arms holding me tight against him. "I'll fight it with you."

"Inevitable. I know you know what it means, but I am going to save you. Or maybe you're going to save yourself, sort of." He kissed the end of my nose. "You are getting a birthday cake. I'm going to make it for you."

"That is really sweet."

He leaned over, kissing a spot on my neck, and I caught my breath. *Oh yes, I liked that.* "I'm not sweet. You make me want to be."

Griffin stepped away just a little bit, putting the smallest amount of distance between us. It felt immense. "Griff?"

"Come on. I need to tell the others about your birthday. Everyone is going to want to see you tonight. To make sure you're okay. It begs the question, Maci, *why* are you so okay? You've had one shock after another."

I took his hand. "I'm not okay. I'm so far from okay, I'm not sure I ever will be again. But I'm not the one who is going to die. I'm not the one they're going to stick in a coffin alive. I'm not... My problems are my own. I'll deal with them like I always do—silently. Let's focus on you guys. You have the more imminent issues."

"Don't deal with it silently. We all have our roles in this little family. Rowan thinks he solves problems but the truth is that its mine. I solve problems. If you're feeling things, I need to know what they are. Please, trust me like that."

I swallowed. "You have trusted me only because you had to. You've all seen me at my worst. I mean... I think you can guess how I'm feeling. At the moment, it's best described as overwhelmed."

"Then let's see to it that you start to find your feet again. Come on. Let's go find out what all those servants were doing in Rowan's house. What could they possibly have been up to?"

I wasn't at all sure I wanted to know.

10

"Hey." I stopped Griff by grabbing his arm before he stepped inside the house. "I know that you set Mrs. Reemus up with a vampire because of what she did to me."

He lifted an eyebrow. There was challenge in his look. "She got bit twice and sent home—enough to give her what she herself had been trying to get for some time and to frighten her. The vampire who bit her is a bad dude, I'll admit it. He's not kind, not that any of them are, but he is particularly bad, so I'm sure it was painful. Nothing about that will leave permanent damage to her except that she will now be watched. Part of the group of people who could be called upon to do things in the event they're deemed necessary. On the off chance that she is already addicted after just twice...well, that is just too fucking bad."

I squeezed his arm. "Griffin, I'm not upset about it. I'm even a little bit...glad?" And if that made me a bad person, then so be it. "I wanted to say that I've never had anyone do anything like this for me before. It's a little bit bad, I guess, but maybe that's what I am—a little bit bad."

"You're not. You're very, very good inside. We all reach a threshold where we don't mind the people who hurt us getting what's coming to them. That just makes us human. Vampires take it to another level. So maybe the vamp soul in me is just a little bit more evil than most and it was already showing itself."

I leaned against him. "We can call Mrs. Reemus my birthday present. Thank you for it."

He scowled at me. "You were tricky with that. No, it's not your birthday present. I'm going to spend money on you. Deal with it."

I matched his scowl, which made both of us grin. Finally, we entered Rowan's house, finding our way to his bedroom. If anything, his mansion was bigger than Caesar's. The vampires did like to have showy houses. There was nothing understated about them. I looked out the window, something I hadn't done the last time I'd been there. The woods were visible, which was funny to think about. The same woods that surrounded my trailer were right there too, just from a different edge.

It was what connected us.

Or maybe I was overthinking it.

All the guys were back, and the room had changed significantly. Six beds where there had just been one. The servants set them up so that they were all in a circle with an open space in the center that seemed a natural gathering area, since that was where everyone sat on the floor.

Tanner had his guitar out, and I walked over toward where he strummed. He grinned at me, so I sat next to him on the ground, finding Rowan's gaze. "Are you okay with this? It's your room, but now it's where everyone is sleeping, even me."

He nodded, leaning against his bed. "We used to have sleepovers all the time. Not for years. It just sort of stopped."

"About four years ago, we started to get a little dour." Ace scooted next to me. "No fun. Just...sort of existing."

The fact they started to commit small crimes made more and more sense to me. "So your fathers have basically forced you to have a good time again."

"They're trying to make sure we can all be watched." Ace put his hand on my knee. "Easier."

"Hey, guys." Griffin sank to the ground next to Rowan and Caesar. "Tomorrow is our girl's birthday."

Their girl. The title felt like a birthday present all unto itself. "It is. But listen, Griffin is insisting on doing something. There really is no need..."

"You'll be eighteen just about the time we wake up. Well, maybe we'll be up earlier." Ace said it like what he said had no ramifications at all. "If we're more like nine-monthers rather than year long."

My stomach twisted. "I...I won't see you for a whole year." I'd known them days, but already, I couldn't stand the idea. Actual pain assaulted my midsection, and I wasn't sure I wouldn't throw up.

"You won't see us then, either." Rowan sighed. "You won't be anywhere near us—not then and not in the future. Can't allow it." He held up his hand. "Don't argue with me about what I can and can't do, Griffin."

Next to me, Griffin shrugged. "I wasn't going to, but we're bumming her out. It's her birthday. We need to make a big fuss."

A knock sounded on the door, and everyone turned to see a woman standing there. She didn't look much older than us. Blonde. Blue-eyed. Beautiful but gaunt, in an unhealthy way. Big dark circles under her eyes. "Sorry to disturb. I've been sent to let you know you aren't going to school tomorrow. Well, Maci is, but the rest of you are to stay home and study the texts. There will be a test tomorrow afternoon. If you don't all ace the test, Maci gets bit."

I sat forward. "What?"

She winced. "I'm sorry to deliver this message. I was sent. Don't blame the messenger." For just a second, she made eye contact with me. "Bye."

Having said that, she turned and fled. For those few seconds, when we'd looked at each other, I noticed she'd had kind eyes. I turned my attention to Rowan. "What is her name?"

"I don't know. I'll admit, once I was old enough to get what was happening around here, I stopped learning them. They come, then they're gone. It was heart-wrenching to make friends with older adult figures, then have them either die, become vampires, or just...fade into shells of themselves. I don't keep track of their names anymore. Maybe that makes me callous."

I sighed. "Maybe it means you're protecting yourself."

"We'll learn the stuff," Ace whispered. "No one is biting you because we fucked up. Besides, tomorrow is your birthday. No biting on your birthday."

There really wasn't much else to say. Tanner went back to strumming on his guitar. It wasn't a song I recognized, but his voice was nice. Low, tempting to listen to, and I was drawn into the picture he sang about. Sunny days, cool weather, long drives with a pretty girl.

Ace put his head on my shoulder. "We're going to have dinner. I've promised it to you. Tomorrow is your birthday, so we'll all do something together, but after that? Dinner, you and me, okay?"

"I'd really like that." The whole image was appealing. All

the birthday fun and then the dinner. I loved the idea.

He lifted his head and jumped to his feet. "I have a surprise. I went by Wanda's earlier today, and I took something. Well, I borrowed it."

I gaped at him. "Ace, do you have a little bit of a kleptomania problem?"

"We all do bad things." He shrugged. "Let's blame the dying and vampire thing, if we want to. Or maybe I'm just a bad guy. No, I plan on putting it back. I don't steal, even if I sort of want to." He shrugged again. "Don't judge lest you be judged. Or whatever they say." He held up a box. "I got the board game that we didn't get to play the other night."

I sat up straight. "Oh, fun!"

"See?" He rolled his eyes at Caesar, who hadn't, as far as I could tell, done anything to deserve the eye roll.

Caesar eventually grinned, and it looked like all was forgiven. They'd been doing this a long time—hanging out together—so much so, they were family. For some reason I couldn't fathom, they'd taken me in, to the point that I was now their weak spot and something their fathers could use against them.

Frowning, I took a deep breath.

"Uh-oh," Tanner said, putting away the guitar. "She doesn't look like she wants to play."

"I do. My frown was about another thought. Don't worry about it. Yes, let's play." I smiled at Tanner and then Ace. They were always watching me, always trying to read me, and I was doing the same to them. I wasn't used to hiding my inner monologue from my facial expressions, since no one had ever noticed me.

Ace opened the box and pulled out a whole bunch of cards. Some of them were characters, attributes on others, and others showed weapons. He quickly mixed them up and started distributing them. In short bursts, he explained the game. We each got a character and two random other cards that gave us an attribute and a weapon. Then we had to challenge the person next to us to see if our cards would beat their cards.

They'd all played the game before, so I assumed I'd catch on as we went. It didn't take long. Rowan and Griffin started first. It was lively and sort of ridiculous. Would a brick monster beat a man made all of needles? Did it matter that one could turn invisible? That one had a giant hand?

I watched them as they went back and forth. Eventually, we all had to vote on which one of them won. This time, it was Rowan. The invisibility just trumped everything else. Griffin threw his hands in the air. "*So* not true. Big giant hand—I grab you, and I don't care if you're invisible, I hold you there and you don't move."

Tanner put his head on my shoulder like Ace had earlier. If this was a thing, I really didn't mind it at all. "Griffin doesn't lose well. It's one of the reasons we don't play with him."

"Bullshit. You just know I win most of the time." Griffin winked at me, our earlier conversation rushing back to me immediately. He wanted to leave a mark. Winning did that, at least in his mind.

But he actually looked amused and not pissed because he hadn't won. We went on, and when it was finally my turn, I lost easily to Ace. I just had terrible cards. A big giant cookie was never going to beat his swordsman. Still, it was fun. Eventually, we redealt and went again. The time passed easily.

"Why did we stop doing this?" Rowan asked all of them, looking around. "Why did we decide to just not do this anymore?"

"I think," Caesar spoke up for the first time that night outside of the game, "things just got heavy."

"I don't want heavy for the next week." Rowan sighed. "I want as little heavy as we can make. As I told Maci, we're going to have fun. Go out with it."

Tanner laughed. "Sounds like a plan."

I liked it too. Before too long, it was really dark outside, and the heaviness that meant I was tired settled on my shoulders. I rubbed my eyes. Although Ace and Caesar were debating their characters, quietly, a glance showed me Griffin's eyes were closed, his head leaning against the bed behind him.

I rose, which caught the other's attention. Rowan touched my leg when I passed him, and I bent down next to Griffin.

"Hey." I stroked his cheek. "Time for bed."

He lifted his eyes slowly. My bet was that he'd really been asleep and not just dozing. "Forgive me?"

"For what?" I shook my head. "Falling asleep? Don't be silly. Time for bed for all of us, I think."

I had to go to school alone. Which was fine, but they had things to study, and clearly, it was late for all of us.

He sort of pulled himself up and stumbled toward the bed. Griffin face planted down on it, still fully dressed, even wearing his shoes.

Rowan groaned and rose next to me. "He gets up hours earlier than the rest of us most days to run. It hits him sometimes, the hours we keep."

I managed to get his shoes off him without rousing him. He gripped on to his pillow and rolled onto his stomach.

"It's a terrible phrase, considering things, but he sleeps like the dead." Tanner walked over to me. "He'll sleep until morning now."

I nodded. "Is it okay that he's still in his clothes?"

"Yeah, he won't care." Rowan ran a hand through his hair. "Let's all get ready for bed. Unless you guys want to keep playing."

I grabbed the bag Caesar brought for me with my clothes and headed toward the bathroom. "Okay if I go in first?"

"Have at it." Tanner threw himself down on his bed. "Do you suppose I should skip brushing my teeth? I mean...who cares if I get cavities now?"

"Well." I scrunched up my nose. "That is sort of disgusting."

He grinned at me. "Yeah, I know. I'm still going to brush my teeth. Can you imagine a vampire in the dentist's chair?"

I listened to their conversation through the door as I shut it. Their conversation became background noise to my getting dressed. I grabbed my shorts and a different tank top from the night before. I braided my hair after I washed my face, and finally, I brushed my teeth, smiling at Tanner's stupid question.

I opened the door.

"No, I think it's a good idea." Rowan shook his head, talking to Tanner. "And I need to think about it. Griffin barely brought it up, but I have to think about the whole thing. Even the logistics of it."

"Hey." Caesar walked right up to me. He took my hand. "Can I stay with you again tonight? Would that be okay? I think we both slept really well, but if you want your own space, then..."

"I'd like that." It sounded awesome. I'd gotten an actual full night of sleep really easily next to Caesar.

Ace walked over, stroking a hand down my arm. "It's a big bed. Can I get in the other side?"

"You can." It should feel overwhelming, but I knew that I'd like being pressed between them. Especially on a night like tonight. My shoulders sagged. The day was getting to me. *Vampires. Death. My future in upheaval. What would happen if I just vanished?* Would their father really exert the effort to find me?

The questions I'd been putting off in my mind reared to life in my head. They could both sleep next to me. I was going to sit up and obsess.

The room fell silent, and I looked around. They were all staring at me in that moment. My cheeks heated up. "Something on my face?"

"More like your legs are a mile long in those shorts." Ace grinned. "None of the rest of them will say it, but there it is."

I swatted at his arm. "Stop it. They're just shorts." Although I sort of loved the description. People didn't look at me like that. Most of the time, it was like I was invisible.

Rowan put his arm around me. "That bed okay? Or do you like the other side of the room better?"

"I'm not picky. That bed will be fine." It was actually in the center, by the window, and next to Rowan's bed. Griffin would be next to him. Tanner on the other side of me, with Caesar and Ace sharing with me, leaving two beds pretty much across the room empty.

They all started grabbing their stuff, and I climbed into the bed we'd just designated as mine. "Is this okay? That I'm here?"

"Yes," the four awake guys all answered me at once, not even letting me vocalize my concerns about infringing on time they needed together. Of course, it wasn't like they really had a choice. Their fathers had set this up.

Ace got in next to me as Rowan turned off the lights.

Caesar was next. The bed was big, but we did all have to cuddle to make this work.

"I call sleeping with Maci tomorrow." Tanner yawned.

"I'm the next day," Rowan finished. The beds creaked as they adjusted themselves to get comfortable. As for the two with me, they might never have shared a bed with a girl between them before, but they settled quickly. Caesar spooned me from behind, his arm slung over my waist. Ace and I faced each other in the darkness. He lay on his side, one hand on my hip, the other supporting his head as he lay on it.

Around me, everyone seemed to settle. Griffin hadn't moved an inch since he'd fallen asleep, but Tanner tossed a few times before he finally seemed to drift off. He was a deep breather, and I could hear him where I was. It wasn't so much that he snored, as he took long audible breaths in the bed next to us.

I'd never know why I was sure Rowan fell asleep next, but as the minutes passed, I was absolutely certain he was out too. Caesar breathed lightly against the back of my neck, each minute his body loosening against me. Sleeping next to me did seem to work for him.

But I was awake, and so was Ace.

We stared at each other in the darkness, the lights from the window illuminating enough I could see he was up too.

"Hi," I whispered to him.

He grinned at me. "Hi. Is this okay, or are you totally uncomfortable?"

"This is more than okay. I like it. Just hard to turn off my head."

He nodded, a piece of his hair falling over his eyes before he brushed it aside. Although we were already very close, he inched farther against me and leaned his forehead against my own. "Would be crazy if you were able to just sleep after this day. It's too much for most people, I think."

I swallowed. "I'm not thinking any particular thoughts. It's more like...I just can't settle."

He kissed my lips, gently. "You're safe here, right now. I won't let anything get you. I know it was awful, but the fact that Rowan's father marked you means no one would dare bug you right now. Do you want to know a secret?"

"Another one? Are there more?" I winked at him. "Yes, tell me if you want to."

"My father isn't as bad as the others. He actually talks to me. Sometimes, when I was very young, he'd hug me. I know that he's aware I'm around. He doesn't just remember me when it comes to the change. I think that as much as he will absolutely make me go through with it, he regrets what's going to happen."

That was really interesting. "Something in him is just different than the others?"

"Yes, and I wonder if it might be different in me too. Like maybe when I'm over being ragingly mad trying to feed off everything, maybe I can come find you wherever you are and we can talk. Like...I talk to my dad. It won't be a great conversation. He's limited in the things he's interested in. Nothing modern. But he likes books."

I nodded. "If that is possible, to see you without you wanting to kill me, I'd like that."

"Good." He yawned. "Try not to worry. It solves nothing. I had to stop worrying a year or so ago because otherwise, it was going to destroy me. If something is inevitable, it happens whether we worry about it or not."

I appreciated that what he was saying was true, but he needed to give me a huge break if I wasn't feeling particularly Zen in that moment. "Ace." I swallowed. "I don't mean to be a bitch."

He winced. "Say it. If I said something shitty, call me on it."

"In the last few days, I've gone from not knowing you guys at all, to having this strange attachment to you, to being nearly raped by my mother's friend, stolen from, and discovering there are vampires. Also, you are all going to die next week. On top of all that, I'll have to be stuck with the vampires forever because of all this. So...I'm not really in a place where I *can't* worry. Not yet, anyway. I'm worrying." In fact, as I'd said it, my stomach panged. "Quite a lot, actually."

He nodded. "You're right. It was a pretty condescending thing I said. I'm sorry. Can you forgive me?"

"Not that big of a deal. No apology necessary, I just wanted to explain."

Behind me, Caesar adjusted himself, muttering something and holding me tighter.

Ace stroked a hand down the side of my face. "It's your birthday now. Happy birthday, beautiful."

I looked at the clock in the corner. He was right. It was 12:01 in the morning. It was, in fact, my birthday. "Thank you."

He gently kissed my lips again. "I like the strange attachment."

"Me too."

Ace's eyes started to close a little bit. "I'm not falling asleep. Just resting my eyes."

I had to try hard not to laugh. He was completely falling asleep. Maybe all of the not worrying—and I didn't believe that for a second—was catching up with him. I was glad his father had been a little different. At least one of us should have a half-decent parent.

He was out cold seconds later. When these guys went to bed, they really knocked out. Seconds turned to minutes, and soon, my own head was fuzzy enough to push away all the things I should be sitting up thinking about. I closed my eyes.

I dreamed about the stars. I walked through dark woods. The winter stole away the leaves, and I could actually see stars above my head. It was cold, but I couldn't feel it. That was a real benefit of being what I was—I didn't feel the cold anymore.

"Wait," Rowan called to me. "Don't go without me. It's not safe, and you know it. They could be anywhere. If they get you, they'll do terrible things."

I swung around to look at him. "Well, they can try. I'm not so easy to get. You know that."

He was older than he should be. Why did I think he should look younger? "You're not indestructible, my love. None of us are."

"I think you know what would happen if they got you." Caesar was next to me. Where had he come from? "I couldn't survive it. None of us could, so be careful. Please don't go in there without me."

"Without any of us," Ace whispered. "We love you. If you're gone, we'll be just like the rest of them."

"Not me," Tanner answered. "Because I won't be anymore."

"So the point here, darling" —Griffin grinned at me. They officially surrounded me— *"is don't go wandering into the woods where the enemy could get you. Drain you. Take you from us. Don't make us the monsters the world thinks we are."*

I dramatically sighed. "Then let's all go look at the stars."

11

"Maci." Rowan's voice called to me as he shook me. I roused, dizziness overtaking me. *What is going on?* I looked around. I was outside, right by the edge of the woods.

"I just wanted to see the stars. We can all go." Hadn't we just discussed this?

He held me against him, breathing hard. He looked young again. What was going on?

"You're sleepwalking." He let out an audible breath. "I almost... You're okay. Come in. Come on. You're okay." He said that twice.

I didn't understand. "What?"

"Come on. I've got you." He put his arm around me, leading me from the edge of the woods. The door to his house flung open and all of them were there, the other four staring at us as he walked me back inside.

My head was foggy. I looked back over my shoulder. I really, really wanted to go see the stars in those woods. It seemed really important.

"This way," Rowan whispered. "Don't fight me. Back to bed where you're safe. Come on."

"How did she get out here without you two waking up?" Tanner addressed Ace and Caesar. "You had her in bed with you."

Caesar ran a hand through his hair, distress written all over his face. "I don't know. I was really out of it. I sort of felt her leave, but I thought maybe she was going to the bathroom."

"I didn't notice at all." Ace touched my arm when I passed. "Didn't know a thing until Rowan shouted. I'm sorry."

Griffin stepped toward me, his arm coming around the other side of me to help me walk. "I don't think she's really awake yet. Look at her eyes, glassy. Unfocused. She's asleep."

I wasn't, really, but he was right. I wasn't exactly awake, either. I...I didn't really know what was going on.

Tanner strolled over and picked me up in his arms, essentially taking me from the other two. "If she's not awake, then we don't want her walking, not even with help. Let's get her back into bed where she's safe. Come on. And I'll keep her with me if you guys don't think you can keep her safe. It's fine. I'm a much lighter sleeper. I'll feel it if she gets up."

"No, it's fine." Caesar shook his head. "Now that I know this is a possibility, I'll wake up if she does. I've got it."

Tanner laid me down on the bed. What was happening? Hadn't we all just decided to go into the woods together?

"What is happening?" I asked him as he smoothed the hair off my forehead.

"You're having a really weird dream. We'll talk about it in the morning." He kissed my shoulder, where my shirt hung down a little bit. "You can go back to sleep. Close those eyes. No more wandering to the woods."

I took a deep breath. "I'm... This isn't normal."

Caesar climbed in next to me a second before Ace did, who drew the blanket back over us. "It was a long day. You learned some very weird, upsetting things. You got bit yesterday. I'm sure it's all related. Just rest now. Come on. And thank you, Rowan, for waking up. For chasing her outside, for somehow knowing to do that."

Ace kissed my neck. "You're okay now."

"I'm just glad I woke up. I woke up, and I knew that she wasn't in the house." Rowan let out a breath. "But she's back. Everything is fine now."

It was. Except I still hadn't gotten to see the stars.

I woke up feeling like hell. My head hurt, my joints ached, and I groaned. Caesar rolled over and turned off my phone, stopping the alarm. Ace pretty much pinned me to the bed, with most of his body weight on top of me, by way of his leg slung over me like a vise that was not going to let me up. He hadn't budged, and his eyes were still closed. I was face down on my stomach. Lifting my head was a lot of effort.

Caesar tugged on the end of my braid. "Wish you didn't have to get up, but you do. And I'm going to cook you breakfast before you go."

"What happened last night?"

He shook his head. "I don't know. About three hours ago, you took off out of the house, fast asleep. Heading for the woods. Rowan caught you. It was really a scene. Do you usually sleepwalk?" He played with my hair. It was soothing. I had to be careful, or I was going to go back to sleep.

"I never have. Not that I know of."

Ace rolled off me, groaning. "How is it already morning?"

I sat up. "Well apparently, I had you guys up all night, so that's why you're so tired. I'm so sorry."

"Don't be sorry." Rowan spoke through his pillow before he lifted his head. "These things happen. We all need to get up to study, since we've been banned from school today. We have to learn vampire things."

I scooted off the bed, my feet hitting the floor with a sting. I stared down at them. Yes, I'd cut them on whatever jaunt I had taken last night. "I've never sleepwalked in my life, that I know about. I've never woken up where I didn't go to bed. It's really strange. I'm—" I cut myself off before I could apologize again. "It might be a good idea to stick me in the other room or something, so I don't keep you all up."

"That's not happening." Tanner got up and smiled at me. "If you're going to go through something like that, I'd rather you go through it where I can see to it you're safe."

Everyone moaned their way out of bed, and with each one, my guilt rose. They were going to have a long day. I hobbled toward the bathroom. How long until I was just the girl who basically trapped them into hurrying along their destiny and kept them from getting a night's sleep?

"Hey." Griffin stopped me before I entered the bathroom. "I can see your feet hurt. Come see me when you get out. I have stuff for sore feet. Runners always do." He winked at me. "Thanks for putting me to bed last night."

That was a better memory than the fuzzy sleepwalking I had done. Why had that happened? I brushed my teeth and changed into school clothes before I stuck my hair up in a loose bun that was bound to be a mess in no time, but I didn't have the wherewithal to do anything else with it right then.

I found the bedroom emptied except for Griffin, who held up bandages. "Come here. I'll fix your feet."

That was sweet. I sat down on the edge of his bed, and he examined the cuts causing me pain. Quickly, he got to work with some bandages and antibiotic cream that also had a pain killer in it. "They're not bad. Just your run of the mill cuts from walking barefoot." He patted my ankles when he was done. I stared at him, most of my bad mood fleeing. I'd never have imagined this about myself, but I really, really liked him holding my feet. It was almost...sensual.

I swallowed. *What is the matter with me?*

"Thanks."

He squeezed again. "You're welcome. Oh, and, Maci, happy birthday. Sorry we all grumbled instead of saying that right off the bat. Happiest of birthdays, baby." He leaned over and kissed me. It wasn't a gentle peck. No, when Griffin kissed me, the few times he had, he meant it. His tongue stroked over my bottom lip before he pulled me onto his lap.

I kissed him back, every ounce of frustration I'd had since I opened my eyes fleeing in those caresses. He ran his hand up my thigh, squeezing my pant leg. Something crashed in the house, and someone—I was pretty sure it was Tanner—cursed. It sounded like they were downstairs and whatever had broken was glass.

We pulled away, both of us panting a little bit. "Best gift, ever."

"That wasn't your gift." He kissed my cheek. "More like one you just gave to me. Go on downstairs. I'll be there in a minute." He thumbed my cheek. "And have a good day at school."

That was right. I had to do that. I had to go to school.

Fuck.

I did get downstairs, just in time to see Tanner cleaning up a broken vase. "What happened?" I bent down to help him, holding the dustpan so he could sweep.

He winced. "Well, I was thinking about surprising you later with a whole bunch of flowers. Grabbed that vase from the top shelf, and it broke. I'm not usually clumsy, but today I am. Go figure. I'm going to come up with another idea."

I took his hand. "I'm glad you didn't get hurt, and I don't need gifts. Seriously."

"You're getting some, so you're going to have to start."

A thought dawned on me. "Sing me something. That would be such a perfect gift."

"Really?" His cheeks reddened. "You like how I sing?"

"I love it." I bumped my arm into his. "Do it again soon?"

He smiled. "Anytime you want, Maci. You are...amazing."

I kissed his cheek. "I think you're the amazing one."

"Do me a favor?" His face fell. "It's kind of a dark one."

I took a long, deep breath. A clock ticked in the hallway, and the sun shot through the window, illuminating Tanner's handsome face, the dark circles I'd been the cause of today showing in the brightness. "Dark favor? Sounds ominous."

"It's not that." He laughed, looking at the ground. "Our birthday, all five of us, happens in the same week in October. The second week. We were born one day after the other. Rowan first. Caesar. Me. Ace. And finally, Griffin. Starts on the eighth to the twelfth. Griff likes to say he's never had to be without the rest of us. I don't know... It's always been this big deal. Well, we made it one. Not from our families or whatever. But we'd recognize the week. Even this last year, when we basically stopped doing anything fun. We still recognized the birthday week. Like it mattered. And it kills me to think no one will remember it anymore."

I swallowed. "You want me to remember your birthday week."

"I do, if it's not too much. Just say it aloud. Today is the week or something. We won't care anymore. Sometimes, vampires remember the day they come out of the coffin, but it's not...it's not our birthday. Like our human lives didn't matter. So would you remember them? For us?"

I took his cheeks in my hand. "Yes. Count on it." I kissed him again. "Your human lives mattered. Very much."

Not to mention we were putting a stop to my birthday recognition because there was no way, a week before they all died, they should be thinking about this. We needed to focus on getting them out of this hell.

The rest of them were in the kitchen. Tanner followed me, and a second later, Griff arrived, so we were all together.

Caesar was making the same eggs from yesterday. They smelled like heaven. If life was fair—which I knew it wasn't —there could have been a lot more mornings like this. But there was a countdown, and I knew it. He quickly spooned the eggs onto the plate in front of me. "I think you'll like these even better. I put feta cheese in them. Even better than yesterday's, I think."

"Thank you." I smiled at him. "You are so nice. You didn't have to cook me breakfast."

"Maybe he didn't," Ace said. "But he totally has to make them for me. I insist."

Caesar grinned. "I made plenty for everyone."

He quickly handed out plates, and I closed my eyes against the utter joy his eggs created in my mouth. Had I ever had feta cheese before? I didn't think I had, but it was heaven. It was perfect. I chewed and swallowed for a long moment before I said anything else.

"This is the best. Really. I...I love it. I've never tasted anything like it."

Caesar lit up like a light bulb. "Really? That makes my day. I wanted to do something nice to start your birthday."

"On that subject," I interrupted him, meeting Rowan's gaze and then Ace's before I continued. "No more of that. Okay? You guys have so little time left, the last thing we need is to focus on some stupid day for me. What we should all be doing is putting our heads together and figuring out how to get you out of this eventuality."

Tanner winced. "This is my fault."

"Brother, what did you do?" Caesar finally ate his own eggs.

Rowan held up his hand. "There's nothing to do. Celebrating your birthday is exactly the sort of thing I want to do between now and the end. I want to have fun. A lot of it."

"When I asked you to remember our birthday, I didn't mean that I didn't want to celebrate yours. Or maybe I made it too dark or whatever. I...I didn't mean to. Anyway, that shouldn't have put you off birthdays. It should have, I don't know, emphasized them." Tanner lifted his eyebrows. "We have to celebrate you. When you get home, we're going to have a whole thing."

Home? This was absolutely not that. My home was close by, but it wasn't this ginormous place where Rowan lived. Even if I loved being here with them. For that matter, this wasn't Tanner's home either. Or maybe it was, because the guys were there with him. Maybe they were always at home together.

"I'll be back after school, I guess." Since my mother had sold me to the vampires. I hadn't even begun to process that yet. I mean, I wasn't entirely sure I ever really could. What the fuck was I supposed to do? A thought dawned on me. "I need a ride, please. Can one of you take me? My car isn't here."

Ace pulled keys out of his sweatshirt pocket. "Take mine."

I blinked. "What?"

"Just take my car. Use it like it's yours. I'm not using it, at least not today, and if I need a car and one of these guys can't drive me, I will steal one from Rowan's father. He loves cars, but I'm not sure he remembers how many he has most of the time."

Rowan tapped on the counter. "True."

No one had ever just handed me car keys. I'd only managed to get my mother's because she got tired of driving me around. Easier for her to let me take myself back and forth to work. I shook my head at the thought. *No more work.* What was I supposed to do about keeping the lights on in the trailer? I rubbed my eyes. "Thanks, Ace. I'm very grateful. If we can figure out a time for someone to take me to get my car, I won't have to impose on you this way anymore."

He kissed my cheek. "It's not an imposition. I'm going to be here all day reading vampire lore."

Griffin made a gagging sound. "What? Sorry? Just the idea. It makes me want to puke."

Rowan tapped the counter again. I wondered if he was nervous or if that was just something he did. "You've got to get going. Be careful today, okay?"

I nodded. "I will. I'm going to my trailer to get the rest of my clothes. My mom will be gone, I guess. I'll need them, so I'll run over there, grab some stuff, and come back here."

They all hugged me goodbye, one after the other. Not one of them, not even Griffin, seemed worried about missing school. I guessed with their looming death date, it really didn't matter anymore.

Ace's car proved to be a challenge. Mine was kind of turn the key and go. There were all kinds of things I had to figure out in his car, and since my phone wasn't hooked up to his Bluetooth, it was next to impossible to operate the radio. That was okay. I finally did successfully drive to school and park at the back of the lot, where I normally would park my car.

No one noticed me. That was also standard.

I stared at the brick building, a strand of hair blowing over my eyes. This was just going to be a normal day for me. I knew how to get through things in that building.

So why does everything feel so much heavier?

Classes dragged. Mrs. Reemus was back, and she looked like she'd been hit by a truck. I was new to the vampire thing, but the way her hand shook when she held her pen told me she was coming down with something. If she'd only been bitten twice, then she must be one of the unfortunate ones hit really hard by it.

I hated the woman, but my heart panged for her. I didn't like to see addiction rearing its head on anyone, not even those that had perpetually treated me like shit. My wrist pained me, but I suspected it was more about me thinking about it and not because of any actual issue at the moment.

She left me alone the whole class.

Eventually, it was lunch time. I didn't have any, so that was fairly standard for me. The library, however, held no interest. I needed sunshine on my skin. I could soak up some vitamin D and not think about anything important for forty-five minutes. Why had I walked in my sleep? What was that about? And there went my brain, not allowing me to turn it off.

I managed to get outside and find a place on the steps where no one was sitting.

"Maci?" A woman walked over to me. I blinked up at her. It was the servant from the night before, the one who'd delivered the news about the guys staying home.

"Yes." I sort of stumbled to my feet. "I... What are you doing here? Everything okay?"

She held up a brown bag. "Rowan remembered you didn't have lunch, so Caesar asked that I bring you this."

"Oh." I took it from her. "Thank you so much. That is so nice of you."

She shrugged. "Not nice. It's my job, and this one was easily accomplished. I thought I was going to have to track you down, but here you are."

She was pretty. I hadn't really looked at her before, but she had perfectly balanced features. Long blonde hair and blue eyes. Her arms, shown in a black tank top, were toned. Still, she had the look I'd seen when Rowan pointed out the servants. Her eyes were a bit sunken in. Her cheeks looked gaunt.

My guess was she was in pain. I put out my hand. "I'm Maci. You know that, but I don't know your name."

She opened and closed her mouth twice. Finally, she took my outstretched offering. "I'm Charlotte."

"Did you already eat lunch, Charlotte? Would you like some of mine?" I opened the bag. I should have known Caesar wouldn't just hand me a peanut butter sandwich. No, it was a whole subway production. And then a brownie. Some water. I blinked and then grinned. He'd written me a note that said *Happy Birthday*.

That was so sweet.

"I can't eat it all." I held up the bag.

She shook her head. "No, thank you, but I'll sit with you. It's such a nice day."

Charlotte was right. I sank back down, and she joined

me. It was sort of awkward to eat in front of people who weren't eating, but I went at the sandwich anyway. It was delicious.

"I didn't mind coming," she said finally. "I wanted to get a better look at you. Everyone is trying to figure out who the girl is that has those guys all tied up a week before they move to the next level of existence."

I almost choked. "The next what?"

"Well, when they get to be vampires, they move to a place above us."

I wasn't one to criticize other people's religious beliefs. Not ever. But I was pretty sure she had this wrong. "I don't think that's how they see it. I'm surprised you still do, after everything you must have seen."

"I can see why you might feel that way." She shrugged. "I want to be a vampire. I want to have that power. I want to leave this world behind me and open the door to the next great thing. I'm hoping someone will make me their paramour eventually, then change me."

My stomach tightened. I wasn't going to be able to eat any more. I set down my lunch. "That's *really* what you want? To have to feed off of people's blood?"

"I do. You don't?" She leaned forward. "That was my theory. That you wanted them to change you."

I shook my head, fast. "I don't want anything to do with any of it. I only found out yesterday. I don't want any more bites. I don't want to be a vampire. I want to be free of this, and I want them free too."

Her face fell. "Maci, you know...that isn't going to happen. If the Great Ones dragged you into this, then you're in it. The best you can hope for is to become a paramour, but you're so young, I don't think they would allow it yet.

Which makes you one of us—the servants. Or I suppose they might..."

Charlotte stopped talking, but I filled in the blank. "Or they could kill me."

"Yes." She shrugged. "Maybe you'll change your mind. I'd love to have you around. I mean, I'm only twenty years old. You and I are close in age. The others are older. I'd love to have a friend. I don't have that many friends. Or any, really."

I had the guys. They were definitely my friends. "I don't have girlfriends."

"Great, so when you come to your senses and you realize you want to embrace this gift you've been given, we'll be besties. When we're not working, we'll watch movies and have fun. Unless they make me a paramour before then."

Charlotte was weird, but then again, so was I. And it had been a really long time since any girls had been nice to me. "Okay. If somehow I am now a servant, I'd like very much for us to be friends."

"Great." She grinned.

Maybe someday, she'd tell me what she was trying to escape. It really was none of my business, but if this life seemed like the one to trade up for, then something was wrong. Lately, there had been so much airing of secrets, I had to remember people were entitled to theirs.

"So what's your favorite food? Because I know the best places to go out for some. I mean, I'm almost never hungry anymore. But when I am, I love Thai. How about you?"

Looks like she decided we're friends already.

12

The rest of my school day was quiet. I enjoyed visiting with Charlotte, even if I knew she'd chosen to become the feeding tool for a vampire in exchange for doing chores and running errands. It didn't seem at all equitable to me.

Ace's car was right where I'd left it, and I figured out how to turn on the radio. It was fun to drive—the steering wheel was sensitive, and the car responded fast. I was grinning by the time I got to my trailer. A man near the entrance waved when I drove by. He'd lived there for years and was just about as out of it as my mother. If he thought it was weird to see me in a car that cost more than I'd probably ever make in a year, he didn't indicate it. I wondered if he even noticed.

For that matter, did he know we lived surrounded by vampires? Did my mother know? Were they at all concerned about it? Did the vampires just avoid this part of town? Were they only willing to feed off the rich? Did their blood taste better?

I had so many questions, my brain was like a train

headed for the station at too fast a speed. I might crash at any moment.

I parked the car before Ace's vehicle took the brunt of my issues. I didn't want to explain how I dinged it up. What was going to happen to their cars when they were changed? *Fuck.* There I went again.

The door to our trailer hung open. *Really?* Had my mother not even locked the door before she left? I'd be lucky if I had anything left. I sighed. Once again, I had to see what kind of mess she made. Did I even live there anymore?

I stepped inside and came up short.

No. It really couldn't be him. The man my mother had tried to give me to sat on the couch. He drank a beer which he set down with a loud clunk when he saw me.

"Well, look who we have here. Mommy's little girl." He was drunk, slurring his words.

I took a step back. "What are you doing here?"

"I'm looking for your mama." He rose. Once again, I was struck by how badly he smelled and how much bigger than me he was. Fear moved through me, and he'd barely even said anything yet. "She owes me a lot of money. Where is that bitch mother of yours?"

I wasn't an idiot. It might have taken me a second too long, but I turned and ran out of the trailer. My heart raced in my ears. I had to get out of there. No one was coming to rescue me this time.

No one would call me athletic, but I wasn't horribly slow, either. I almost made it to the car before he caught me. Sheer size let him cover longer distances than me. Holding my arm in a vise grip, he glared at me. "I asked you a question, bitch."

"I don't know where she is. Once again, she's skipped

town." *Why the fuck did I come here? I didn't need my stuff this badly. I could have just done without.*

He stared at Ace's car. "That's a fancy ride. Looks like you've traded up. One of your rich boy toys give you that car?"

"I borrowed it. It's not mine." He pushed me back against it, his unclean body pinning me to the door. With weight alone, he kept me pinned.

"Ah, but they'll have ten grand. I bet they have it in their pockets. How much would they give me for you? If I sent them, say, your pinkie, would they send me ten grand for it?"

This wasn't going to end well. All my life, I'd been terrified of becoming a statistic, ending up like my mother. Dead because of this douchebag never hit my list of possible endings. *I'd almost rather be taken out by the vampires. Almost. Maybe not.*

As fast as I could, I raised my knee and jammed him in the balls. He made a sound like he wanted to vomit and gasped at the same time. I shoved at him, and he fell back two steps—enough that I could get past him. I ran for the woods. I was never supposed to go there. *Mom's fucking rules. Who cared now?* I had to get there as fast as I could

I wasn't so lucky. Even in his stumbling, he grabbed onto my leg. I fell forward, my head hitting the ground as I failed to catch myself. Right onto a rock, my forehead cracking like a dish breaking on the ground. Stars passed behind my eyes. I didn't know what happened. I couldn't see anything, but somehow, despite the world spinning, the man gripping my leg, and at the overall sense that I'd just been destroyed, I kicked backward, hitting him in the face.

Vision returned but only barely. Blood rushed into my

eyes, coating my face like ice cream melting down a cone. I pulled away, and after crawling for a second, stumbled to my feet. Somehow, not at all sure how I could function or even think, I ran to the woods.

"You bitch!" he called after me.

The asshole was not going to let this go. I wasn't okay. Nausea rushed through me, but I knew—somehow, even though I couldn't think—I knew I couldn't puke. He'd catch me if I did.

I ran forward, hoping the trees would hide me. Really, I had no idea where I was going. None whatsoever.

"I will bury your body so deep, no one will ever find you."

He was too close. I tripped. *A ledge.*

Falling.

～

"Open your eyes, Maci."

A voice called to me. Deep, unsettling. I'd heard it before, but I could never seem to place it anytime I heard it. I wrenched open my eyes. My head pounded. I was on the ground, leaning against a tree, with no idea where I was. My face was sticky. Hot. My stomach turned.

What is happening? Where am I?

A man stood over me. He was tall, dark-haired, his eyes cold in the moonlight illuminating him. Was the moon full tonight? It was so bright. Everything hurt.

"Who?" I found my voice. "Who are you?"

He knelt beside me. "You never know. It's better that way. We don't have time for the long explanation, and you won't remember it anyway. But those you are with, those who stopped you from arriving last night at your designated time, would call me the Betrayer." While his voice held emotion, his eyes didn't. They were cold. Or maybe it was just me. I was so, so cold. A violent shiver racked my body.

The Betrayer. I'd heard that name. *Once. What was it?* I couldn't remember.

"You will feel better soon, and if I'm not mistaken—and I never am—they will find you shortly. Things couldn't be going more according to plan. Finally. So many years under their nose, and no one speaks to you." He smirked. "You need your precautionary dose. I can't have anything happening to you without it. For a few years more. Then all will be clear. Besides, this will help you now. Which you clearly need." He scowled. "That man has been dealt with."

I didn't understand. "What?"

He extended his hand where he held a cup. *Where had that come from?* Everything was so confusing, and my body hurt so much. Tears leaked from my eyes.

"Now, none of that." He shook his head. "I didn't know what to do with tears when I was human, and I certainly don't know now." He bit into his wrist and blood oozed into the glass. "Drink."

What? Absolutely not. "You just bled into that cup," I pointed out numbly.

The man cupped my cheek. "And you have drunk it many times. Once a month. Since you were twelve years old. You'll drink it now. You know you will." There was a compulsion to his voice, like I would obey him. Maybe he was right? Maybe I had drunk it many times. He handed me the cup.

Despite every part of my body wanting to fall apart to make the pain stop, I did as he asked. I swallowed. And swallowed.

Until the cup was empty. It tasted like milk. He'd dropped his blood into the milk and I'd... What?

What have I done?

He dropped his hand. "Like every other night, now you will forget. When the time comes, you will remember, but that isn't now."

I blinked. *Wow.* My head hurt so much. What had happened? I didn't understand. I couldn't...couldn't... What?

Someone had been there. Or no—*no one* had been here. I was alone. In the woods. *A man tried to get me. He'd tried to...*

A noise to my side caught my attention, despite my blurred vision. I tried to turn my head. My neck objected. *It hurts. No turning it right now.*

"Maci." Ace's voice struck before I could clearly see him. "Found you. Fuck. Yes, found you." He bent down. "What happened?"

"Ace?" I had to make sure it was him. Everything was just...wrong.

"Yes, sweetheart. It's me. I knew you were here. I could just feel it. Like, I knew how to find you. Another weird thing that I'm grateful for. Can you put your arms around my neck?"

Could I? "Everything hurts."

"I know it does. I can see that. I'm going to get you some help. I promise. We'll make this okay."

I hoped he was right, because I was pretty sure I could close my eyes and never wake up again. I didn't want to do that. It was my birthday. Or maybe it wasn't anymore? How much time had passed? I didn't even know. Where was my phone? I could check the time. Instead, I concentrated on lifting my arms.

He needed me to... *What?*

I must have done it, because he lifted me up like I weighed nothing. "I've got you. I promise."

Maybe I passed out, maybe I just didn't remember, but the next thing I knew, I was on a white bed in a bright room with someone shining a light in my eyes.

"Maci, can you hear me?"

"What does it mean if she can't?" That was Rowan's voice. It sounded strained.

I blinked. "Yes, I can hear you. If you could put down that light, I'd be grateful."

The light extinguished, and I could finally see the faces around me. All five of the guys were there. They surrounded the bed, except where a strange doctor stared at me.

"Glad to hear that. You seem to be coming back to us." He was dark-haired, dark-eyed, and he had a well-trimmed beard, but he wasn't who I wanted to see right then. "Do you remember what happened?"

Did I? I chewed on my lip. "That man attacked me. He wants money. From my mom. He said some things." It was hard to remember all of it. In fact, it made my head hurt to try.

"He's dead." Griffin's voice was low. "Found his body. I wouldn't worry about him anymore. He isn't going to want anything going forward." There was a long pause, and Tanner shot Griffin a look. "What? I didn't kill him."

The doctor shook his head. "Boys, that's not helpful right now. What about after that? What happened to you? How did you end up where Ace found you?"

"That would imply I knew where I was."

He laughed. "That's true. All right. Listen, I know you're concussed. But we need to take a look at you. I'm going to run a lot of tests. Gentlemen, you might as well go home. I know your father has things for you to do."

Tanner shook his head. "They can wait."

The doctor lifted an eyebrow. "I don't think so. I'm not losing out on my change soon because I let the five of you ignore his order to return home. She'll be okay. I get that she's important. I'll take care of her, and you'll probably be able to take her home tomorrow. I'll let you know."

"No." I grabbed the doctor's arm. "I can't afford you. I can't ever go to the hospital. Please, I can't stay here."

The doctor frowned. "There won't be a bill for any of this. This is a special hospital, only used for the people under the vampires' care. You won't owe us anything. My name is Doctor Lamar. We're very informal here, so most people call me Archie. You can call me whatever you want." He rose. "Time to go, boys. I promise to take care of her."

Understanding was slow, but it finally caught up to me. The doctor knew about vampires, and he wanted to be one of them.

Would that make him a servant? I didn't know if that was something I could ask, so I didn't. Besides, the less I had to talk, the better. I closed my eyes.

HOURS LATER, my head still throbbed, but I was awake and in better shape than I was earlier. My room was white, clean, and the bed was bigger than the average hospital bed. I'd only been in one once, years ago, when I'd broken my ankle. Even then, my mother had insisted we leave early because of the bill.

In the mirror hanging across the room, I could see a huge bandage covered my forehead. That must have been where I'd gotten struck by the rock. Where was my cell phone? I guessed it didn't matter. Archie didn't want me looking at it for a few days.

The tiniest noise had me looking at my windows a second before it swung open. Tanner stuck his head in and stared at me. "Good. You're up."

He hopped in, and I sat up, glad that doing so no longer made me want to puke. "Tanner? Isn't this floor high up?" It looked like it, based on the view out the window from my bed.

With a shrug, he closed the window. "Heights don't bother me, and I'm a good climber." He swung his backpack off and set it down. "I couldn't leave you here alone. Archie's home for the night. I saw him arrive. The nurses won't send me home or rat me out. They're too anxious for the change. Not only are you hurt, but it's almost not your birthday anymore. I can't let you do that alone. So, yeah, I'm staying."

I lifted my eyebrows. "Do the others know you came? That you were going to scale a wall?"

"No. They're sleeping...badly. Caesar is prowling around the hallways. Can't sleep at all. The others are trying. If they noticed I left the room, they probably figure I'm with Caesar. I don't care what they think right now. Love those guys, but I want to be with you, so I'm going to be."

He opened his bag and pulled out a plastic container. Seconds later, he removed a cupcake. "We baked earlier, before we started to sense something was wrong. We all knew. Ace found you, but we were all looking. I'm just relieved it didn't take too long once we came looking. I wish we'd trusted the feeling and left earlier. I'm sorry, Maci. This is all really new to us."

I understood the feeling. "Why is it happening?"

"I don't know. None of us do, not even Griff, and he thinks he knows everything. I don't really care. I like it."

Another dig into the bag came out with a candle, which he quickly lit with a lighter. "Happy birthday, sweetheart."

Tanner sat on the edge of the bed. I gripped on to his arm. "Tanner." I could hardly speak, emotion clogging my throat. "This is incredible. One of the nicest things ever done for me. I mean..." A tear leaked out of my eye. "I'm sorry. I can't adequately express."

He leaned over and kissed me. "Blow out your candle. You need to make a wish."

I did as he asked, wishing beyond anything in the universe that they didn't have to go through their pain, that they didn't have to be vampires. That they could stay these guys.

I raised my eyes to meet his gaze. "Thank you."

"You're my girl. All of ours. But right this second, you're mine, because we're alone. I have so little time to spoil you." He lifted the cupcake. "Want to eat it?"

"No." I smiled. "My stomach isn't great yet." It might be whatever they were pumping in my IV, but I had no intention of eating just yet.

He set it down. "Let me know if you get hungry. Tell me your injuries. You look better, but it would be hard for you to look too much worse. I don't ever want to see anything like that again on you. I thought... Never mind. Just so glad you're sitting up looking like this."

"They thought I had a lot of things broken, but nothing was. It was weird. Like as the hours passed, I seemed to get better in ways they didn't anticipate. I guess I was just really lucky. Anyway, my head is really concussed, but otherwise, I'm strangely sound."

He nodded. "Such a relief. Would it hurt you if I scooted in next to you, just to hold you? Make my heart rate slow down, feeling you in my arms, I think."

I scooted over. "Yes, come on, but I think I smell bad. They cleaned me up, but I need to shower, and I'm not allowed yet."

"You don't smell bad, and even if you did, I promise you I wouldn't care." He smiled, sitting down before he stretched out next to me. The nurses had turned the lights down for me so I could sleep. It wasn't totally dark, but it was better than nothing. My arm ached from the IV, but it was hydrating me, and maybe they had some sort of magic feel-good things in it. I really didn't know.

Tanner smelled fantastic. He must have showered, because his soap, which had a hint of sandalwood in it, was right on the surface. I nestled down against him and only winced for a second at my head pounding. It eased just a little bit and then cooled. Yes, Tanner was exactly what I needed right then.

"I thought I might read to you. How does that sound? I know you can't watch anything, but I could read to you." He shifted a little, so I was on top of his chest. "How does that sound?"

I loved the idea. "Please."

He picked a book out of his bag. I didn't know what it was, and he didn't tell me. It took me a second to realize what it was. If my head weren't pounding, I'd probably start quoting as he read. I loved that book. Tanner was a music loving, voice of an angel, Gatsby reading guy, and all he wanted to do right then was to hold me.

I closed my eyes and let his voice lull me off to sleep, where my head wouldn't hurt anymore.

"I told you he was here." Griffin's voice filled the room. "I told you this was where he was. Tanner, brother, when did you get here? How early did you get up?"

Next to me, Tanner shifted. I opened my eyes. We hadn't moved since he'd started reading. Maybe the nurses had come in? I had a new IV bag, but I hadn't even woken when they'd changed that out. The book was on the table next to him, and otherwise, Tanner had held me all night.

"I got here about eleven o'clock, right before her birthday was over. What are you all doing here before eight?" His voice was scratchy. He'd just woken up too. "And why come in like you're pounding on things with noise?"

I pointed at the window. "He came through the window."

"Ooh." Ace laughed. "He's back to climbing. I haven't seen you scale a building in years."

"Well..." Tanner put his head on top of mine. "The motivation was good."

They all took seats around the room, Griffin abruptly stopping at the bedside table. "You brought her a cupcake."

Some mildly funny bickering took place, but I sort of zoned out. My head was clear, but I still wasn't right. This wasn't a new feeling, though. Every so often, I felt this way, like I was just a little bit out of it for a day. Then it would pass. This time, I could call it part of the concussion symptoms, or I could acknowledge it was just that kind of day.

It didn't seem to come around my period or anything I could chart. *Just so strange.*

Rowan touched my leg. "You okay?"

"I'm doing much better now, thanks for asking."

"Good, Archie said we can bring you home, but you can't go to school for a while. You need to rest, so they're going to excuse you from your finals. It's all taken care of. One of the benefits of being my father's ward. Anyway, you'll be home with us. We'll be learning things so that they will be fresh on our minds when we wake up as vampires. The things we learn right before stay with us, so you can watch us do that."

I smirked at him. "What if I fucked with it? Like I told you a lot of dirty jokes right before or something?"

"Rowan, can I see you in the hallway?" Archie came to the door. "I need to talk to you for a second."

Tanner groaned after Rowan followed the doctor out. "I hate that man."

"You do?"

"I do. He's the one who is going to dose us right before we get in the coffins. Drug us so we're less scared. I've dreaded the sight of him my whole life. He'd show up to give us shots, and I'd want to have a fit, even before I really understood. He's Doctor Death."

The door slammed back open, and Rowan stalked back into the room. "Come on. We're getting her out of here."

I sat up. *Well, that's abrupt.* "Everything okay?"

"No, it's absolutely *not* okay." He shook his head. "Griff, give her the clothes we brought. Out of here, now."

Ace put his hand on Rowan's arm. "Talk to me. What's going on?"

"He just asked me if I wanted him to kill Maci. To do her a kindness and put her down gently, since my father is going to kill her so badly. He just asked if I wanted her to die right this second. Obviously, I said no. We have to get out of here."

Caesar jumped up. "Immediately out of here. How do we get the IV out of her arm?"

Tanner leaned over and ripped it out. The pain was jarring, and I cried out, blood going everywhere. "We don't know what's in that thing."

"Fuck." I grabbed on to the wound as Griffin pressed a

towel down on my sore hand. I tried to swallow my fear to ask the obvious question. "So, it's a given then, he's killing me?"

"No," Griff answered. "He's absolutely not, trust me on that."

I wanted to, but my doctor had just asked Rowan if he should euthanize me. I wasn't filled with a lot of confidence.

13

There was a huge amount of fuss over getting me out of the hospital, but it resolved pretty quickly after Rowan started barking orders at the nurses. He wasn't a vampire yet, but you wouldn't know it from how they behaved around him. My hand was bandaged, instructions on my care given—although I felt remarkably fine— and I was sent home, this time in Caesar's car.

A thought dawned on me. "Ace's car? It was…"

"We got it. Don't give it a second thought. A vampire got the douchebag who went after you. He was drained. I mean *really* drained. No blood left in his body. From what I understand, that's hard to do. Every last drop takes more energy than most of them want to apply to any given feed. That's personal."

I didn't have an explanation for him. "Maybe I'm not the only one he's hurt. Maybe there's a vampire with a grudge, and I just got lucky."

Caesar reached over to take my hand in his. "*We* got lucky. If he had killed you, I might have begged for the change tonight."

"Seems we might both be dying." I meant to say it light-heartedly, like it would be funny, since we both knew now that the death was coming, but my voice cracked, thus ending the idea that I was at all lighthearted about the situation.

He squeezed my hand. "Absolutely not. You're *not* dying. We worked out what to do about that. Can't let the whack job who wants to be a vampire, Doc Archie, accidentally get in the way, but no, you're not dying. The less you know, the better, but trust me. Okay? Trust me."

I did. I completely, absolutely believed every word he said, like I always had. "I do."

"Good." He brought my hand to his lips. "You look so much better."

"Like nothing happened. That can't be normal."

He frowned. "No, it's not. But what is normal anymore? It's like... It's like everything that should be both is and isn't. I don't know. I don't get it. And on top of that, I don't care."

I leaned my head on his shoulder. "I'm still tired. That's pretty much it."

"Well, it probably doesn't help that you were out cold in a healing sleep. We barged in because we were sort of annoyed Tanner took off to see you and didn't take us with him. You needed to sleep longer. Well, maybe we were also really anxious to see you again, since we were unceremoni-ously kicked out of your presence when you most needed us." He frowned. "And maybe I'm annoyed at myself because I didn't have the same idea as Tanner when it came to sneaking in."

I shook my head. "We all have things we're good at. Sounds like Tanner knows how to be sneaky. I think you'd probably be more likely to kick down the door."

His body shook as he laughed. "For you? Yes, I'd kick down the door."

I liked that image. "Maybe we could keep driving? The others could come in their cars too. We'd all just keep driving. To a place where there is sunlight almost all day and no vampires. We'll just drive and drive. Surely there must be such a place."

"I looked it up once. Would you believe it's in Arizona? Anyway, there are vampires there too. They battle on our side, so it's not even someplace we could go to escape." He shook his head. "Good thought, though."

I lifted my eyebrows. "The Betrayer? That's what Rowan's father called the guy on the other side. What's he about?"

"He and his people are the enemy. That's all I know too. I'll get to know more when I've got fangs to use against people. There are more of us than them, but they just continue to survive. My father runs the war. That's why he's not here most of the time. He's their general. I think they intend for me to take on the role when I change. I don't know. They call the other side cockroaches."

The Betrayer. The name banged around in my head, and I wasn't sure why. "The title would indicate he somehow betrayed someone or something."

"Yes. How, who, and why? No idea. Big giant secret. How does one betray a vampire?" He shrugged, which moved my head and made me giggle. "I could listen to that sound all day long. Hate to tell you what it does to me."

I lifted my head, all thoughts of the Betrayer fleeing. "What *does* it do to you?"

He visibly swallowed. "The same thing that happened the other morning, when you were pressed up against me, alone in my bed. I mean...I know your boundaries. You were clear about them from the start. There is no pressure from me. I shouldn't have even brought it up. But, yeah, you have to know what you do to me. The only person really to get me so worked up. I used to think it was because I'm a vampire that I was sort of blasé and uninterested in things guys my age are supposed to be really into. I know now, I just needed you. Just you, Maci. Now I know how the rest of those guys are always feeling—the ones in school who can't talk about anything else."

His words heated me up inside. Yes, I'd set a limit with them. Kissing, yes; sex, no. But they were essentially vanishing from my life in a week. I couldn't be left more of a mess than I was already going to be, if I lived at all. God forbid something went askew and I was left with a baby. I didn't want to even consider what choices had to be made then.

No, it was better if we just didn't do that. That didn't mean, however, that I wasn't really, really interested in what he was saying to me. "I have...the same reaction to you. It's not a good idea. Maybe if we had more time? I just thought you should know."

The tension in the car had upped considerably. I breathed heavily, so did he. Finally, and too soon, we reached Rowan's house.

He grabbed me by the shirt, pulling me to him to kiss me, hard. Over and over again. It was only Rowan knocking on the window that finally broke us apart. Rowan lifted an eyebrow and grinned at us before he walked away. His point had been made. We were taking too long to get in the house.

"If vampires dream of their human lives, if they hold onto memories of any kind that matter, you can be sure what just happened in the car will be all I'll ever be dreaming about." He kissed my cheek, lingering there.

"Sweet Maci, who for just a few short days, was all that crossed my mind all the time."

I loved that. It was so meaningful to me, touched my soul so deep and profoundly, that I couldn't even find something to say in response. It was too much to speak about. And I was sure that Caesar understood.

I'D NO SOONER FOUND my footing about being back at Rowan's than I was struck speechless again. The guys had bought me birthday presents, and they were strewn all over the bed that I'd slept in two nights earlier.

"What did you guys do?" I could hardly believe what I saw.

Rowan cleared his throat. "We bought a bunch, then when you got hurt, we bought a bunch more. Maybe overboard, but we just wanted to spoil you. A lot."

Tanner walked over to me, handing me the book he'd read to me last night. "This is one of them. I didn't wrap it because I used it."

I brought it to my chest to hold on to it. "I'll never forget it. I've read Gatsby many times. I love it. I loved it even more when you were reading it to me."

His cheeks brightened a little bit pink. "I loved it too."

"Open the others." Ace brushed against me. "See what we got you."

Griffin met my gaze. "I hope you like what we picked. Just things we thought you might like, want, or need. You've already seen the cupcakes, but we'll cook you dinner too, if you're feeling up for food."

Someone cleared their throat, and we turned around

almost all at once. One of the older servants stood there. "Your fathers need you now."

Rowan held up his hand. "We're going to need a few minutes."

"Sir." She sighed. "They said very specifically now or there would be a huge problem."

All of the joy in the room fled. A muscle visibly ticked in Rowan's jaw. He rubbed at it. "Okay, be right there." The woman turned and fled. "Maci...I am so—"

"I think she is probably sick of our sorry," Griffin interrupted him. "She gets it. We're sorry. We suck. It's going to be like this from now until it's over, and then she won't see us again. We ruined her life, and we can't even give her birthday presents the day she is released from the hospital, where the nutjob who will dose us with sedatives before we get in the fucking coffins threatened to kill her. Please don't tell her we're sorry, because if I were Maci, it would make me want to hit us in our fucking faces."

I reached out and took his hand in mine. He'd gotten increasingly loud as he'd hollered at Rowan, but I didn't really think it was Rowan he was upset with. Nor was he really concerned that I was going to hit anyone in the face. He was just mad because this was life, and he had no say so in what happened to us at all. Whether Griffin liked it or not, this was fucking happening. Sometimes when the world got to be too much, what I really wished for was someone to just hold my hand.

Actually, there *was* something I wished more. I dropped his hand so I could hug him tightly. He froze for a second but quickly hugged me back. The room went quiet, and although I closed my eyes, I could feel everyone's gaze on me.

I couldn't make this better, but I was getting good at hugs.

THEY INSISTED I open all my presents without them there. I'd never been so overwhelmed in my whole life. I had more clothes than I'd ever owned, all different kinds, and they got my sizes right. Someone bought me earbuds, so I could listen to music with my new phone. I had four different books to read and a gift certificate to the restaurant Tanner had taken me to. They'd also baked me the cupcakes that were in the kitchen, and if I weren't mistaken, gotten the ingredients to grill steaks and make baked potatoes.

I sank into one of the stools by the counter. How did you say thank you for all of this? How did you even begin? As I pondered that, with no answer in sight, I took a bite of one of the cupcakes. It was delicious. Who baked them? Was it Caesar? He did like to cook. Did that include baking?

Arguing the birthday presents were too much seemed really rude. If a person spent time and money getting you something, and didn't have anything nefarious planned in the gifting, then it seemed the right thing to do to just say thank you and enjoy the gifts. But it wasn't like I could ever reciprocate this, assuming we kept them from becoming vampires next week.

I was going to go with thank you and hope I got a chance at some point to make them feel as special as they'd made me feel.

Even if they hadn't been here to watch me open them.

"Hey." Ace rushed into the kitchen. "I finished fast. Passed all my tests. Helped that my father has spoken on these matters before, so I had an edge. Anyway, you're here, in the kitchen. Can I please make those steaks I was going to make for you? Right now? It'll be like I got to take you out, even though I didn't get to."

I stepped toward him. "Ace, I don't know how to say thank you for those gifts. I really don't."

He hugged me, and I wrapped my arms around him. "This is thanks enough. Okay? I wanted to hug you all day after I saw you hug Griffin. Not jealous, just wanted one of my own."

I smiled against his chest. Ace did like to speak his truth and not worry about how it came out. That was amazing about him. Most people were guarded, even when we didn't have to be.

Finally, we pulled apart, and he hustled to the fridge. "Making those steaks."

"Thank you. Sounds great. Can I make the salad? Or the baked potato?"

He shook his head. "No. This is me. Part of my gift to you, so no. There's something else, actually. It's sort of a regifting."

I didn't understand, so with nothing to do with myself, I sat down on the stool again. It was awkward not being busy all the time. He went out the side door with the steak. I had no idea what he was going to do to grill it. We almost never had steak. A few times when I was younger, but that was it.

My mother hadn't cooked it. One of her nicer boyfriends had. Funny memory I hadn't thought of in a while. He'd been kind to have around. A little cold, distant, but pleasant, and he hadn't tried to hurt either of us. When I said I was hungry, he'd insisted on grilling steaks.

What had happened to him? It was like one day, he'd been gone, with no explanation. My mom had been put out, but she'd moved on fast after that. What had his name been? I couldn't really remember. He was the dude who made us steaks.

"I lit the grill. It'll be a minute or two until I start. I want to get it perfectly right, so I want to give you something that someone else gave to me." He preheated the oven. Ace moved like he knew what he was doing in the kitchen. Caesar did too, but then again, they'd been feeding themselves for years. And unlike me, they had the means to spend whatever they wanted on food. I didn't know how to cook because no one taught me, and what I could afford couldn't be wasted attempting to make things that might not work out.

He pulled a salad bag out of the fridge next. It was one of the pre-made ones. "See why I don't need your help making it? I let someone else do it already."

That was cute, but he was being really hesitant with this giving-me-something-that-was-his thing. "Ace?"

"I want you to take my car when I'm gone."

No. That was absolutely too much. "I'm sorry, I can't do that. That would make me very uncomfortable."

"Please listen to my reasons?" He was messing with the baked potatoes, putting them on a tray. "No one will drive it. It will end up in a garage, one of a hundred expensive cars no one drives. It'll just die somewhere, with no one using it. I'd rather it go to you and be driven around."

"Ace, you're going to be awake in a year. I can drive it around to keep it going but leave it for you when you come back."

His face fell. "Sweetheart, I won't be awake during the day for years. Maybe fifty to a hundred of them. And once I'm up, I won't be driving around for decades. I'll be feeding and fighting. Or whatever. But not driving. Trust me, it will die." He visibly swallowed. "Like I'm going to die."

"Ace." I put my head in my hands. "Let's all run away tonight. Let's go now. Get the others. Just fucking go. Where does the Betrayer live? We'll go there. He can have a big win, the children of his enemy, with the stipulation he doesn't make you change."

"No one knows where he lives. They can't track him. Or yes, that would be a good idea. I only know that much because my father talks. We can't count on the Betrayer. Besides, with that name, he doesn't seem real trustworthy."

That was it. I let the tears I'd been holding fall. I gave up. All of it was too much. Ace rushed over to me, dropping the potatoes as he did. He had his arms around me. "Never mind. Don't take the car. Forget it."

I shook my head, definitely getting snot all over him, but when I would've pulled away, he stopped me. "It's not the car. It's *everything*."

"I know it is." He kissed my temple. "I'd take all of this from you, if I could."

"Fuck. His cooking isn't that bad." Rowan entered, approaching us slowly. "Arguably, Caesar is better. And I'm not half bad, either, but he can handle this."

I couldn't help it. My tears turned to laughter. Ace followed me, and we were both soon hysterical. Rowan ran his hand through my hair.

"So I'm not going to apologize, because Griffin might show up and bite off my head. I'm simply going to ask...what can I do to help?"

I wiped at my eyes. "Nothing. That is very sweet, but nothing. I'm okay. Just having a moment. And I totally soaked Ace's shirt."

For his part, he shook his head. "Use me to cry on anytime."

"Let me think about the car, okay? I'd rather we all get in

it and leave. Right now."

Rowan's face fell. "Did you not tell her?"

"No, it seemed a little bit much. I wanted to give her steak and celebrate her, not make it even worse."

I put my hands on my head. "All of the constant hedging is getting old. What didn't you tell me?"

Rowan held up his arm. "I think they must have been getting worried that we were legitimately considering a run. The funny thing is we seriously talked about this a few years ago. Not currently. But they tagged us." He pointed to the specific place. "Yesterday. Like we're animals. So unless we dig it out of our skin—which I would be willing to do if I didn't know it was pointless, since the vampire network is such that I'll never really be able to get away from my destiny—they'll be able to find us. We are completely trackable now."

Not only now. "That will be after you're vampires too. I mean...they could conceivably track you from this point on for however long you guys live. I guess I'm saying that is... intense. Is this because you're carrying around the souls of some dead vampires? Or is there something else going on? Have they ever done this before?"

"Have they ever done what before?" Caesar entered, followed by Tanner and Griffin.

Ace winked at me as he walked to the fridge and grabbed the other steaks. Looked like he wasn't getting his dinner alone with me after all. Was that something we could actually do? It seemed important to him, and I wanted to make it happen. In fact, I wouldn't have said no to spending alone time with all of them.

However, I'd lived long enough to know most of the time what I wanted absolutely didn't happen.

Besides, I didn't mind all of them together as a group

either. It was so normal, so comforting, like we had been together like this a hundred times when we absolutely hadn't. Internally, I shook my head. Would I ever understand any of it?

I just loved it. That was all there was to it. Every moment I was with them, I loved. The thought should have scared the shit out of me, but it didn't. It hadn't, and I doubted it ever would.

Oh man.

It looked like we were having steak.

It was delicious, but I liked the company more than the food. I loved the laughter. The quiet moments that didn't last long because one of them would usually fill the space. And when they sang happy birthday to me, it ranked among the happiest moments of my life.

"Gotta go." Caesar sighed. "Griffin and I have a task to take care of at Wanda's. I'll see you all later."

"Yep." Griff jumped up, kissing me on the cheek as he passed by.

The rest of us cleaned up and ended up getting ready for bed. It was very quiet after that. I wasn't sure exactly what had happened, but they all seemed to have things on their minds. That was fine. How could they not?

I put on some new pajamas, which earned me a grin from Tanner before he pulled out his guitar. "Good taste there, Rowan."

I touched the strap of the pink tank top I wore. "You?" I asked Rowan.

"I thought you'd look pretty in the matching set. I was right." He ran a hand through his hair. "I know it's technically my turn, but you're not a toy we're passing around. You can decide who you sleep with. You can also decide to sleep alone. What would you like for tonight?"

I gestured toward the bed. "Please. Join me."

His smile was huge, and it lit up my soul. Rowan so rarely grinned like that. I wanted to roll around in it. We climbed into the bed together, but it wasn't really time to sleep yet. Ace flipped on the television, and a movie came on that I didn't recognize. But while Tanner strummed quietly on his guitar, we watched a story about a man who had to solve a mystery even though he couldn't remember what happened to him.

"What should I do as a last hurrah?" Rowan asked me quietly. "What last thing should I do?"

"Are you a last hurrah person? Do you have a bucket list?"

He played with a string of my hair. "Lie in bed with a beautiful girl. Check. But I feel like I should do something else."

"Well, if you get a tattoo, you won't know if your vampire self will like it. You could really fuck that guy by doing something terrible he has to live with for a very, very long time."

I'd been kidding, but he sat up straight like he intended to dash from the room. "I am going to fucking do that."

"Really? I was not serious."

"Well, I am. I am going to go get a big, giant rose on my back. Or a daisy. Or a cat. Or something. And that dude is going to have to walk around wearing my body in whatever I pick out forever. That is what I am going to do."

I guessed we knew what he was going to do for his last hurrah. "Should I do something?"

"Not as a last hurrah, because trust me, gorgeous, you're not going to die." He took my hands in his, then a second later, he kissed me. It wasn't goodbye, but it felt that way.

14

Rowan held me in the comforting darkness when the bed dipped. I knew it was Caesar. I'd gotten so used to him being in the bed that, as his scent moved over me, it tried to drag me even further into dreamland. I smiled.

"Did you get them?" Rowan's voice was low, almost a whisper.

"Wanda took care of us. It's done. Griffin set them all up, and we tested them in the forest. All is good to go. They'll work, if we end up needing them to."

Rowan pressed his nose into my neck. "Last resort."

I wanted to wake up to see what they were talking about, but the night was cold and my brain refused. When Caesar threw his arm over me in the way he always did, I quit fighting the urge to dig deeper into my dreams.

Morning came too fast.

Being concussed, even though I felt fine, meant that I had a lot of down time to wander around the grounds while the guys studied whatever vampire strategy and history they had to have stored in their brains minutes before they died. I cooked in their kitchen. I watched movies. Napped, like I was a lady of luxury.

It was ridiculous to be so at odds, especially considering the best I could do was hope that I'd soon be responsible for the upkeep of the place. I almost begged to go back to school, but it was ridiculous too. I got to see glimpses of them in odd times. I'd lose that if I were gone.

It wasn't until I stood watching the rain pound the pavement from the inside of Rowan's garage that I really considered running. I had no doubt that the vamps would come for the guys if they ran. They were worth too much for them. Would they really waste that kind of time and resources on me? They planned to kill me anyway. Probably they wouldn't.

I was just a girl they were using to get what they wanted. It was only days until the guys would die. They weren't going anywhere, and they were obeying—something they would do whether I was there or not. Would it make any kind of difference if I ran? The guys would be upset, but they'd understand. They might even like it that I wasn't there to see them die.

Could I live with myself if I did?

No, I absolutely couldn't. I hadn't known them long, but I knew I had to be there with them until the end. That in the same situation, they never would've left me. I would be there to see this through, and I'd run afterward.

Yes, that was what I would do.

The day they were dead, I would get the hell out of there and be done with fucking vampires forever. I stepped out into the rain, letting it make me wet.

Despite the fact we were all pretending really hard

otherwise, tomorrow was graduation. Even if it were pouring rain, there would be no postponing what the guys had to do.

No rain delays for becoming a vampire.

I hated the vamps. I always would.

GRIFFIN HELD ME AGAINST HIM, both of us wrapped in blankets on the floor, while the television played an action film softly in the background. Everyone else was asleep in their beds. Tanner wasn't sleeping well. He lay in bed next to Caesar, where I would soon join them.

I didn't know how they were sleeping at all. I was wide awake.

"You got yourself soaked today. You're going to get sick like that, and I won't be around to take care of you, so you have to be careful not to do that again."

I looked up at him, leaning on his chest so I could. "It's sweet of you to worry, but you don't have to. I promise I know how to take care of myself."

"I know you do." He cleared his throat. "Maybe it was a past life, how we knew each other? Maybe that's why it feels this way —like we already had the basics all done the day that we met."

At the end of the day, we could believe whatever we wanted. Who was going to tell us we were wrong or right? "Sounds good. Let's go with that."

"Okay."

"You didn't get to make a speech. You didn't get to go show off being valedictorian."

He laughed, a low sound. "I was never going to get to go."

I could hear the ache in his voice, and it moved through me like he'd taken a knife and sliced at my soul. "What would you have said?"

"I don't know. Something about living your best life. About making sure every day has some meaning. Not that every day has to be filled with purpose and drive, but that at least a small moment of every day counts for something. Like just taking the time to appreciate how cool a cloud looks or something."

I loved that. "I'd have stood up and applauded."

"I love you, Maci," he whispered in my ear. "Too soon to say it, but I'm gone tomorrow, so I'm not going to hold back the words. I love you. Thank you for coming into my life when you did so I'd know this feeling, just once."

Tears flooded my eyes. "Oh, Griffin. I love you too." I really did. I was young, it made no sense, yet there it was. My feelings were real. Maybe we really had loved each other in a past life. Or we were all crazy in this terrible time. I didn't suppose it made much of a difference. I loved all of them, and I was the lucky one, because whatever happened next, unlike them, I wouldn't lose the memories. I'd always remember what it felt like to love them and be loved in return.

The next day was filled with all of them getting tattoos. A funny way to spend a last day alive, but it was what they wanted to do. The idea was to get ones they were sure they would someday hate. The artists doing the ink must have thought they were all crazy but seeing as I was pretty sure they were aware of who they were giving their work to, they didn't say a word.

Had it been easy or hard to live with people always nervous around them, knowing they were afraid of them even though they hadn't really done a thing? Maybe it was a little bit of both.

Rowan settled on a butterfly on his wrist. Griffin had a peace sign done. Tanner picked the mascot for a hockey team, even though he didn't follow the sport. Caesar got the rising sun. Ace selected the card symbol that was his name. They were all beautiful, and I was actually disappointed I wouldn't get to look at them over time.

I didn't see other inked vampires. It might be a big problem that they got tattooed someday, but it wasn't going to affect my guys. It was their message from beyond the grave. They existed, and they were here.

Finally, we were back in Rowan's room, their healing tattoos covered up. I didn't know what was going to happen to that newly inked skin. Would it drain off when they died? How did it work for vampires?

I wasn't going to ask them. They didn't need to be thinking about their dead skin. I really shouldn't be going there in my own head either. It was yucky. Gross. It was like each day, I had to get a little more used to things that might have made me gag just weeks earlier. Blood in general had never been something I'd been all that comfortable around. Now I'd been bit by a bloodsucker, yet it was the least concerning thing I had going on at the moment.

"Time to get changed." Rowan rocked back on his heels. "Maci, can you give us a minute?" He stroked his thumb down my cheek. "Don't be hurt. Just a minute. It's easier if we all just get it done."

"Oh!" It hadn't occurred to me, but they'd all have to change in the bathroom if I stayed, because they weren't going to get fully naked with me in the room. "Of course. Sorry."

Tanner shook his head. "Don't be sorry. If we had more time, maybe that would be something that would have happened."

"In smaller doses." Griffin laughed. "I was so not going to have sex with her with all of your asses watching."

I balked at them. This was new. A touch of this kind of talk right before the end. I grinned at them. "What makes you think I'd be into the group thing?"

"Maybe we know your kinks better than you do?" Ace winked at me. "And yes, I just said that. Ugh. Sorry. Being ridiculous."

I tapped his arm as I passed by him. "It was funny. It's just not a funny night."

"It can be." Caesar grinned. "Seems like the perfect time for the dark kind."

"Well...let me know if you come up with any jokes." I went into the hall and leaned against the wall. *Okay. I can do this*. They were setting the tone for how it would go, and I had to follow suit. It wasn't *my* death day. Or maybe it was? I hadn't really let myself consider the idea they could kill me tonight too.

But I supposed they could. Rowan said they wouldn't because he wouldn't let them, but he would be dead.

I rubbed my eyes. He said to trust him. What did that mean at this point?

If things went askew, I was getting away. He'd understand. Or at least *this* version of him would.

They all would.

Minutes seemed to drag, but I didn't move from my spot. Where would I go? That was the overall question for both now and later. I'd grab Ace's car and go... That's where I drew the blank.

No fucking idea.

"Hey." Caesar leaned against the door. "Come on back in."

He was wearing a blazer over his jeans and a black T-shirt. I followed him back inside. They were all dressed that way, the same black blazers over the rest of their outfits. White T-shirt on Tanner, red on Rowan. Light blue on Griffin. Ace matched Caesar—black on black.

"You guys look so nice. I didn't know it was a dress-up thing." I wished I hadn't spoken the second I did. That was pretty much the stupidest thing to say ever.

Tanner pulled me into a hug. "Thank you, Maci."

I took a deep breath, bringing the scent of Tanner into my senses. He was clean, and he always had the aroma of cinnamon on him. I'd no sooner thought that than I got passed to Caesar. It startled me, but I hugged him back.

He kissed the edge of my neck. "Miss me sometimes, but not all of the time. Okay?"

Tears flooded my eyes, but I didn't get to cry, because it was Ace's turn to hold me. "I swear it would have been the best date ever, but I liked the few minutes we got."

"I..." Whatever I would have said, I didn't get to finish, because Griffin was there.

He stared into my eyes before he smoothed the hair off my forehead. "So we agreed, past lives, right? That means we'll get to do this again sometime. In some life when I won't have to die at eighteen. You'll get to have this life, live to be an old woman, have eight kids or some shit. And then the next go-round, we'll be on a path that keeps us together. That's how it works."

Was it? "Griffin..."

"Sorry, I have to have my hug." Rowan gave me a strong embrace. "I don't have enough time to let you answer what

Griff just said, or for any of us to digest it really. We have to go now. You need to come, and you need to stand behind me. The whole time. Okay? Until I get in the coffin, you have to stay behind me. Promise me?"

It didn't seem a hard thing to agree to. "Sure." I was certainly not looking to be out front.

"Guys... I... This was the best..."

"Don't," Rowan whispered in my ear. "Thank you for talking to us. This was not the way I'd pictured the last week of our lives. It was so much better."

Really, he had no idea how true that was for me too.

THE REALITY of what was happening struck me the closer we got to the coffin room. It had another name, but I couldn't think of it at all. The crickets sang. That was such a strange thought, especially while every vampire in the town stood outside the area. The moon was huge, not quite full, but bright and almost there.

I shivered and rubbed my arms. Across the way, Charlotte nodded at me, then smiled. She was happy about this. It was hard to come to terms with the fact that everyone wanted this to happen except for the six of us.

So much so, that they'd been looking forward to it. I swallowed. Rowan turned to look over his shoulder at me. "Don't run. I know you want to. I don't blame you, but almost everyone here is a predator. If you run, they will chase you because they get so little chance to do that."

It made sense, even if I hated it.

"Dad," Rowan called out, shooting a look I couldn't decipher at Caesar before he said it. Ace changed his stance, broadening how he stood, while Tanner shoved his hands in his pockets. I couldn't decipher Griffin at all.

His father stepped toward them. "The ceremony takes place inside. You know this. You've seen it many times. I'm glad to see you're not just on time but you're early."

Rowan took a deep breath. "We still have things to talk about."

They stood just far enough from their fathers that they had to shout to be heard and their vampire dads had to do the same. I blinked. That was odd...wasn't it? What were they doing?

"I don't think so. Come."

Rowan barely let his father finish speaking before he answered him. "We understand you intend to kill our friend. Now that you have us here, her usefulness to you is over. That's true, yes? You never lie, so I'd like an honest answer."

Rowan's father didn't answer, but Ace's did. "I think that was always the intention."

"Not acceptable," Ace answered his own father. "She has to be protected. No one is going to kill her."

Around us, the vampires started to laugh. I'd never heard the sound before. Oh, they were amused. In that moment, I hated them—hated them so much more than I already did. I hadn't known before then that it was possible to have levels of hate. I'd just pushed up a degree to the point that my hands shook. *They think this is fucking funny?* I clenched my fists. If they were going to kill me, I was going to break some vampire noses before I went out. And I bet it would hurt them.

Rowan's father waved his hand. "Stop this nonsense. You have no say here."

"Oh, but I do. We all do, because you have moved heaven and earth to get to this moment, so that the five of us would be standing here right now. Together. We had to be born within a period of time. We had to fit what you needed, so that we could carry these souls, right?" His back was so stiff that I swore I could see a slight tremor in it. I doubted anyone not standing directly behind him could see it. His blazer would cover all of that from the front.

The elder vampires looked at each other. "What is your point?"

Rowan pulled a gun out from under his blazer. It had been covered, and I hadn't seen it. I gaped at him. They hadn't had that on them when I'd hugged them. Was it just Rowan? Was it...?

My question was instantly answered. All five of them had guns pressed against their temples.

"Let me ask you, Dad...if I shoot myself in the head, will I wake up the way you want? Can I? Because I read in those books that some deaths kill the humans completely. Seems to me this is one of the ways. And I know you're fast, but not so fast we can't all pull the triggers. Even if you stopped one of us, what happens if all five of us don't make it? What happens to your best laid plans?"

I couldn't breathe. Couldn't even draw breath. *What are they doing? Are they actually threatening to off themselves? Where did they get those guns?*

It was Caesar's father who spoke. "What is it that you want exactly?"

"I want Maci to be alive and well when I come back. I want her brought to me at the first meeting where you reintroduce me. You are going to give her to me then. She will be mine. And alive and well when that happens. That's what I want." His hand was steady. "You never lie, Father. I want your word. Now. In front of everyone, swear that is what you'll do. We know what could happen to you if they think you're a liar."

What could happen to him? I had so many questions, but all I wanted to do in that moment was to call out for them not to do this.

"You think that you will care when you see her?" Tanner's father had a low, scratchy voice. "But you won't. At best, she'll be interesting to you to feed on until she's dead. At worst, you'll want to torture her for fun. The early years are brutal. If you care for her as much as we think you do, and I see that you all do, you'll let her die now."

Rowan didn't falter. "Those are my demands."

His own father nodded. "I don't like being held hostage, but I will be amused to see her at your mercies at that time. It will be a lesson for the others. Humans don't matter other than as feeding tools. You'll understand when you arise and you are finally one of us. Fine. She will be alive and brought to you at that time. You have my word."

It was a long, poignant moment. With everything he could have demanded, it was actually brilliant what Rowan had done. And it had Griffin all over it. This had been his idea, and Rowan had executed it. Well, they all were. No way would his father ever let me go. I knew too much. He'd said that. Once you were in, you were in, whether you wanted to be or not. I had to stay, but he'd kept me alive.

I could hardly swallow. Tears clogged my throat. He'd asked me to trust him, and I had. They hadn't let me down.

Almost at once, they all dropped their guns from their heads and set them on the ground. Tanner turned to me. "If it wouldn't get you killed, I'd have taken them out."

"Tanner..."

There was a flood of action then. Five vampires I didn't know grabbed them by the arms and hauled them inside toward the coffins. Charlotte ran to me. "I can't believe they did that. Would they actually have given this up?"

I nodded. She'd never understand, though. From that moment on, I was certain I'd only be surrounded by people who would never get it.

They all wanted this.

With Charlotte pulling me along, I went into the room where it would all end. Doctor Lamar stood inside. The lighting was low, almost resembling candlelight. He had five glasses in front of him.

That was the medicine they'd ingest to make them less likely to fight to get out of the coffin. It took everything in me not to rush to the tray and knock it over. What would be the point of that? He probably had more in his car or wherever he stored the stuff.

"You're all murderers." I had to say it. "And there will be an accounting. Somewhere. In this life or the next. I don't care what you are. There will be. I know it." I didn't. Not really. I had no spiritual life to draw on, no sense of anything other than what I saw day by day. But right then? I believed it. In all of my body, in every cell in my body.

Caesar caught my gaze. He smiled at me before he took the cup in his hand. Tanner was next. Rowan after him. Griffin. Then Ace. They all stood together. In silence, they stared at their cups. Then, one by one, they drank them.

I closed my eyes. *This is happening. I can't do anything to stop it.*

Chairs squeaked; bodies moved. The vampires settled in to watch, to be there to see these five die in the next five hours. *Faster, if they struggle.*

"It's going to be okay." Lamar walked over to me. "This is a beautiful tradition."

"Drop dead." I wouldn't pretend it was okay. Not for anything in the world.

He sighed. "You'll understand the beauty of it. I promise you will."

It wasn't likely. Not at all. "I'll make you pay for this someday."

This was happening because of me. I'd spoken to them in the library, and then they'd used me to make sure the five of them didn't take any out they might have had to get away from this. I'd been the pawn in their deadly endeavor.

"I'm sorry." I spoke low, but I was sure they could hear me.

Caesar climbed into his coffin first. They were all the same. Mahogany. Big. Daunting. The stuff of nightmares. Human beings shouldn't have to see their own coffins unless they wanted to. They certainly shouldn't be alive when they got in them.

Ace went into his next. He paused to clasp Rowan on his shoulder before he got inside. None of them looked at me so far, and I doubted they would. My part with them was over. They had to do this, and they had to do it alone. Even in a crowd.

Tanner. Then Griffin. Finally, Rowan. The lids were closed by vampires I didn't know. Charlotte squeezed my arm. "It'll be okay. They're going to be like gods when they come back."

I didn't want gods. I wanted the five of them, just as they were. As they were meant to be. Not this nightmare. Not whatever monster was going to wake up sometime in the next nine months to a year.

A tear slipped from my eye, and I wiped it away. I couldn't cry there. Not in front of these people. The lids were locked.

They'd lived their whole lives knowing they had to do this. And as I stood there, I knew one thing, even though it didn't make sense—I should be doing it too. They shouldn't be doing this without me. Their death should have been my death. As it was meant to be.

I shook the thought away. This was no time to lose my mind.

15

They didn't go quietly. I didn't know whether to applaud the Dylan Thomas quality of it or to wish they had a way to knock themselves out so they never had to endure another minute of living. Yelling. Screaming. Banging. At the end of it, the need to survive won, and they tried. Everyone but Rowan. He was silent. What was happening with him? I just didn't know.

And then it was over. I didn't know that I'd be able to tell who died first. I really had no idea. My mind had become mush. Their coffins were silent.

I was going to run now. I'd stayed, witnessed their hell, and now it was time for me to get out of there. Charlotte rubbed my back. She might not get it, she might be one dose of crazy away from being a Manson chick, but she wasn't cruel. Rubbing my back was kind. I wouldn't forget it.

I stumbled to my feet. "I've got to go."

"Hold on." It wasn't Charlotte who spoke to me but Rowan's father. He stared at me, as he grabbed my arm, hauling me to him. He smiled, slowly. There wasn't an ounce of grief in his gaze. Not even a little bit. Right that second, he was every bit the monster I knew him to be. *How can anyone want this?*

"They backed me into a corner. It was rather clever. Much more so than I would have thought they could do. It makes me feel even better about exactly how ruthless they will be when they are finally who they were born to be." His smile broadened. "And they said they wanted you to be alive and well. I didn't agree to the second part. No one noticed. I don't care if you're well. You'll be alive, and they won't care. In the meantime, you're ours. And I intend to make the time worthwhile. We are going to feed on you. A lot."

I tried to wrench my arm away, but it was futile. His fangs elongated, and he bit my wrist. Hard. I cried out in pain. Unlike the first time, it wasn't an easy, quick bite. No, he prolonged the agony as I struggled. The more I did, the more he liked it. Finally, he let go.

"Any vampire who wants to feed from her can. She just has to be alive for that meeting. That's the law. If she tries to run, find her. She's ours. It's been so long since we had someone we could really play with." He shook his head. "So glad to have a feeding tube for a while. Just keep her alive."

That was when I knew I was really fucking screwed. I struggled, but it was for nothing more than the show of it, so that I could live with knowing that I had done everything I could to get away. Even in that moment, I knew it was fruitless. But it wasn't until Tanner's father bit my other wrist that I truly believed it.

They had me.

It turned out it took five bites to addict me. And for that, I had Caesar and Griffin's fathers to thank. The pain was horrendous, even as the numbness started to take over. I was fully aware that everything hurt, even as the vampire venom made it so I really didn't give a shit that it was happening.

Run away? How could I bother when nothing mattered at all? My mind slipped into the chemicals that I'd avoided my whole life.

I'd lost my best friends. Now I lost myself too.

BITE. Work. Sleep. Bite. Bite. Bite. Bite. Work. Sleep. My days blended into one moment of a vampire feeding off of me to another. In between, I did their chores.

Wash. Rinse. Repeat.

Wash.

Rinse.

Repeat.

SIX MONTHS later

I THREW up for the fifth time, holding my head over the toilet to see if there was anything left to come out. Charlotte pushed her head in the bathroom, then came over to kneel next to me. "You should be about done now. I can't imagine you have anything left in there, considering you don't eat."

Lifting my head to stare at her, I tried to find her amusing and not interfering. "I'm sorry that I've been puking so much lately that you've become an expert on my vomiting."

On days when I got bit more than eight times, I tended to spend the next day throwing up. It was like my body desperately tried to rid itself of the poison, but it was to no avail, because I would get bit again and it would just start back up.

She slid to the ground. Lately, the glow usually in her gaze was gone. Had the shine finally been rubbed off in Charlotte's eyes? Did she finally see how sick and messed up this was?

My friend sighed. "I was thinking about running." She kept her voice down. "But then I changed my mind."

This was new. I'd never heard her even suggest it before. I wished she would actually do that. She was hardly ever fed from anymore. They might not even notice if she left. The servants were really all the same to them.

Charlotte was never going to be anyone's paramour. They picked them out from other places, not from within their own community. It was sad, really.

I had no legs to stand on when it came to being pathetic. My arms were a really good indication of just how far I had fallen in life. Rowan had arranged for me to live. It would have been better if they'd just ended it that night when they'd all left this world.

Vampires could make it so you never scarred when they bit you. No one took that time with me. I stared at my wrists. What would anyone who didn't know what was going on think was happening to me? I hadn't left the vampire area since it started six months ago. I really had no idea how anyone would react to me.

"Ladies." Bethany, one of the older servants, walked over to me. She knelt. "We have things to do. Charlotte, I want you to clean the main room in Fredrick's house." That was Rowan's father's name. I'd never known it until the women servants started using it. She smoothed my hair off my face. "Bad one?"

I nodded. "Bad one."

Fredrick had miscalculated just a smidge with his *abuse Maci* plans. The servants were less enthralled seeing what he was doing. Maybe he didn't care? They could probably always find women who wanted to serve them, for the chance of being eternally a vampire. I still didn't understand it.

On their own, in moments like this, the women I now lived with were lovely human beings. For moments, I could forget that they had chosen this life, that they had left their old lives, came to this place, and decided to work for these monsters so they could have the potential of becoming one themselves. They got bit every so often.

But all in all, they were better off than the paramours.

Those women were in the pits.

Prancing around in their expensive clothes, showing off the bites on their neck like they were some kind of new accessory every time it happened. Willingly deciding to have sex with the creatures that would ultimately kill them when they'd had enough. Well...maybe not. Maybe they'd impregnate them, then change them into monsters at that point.

My head always hurt when I gave it too much thought.

There were things I knew about vampires that I hadn't known before. Yes, they never lied, but they watched their words carefully. They could easily change what they said to mean what they wanted.

Only the older vampires had sex. They had to be at least a hundred years old to have the urge again. Interestingly enough, they were monogamous. They only wanted their paramour. Until they didn't want her anymore. I hoped their time was worth it.

"I'll help." I pulled my legs to my chest in the hopes of hoisting myself up that way. I had become more adept as time had gone by.

She shook her head. "No, you sleepwalked again last

night. I saw you come back inside. Now you're puking. They're taking too much from you. Rest today. You can help tomorrow."

I shook my head. "Better if I have something to do so I don't have to think about it."

I'd never told them that I used to sleepwalk before any of this happened. Or at least I had that one time with the guys. Maybe it was vampires? In their presence, I sleepwalked like some kind of allergy. I was, in my sleep, trying to get the fuck away from there.

But I always came back. Wherever I went, I returned. It was really odd. And I tended to puke the next day too. I couldn't make sense of any of it, as though there was a piece I was always missing and couldn't work it out because I was never going to see the whole picture.

"Not today." Bethany smiled at me, then she frowned. "When you first came to stay with us, it was such a shock. I don't think any of us thought they'd do to you what they have. We've all come to really like you. We appreciate how hard you try to help, even though this has been hellish on you. Frankly, I'm not sure how you're still alive. They bite you too much. It should have killed you by now."

None of it was news to me. "Bethany, you're giving me kind words, but if you don't have a point, I'd really rather not bang around with the *you should be dead* motif."

She grinned. "I do. I guess I'm wondering what you think is going to happen when they wake up? What are they going to do with you?"

"That is the million-dollar question. If their fathers are to be believed, they won't care about me as anything other than a feeding tube. So...I guess we'll find out."

I needed to leave. That much I knew. But I was addicted. I had to find a way to detox in a place where they couldn't find me before I could accomplish any kind of real escape. I woke up every day with my hands shaking, needing someone to bite me so I could function again. I was my mother, but ten times worse than I'd ever seen her before.

"We're all here for you. I want you to know that. Get some sunshine." She squeezed my knee. "See you, lady. Charlotte, with me."

She waited until Bethany was out of the room before she rolled her eyes. "I don't know who put Bethany in charge, but I wish they'd demote her." She winked at me. "See you later."

With a bounce in her step I wished I still had, she rushed from the room. Bethany was in charge because she'd been there the longest. Did she know yet that she'd never be turned? Or was she still holding out hope?

She asked me things, so maybe I could ask her? By nature, I was cautious, and the last time I'd stepped out of my comfort zone, I'd landed in this mess. No, I'd just keep my personal intrusions into the lives of those around me to a minimum.

On shaky legs, I made my way outside, avoiding looking at the coffin room. Everyone called it the rebirth room. As far as I was concerned, it was a place where they murdered people. Not that it mattered what I thought. It was windowless, and guards walked the outside of it all day long. Bethany and a woman named Laura usually cleaned it.

I stayed as far away as I could. Even looking at it broke my heart.

But the rest of the compound stayed as it always had been. I imagined, if I lived to be two hundred years old, if I came back there, it would still look the same. They'd modernize enough that no one would notice that the majority of it never changed. Just rich people doing rich things, that's how they wanted to seem from the outside.

Laughter caught my attention, and I side-eyed the people doing the laughing. It was the paramours. Well, three of them. Last count, there were ten, but there could be more. Or fewer. Depending on what was going on. Sometimes we got asked to clean up after them or straighten their rooms in whatever mansions where they lived.

Rowan's house wasn't his father's house anymore. Once Rowan was gone, others moved in with human children. It was like the houses rotated once the human was no longer alive. I hadn't been asked to interact with those kids. It was easy for me to imagine their lives, since I knew what the guys had once told me.

It wasn't happy in there.

Across the yard, with the sun setting, I met the gaze of Ace's father—Gilbert. They were always first and foremost *the fathers* to me. They belonged to the guys first and their actual name second. I didn't even know if those had been their given names or if they'd adopted them over time, the way they added electronics to the compound. They were old-fashioned enough, they might need to be updated again soon.

Or maybe I was overthinking it.

Gilbert never fed off of me. Not once. He didn't have a paramour and regularly used the servants, but never the same one over and over. Sometimes he took random humans too. As far as I knew, those folks lived through the experience. Not that anyone would tell me if they didn't. Some vampires still killed regularly, and there was an entire section of vampires whose job it was to hide the evidence.

He furrowed his brow and looked away. Ace had always

said his father was different than the others. Maybe he actually cared what was happening to me?

Maybe he was my way out?

I didn't know what made me decide right in that moment to run, but I turned on my heel and walked toward the exit the vampires used to get to their cars when they came and went from the compound. I grabbed a broom. No one would question me if I held onto the broom. I lived with the servants, and when I could move, I did their jobs with them. I was basically a part time servant, waylaid only by my constant blood loss and addiction issues.

Without any money, car keys, food, or even a jacket, I rushed out that gate. It was my first time through them since the guys had died. I looked left and right. There was nowhere close to go if I didn't grab a car. Ace had given me his, but the keys vanished that first night. That meant there wasn't anywhere to go but into the woods, so that was where I was going.

I ran, stumbling twice before I made it through the trees. Weakness wasn't a joke. I gripped onto the tree trunks as I passed them. The wood splintered my hands as the touch offered brief moments of knowing I could absolutely stay upright.

But even that didn't last very long.

I sank down finally next to a tree to catch my breath. Dizziness, my constant companion these days, swelled to a crescendo. I put my head between my legs. *Everything eventually comes to an end.*

This too will pass.

Maybe if I said it enough times in my head, I'd believe it.

"Don't run. I doubt you could. Don't try." Gilbert spoke to me, and I gasped. Where had he come from? I dug my back into the tree, trying to stand. I didn't want to be down on the ground, not at this moment, with him standing over me. He bent over, his eyes red-rimmed like all vampires, yet I didn't see any of the hunger I'd gotten so used to identifying in the others.

"Just do it." I didn't know I was going to speak the words until I did. "I can't do this anymore. It's killing me anyway. Why not just do it? They won't care when they wake up. And Fredrick can just say he didn't know because he won't. You can do it. They won't ask you. It's not a lie. You can simply let it go. I'm just a girl. I didn't mean to get in the middle of this. I spoke to them, and it all just happened. Please. I don't want to live like this. I don't deserve this. I didn't tell them to take the guns. I didn't even know..."

He knelt in front of me. "You are not *just a girl*. And yes, you are tangled in this. Now is not the time for you to die. We all have a time when we die. Vampires do it twice. You are going to come back, and you are going to rest. There is no one who can save you in these woods right now. You're not eighteen yet. It's not time."

I didn't understand half of what he said to me. That was true for a lot of vampires, unfortunately. Their minds didn't always run in the same direction as mine. They zigged, and I zagged. Some vampires were entirely mute. They didn't seem to be able to speak at all. Ace's dad was spurts and stops. Fine, I tried to interpret what had been said to me. The gist of it was that he wasn't going to kill me. The whole bit about me turning eighteen? I didn't know what that meant, not at all.

"I can die just as easily at seventeen."

He shook his head. "Doesn't turn on until you're eighteen, and I made a promise. A long time ago. A deal. So you will come with me now. Back to the compound, and you will rest. There is movement in the coffins."

I stared at him. That last bit... I was pretty sure I understood it. "They're waking up?"

He nodded. "Yes. They say the longer we sleep, the more powerful we are. That's a falsehood. The truly powerful wake sooner."

I didn't give two shits about vampire power. My heart rate kicked up. "They're all moving around in their coffins?"

"Yes. Just started. They'll likely not be even aware of what's happening yet. Then they'll start to fight to get out. Days. Maybe a week. I don't think you want to die without seeing them wake." He took my hands and helped me get to my feet. "You need to rest. Tomorrow there are meetings. They will likely leave you alone."

That was even worse. "When they don't bite me, I go into withdrawal."

He didn't respond to that. "Come. Before anyone notices you left. They will hunt you then."

"Why don't you feed off of me?" That was something he could answer. The rest of it was going to remain a vampire mystery that I was stuck in the middle of, whether I wanted to or not.

"You are a child." He looked away. "I have other arrangements."

There it was. The vampire didn't lie to me, but he didn't tell me the truth, either. Did he have some kind of hidden paramour he saw sometimes? When he wasn't feeding randomly off servants, just to make do? That was interesting. My head started to pound. That was fast. My running had probably brought the need for venom on more quickly.

We made it back to the compound, and he let me go. "Rest. That is my advice for you right now. Rest. Things will be changing."

In the way that vampires glided, he took off.

"Hey." Charlotte walked up behind me. "Where did this broom come from?" She held it up, and I stared at the broom like it was a foreign object. That was the one I'd grabbed. I guessed I dropped it and I hadn't even noticed.

"Someone must have dropped it." I was pulling a vampire and being vague.

She shrugged. "Come on. Let's go back inside. You know what I heard? There's movement in the coffins. Do you think that means they won't be very strong?"

I widened my eyes and sucked in a breath as though this was the first time I'd heard of it. "Wow. I'm shocked. So soon. And...maybe they're actually just so strong, they don't need the extra time."

"Anyway, it's exciting. Whatever is going to happen, it will happen soon. After they go through the wild, animal-like raving need to eat and kill every human they see, of course."

Certainly, after that. Gross.

Caesar's father appeared before us, gliding into my view faster than any human ever could. He grabbed me, yanking my wrist to his mouth and biting without so much as a word spoken. I winced and looked away. It was always my arms. Paramours got the neck. I was lucky I didn't have to put up with that.

My headache passed. Blissful nothingness overtook my body. Charlotte hadn't moved, her gaze on the ground. Then it was over, blood pouring from my wound onto my hand and dripping onto the ground. I didn't merit them making the effort to even lick the wound, which would close it and prevent the bleeding.

Charlotte grabbed my wrist, and with a rag she must have had on her, she wrapped the fresh wound. "Come on. You need to rest. This will all be over soon."

That was what I wanted. One way or another. The torture had to stop. Although I had no idea how that could be. I was still going to be addicted when the guys broke out of their coffins. And after that too.

I SCRUBBED the floor of our living quarters on my hands and knees. It was raining outside, and the sun going down hadn't stopped that. The compound, always lit well, had a sort of surrealness as I glanced out the window. The water hitting the lights made it look as though everything was sort of not real.

Humming, I scrubbed some more. While I had energy, I had to use it.

A noise caught my attention. Outside, someone was yelling. I pulled myself up to stare further through the old glass. The outside door of the coffin room gaped open, and right outside of it stood Caesar. I caught my breath and placed my hand on the window like I could touch him from a distance. Three vampires held him, but he struggled against them, yelling loudly. It looked like he was going to break through.

This was unheard of. Vampires stayed in the coffin room until they were fed enough, then they could be safe to roam the compound. Humans were brought to them. I hadn't heard that any had been going in, but it wasn't like I had seen anyone today to tell me.

I could hardly breathe. Another figure emerged from the coffin house. Rowan. He strode to Caesar and placed a hand on his arm. The latter stopped fighting, grabbing his head instead. I couldn't hear what they said, but after a long moment, the three vampires holding Caesar let him go and they all went back inside.

"They woke up. Two days ago," Laura, one of the older servants, said to me as she entered the room. "So far, they've been fed twice. That's all I know. I thought someone would have told you."

It had been a week since Ace's father warned me this was happening. I'd lost track of time. It didn't matter how long they'd been up. They'd risen from the dead.

They were vampires.

16

For all that I'd avoided looking at the coffin room for six months, I couldn't take my eyes off it now. But not much happened. At least not that I could personally see.

Days passed before I could find the guts to ask Bethany what she knew. All the servants were home, lying on their beds, when I turned to her. As Charlotte braided my hair, I found my voice. "Bethany, do you know what happened? Who woke up first? Or maybe never. Maybe it doesn't matter." She rolled over onto her stomach. "I do have information, but I don't know if actually hearing about it is going to make you happy."

"I'm never happy." I paused. "Are you?"

I might have hit a nerve, because they all shifted in their beds, and Charlotte's hand faltered. It was she who answered me. "No, but we all hope to be. I know that's not what you want, to be a vampire. It is what we still hold onto, even when we sometimes falter."

So there it was. The answer I would have expected to get

from them. "We don't even know what female vampires are like. I've never seen one. Have you?"

Bethany sighed. "Maybe we should get back to the original topic. But yes, I once saw a female vampire. She was so stunningly beautiful. For just a moment. Then they had her out of here because the rule for this location is there aren't female vampires around." Charlotte started to braid my hair again as Bethany spoke again. "It was Ace who rose first. I heard the pounding in his coffin. Then Rowan. Caesar. Tanner. Finally, Griffin. He was a day later. Unless he just lay there in silence and was up for a while first? That could be true for any of them, actually. Maybe Ace just complained about it in a way we could hear. The vampires would know for sure. They'd be able to sense small movements we can't because they're closer to perfection than we are."

Okay. I was done with this. "Thank you."

"You know what? Out of all of us, you're the most likely to be made a vampire. And I don't think you appreciate that." That nasty gift was thrown at me from my least favorite servant, Tally.

"No one is going to be making me a vampire, I promise you that." Charlotte was done, so she rose from my bed and went back to her own. This whole being together every night thing could get old. So now I knew the most likely order that they had woken up. Did that mean anything to me at all? No, it absolutely didn't.

They are awake. I'd seen Caesar and Rowan. I hadn't seen their fangs, hadn't watched them drink from anyone. But I'd seen three vampires try and fail to take Caesar down. I'd seen the way they glided, like the vampires, when they moved. It had happened. Intellectually, yes, I'd understood it. Seeing it was a whole different thing altogether.

Bethany's phone dinged. It usually meant that someone had a job for us. It was late in the evening for that. Usually, the vampires were enough involved in their own things by now they wanted nothing to do with the servants. She looked down at her phone.

"There is a huge mess after a party in the second house. The paramours got out of control. Little drunk. And now they want it cleaned. Probably one of the vampires is fastidious. So we've got to do that."

I raised my hand. "I'll go."

I needed air, and I had to get out of the room before I caught whatever it was that made these women want to be vampires. The female was beautiful? She'd probably been that way before she changed. I doubted very much there was a sudden dive into gorgeousness just by becoming a bloodsucker. And even if there were, who cared? Not if you had to live by feeding off someone's blood. Yuck. Gross. It never stopped being that way to me.

"We'll go." Charlotte rose. "If we need more help, I'll call for it. How much of a mess could they have made?"

Bethany got off her bed. "I'll come too. If a vampire sees Maci, they'll want to feed, and then you'll need help anyway."

And there it was.

Just another sucky aspect of my life that might never go away. My dead friends were vampires. They weren't getting me out of this mess. I'd proven I couldn't leave on my own. I was hitting walls everywhere.

The wind hit when I stepped outside, a storm rolling in. I rubbed my arms. There were eyes on me right then. I knew it. I might never be able to say how I did, but I did. Maybe it came from six months of becoming accustomed to this kind of thing. There were vampires watching, and while it was mostly the big men in charge who bit me, any of them could take a turn.

Bethany put an arm around me. "If they kill you, I'll miss you."

That shouldn't have made me laugh, but it did. "Thanks. I'm not sure I'll miss you at all."

"That's what I'll miss most—when your mouth shows up, and it's like you're not on the brink of death. Then I can see who you were before all of this screwed you up."

We made it to the mansion—which had been Caesar's house before he died—currently the home of one of the silent vampires and his paramour, Andrea, who never stopped talking. Or drinking. Or, like tonight, making a huge mess. She was alone in the house, singing when we got inside. I stared at Charlotte, hoping we could share an eye roll, but all I saw was longing in her eyes. This was what she wanted. When it came down to it, she might think about leaving, but she never would.

Not when there was the possibility some vampire would see her and give her this.

Of course, I had no idea how any of this worked for Andrea, when her vampire, whose name I didn't even know, couldn't speak. His muteness wasn't even a problem for the vampires. If anything, they seemed to consider the mute ones even more powerful.

We'd started to clean, picking up the discarded bottles of wine and liquor, when Andrea appeared. "Thank you, ladies." She always spoke with a singsong quality, like she wasn't sure if she should be singing or talking and decided on something in the middle to handle both possibilities. "Guess things got a little out of control."

"Oh, don't worry, we've got this." Charlotte must have been trying to sound breezy while she walked quickly into the kitchen to start scrubbing in there. Bethany didn't say a word, heading upstairs to face that mess, and I took it upon myself to keep grabbing bottles. How many had they polished off? *They're really taking day drinking to a new level.*

Andrea strolled toward me. "I've always wanted to talk to you, Maci. Ever since that display the night The Five were changed. I thought maybe you could use a friend, but then I thought...my man might not like that."

Every time I talked to the paramours, I disliked them more. It was impressive, really. I lived constantly surrounded by people I hated with varying degrees of disgust. I'd thought living on my own when my mother came and went was hard, but now I'd take my own company any day of the week.

"How do you know what he likes? He doesn't talk." We were supposed to be polite to the paramours, and I tried. I really did. I guessed I just failed. *Whoops.*

She put her hands on her hips. "If no one told you there is a way to understand what a man wants that has nothing to do with the ability to speak, then they have failed you, girl."

Andrea was beautiful. If they did make her a vampire, she'd certainly fill Bethany's beauty dream. Blonde hair cut in a bob that wasn't fashionable, that looked more like it belonged to a flapper girl in the nineteen twenties, I wondered if she'd cultivated the old-fashioned look purposefully. After all, she was dating a vampire. Living with him. He couldn't talk. Who knew when he'd been human? How long ago was that? To want sex, he was prob- ably a hundred years old at least. So... he was alive before there were airplanes, probably. Or maybe just as they were being invented.

It was so strange to think about it. The vampire versions of my guys were going to live to see so many changes they couldn't even imagine when they were humans. Life would just keep moving.

And they would stay vampires.

"I understand how that works. What do you do when he's not feeding on you and fucking you?"

She smiled brightly at me. "Oh, how I wish they'd wake up wanting sex and one of them would make you a paramour. I'd love to have you around. We could go shopping together. Spa days. Parties. You find them attractive, but you already know that. It could be fun." Her face fell. "But they might not find you that way anymore, even if they could. You look like death. Such a shame what they've done to you. I mean, not my guy. He only feeds off me, and only once or twice a week at that. They are going to drain you dry."

I was pretty sure that was the idea. "Are you going to have his baby and become a vampire?"

"That's the plan." She leaned over to whisper to me. "So the sex will stop at that point. Then I can be this gorgeous forever."

If these were the women being made vampires, I hoped I never ran into any, ever. "I'll get this cleaned for you and get out of your hair."

"I heard they're all brutal. That the number of unsuspecting humans they're having to find to bring in there to keep them fed is beyond belief. They're traveling hours to find people no one will miss. They were sweet guys, weren't they? That's what I heard. We lived a distance from here, but talk about a complete shift. They're everything the elders hoped they would be. Oh, and as for silent vampires, so far, it seems Tanner doesn't talk. Not one word. Not at all. They're so excited about it. The silent ones are always extra-ordinarily deadly."

I nodded and left her where she stood. I didn't need to let her throw her vitriol at me anymore. Passive aggressive nonsense had never been my style, not even when I'd been able to go to high school. She could choke on it in her own head, as far as I was concerned.

I didn't have any illusions they'd wake up and be vege-tarian vampires. They were going to kill people. A lot of them. Probably me, before this was done. Tanner was silent. The one who had loved music, who had sung to us with his guitar. He'd lost his voice. Life was so fucking cruel.

I'D NO SOONER LEFT Andrea's than I saw her gliding, silent vampire enter to greet her. I had so many questions about exactly how that worked without speech, but speaking to Andrea was too much punishment. She wanted to be a vampire, to give birth to a vampire, and be beautiful forever. Spa days aside—I'd never had one—I didn't want anything to do with her life.

Fredrick stepped in front of my path toward home. Charlotte and Bethany took one look at him and scampered away. That was the general rule with him. No one got near him, not even those who wanted to be like him.

I swallowed. "Need something?"

He grabbed my wrist and bit hard. I closed my eyes. I'd had a pretty good day. Only three other bites. The numb-ness moved through me. Finally, he dropped his mouth. "It won't be long now until you'll see how much worse they made it on you by not killing you all those months ago. They're going to tear you to shreds."

"They might." I smiled at him. What did I care? "But you'll always know that, in that moment, they bested you. Even when you win, and I'm dead...when they were human, they beat you."

He slapped my face, and I hit the ground. Even in my haze, I could feel the smack of the ground and the ache forming on my back where I'd struck the pavement. *Yep... that is going to hurt.*

Strong hands hauled me up. It was Ace's father again. He seemed to be around to rescue me a lot. Maybe he *was* the nicest of the bunch. "Let's get you back inside. Come. Now."

Fredrick left without another look as I was quasi-dragged back to my residence by a vampire whose motives I couldn't discern. "Why do you keep helping me?"

"I explained already."

Once again, I had no answers. Just a throbbing cheek and another feeding to add to my never-ending list.

IT WAS funny how fast the next three months passed. Every day, I anticipated being hauled to the meeting to see the monsters inhabiting the bodies of the guys I had once loved. The days went by, yet the moment never came. I'd almost come to believe that it wouldn't.

Until it did.

Life was funny like that. The last few months had felt like I had to hurry up and wait. Or maybe that hadn't happened at all, and the whole feeling of urgency had only been in my own head. As sunset started to descend on a random Wednesday, three months before my eighteenth birthday, Charlotte shoved me in a seat to do my hair and makeup while Bethany arrived with clothes that looked like Andrea had picked them out.

"Why are you doing this?" I batted Charlotte's hand away.

"We want you to look fierce for whatever this is. Not defeated. Not like they've spent the last months defeating you. When you stand there, we want you to be the girl you were nine months ago."

That was sweet, surprisingly so. "You guys have been good to me, and you didn't have to be. You could have made this even harder. Thank you."

I didn't have to agree with everything they believed to recognize they were good people inside. Lost, for sure, but kindhearted.

"Maybe there will be a happy ending for this." Charlotte squeezed me from behind while I stared at myself. Even before the mess started, I'd never had clothes like the ones I wore. Jeans that fit perfectly and made my legs look long. A soft white turtleneck that felt expensive. There were no holes anywhere, nothing that would make anyone judge me as anything other than a well put together teenager. Even my shoes, the boots they'd put me in so that I could avoid getting wet from any leftover snow on the ground, were expensive.

"Where did you get these?"

She shrugged. "One of the paramours has nice taste, and you're tiny like she is. Well, you are now. You didn't used to be."

She hadn't said it, but I'd bet it was Andrea. She had the

nicest taste in clothing to go with her bad attitude. It had been so long since I'd looked in the mirror. I was almost waif-like, and it wasn't a natural look for me. She was right —I was tiny. I didn't have a lot of curves to begin with, and even that was almost all gone.

My eyes were older than they'd ever been.

So much so, that I didn't recognize my own gaze.

"It's three months until my eighteenth birthday."

Bethany took my hand. "If you're still here, we'll get you a cake."

Was the turtleneck meant to dissuade anyone from biting me? Because I sincerely doubted the soft fabric would stop a vampire intent on delivering me a death blow to the neck. That was why feeding from the neck was only for paramours. It implied an ownership to other vampires, that only the owner of the paramour could end their life.

Or at least that was how it seemed to me.

That evening's meeting was a big one. New vampires were regularly introduced, but not ones who were the sons of the monsters in charge. They'd really dragged out the whole group to reintroduce them to everyone. Fires were lit, which said a lot. Vampires could die in fire. To do this meant they weren't afraid, not even of that which could kill them.

As we approached the blazing bonfire, conversation hushed around us. Some of the vampires actually smiled. They must have been expecting this moment, waiting for it, enjoying my discomfort. I lifted my chin. I wouldn't be meek.

The monsters in my guys' bodies stood in a semicircle around the flames, their fathers interwoven around them.

I let myself look at them for a long second.

The changes were evident in their bodies. They were

bigger, stronger, as though their months being dead had increased their muscle mass rather than decreased it from disuse. I wondered how that worked. *Oh well. Another question I'll never know the answer to.*

Their eyes were red-rimmed—they needed to feed. That look would lessen when they were well fed. I was sure that was purposeful. They'd been left hungry so they could easily feed off of me.

Caesar rocked back and forth on his feet. The others were still, regarding me silently. Every second was like a piece of hell jabbing into my heart. I needed this over.

"I understand that you're all waiting for this, and I want you to know I'm not afraid." I spoke the words because they were true. "Whatever happens now, I know who you are, and you can kill me, but I'm not the same person I was when this all started."

I met Bethany's gaze, and she nodded. I'd done it. They'd wanted me to seem fierce. This was the best I could do. I hoped it was enough for them to remember me well, if it came to that. My knees might give out. It had been too many hours since someone had fed off me.

"Is she done?" Rowan asked his father. "Or am I supposed to let her make some kind of speech?"

The last best bit of hope I had died. It burned in the flames. Rowan's voice was different. Sinister. Sneering. So much like Fredrick's, they could have been the same person.

"I think she's done. I told your foolish human self you wouldn't care about this. That she wouldn't matter to you, but I keep my word. She's here. What will you do with her?"

Rowan nodded. "Yes, you did. I only wish I had understood then what I understand now. I was always a vampire." He turned toward the crowd. "Those of us born this way are always creatures of the night, even when we are in our young, human bodies. Amazing how I can see all of that now. My father has put me in charge of what we will do for the next bit of this battle, and I've decided that first and foremost, we will leave this place. We've been here too many years. The Betrayer and his foolish followers know it too well. We are moving to a new location."

Low whispers sounded. That wasn't what anyone had expected him to say. I swallowed. Did he remember I was even there?

He continued, "In this vein…" There was actual laughter when he said that. *What a stupid fucking joke.* I rolled my eyes. "We will proceed forward. We will leave that which was here behind. A few of you will stay for a few years, to make sure things here are closed down properly. The rest of us will move on. Maci…" Finally, his attention returned to me. "I was always a vampire, and vampires don't lie. I promised you something. I intend to deliver on that vow. You're to leave here. Now. No one will see you again. Ever. If you speak of us or your time here, those who are left have permission to kill you. Otherwise, you will never be viewed by a vampire again. You are something we are done with."

What? I widened my eyes. That wasn't at all what I'd expected. The realization dawned on me. *No, they can't do that.* I needed to be bit. Yes, I wanted freedom, but I couldn't live without the vampire bites. It would kill me. Fredrick smiled slowly. He understood. He had known. All of them looked away then. Caesar. Tanner. Ace. Griffin. Their gazes moved from me like Rowan, proclaiming it meant they couldn't even view me anymore.

They were done with me.

"Rowan, please…"

They never let me finish. In one quick movement, Tanner's father ripped me from the circle and hauled me to the street, through the door I had myself tried to exit once, when I had collapsed in the woods.

With a shove, I was on the ground. "Go. If anyone sees you again, we'll take that as a sign you're talking out of turn. Not that you'll be able to do that, will you? How long can you survive? Days? We're done with you. We won."

I shook my head. "It was never a contest. I'm just a human girl. I didn't do anything. I wasn't in some kind of competition."

"Small human, you were a gnat to us. But let me give you a piece of advice. If you happen to live through this, it's always a competition and we will always win. It's best if we all know our place in the world."

He disappeared then, back into the vampire compound that I'd just been banned from. My hands shook. It was seconds since the proclamation, and already, I was withdrawing. What was I going to do? Tears leaked from my eyes.

"Maci." A woman I didn't expect to hear from walked out from behind Rowan's garage. "Do you remember me? I'm Wanda. I own the bar that you went to once so long ago."

I blinked. "Um. Sure. Yes. I..."

She put out her hand. "We have a mutual friend who asked me to help you. Ace's father. He said if this happened, I should come get you. That you would need help. Come with me. Now. I need to get you away." She looked over her shoulder. "Please."

I took her hand.

What other choice did I have?

~

DEAREST READER,

Does it help that the next book is called *Paramour*? Maci's journey toward happiness and love isn't nearly over. Please grab the next book to see what happens!

ALL MY BEST

RR

PARAMOUR

For Lynda Quintana—grateful to you for so many things, my friend. Let's keep fighting the good fight together and laughing the whole time!

1

Descending the steep stairs from my apartment was easier said than done while jonesing for another vampire bite. It would be hours until any of them were awake and willing to comply—good news, because I had to earn the money to pay them to bite me. *I'll get paid tonight in cash then they'll give me what I crave.* Four bites a day was ideal, but I'd have to get by with just two.

It was going to be a long night.

A gust of wind lifted the strands of my hair and scraped icy fingers across my skin, so I pulled my jacket tightly around me. The coat might be two sizes too big, but when Wanda left it for me, I'd been grateful. She delayed following the vampire compound—as she'd been ordered to do—for as long as she could in order to make sure I'd be okay.

I obviously wasn't, but things were probably as good as they were going to get.

I was officially eighteen years old, not that anyone in my life celebrated the event the day before. The past year and the changes it brought were a really strange time in my life

—the ramifications of my seventeenth year would stay with me until I died.

But at least I made it to legal adulthood. *Whatever that means.* I'd been an adult since birth; now I felt ancient.

The sun burned my eyes, so I lowered my gaze. I actually slept about four hours that morning. One of the few things that had gone my way was finding a job where I worked from afternoon until nightfall. The hours meant I was awake at the same time as the vampires who still lived here, and they were why I hadn't completely fallen apart.

Not that they helped me out of the goodness of their monstrous, evil hearts. *Ha!* No, I paid them, and since they were the low hanging fruit in the vampire world, they gladly took my money to betray the order they'd been given to leave me alone.

Rowan's directive placed me in this situation.

Banished, abandoned, yet it didn't really surprise me. *Rowan is one of the monsters now.*

Rowan. Griffin. Caesar. Tanner. Ace. As humans, they were my friends. Not anymore. Now, they were nothing to me except other vampires to destroy my life.

I sighed. Thinking about my situation did me no favors. I needed to keep my concentration where it belonged—on putting one foot in front of the other. Instead of focusing on things I couldn't change, I reminded myself of the things I did have going for me. I was lucky to have the job at the gas station, grateful for the pitiful amount of food I managed to get, and lucky that Wanda put a roof over my head and didn't make me pay rent or utilities.

Not that Wanda helps because of her charitable desires. No, she owed a favor to Ace's father, who'd been preoccupied with keeping me alive. *He's gone now. They all are.* It had taken just forty-eight hours for the majority of the vampires and anyone associated with them to disappear when they were ordered to move. Our town became ghost-like practically overnight.

Restaurants closed. Half of the shelves in the grocery store stood empty. The bars were gone. Although we were always a small town, it looked as though the end of the world descended on us. I thought I knew what it meant to be lonely before, but I hadn't understood the meaning of the word.

I was completely alone.

Addicted.

Even my future hung like a desolate void.

I couldn't go back to school because of my issues. The teachers didn't know about the vampires or they would have left with the compound. They'd probably think I was on drugs, and the last thing I needed was a well-meaning social worker to make things even harder.

I nodded to Jim as I pushed through the door to the gas station where I worked. He worked the shift before mine, so he grabbed his bag and sent me a polite nod as he clocked out. I liked Jim—he was organized, and he kept the shelves stocked and laid out exactly as we had been instructed to keep them. A small television in the corner kept a constant stream of news going in the background, and I appreciated the noise once Jim left.

Afternoons were the slowest part of my shift. A few customers might drive through for cigarettes and soda. Otherwise, the monotone drone of the news kept me company until night fell. At dark, the soda changed to beer and condoms, but good for them. I was glad other people were having fun.

I certainly wasn't.

I CLOSED AT MIDNIGHT. The pumps might stay open twenty-four hours a day, but the market didn't. I yawned and locked up as I did every night. At least my hands didn't shake anymore, the tremor replaced by a constant body ache that would remain until I could get bit. I preferred the shakes to the pains, but it was all the same, really. *Just the way things are for now. How long can I live like this?* I didn't know.

My clothes hung off me more and more every day. I tried to eat, but it was a struggle. My body rejected food, especially if I tried to eat too much. *All in all, I'm a mess. But, hey, time to get bit!* I hated them, but I felt so much better afterward. I'd get bit, go home, and try to eat, and then come out for two more rounds with other vampires. After that, I'd try to sleep, rinse, repeat. I knew the routine, and it might suck, but it was *so* much better than the full-on all-consuming pains and withdrawals I experienced right after the vampires left.

They'd been biting me ten times a day or more, so getting down to these few bites was a triumph. The downfall? I couldn't get past this few and probably never would.

This is as good as it gets, and it fucking sucks.

I cringed, seeing the vampire waiting for me ahead—Samuel. That was all I knew about him, really. I'd discerned some other things over time from observation, like he wasn't well thought of in our community. Wanda rolled her eyes when she'd introduced me to him, so I picked up on it immediately. Plus, he'd been left behind. Despite all of Rowan's claims about how people needed to handle things aside, they only left vampires they didn't want around behind when they'd gone. Basically, it was a slap in the face to those they left behind; they would never be powerful or part of the inner circle. They were nothing. Expendable.

And they were also all I had to keep me alive.

Samuel liked to wear bell bottom jeans and plaid t-shirts.

Some of the vampires were ethereal looking, mystical, but this one hadn't changed well. He was gross, though my definition of that word seemed to be ever changing. A lot of things that used to gross me out didn't make me blink, so it had to be really bad to qualify.

Still, Samuel is gross.

I sighed. "I'm here."

He nodded. "I knew the second you left the store."

It wasn't my first time meeting him or someone like him in a back alley. Nothing good ever came from these sorts of encounters. Fortunately, I knew he'd be painful but fast. I'd get what I needed, and so would he.

With his hand outstretched, he beckoned me forward. "Money?"

I pulled the fifty out of my back pocket. *Oh, the things I could do with fifty dollars if I didn't have to do this.* "Here you go."

"I should start charging you more. The amount of trouble I could get into for even speaking to you is enough to charge more. If questioned, I'd have to tell the truth. I can't lie. It's not like evasion would work with someone as powerful as Rowan."

He said it with such reverence—*ridiculous*. "How do you know he's powerful? He just changed. Maybe he's not." Samuel might not want to evade, but I did. Changing the subject before he made it one hundred dollars a bite seemed pivotal. It already cost me one hundred to get what I needed each night. I couldn't afford more. I could hardly afford what

I was doing—soon I wouldn't even be able to get by on that. The little emergency money Wanda had given me was almost gone. Panic sent my pulse thudding in my already aching head.

He shook his head. "Human, you'll never understand. He's *powerful*."

"Okay." I held out my wrist, and he grabbed it.

His breath whispered across my pulse. "I want you to know I do this out of pity. I should let you die."

Pity? Yeah, right. He did it for fifty dollars to keep himself in bell bottoms or maybe blackout curtains for wherever he spent his day. I didn't argue with him, though. *Let him insult me. I don't care. Just bite my skin and suck my blood.*

After his last verbal jab, he gave me what I wanted, what I needed. *One bite into me.* It pained me, but I knew what was coming.

Only... it didn't.

A blur of something passed by me, and the vampire about to suck on me was thrown away with as little regard as one might toss aside a crumpled bit of paper. A roar sounded, one more animal than man. Instinct had me backing up, and I would have run. I wanted to, but my knees gave out, once again making it impossible for me to do what I needed to do.

The streetlights illuminated the dark blur as it slowed enough to have shape and substance.

Caesar, his face filled with vampire fury, and his gaze red in a way which told me his monster was ready to strike.

"No," I cried out. It wasn't that I didn't want him to hurt Samuel, but I was very worried I'd lose one of my few remaining resources.

Caesar ignored me, picking the other vampire up by the

collar. "You touch her? You think you can put your fangs on her skin?"

Samuel's voice whined quickly, "I... I know it's wrong, but I need the money. She pays me. Things aren't easy now."

Apparently absolutely the wrong answer as far as Caesar was concerned, because he threw the other man across the alley. With a thump, Samuel hit the wall. Seconds later, he took off running, prey to the predator that looked like my former friend.

Rage filled me. It was unreasonable. Stupid. I couldn't get angry at a vampire. It was a death sentence, only right then I didn't care. Not even a little bit.

I got to my feet despite my shaking legs to holler at him, "Why did you have to do that? Why?"

I didn't really expect him to answer. He was a vampire in a temper. I might only be human, but I'd had more than enough. I shoved at his chest. "Do you know how hard it is to find anyone who will even bite me? Do you have any *fucking* idea?" I screamed like a banshee, and I tried to shove him again. He didn't budge. Caesar was solid muscle. I didn't have a chance against him physically, not in any world, but I didn't care.

He took my wrists in his hands before regarding me with cool vampire indifference only betrayed by the fact that his eyes glowed red. I didn't care what raged inside of him. "How dare you do that?" I demanded. "How *dare* you come back here and do that?"

"Why would you let him debase you? Why would you let that nothing of a vampire put his mouth on you?" His voice was low, the disinterest I was used to from these monsters not there.

Why? That was his only question? *Fine.* I would remind him of the realities for a human addicted to vampire venom.

"Because your father and others bit me at least ten times a day for nine months and left me a shell of a human being. Afterward, your precious leader Rowan sent me out to never see a vampire again. I almost died. Three times, actually. I still have to be bit four times a day to feel any semblance of normal, and at least twice to not die. That's why. Yes, it's disgusting, but this is my life."

My heart raced and my fight died. I wasn't strong enough to keep struggling. I simply didn't have it in me.

"What?" He tilted his head.

Nothing was wrong with his hearing, I was certain of that. "This could be a good thing. Finish what they started. Put an end to this. The guy whose body you wear would have understood. He would've gotten why this isn't a scenario I could survive. I'm bleeding where he bit me—take my blood. Take too much of it. End this. Maybe there's an afterlife. If not, I don't care. I just know I can't keep up this charade of existence anymore. You all abandoned me. Threw me out on my own after leaving me to suffer at their fangs for nine *months*. Do it. I'm sure you must be hungry. I'll be an evening snack."

He didn't move, but instead of grabbing my wrist to bite me, he licked my wound closed. I gasped, warmth moving over me. Their saliva was addicting, but it could heal if that was what they wanted.

"Why did you do that?" He needed to answer me. "Caesar?"

With almost no effort, he picked me up in his arms, holding me like I was a baby. "Stop fighting. You'll hurt yourself."

I tried to roar, only it sounded so much like a whimper. It was pathetic even to my own ears.

We ended up in the basement of Rowan's old house. I'd

cleaned it many times in my months as a servant. There were plenty of bedrooms with no windows downstairs. When I'd been a resident on the compound, it was clear they used these rooms for important guests.

The house was cold because no one had used it in months. Caesar turned the lights on in the basement, leaving the rest of the house dark.

"Sit." He placed me in a chair before going into a room and retrieving sheets.

I was done. Where he'd put me, I would stay. What other choice did I have? "Those sheets, what will you do with them?"

He didn't answer. Instead, he methodically made the bed before looking at me again. In one move, he'd lifted me from the chair and placed me in the bed, taking off my shoes a second later.

Did he want me to sleep? "Why are you doing this?"

"They bit you ten times a day?"

Oh, we're back to that? I lay on the pillows. I hadn't gotten what I needed. Everything hurt. Like death. "Sometimes more."

"Fredrick can't lie. He said that night you would be alive and well."

"No, that's what Rowan asked for, not what Frederick agreed to do. I was *alive*. That was all he promised. Obviously, I wasn't well, and then Rowan sent me away. As you can see, this is what I am now. Worse than my mother ever was." I stared at him. "What do you intend to do to me?"

He sat on the edge of the bed. "You pay them?"

"Sure. I'm not supposed to be around vampires, so they have to be incentivized to bite me. They're poor for vampires, but there are a few who will do it."

He scowled. "Maggots."

"Be that as it may, I'd be dead without them." *Why are we even discussing this?* "What are you doing here?"

He climbed onto the bed, covering my body with his in a move that would be sexy if we were lovers but felt aggressive considering our current circumstances. "I came looking for you."

That told me nothing but then again vampires never did. "Why?"

"I had to." He rolled next to me. "You have to be bit several times a night or you will die."

It wasn't a question. I didn't answer him, just stayed where I was, staring at the ceiling. "Why did you have to?"

"I will feed from you tonight. Tomorrow, we'll figure out a better solution than this. Those vampires don't have the right to touch you."

Have the right? I was pretty sure every vampire alive had the right, but it didn't matter right then. I held out my wrist. He could have at it. I'd even be grateful. Caesar was many things, but gross wasn't one of them. He was beautiful. As a human he had been, and he continued to be so now.

Caesar ran his finger over my wrist. The scars must be obvious. It was hard for me to look at. In a swift move, he dropped my wrist and pulled me to him, seating me on his lap. I realized what he meant to do a second before he did it. Gentler than anyone who had ever bitten me, he nipped onto my neck.

This was unheard of except with vampires and their paramours. They didn't feed randomly from the neck. Heat exploded inside of me, and I had to close my eyes against the onslaught. *Yes, I was so cold. Yes, this is warmth. This is tender.*

Caesar moaned, bringing me back to the moment as he laid me down beneath him. I shook in his arms. *Feeding shouldn't feel like this.* One second a warm bath, the next as though my body woke up and took note of what was happening.

He was strong, hard, and I'd always been attracted to him. This body used to hold me in bed. I wrapped my arms around his neck and drew him closer. There were things I should be afraid of but none of them mattered right then. Not as he sucked and sucked on me.

My insides started to throb. Sex hadn't been on my mind since the night the guys died, yet right then, as an ache I'd really never felt so intensely took over inside of me, I would have gladly pulled my pants off and invited him inside of me. Begged him to make it stop with his hand or his cock. I squirmed. That was when I felt him. He wasn't unaffected. His body was hard, and an erection pressed against my abdomen—something that shouldn't have been happening with him as a new vampire.

Not that I cared if it was unheard of in the moment, with the sensations vibrating through my body. The velvety hunger of passion sliced deeper after the grinding agony of the pain of addiction. I ground against him, needing him, practically ready to beg him for relief.

He squeezed my hand, stopping me when I would have reached for his cock. When he held me in place, I whined. Maybe he would understand?

The world started to float around me. *Peace. Nothingness.* Yes, I knew this feeling—craved it, needed it—only it had never felt exactly like this before. Usually, it was a sick emptiness I just didn't care about. This sensation was different, more somehow. *What is it?* Just a sense of rightness. Of finally getting what I needed.

I drifted away.

Sometime later Caesar's voice pulled me back to him. "Maci, wake up. Look at me."

I lifted my lids. He was still hard, and I still wanted more. "Why?" Maybe he'd know what I meant. I was only half-sure that I did.

"I don't know. Does that not happen when others feed from you?" He pushed my hair off my face. "I didn't take that much from you. More than I intended but not enough to knock you out. You're anemic. Weak."

His words sounded like an accusation, but I ignored that part. If he could divert, so could I. "Never. Is it because you drank from my neck? Is that why it's reserved for paramours?"

"It's not really. We frequently tear the throats out of people when we feed. And, no, that doesn't happen. What happened to me... it shouldn't have. I'm not complaining, I'm just unsure what happened here."

Well, if he thought he was confused, then he should try it from my end. "I hate you a little bit." Tears flooded my eyes. "I hate that you all didn't just get up and leave the first day I spoke to you. I hate that you all made me care about you. I hate you. I wanted you to know that."

He stared at me with as much emotion as if I'd just told him it was cold outside or it might rain. "Hate me if you want. It's a wasted emotion because I don't care one way or another about such things. Hate? Love? There is nothing, but don't hate the human I was. He died loving you."

A sob racked my body. After so many months, I'd forgotten that version of Caesar. I tried so hard not to let myself think about what any of them were like before they changed. Necessity forced me to bury them in my heart and mind, to destroy what they meant to me. *How else was I supposed to survive?*

His few words had undone all of that. I cried, pulling out of his embrace so I could weep into the pillow beneath me. *I shouldn't be feeling this. I should be wrapped in nothingness. I'm not supposed to be able to feel this right now.*

He placed a hand on my back. "You're weak beyond belief. Anemic. You need to be fed, and you need to rest."

I laughed. "I'm going to have to have someone bite me again in a matter of hours. At least once more tonight so I don't have a seizure and stop breathing."

"Hours? Fine. If that's what has to happen, then I'll do it again. In the meantime, I'll get you food." He rose from the bed and stepped away. "Don't move from this bed while I'm gone. I have to consider some things. Chasing you would not make me happy."

I rolled over to stare at him. "I'm not in any condition to run away."

He didn't indicate he heard me, instead gliding from the room. He left me in the basement of a house I'd once cleaned, lying in a bed that wasn't mine, with no understanding of what just happened. My body still ached, only not from the venom. I needed it, and I hadn't gotten any satisfaction. *But he is gone, right?* I tucked my hand in my pants, dove under my panties, until I found my clit. It had been a long time since I'd had any interest in these sensations. Still, I rubbed at myself until I came around my own fingers.

It was a hollow victory. *Not what I wanted.*

Caesar had gotten hard but he didn't react like a man craving satisfaction. *What does it mean?*

I rolled back over onto my stomach. With a groan, I

decided that I'd just lie there and not think. What other choice did I have?

My eyes closed.

With no idea it was coming, I fell asleep, darkness sucking me under. It was peaceful and I didn't fight the sensation.

"Maci." Once again, Caesar's voice called me from wherever I'd gone. I wrenched my eyes open. They felt glued shut.

"Caesar?" *How is he here? He's dead.* Everything rushed back to me. "Sorry. I guess I fell asleep."

"Drink this." He put a straw in my mouth, and the sweetness of orange juice filled me. "Swallow these."

I stared at his pills. "What are they?"

"A multi-vitamin and an iron pill. Swallow."

I did as he said. *Why is he doing this?* He spooned eggs into my mouth, and even though I absolutely could feed myself, I let him. Things were so unclear right then. Like, I was in a haze, not really awake.

"Do you need me to feed from you? Are you aching?"

Funny enough, I absolutely wasn't. "Not yet."

"Okay. Sleep. If you wake up and it's daytime, I won't be awake." He kissed my cheek. "I don't understand what's happening. We will figure it out. You need to rest."

As he'd ordered, I went back to sleep.

2

I woke up in a haze. It had been a very long time since I'd slept during the night and into daytime. *What time is it?* The quilt Caesar covered me with fell off my chest when I sat up. I didn't have my phone and there weren't any clocks in the room. I rubbed my eyes, pushing sleep from my mind. I hadn't dreamed, not that I could remember.

Looking down, I stared at my hands. They weren't shaking. It took me a moment to digest that feeling. I wasn't in any pain, either. When was the last time that happened? The morning I'd woken up when they had all died? After that, it had been a steady series of hellish wake-ups ever since. My stomach grumbled. *Am I hungry?*

It was daytime, so wherever Caesar had gone—as he wasn't in the room with me—he wouldn't be around to ask about food, but he'd fed me the night before.

Maybe there was something left? Where had he gotten the food, anyway? I pushed my blankets aside and stopped to stare at the bed. I cleaned this place more than I cared to remember; making the bed was almost habit. Even my tiny little bedroom above Wanda's bar was spotlessly clean. When I had any energy, I got busy keeping things straight and in order. *Something in life should be that way.*

Fuck it. I'm not making this bed. My own personal passive aggressive moment that no one would ever know about except me. *I'm not making any more beds in this vampire compound ever.*

Period. End of story.

I didn't know how long feeling not-shaky and not-sick might last, so I made my way upstairs. The lights were all off, so from the outside, it would look like no one was home. Maybe. That's what I imagined anyway, I really had no way to know. I couldn't be sure, but it seemed like he'd been deliberate in his use of light, perhaps trying to avoid letting anyone know he was in residence.

He said he had to find me. Well... he found me, but why did he want to find me?

I opened the fridge and caught my breath in surprise. It was packed with food, more than I could probably eat in a week. Maybe a month. Where did he get so much food? It was well after midnight when we'd arrived. The grocery stores weren't open, not that vampires particularly concerned themselves with things like business hours. *He probably robbed the place.*

I should feel morally offended, but I was too hungry to care. I grabbed one of the sliced hams and started to make myself a sandwich. It was breakfast but who cared anymore? I ate over the sink, not even making it to the chair to sit down. For just a second, everything felt heavenly. A full stomach was such a gift.

Then the pain started. I winced. *Yep.* My stomach wasn't used to so much food. I should have known better. Starting small was key.

Puking sucked, but I had no choice. It looked like I was missing work. My phone was on the bathroom counter, plugged in and charging, where Caesar must have put it, so I shot a text to my manager. Maybe it was the only available outlet? Who knew how vampires thought. My manager would have to come in and handle things. I didn't have a car and this location was too far for me to walk. As I puked into the toilet, my good mood fled. *Yeah... this fucking sucked.*

I was drinking tea when Caesar appeared in the kitchen. I never actually looked around the house to find him, as it seemed like a good idea to let the vampire keep his sleeping area private. So far, Caesar hadn't been threatening. That didn't mean things wouldn't change.

He stared at me a long moment. "You don't feel well."

"I woke up hungry then ate too much too soon. Forgot I needed to be really, really small with portions, so I spent the morning into the early afternoon puking." I winced at the memory. "I'm settling my stomach now."

I lifted an eyebrow at him. He was so cool, so passive. "Does that happen to vampires? Can you gorge yourself on too much blood?"

"No. We are always hungry. It's a constant ache. We learn to take enough to be sharp, to be strong, and then to leave the need alone unless we are in a rage, in which case it usually ends up in a bloodlust frenzy. It can be hard to be pulled back from that. We all wake up the first time in a frenzy, and it doesn't go away for some time. Months at best." He tilted his head in the way that vampires do. "Actually, at this moment, I'm not noticing my hunger. It is very much at bay, so small I am hardly aware of it. How is your need? Are you craving the venom?"

That was interesting. I'd never heard that about how they fed before. "No." I shook my head. "Surprisingly enough, I'm absolutely fine in that regard for the first time in a long time. Why is that? What did you do?"

"Nothing." He stepped further into the kitchen where I sat. "Last night is a mystery. What happened to me and you during the feeding doesn't make sense. Even vampires in serious committed paramour relationships don't want to have sex during feeding. Sex and food are separate things."

I was glad he wasn't avoiding or redirecting the subject. "Why didn't you act on it then? I tried to touch you, but you stopped me. If it's such a unicorn of an occurrence, why not... I don't know, use it?"

As soon as the words were out of my mouth, I wished I hadn't uttered them. *What is the matter with me?* Having sex with the vampire Caesar was *not* on my to-do list. Still, I'd already said it, and it wasn't like I could take the words back, so I swallowed.

He shrugged. "First off, you were minutes from death. Even in that state, I knew it wasn't a good idea." *I was what?* I sat forward but he was still talking. "You also had rules about sex. I remembered them and recognized that, despite what we were both feeling, it wasn't going to happen."

I tried to swallow. "I'm not minutes from death."

"You might be underestimating how worn out you are. We'll fix this." He passed me to stare out the window. "I can't stand the smell of cooking food, but I will continue to feed you appropriately until you are better."

I got to my feet. "Why are you doing this? And you can remember my rules?"

"I haven't suffered amnesia. My life before I was as I am feels lived by someone else, but I'm in possession of their memories. Yet it also touches me as mine? You wouldn't understand. Humans live one life; vampires live two."

I laughed and he turned, then tilted his head back as he

regarded me. "You think I haven't lived a before and after life? Trust me, I've lived two lives, too. Things were hard before. They're impossible now. I didn't realize you could even really think about that time."

He stepped toward me. "Disdain and sarcasm are new to you. I can remember everything. I just don't care about it very much."

Well... he cared enough to keep us from doing anything last night. Or maybe it was that first part really motivated him— he thought I was really close to dying.

I *had* been feeling particularly bad lately.

"Why did you come here? You said you had to see me. Why? And *don't* pivot. Vampires tell the truth. Why are you here?"

He moved so fast, I didn't see him approach before he was in my face. Unlike pop culture manifestations, vampires breathed air. They had hearts that beat. They were just monstrous blood drinkers walking around in the bodies of people who used to be humans.

And I just pissed this one off.

"From the second I woke up all I could think about was getting to you. That's not normal. It's not what happens to vampires. I even tried to get you once in a haze. If I'd found you, I might have torn out your throat. I've tried to stay away. You're just a human. I don't care about humans. But here you are, and I had to see you for myself. I came back intending to do that and found you with that less than nothing male about to bite into your wrist. Now we both fucking find ourselves in this situation."

I might have been close to death or whatever, but I wouldn't be intimidated. This had gone on for too long. "No one asked you to come here. In fact, I think you're breaking rules by doing this, so go home. You've seen me. Thank you for your help last night. Go wherever you all live now. You don't care about humans, and I absolutely detest vampires." I shrugged. "Whatever last night was, we can both forget it. You're such a superior being, so you can feel free to forget I exist."

He put his hands on my cheeks. "If only that were possible."

Caesar kissed me. I hadn't seen it coming, and from the way that he pulled back to stare at me for a second, he hadn't known he was going to do it, either. We both breathed heavily, despite having only been seconds that our lips had touched. In seconds, we were kissing again. I hated him, yet for some reason, I wanted this—more than I possibly could have imagined I would. No haze blurred my thoughts, and I wasn't hungry for a bite. He just kissed me because it's what we both wanted.

He picked me up and put me on the counter, tugging me closer to his solid body. I wrapped my arms around his neck and tried to follow where he led. Caesar took control of my mouth, so I could hardly catch my breath between caresses. Besides, the need for air seemed to get in the way of what I wanted right then.

He pushed me down on the counter, coming on top of me in seconds. Caesar stared down at my face. "I was afraid every day when I was him. Every fucking day. That much I remember."

I caught my breath, reality dashing ice water on the moment. I pushed against his chest. "Off."

Caesar didn't fight me, leaping off the counter in a smooth move.

I spoke to his back, since he didn't turn back to face me. "I loved you, even with the fear. Fear is real. It makes us human."

"Then I'm glad not to be." He walked to the fridge. "I am going to feed you again and ask that you don't screw it up tomorrow when you feed yourself. Surely, you can handle that much, can't you?"

Caesar was a whirlwind of discontinuity. I didn't know what to make of him. "You can go. You can leave me. There is absolutely no rule that says you have to feed me for another minute. In fact, my guess is you could get in serious trouble for what you're doing now."

"I'm not sure what will happen to me if they find out." He grabbed eggs and bread, starting to make the same meal he'd made for me the night before. It did seem appealing. Lightweight. I was pretty sure I could digest it.

"What did you tell them you were going to do?" I needed to get off the counter. It was starting to get awkward, not that Caesar seemed to notice. Maybe things like awkwardness no longer mattered to him. I swung my legs over and got back on the floor, retaking my seat as though that strange interlude never happened.

He looked over his shoulder. "I didn't tell them anything. I just left."

"They just let you leave? Rowan didn't object? Fredrick? Your father?" I shivered at the memory of those men. I never let myself think of them. Those vampires had been hell on me.

Caesar was quiet for a moment. "Vampires come and go a lot. We have to fight and come back. The Betrayer is always waging war, and he won't give up when he should know by now that he's lost. It's frustrating. I've been to battle twice. They will likely not cue into the fact that I'm gone for some time. By then, I suppose I'll have made some choices."

I walked toward him. "What choices?"

"About exactly what I am going to do and where I am

going to go. I cannot be separated from you, at least not currently. I need to figure out why. Rowan leads well. He is certainly better than his father. He makes better choices. I would gladly follow him, but I cannot currently." He scowled. "Vampires left on their own die. Fire. Stakes through the heart. The ones left here are considered expendable. I find myself in an untenable situation."

I had an easy answer for him. "Go home, Caesar. I'm not staying here with you, and I'm not hiding in this basement. I can take care of myself. I'll find vampires to bite me. You've done what you needed. Perhaps you just had leftover business with me. It's done. Go."

My back hit the wall as he pressed me into it. I squealed. "What?"

"When you tell me to leave, it makes me want to rage. You don't want that. That's not a threat; it's a reality. For whatever reason, I'm in control, but I can feel my hunger rising the longer we do this dance. It won't end well if I lose it."

My own need hit me suddenly, strong and all encompassing. My hands shook but only for a second before I cried out in pain. Oh, this was bad. I hadn't been bitten, and it was hitting me hard.

He widened his eyes. "Maci?"

"It's bad." That was all I could manage. "Please."

His mouth came down on my neck and he bit me—still gentler than anyone else ever had, despite the urgency. My pain cooled, and he sighed against my neck. I wrapped my body around him, with my back still pressed against the wall. I closed my eyes. Caesar only fed from me for a long moment before he licked the wound closed.

I shook in his arms—not in pain, but in the contrast of pleasure rushing through me after the sudden onslaught of pain. He rocked me in his arms. "I'm not leaving, and you aren't going to tell me to again."

"You didn't drink much. You can't be done already." I didn't want to open my eyes. It felt too nice. Pleasure not nothingness. I could drown in the sensation and be happy to do so.

"I'm full." He set me on the counter. "Eat your eggs."

Caesar fed me as he had the night before. I chewed and swallowed. Took my pills. Drank my orange juice. It was quiet but not uncomfortable, probably an aftereffect of his venom. Maybe that mattered, and was something he should know?

"I don't feel the same after you bite me. I don't get numb. I become happy, relaxed. Maybe that's what's different between us."

Caesar strode from the room. "I've fed from hundreds of people before. That's never happened with anyone but you. And it's not your blood, because the bottom feeders you give your blood to would have certainly noticed if they were suddenly sexually alert. Presumably one of the elders would, too."

With that parting shot, he left me in the kitchen. *Where is he going now?* It didn't matter. I needed to go home. Tomorrow I had to go to work. Caesar could stay if he wanted, I wouldn't tell him to go. That was fine. We hadn't said anything about my needing to stay put, too.

It would take hours to walk home. *I might as well get started now.* One thing I'd like to be able to do like the vampires was glide and move at their speed. It was impressive.

I opened the front door, but a second later, it slammed in front of me. Caesar closed it right in my face. "You're not going out there tonight."

Well, that is annoying. I lifted my eyebrow. "I missed work today. I can't tomorrow. I have to go home so I can get there on time."

"Quit your job. Text them, tell them you won't be back. Or just don't show up, I don't care. You're done with working for the moment. You're in no condition for it."

Strong doses of pleasure aside, him ordering me around wasn't really going to work for me. "I have to work. You'll leave at some point, then I'll still have to make a living." I put up my hands. "I'm not telling you to leave, I'm simply acknowledging that you will. Due to reality, I can't just quit my job."

Caesar pulled a wallet out of his back pocket then handed me a credit card. "Here. You never have to work again. Buy whatever you like. Forever."

I stared at the card in my hand. "You can't be serious with this. You have vampires under your service who need money, that's why they took it from me. You can't just *hand* me an endless pit of cash."

"It is simple for me. I'm very important, and I have no interest in monetary possessions unless they make my life more manageable. Take it."

I handed it back to him. *Not today, bloodsucker.* I wasn't going to be under his command, even if it was only money related. Everything in their world came at a price, and I knew I couldn't afford whatever strings came attached to his card. "No, thank you."

"Fine." He put it away. "Then I will buy you whatever you need. You're still not leaving. Come with me."

He really wasn't understanding me. I hustled to keep up. *Where is he going?* "Slow down if you want me to keep up."

"Sorry." He waited until I reached his side. "I forget you're only human."

I cheerfully replied, "Better *only human* than a cold, heartless bloodsucker who ruins people's lives."

He smirked. "You're very amusing."

I really wasn't trying to be. We ended up back in the basement, in a storage room filled with the former household items. Sheets—which at least explained where Caesar had found them the night before—sat stacked in the corner. But there were lots of other things. Clothes. Televisions. Books.

"Things were stacked away fast in here. We obviously took all the original manuscripts with us, but they left copies of things in their rush to finish. We're going to locate those manuscripts and read them until we figure out what is going on with us."

I rubbed my eyes. "Caesar, you read all of these before you died. Surely you'd know if there were answers there."

"I didn't really read them. I was too busy thinking of you. We all passed because Ace read some of them earlier, and Griffin did the rest. We cheated. I need to read them now."

Okay, it sounded reasonable. Plus, I sort of loved knowing they'd spent as much time thinking about me as I had them. My days had been consumed. I scooted into the tight squeeze and started to pull out any books I could find. I handed them to him. He looked at each one and started sorting them into piles.

"What were you thinking about specifically? Back then?"

He shrugged. "What does it matter? It's the ridiculous romantic ramblings of a dead man. We have something to do here."

"Fine." I continued to pass him books. Eventually, once I was pretty sure I'd found all of them, I met him in the hall. He carried them to the bedroom where I'd slept and, still in silence, we looked through the books.

I wasn't much help. The language was old, hard to push through, and it took some time until my brain adjusted to the cadence—a little bit like when I'd decided to read the original Chaucer. Still, eventually I got there. Caesar left and returned with more food. This time, he'd made a sandwich.

"Chew and swallow slowly while we read," he ordered.

He smelled good, like soap and cinnamon. Vampires showered the same way we did, but I'd never noticed one smelling so lovely before. I cleared my throat. *This kind of thinking isn't going to help.* Maybe we'd find more answers in these books than the ones he sought. Maybe I could figure out how to cure myself from this mess, and find a way out for both of us.

With my stomach full, it became harder to read. Tiredness threatened to pull me under. I hadn't done anything but eat and puke all day, so why did I have to be so constantly weak?

Caesar pulled the book out of my hand. "I continue to have the same problem. I can only think about you. Put your head down and rest. You aren't even seeing the page."

"How did you know?" He was right, but how did he know?

"We're attuned to you humans. We tend to know things about you even before you realize them, not that we advertise it. For example, I could probably tell if you were ovulating. That's a trick I seem to have. You're not. Every vampire has different talents. It helps us to feed."

Gross. Just when I thought I couldn't find anything else that could disgust me, I learned something new. "I don't ovulate anymore. I haven't had a period since this all started."

If the news surprised him, he kept it to himself. "Lie down. I'll wake you to feed you before dawn again. If you could keep going through the books during the day tomorrow, I'd appreciate it." He lifted his gaze. "Since you are going to make no effort whatsoever to do anything else but rest, eat little amounts, and start to get better."

"And if I do something else? What happens?" I wanted clear repercussions so I knew what was at risk.

"You'll just have to see. It would be better if you stayed home."

Home? Whatever this was, it would never be a home again. For a week and a half, it *had* been a home when I'd lived here with the not-dead version of Caesar and the others. "I don't like being threatened."

"I don't like being disobeyed."

I really don't have the energy for this. Scooting away from him, I made my way back to my pillow. "We used to sleep together all the time."

He turned off the light, bathing the room in darkness. *Can he read in the dark?* Caesar pulled the covers back over me. "I know. I remember it well. It was the last thing I thought about before I died. I tried to picture lying in the bed with you, to pretend I was there."

"I stayed outside the coffins the whole time. I didn't leave until you were dead." I wanted him to know that. If there was any part of the Caesar I knew still in there, I wanted him to know I never left him alone in the dark.

3

"Where did you go?"

Caesar called to me, so I turned around. The dress I wore blew in the wind, and it was going to be embarrassing if I flashed anyone, but I loved it. Wearing the long, blue dress made me feel beautiful.

So few things did that in this time of war.

I put my arms around Caesar when he approached. He didn't like when I was out of his sight, and he hated it when none of them knew where I was. It created a constant battle because I needed a lot of alone time to think. I always had, even before everything went to hell.

How could vampires be so split on this issue with me that we couldn't come to terms at all? I had to fix things. It was in my nature to make things right, even if I had to spill blood to do it. I wasn't going to let the schism turn into outright war.

"Well, I went here."

He made a grumbling sound in his chest. His monster rode him hard, his hunger moving inside of me. Caesar needed to feed again. Probably his worry pushed the frenzy a little bit forward. I knew the feeling well.

"You weren't here a few minutes ago. This was the third time I checked here."

He had the need to find me. Always had, always would. "I had to think, and we know I can't do that with you guys around sometimes. When you're around, I just want to make everything right. I want to snuggle into the way you all love me and never come up again."

Caesar smoothed my hair away from my face. "What's wrong with that? You don't have to fix everything on your own. You aren't responsible for the entirety of vampire society."

"Fredrick and the other young ones? They're going to get us all killed. We've lived surrounded by humans since the beginning of time. What they're proposing? It's only a matter of time until they get us caught and hunted."

He nodded. "I know. And they're not just young and foolish, they're also dangerous in their power. They want to win at any cost. They're reading old, long-forgotten prophecies that are best left that way. I think they want us all dead."

"I might have to kill them. All of them." I hated to say it, but I couldn't think of another solution. Vampires very rarely killed other vampires. We had few rules when it came to death, but that was a pretty big one.

With a brush of his thumbs over my cheeks, he nodded. "I'll do it, then. Not you."

Caesar wasn't a killer. Only during the frenzy did he really ever lose control. He would hate to do it consciously. "No, you won't."

It might not be me, but it wouldn't be him. I offered my neck, turning so he could see my pulse. "Feed. You need it."

He ran his nose over the spot before he placed his teeth there, grazing but not biting. He liked to prolong the moment. "You need to feed, too."

Not like he did. "I will after you."

"Here?" He and I both knew what would happen to us when we fed. It did every time, with all of them—just part of being soulmates. Every vampire could have the same kind of happiness, if only they didn't want power more, which meant changing things. No more seeking lives of quiet love, feeding off each other, of keeping the human lives lost at a minimum. What I had should always have been the goal, so why had it changed?

I nodded. Let others see it. I wasn't shy. I never had been. "Feed on me right here."

"Yes, my love."

I woke up as the sun was setting. Blinking, I looked around. *Did I sleep through an entire day?* Sure enough, the clock on my phone—which, thankfully, had not been left in the bathroom—said it was just after six in the afternoon. *I slept all day.* Not only that, I'd done it next to a still-sleeping vampire.

Clearly, I was fired. I couldn't even blame them. I would have to find another job.

Caesar shifted on the bed, waking. Vampires slept still, like they were dead, and then came to alertness instantly. I'd seen it, unfortunately, on several occasions while cleaning. I'd also ended up being their breakfast.

This seemed different. *Is he dreaming?* I scooted closer, a haze taking over my good sense. Instinct curled me closer to him, and my body throbbed with the need to give into it.

I dreamed about something... I couldn't remember it, but it was there, like a lost memory. I tilted my neck, our bodies flush against each other. "Caesar, feed."

He shifted, his nose coming down to my neck, as if he

intended to breathe me in. Familiarity was a strange companion to the moment. *We never did this before... did we?*

"Maci," his voice was low. He nipped at my neck a second before he bit down fully. My body came alive. I closed my eyes, the fog continuing to push down my reservations. I could fight it. There was a moment where, if I wanted to, I'd send it flying away. I decided in that moment that my good sense could go somewhere else until later.

I wanted Caesar.

Molten heat traveled through my body. My breasts ached a second before my nipples pebbled. It didn't stop there. A bundle of nerves in my core started to throb. I had to find relief. Between us, I dropped my hand, brushing the tip of his very hard cock when I did. I pushed my own pants aside, then my underwear, and easily pressed against my clit.

Caesar knocked my hand aside. With a grunt, he replaced it with his own. I cried out. *This is a new touch.* An invited one, but not something I'd ever experienced before. *Only my own fingers up until now.* His were rougher, callused, and I cried out. The extra sensations were exactly what I needed. I dropped my hand, this time unzipping his pants. It took a strong tug to get his pants off, made harder by the fact that I ground against his fingers. *He is using two now.*

His mouth pulled back and he licked my wound closed. He sighed against my ear in the same moment that I took his cock in my hand. Although I'd never done it before, it didn't mean I didn't understand how. I squeezed his tip and his sigh turned into a moan.

We moved together. He stroked, and I ran my hand down the large length of him. "Caesar."

"Maci." His voice was low as he palmed my breast under my shirt. "I want your clothes off."

I wanted his off, too. Each piece of clothing removed from each other was a moment either of us could have called it off, but soon we were both naked. He was still a vampire. I just flat-out didn't want to, and he must have felt the same, so why was this happening? I didn't know, but I gave into it since it had been given to us.

Caesar was hard, huge, and I had no doubt there were parts of the moment that would be filled with discomfort, yet I still ached for him inside of me.

He slipped a finger back into my pussy. "You're so wet for me."

I had never done this before, and I didn't think he had either, not even when he'd been human. I gave him a long stroke, and he closed his eyes, leaning his forehead against mine. "Why does this feel the way it does?" he rasped.

Like we'd both come home to something? I really had no idea. We only had questions. Right then, I wanted to feel, not think.

"Inside. If you want." I didn't want to presume, but I wanted to let him know I wanted him.

He nodded then tilted his head in the uniquely vampire way. *What does he see when he looks at me like that?* Caesar kissed me, our lips meeting in a gentle caress. I closed my eyes and let him make love to my mouth. That word I'd thought should make me nervous. It would later, I was sure of it. Right then, I bathed in the knowledge that nothing would come between me and what I wanted—Caesar.

He pressed himself inside of me. As he hit my small barrier, I winced. I expected as much, and I'd known there would be a little bit of pain.

I could see by his expression the second he recognized my discomfort, because he abruptly stopped moving. "Are you okay, Maci?"

Nodding, I kissed his chin. "Normal for the first time."

"I... I think I knew that somewhere. A lost memory? Not one that I had to hold on to. The discomfort. My apologies. What can I do? Stop?"

He apologized? I wasn't aware vampires *could* apologize. Saying that would spoil the moment, and it didn't matter right then. "Keep going. It'll pass with time. Just have to adjust."

Caesar nodded, moving, but much slower than I would have liked. Eventually, he fit himself inside of me and thankfully had the presence of mind to pause as my body got used to the intrusion. Suddenly, what had felt stretchy and off wasn't enough. I wanted more. I lifted my hips, wrapped my legs around him.

"More."

He smiled and pulled out before he pushed back inside. *Yes, there's the rhythm.* I pulsated, getting even wetter with every stroke. I dug my nails into his back, holding onto him as the explosion got closer and closer to the surface.

I had no idea what would happen to me when it came, but I grasped for it just the same. *Yes, this is what I needed.*

"Maci." He said my name as if it was a prayer before he took possession of my lips once more. Each second was a gift I was sure I would never have again. Finally, and too soon, I exploded around him. My back arched, and he grabbed me to hold me against him. He pulled us both into a sitting position, with me straddling him as he emptied himself inside of me. I collapsed, my head against his chest as I panted in his arms.

My whole, sweat-drenched body buzzed, my ears rang, and I giggled against him, unable to stop as joy resonated through each tremor of my body in the aftershocks of pleasure.

He kissed the top of my head. "Are you okay?"

"Little giddy, I think."

It was awkward, but he pulled out of me. Pregnancy might have been a concern—if there was any indication my reproductive system was in working order, which it wasn't. I didn't think vampires could carry STIs, or at least I'd never heard of such a thing. Plus, Caesar hadn't had sex since his rising, that much I was sure of.

I kissed his chest, listened to his heartbeat.

He rolled me beneath him to stare at me for a second. "You haven't eaten today. I can tell. Vampire thing."

"I just woke up right before you."

The head tilt again. "You must have really needed the rest. Much as you are unfed, you are brighter eyed today. You look better."

"Thanks?" I rolled my eyes at him. "*Not* sexy pillow talk."

Caesar got off the bed. "Come. Let's feed you."

"I need a shower." It wouldn't hurt to change my clothes, either. "All of my things are in my apartment. I have to go there eventually, Caesar. I can't just stay here."

He nodded once. *Finally, I made a good argument for leaving*? "We'll go there after you eat. I need to shower, too. As for clothes, I will get some for myself while we're out, too."

Caesar was really unconcerned about paying for things. He completely robbed the grocery store, and he wanted to most certainly steal himself clothing. Vampires cared little for that sort of right and wrong, so I needed to learn to be okay with that. Otherwise, I'd forever bang my proverbial head against a literal wall.

"Okay." I dressed in my dirty clothes. By the time I made my way to the kitchen, he was already standing over the stove. "I can cook. I know you hate the smell."

"I have a very serious diet plan for you. I don't want you fucking it up."

Ah, we're back to this. I jumped onto the counter and crossed my legs, a feat I was proud that I could do. The fact that I was being so incredibly nice and quiet was probably why it was shocking to me when he rounded on me, his face in mine again. "I'm broken. You understand that, right? I am not as I should be. I don't know why, and what's more, I am becoming more and more comfortable with the distortedness of my nature. I'm not fit for other vampires because my mind is constantly at war with itself—knowing what I *should* do versus what every instinct inside of me *begs* it to do."

I swallowed. "That has to be exhausting. I'm sorry you feel that way? If it helps, and I'm sure that it doesn't, but I don't think you're broken. You're the only vampire I've ever... liked."

He lifted his gaze. "I thought you hated me."

"And I thought you didn't care about such things."

Caesar frowned. "You confuse me to no end, but I won't be separated from you. I give in to it. I am a terrible vampire, but I will be yours until it's over for me and they burn me for my distortion."

I took his face in my hands. "Caesar, I am way more likely to die first. I'm a mess. If I do live to somehow survive long enough to be old, I'll *still* die long before you. I'll look old, and you'll be hardly aging."

I meant him to smile, but instead he furrowed his brow. "I don't like that." He turned away from me and back to the stove. "Get off the counter before you hurt yourself. Go sit on a stool. I'm making you chicken."

"Is this one of those times, where if I argue with you, then you're going to tell me about how you don't like to be disobeyed?"

That earned me absolute silence. I jumped off the counter. Caesar was dealing with a lot of internal strife, but at least I knew who I was. *Sort of. Does anyone ever really actually know themselves?* Boy, was that a road of pain I wasn't going to wander off on at the moment. Instead, I did as he wanted—I got down to get on the stool.

"I could just as easily fall off the stool." I didn't know why I was jabbing at him verbally except that he seemed to need it. If I left him alone in that head of his too long, he would say something that would ruin my mood after the really good sex we'd just had.

"Keep it up and I'll make you sit on the floor."

I grinned and he walked over, placing grilled chicken on a plate in front of me. Caesar used to be a good cook, and he'd actually done a good job with the eggs. But the chicken didn't look particularly well prepared. I was pretty sure it was raw in the middle. "How about if we grab another piece and I cook it? You can watch me to make sure that I don't do anything to spoil the nutritional value?"

He stared at the chicken. "No good?"

"I'm worried about salmonella poisoning." I rose. "No big deal. I'm feeling stronger. I can do the chicken. You can even stand back so you don't have to smell it so acutely."

I kept my back to him on purpose as I cooked the chicken. He hadn't said anything about what we'd shared except that he felt broken. *Does that mean he regrets it?* I didn't want to fight with him, not while I still buzzed from what we'd done together. I grinned at the memory. Yeah... that had really been something.

As I plated the chicken I cooked appropriately, I saw him watching me. "Does it screw anything up if I add some fruit?"

"Fruit would be fine. Vegetables, too, if you can stomach

them. Nothing too much. Small bites. We need you to be stronger bit by bit so we can leave here."

I sat at the counter and proceeded to cut the chicken into small pieces while I considered what he said. Caesar never misspoke. He'd proven himself to be a vampire willing to play around the truth problem. He avoided and didn't answer things. He redirected. No lying but not necessarily out there with things. Still, I could understand him. His mind was jumbled in spurts and stops. If he said we were leaving, that was what he intended to do.

"Where do you propose we go?" I wasn't agreeing without a conversation. Since I lost my job, staying wasn't necessarily ideal. Previously, I lived nearest the blood-suckers who would feed on me, but he said he would stay with me—my own personal vampire. We could really go anywhere he liked, unless it was really, really cold. As it was, I was always freezing because of blood loss. Too much worse and I would freeze to death in a winter coat.

I chewed and swallowed a piece. It wasn't bad. My stomach clenched, so I stopped. *Slowly.* I was going to get this food down, but I couldn't do it all at once.

Caesar took the seat next to me. "One bite at a time. If chicken is too much, we'll go back to eggs."

"I'm determined to make this work." I took a second bite, chewed like my life depended on it, and swallowed.

He stroked the back of my head. "After we go get you clothes and shower, you'll rest while I get myself more clothes, okay?"

"I hate that I can do so little. I was working full days before you got here."

Caesar put his nose against my neck and breathed in my scent. "You were dying, but now you're getting better. I can feel it inside me. Smell it on your skin."

I shifted slightly so he had to pull back. "Are you sure you're not just smelling yourself on my skin?"

His smile was slow then it fell away quickly. He jumped to his feet. "Wrap your arms around my neck from behind, and stay there. If he attacks me, I want you to go, fast. I'll keep him occupied at least long enough for that. Car keys are hanging in the garage. Yes, I should have told you that, only I didn't want you leaving. Get out of here, fast."

I obeyed, despite not understanding what he was talking about. "Who's going to attack you? Who's coming?"

Caesar backed us up until I was on the counter again, my arms around his back and neck, his body a huge blockade between me and whatever—*whoever*—was coming.

"Griffin."

The door to the house flung open and Griffin strode inside. He wore all black, including a trench coat and boots I would've never imagined him wearing as a human. His hair hung slightly into his eyes before he flipped it away.

Shock hit me, but I couldn't dwell for long, because the need for venom filled me like I didn't just get bit an hour or so earlier. My body threatened to seize, every muscle inside of me tightening. Pain struck me, my head pounding so hard it might actually explode.

"Easy." Caesar squeezed my hand. "That is the last thing that we can handle right now. We will, but, not yet."

Griffin tilted his head. "Handle? And what would you be *handling* with this woman we're forbidden from seeing?"

"Her pain." Caesar squeezed my hand. "Yes, I've broken his commandment. I will take whatever punishment he dishes, but it won't be from you, Griffin. You have no say over what I do or don't do."

The other vampire lifted his shoulders in a nonchalant

shrug I knew was so far from that, it was akin to him telling Caesar to fuck off.

"Why are you in pain?"

Griffin addressed me, ignoring Caesar. It was hard for me to speak. Every second was agony. The last time it had been so bad, I had a seizure—Wanda feared I wouldn't wake up from it. *Before today, I wondered if it would've been better if I hadn't.* Depression proved as much of a monster in my head as the real ones standing before me. Grief didn't ever go away; maybe we just got better at carrying it around, although arguably I hadn't yet.

"I..." I had to close my mouth, because my teeth chattered. I leaned on Caesar's shoulder. He wanted me to run? I wasn't even going to be able to *move*.

"Our fathers bit her every day for the entirety of our death, sometimes up to ten times a day. She's addicted, but she managed to get it down to fewer times by letting the castoffs bite her. She paid them. I found her near death, although she didn't realize it, and I've been taking care of her ever since. She was doing remarkably better... until you showed up."

He was leaving quite a lot out. Griffin had his own head tilt, and he used it right then. "I don't think Rowan knew that."

"If he did, he didn't share with the rest of us." Caesar squeezed my arm, a gesture meant to be soothing.

"He likely wouldn't have sent her off so abruptly if he had. I see why you thought this was a rule to disobey, yet you couldn't have known that before you got here. Semantics, I suppose." He approached us. "She's in pain now. Have you not bit her yet today?"

Caesar let go of me, leaving me on the counter, though he didn't move too far away. If I fell, I imagined he'd catch me. Agony was my best friend. I lay down on the granite, bringing my knees to my chest. "It's going to be bad."

I hoped they understood what I meant.

"I did." Caesar nodded toward me. "There are some unusual things about that. I'd love your opinion. Maybe you'd like to give her what she needs and then we can all talk."

Griffin threw his coat on the table. "I am hungry. I've yet to feed. Fine, I'll do it, and then we'll discuss exactly where to go from here. I've saved your ass again."

I didn't care what he meant. No, all I knew was Griffin pulled me upright. I cried out, pain jolting me as his teeth came down on my neck, the opposite side from where Caesar had been biting me. Immediately, everything that hurt stopped.

Yes, this is better. I closed my eyes as Griffin's body softened against me. He moaned. I couldn't do more than float in bliss.

4

My floating didn't last long. Soon enough, I was thrust back into reality—my body awake as earlier and needy. I moaned. Griffin pulled me against him so that he held me up instead of my sitting on the counter. I breathed heavily. *What is he going to do?* I desperately craved relief, but not like with Caesar. It had taken days to get to where we both wanted it.

Griffin pulled off me, licking the wound closed, but he didn't move right away. Instead, he held me against his hard body, his erection evident and probably painful. For just a second, he nuzzled down on my shoulder. "How?"

"We don't know," Caesar answered. "It doesn't happen with the others. I wondered if it was just me. That's why I let you feed from her."

"*Let* me?" Griffin's eyes shifted to a threatening red. "You think you could stop me if I wanted to bite her? You think I needed your permission?"

He stepped toward Griffin. "No, when we were humans, we shared her. I remember that."

"As do I." Griffin nodded. "You think that has changed? You're taking ownership of her?"

Caesar's smile was without any mirth. "Not at all. I'm warning you that she has me to protect her should you decide that you don't like what's happening here."

Griffin turned slightly, setting me down on the counter again. "Don't fall," he left his hand on my leg. "I don't understand what's happening yet, so I don't know if I like it or not. I know that you'd be dealing with a lot more than me if Rowan had been home when that nothing of a vampire showed up to tattle."

I blinked, coming fully back into the conversation. "Which vampire?"

"I guess Caesar threw a vampire into a wall to stop him from biting you." He lifted his eyebrows. "He came to complain. Looking for Rowan, who is away dealing with the war. The elders refused to see him, so he was sent to me. He told me his story. It's why I knew where you were."

I frowned. *This must have been why Caesar wanted to get out of here.* "So, you're caught."

"No, I killed him. He threatened Caesar. He matters, that one didn't. He's gone." Griffin shrugged. I would be shocked except that Griffin had been the same way as a human, too. He'd been the one to turn my teacher over to the vampires because she'd picked on me. She hadn't mattered to him as much as I did.

He had always ranked people like that.

Caesar nodded to him. "Regardless, we should leave. Maci and I were on our way out. She needs clothes. We're going to her apartment, then we'll be on the road tomorrow. Message delivered, Griffin. You can leave now, if you want."

The other vampire didn't move an inch. "You think I would leave? Now?" He turned to me. "After what just happened? And how she made me feel?" He squeezed my knee. "I'm not leaving. That isn't a normal reaction."

"When did we ever have a *normal* reaction? The way that it was with the five of you and me? It wasn't standard. We were all way too attached too quickly." I leaned back on the counter. *Maybe I'll just lie down right here.* Why not? It seemed as good a place as any.

"I always took that as the presence of death making it intense." Griffin took my arm and raised me to a sitting up position. "Have you been feeding her?" The question was to Caesar.

He nodded. "At least until you showed up. We were working on the chicken. Come on." When Caesar would have taken me from Griffin, the other man set me in the chair instead. Caesar smirked. "Back to the chicken, then your iron pills and vitamins. Then clothes. Shower. Sleep. We leave tomorrow. Griffin is apparently coming with us."

"Apparently? Yes, I'm coming. You can get off your high horse with her. Just because you found her first doesn't give you special rights. I was thinking about her, too. A lot. I was going to work on getting Rowan to change his rule. There are easier ways than blowing everything to hell."

I took a bite of my chicken, which had gone cold. Getting it down wasn't easy, but I worked on it. "There's no impending death," I told Griffin, bringing back the old topic. "So I don't have any explanation any more than you do. Sorry."

He rubbed the back of my neck. "She needs a lot more time. Paramours can take up to two to three bites a day. If we can get her healthy, there is nothing wrong with keeping her like that. You bite once, I bite once. Done."

"I'm not hungry. Not even a little bit, right now. I fed this morning, but only because she offered." Caesar took my hand. "Another bite. I don't feel at all hungry, and that's after three mild feeds. You tell me how you feel tomorrow. We may not need to feed for ourselves. We may just need to feed for her. That's fine, by the way, Maci. Don't worry about that."

Griffin sunk into a chair. "I have been constantly hungry since I woke up. Desperate in that coffin to be fed. Then it was such a haze. Feed. Feed. Feed. Feed. Pass out with the dawn. Wake up. Do it again. A need to survive beyond which I could handle."

That sounded like hell. "I'm sorry it happened to you."

He blinked. "Your sorry is unnecessary. It's what happens when we change. I wouldn't go back to being a human."

That broke my heart a little. *I'd change him back any day of the week.* "I can't fit anymore. Let's go. Get the clothes. Shower. All that stuff."

"Right." Caesar grinned. "I've been trying to get answers from books we left behind."

Griffin rolled his eyes. "They're not the important books. You won't find anything in them."

"Well, it seemed a good place to start."

They were silent the whole way to my apartment. I had no idea what two vampires sitting in silence meant exactly. Were they annoyed? Bored? Upset? Just quiet? Was it something I'd done? I rolled my eyes and decided I didn't care.

When we got to my place, I jumped out of the car. I certainly had more energy than before, that was for sure. In fact, all in all, I couldn't remember the last time I'd been so great. A song came to my soul, and I started to hum, going upstairs to my apartment.

"This is Wanda's bar," Griffin said in a low voice. "You live above a bar?"

I looked over my shoulder. "Wanda helped me for a while, and then she let me stay here for free so, yes, I live here."

"Lived," Griffin corrected. "You don't live here anymore. We're leaving tomorrow."

"That's fine." It really was. "If I don't have to pay for feedings, then I have no need to be here. But if you vampires drop me off in the middle of Iowa where there are no vampires so that I die in terrible pain, I'm going to be pissed at you."

He blinked. "Why would we do that?"

"I don't know. I'm never exactly sure why any of you do anything." Inside my apartment I didn't have too much stuff, but I did have a working bathroom. They needed to shower and change, too, so I turned to regard them. "Why don't you two get your clothes wherever and however you're going to do that? I'll shower and pack, then I'll wait for you here. We can get back to the house before daytime and leave when you wake up tomorrow. How is that?"

Caesar nodded. "I suppose you're safe enough. You've been here alone for some time."

"There's no such thing as safe, and we all know that."

Griffin grabbed my wrist. He stared at it for a second before he licked it. I tried to pull back. What was he doing? "Are you going to bite me?"

"No. I'm going to make those marks go away. I don't like them. I don't in any way want to see the evidence of others having bit you."

I took my hand back. "While I appreciate the sentiment, I think the damage is done. I don't think you lick it and make it go away like it's some kind of ice cream cone."

He shook his head. "I'm going to lick your wrists once a

day and the scars will fade. Eventually, they'll be entirely gone."

"Griffin..." *It has to be said.* "Even if you could make them go away, and I'm not sure it works like that, I don't want you to touch my scars. They're mine. I earned them. I survived. They're mine, and when my wrists hurt, which they do a lot, I can look down and remember why. I don't really care how you feel about them."

He lifted his eyebrows. "You don't care how I feel about them?"

"She hates vampires. And maybe the boys we were, too." Caesar crossed in front of me to look around. Without another word, he left the living room and went straight into the small bedroom. *What is he doing in there?*

"Do you?" Griffin tilted his head. "Hate us and the boys we were?"

I stared at him. "Do you care?"

"Emotions like hate don't really matter. They're human and pointless."

I thought he was going to say that, so I smiled at him. "Then the conversation is pointless." I walked into my bathroom, stopping to call over my shoulder, "Go get whatever stuff you guys need. By the time you get back, I'll be done, you can shower, and I'll be ready to go."

"Fine." Caesar called from my bedroom. *Seriously, what is he doing in there?* I left the bathroom to find him standing in the center of my room, staring at the walls. "You lived in here?"

That seemed obvious. "I did. Why?"

"It doesn't seem like you." He turned to me. "Even your room in the trailer had more stuff. Why didn't you go there and get your stuff?"

I shrugged. "Seems like the life another girl lived. I didn't live here as much as I was grateful to survive. I don't need stuff. I would think that was something a vampire could understand."

"Maybe some vampires but, truthfully, vampires love stuff," Griffin said, walking into the room. He shrugged. "Why does it bother me that she hates me?"

Caesar lifted an eyebrow. "It bothers me, too."

Okay. Enough of this. "I don't hate either of you. Better?"

I had to be careful. I couldn't let myself soften too much to these guys. I had no illusions about vampires being warm and loving. I wasn't one of the servants who wanted to be them or even a paramour who liked what she could have in their presence. I'd seen firsthand how callous and uncaring vampires were as a rule. I couldn't fall for them like they were still who they'd been. They'd died and been reborn as a different creature. I was certainly not the person I had been before all of it started.

My shower called to me, so after getting the hot water going, I got inside. Luckily, Wanda's bar never ran out of hot water. It was lovely. My current shampoo smelled like strawberries. Although I used whatever was on sale, I liked this one. I scrubbed my hair, applied a conditioner that had no scent, and then soaped up my body. It took ten minutes.

By the time I got out, I hummed to myself again. It wasn't a song I even knew, just a melody that came to me. My body didn't hurt—a remarkable gift I'd never get over. Gratitude of just being fine was a real, palpable thing.

Enough to hum over. If I knew the words to the made-up song, I'd even sing, and I had a terrible singing voice.

I ran my hands through my hair, wincing as each knot came loose. *When was the last time I did this?* I couldn't even remember. Lately, it had been too much effort, but tonight I felt like taking extra effort. I blinked. If this became a thing

—me hanging out with those two vampires—would I start thinking of nighttime as daytime? It was something to ponder.

A noise of someone coming through the front door caught my attention. A second later my bathroom door swung open.

"Hey," I yelled. "I'm not dressed yet."

"Then you can die naked."

One of the vampires—Bash—who I'd been paying to feed off me stood in my apartment. His eyes were bright red. *Fuck. He's in a rage.*

"W-what are you doing here?" I didn't know any of them knew where I lived. I tried to grab for my bathrobe, but he took me by the neck and slammed me against the wall.

"You missed your appointment, and I want my money, bitch."

I winced. "I don't have any. I'm sorry. I have no way of canceling you or anything. I mean, none. I have no way to pay you. I'm sorry. I can't do that." My last fifty dollars had gone to the now dead vampire. I hadn't showed up at work, and I hadn't been paid.

He scowled at me. "That's really too bad, because now I'll have to take my payment in blood. Fifty dollars' worth of blood will kill you.

With a twist, I tried to knee him in the balls. Tried was the key word, because I failed. It only resulted in him squeezing my neck harder. He loosened his hold only enough so that he could tear into my skin. I screamed. It wasn't pretty, and for the last thing I was going to do, it was really pathetic. I clawed at him. It did nothing.

He was wrenched off me and thrown to the side. Griffin breathed heavily, his eyes blood red. He roared, a completely non-human sound as he pulled Bash off the floor. His fangs elongated, but he didn't bite him. No, using one hand, he broke my kitchen chair in half, separating the leg from the rest of it. With the pointy end he staked Bash right the through the heart.

I'd never seen anyone staked before. Sure, I might dream of becoming a vampire hunter, but even trying would make a vampire laugh at me. Bash's body flopped once before he died on my floor.

A great time to get up and say something pithy. Not that I could, because blood dropped down my neck, and it took every bit of my energy to try to hold my neck together. *This is bad, nothing like when they bit my neck.*

Griffin knelt in front of me. "You're very injured. Move your hand."

I wanted to explain—if I moved my hand, I was dead. That's all there was to it. He gave me a kill injury, as he'd intended.

"Come on. Your hand." With gentle figures in contrast to his red eyes, he took my hand away. Bending his head, he licked the wound. Once. Twice. A third time. It tingled the way that it usually did when one of them cleaned up their mess, but even more so. The tingle changed to a burn and tears leaked from my eyes.

"Why does everything have to be so hard?" I didn't know why I asked him. Griffin certainly had no idea why the universe did what it did. If he had, he would've never been made a creature of the night.

He smoothed my hair away from my forehead. "Don't move for a second. It's closed, but your skin is going to need a second to adjust. That was close. Low life vampire. He should have been staked the second he woke up. I'm going to get your robe."

He left and returned with my bathrobe, carefully putting

me in it.

I grabbed his wrist. "Thank you. I don't think I can ever say that enough. Thank you. And I don't hate you. I want to. It would be so much easier if I could hate you, but I don't and I never could."

"You make me want to be gentle as a war rages inside of me, craving violence and destruction. He had his mouth on you. He would have killed you, and you don't belong to him. He had no rights. I wish I could kill him again."

I swallowed and it hurt. "I'm not... okay."

"You will be. Healing will take time. The same venom that addicts you will fix you because I administered it." He held my gaze. "Sleep until tomorrow, Maci."

Some vampires could compel. I knew it. I'd never seen it, but I nodded my head. I would sleep. *Hopefully when this is over, this could all feel like it was a bad dream.* I liked the feeling of wanting to hum. *Why couldn't it have stayed like that?*

"What happened?" Caesar yelled, but my eyes were already closing as I leaned against Griffin's strong arms.

It was a day for firsts. Lots of them.

"GRIFFIN? Still with your head in the books?" I leaned against the door to the library and watched him.

He jumped, showing how out of it he was. "What? No, actually, I'm writing a story. Our story. All of us."

He was doing what? I walked toward him. "Why?"

"All the great vampires get things written about them. I think our story should be told."

He wasn't kidding. I leaned my head on his shoulder. He was writing about us. A long story about how we met and all the things we'd done together. "I don't know if we're important enough to warrant our own story."

Griffin sighed. His hunger hit me. It had been way too long since he'd fed, but when he got focused on a project, he forgot basic things—like the fact that he should eat regularly to maintain his best levels of power.

Or at least avoid going on a rampage and killing everyone within walking distance.

"After the battle tomorrow, we'll be great. We'll be the most famous vampires alive. Putting down rebellion, holding to our values, with great strategy? There are prophecies about us, so why not write our stories?"

I kissed his neck, breaking him in, and because I liked to feel him react to me. Yes, I was getting his attention, and I wanted it that way. "For those prophecies to come true, we all have to die and be sort of reborn. That doesn't sound wonderful to me."

He turned in his chair. "Everyone dies. It'll be someday far in the future, and then we'll wake up and all be together again. Just like now."

I doubted anything was that simple. "I don't think it's us. Don't get cocky. We're just normal vampires. By all means, write our story, but not because you have grandiose dreams. We're doing battle tomorrow, then we'll go home. Have a life. Maybe a family."

He shot his eyebrows skyward. "Really?"

"Yes. But first you need to feed." I tilted my neck. "Come on."

He stared at me for a long second. "When was the last time you fed?"

Redirection was always his middle name. "This morning. Feed, my love. Come on." I wrapped my legs around him, climbing onto his lap as I did. "Please. You won't leave me hanging, will you?"

Griffin kissed me. "Never."

I woke up back in the mansion. Suitcases sat around the bed, but I was alone. They must have brought me back. I tested swallowing. *Yes, better. Much better.* Sitting up didn't cause dizziness, and I rubbed at my eyes. Coffee would be wonderful. Did we have any or had Caesar thought that wasn't on my healing plan?

As the sun streamed through the window, I couldn't ask him anytime soon. Where had they put themselves? I stared down at myself. One of them had dressed me, too. It should have been humiliating but maybe getting my throat torn out by a vampire I used to pay meant I was above things like embarrassment.

I padded down the hall wearing my yoga pants that had a hole in the bottom and an old tank top that had seen better days. Most of what I owned was worn out in some way or another. The gifts the guys had given me had been taken away. I had no idea what happened to them.

Stacks of books littered the counter, and I glanced at them while I walked to the fridge. What I saw in there made me grin—Caesar clearly thought ahead. There was a turkey sandwich ready to go for me and a glass of orange juice. I grabbed the plate. *That is really sweet of him.*

I jumped onto the counter to eat and grabbed the book on top of the nearest stack. I hated reading these things. The old language was hard to comprehend. Still, I'd been a good student before it had been ripped away from me, so I'd give it a go.

Maybe it was the turkey sandwich, but it didn't take me long until I could understand what I read. When I'd tried with Caesar, the books had been dense and mostly about counting blood supplies and feeding servants. This book was more interesting, a history of great vampires. That seemed familiar to me, though I had no idea why.

How interesting. Vampires sometimes did things besides feed and ruin lives. According to the book, some of them made art, wrote books. They lived lives. *Of course, they were all men.* The vampire females were never included. I flipped through a few more pages, but I didn't spot any record about anyone getting sexually aroused by feeding.

That's too bad. If one of these great vampires went through this, it would be helpful.

I didn't know who'd authored the book, but the way the wording kept changing, I wondered if it was more like a diary that got discarded and then picked up by others, with the narrative changing authors every so often. I chewed and swallowed.

Pages were missing. I flipped through more of the book. A whole chunk was missing, like someone took a section of pages from the book. *Weird.*

It probably doesn't matter. I kept reading. We were almost to modern times when everyone stopped writing. *Well, that isn't surprising, since there aren't any great vampires anymore.*

Caesar placed a hand on my shoulder. "Hello."

I jumped. "You startled me." *How much time had passed?*

He picked up the book. "Worthless book. It's staying here. You're well?"

I wrapped my arms around him. He didn't return my hug, but I hadn't expected him to. Vampires weren't affectionate, not even when they cared about me like I was sure he did. "I'm well."

"I wish I could have killed him. Let Griffin kill him, but revive the son of a bitch, so I could kill him again."

I did, too. He could kill him every day if he wanted.

5

"You've eaten?" Caesar stepped out of my embrace and headed toward the garage. "If you have, you should wait in the car. I'll bring Griffin and the bags outside."

Well, that makes no sense. "You're going to *bring* Griffin? What's wrong with Griffin?"

"He's not awake yet. He's a later riser than me. I'm actually among the earliest. It's dark outside, so the sun won't hurt him. We don't need to wait for him to awaken. I'll simply put him in the car. Go wait for me there." He stopped and turned toward me. "Lock the doors and unlock them when I get to the car."

I sighed. "I don't think I'm going to get in trouble in the car. I mean... granted, I got attacked in my apartment, but it's not like there are a whole lot of people after me. I probably don't have to lock myself in like my life depends on it."

Caesar tilted his head in the vampire way. "People will be after you. Soon. I think we can guarantee that. As soon as anyone important gets wind that you're with us, they'll be after you. My only hope is that we can get you home before then."

Dread filled me and goosebumps broke out on my arms. I rubbed them away. "Home?"

"We're taking you close enough to come and go and no one will notice. We've bought you a house where we can be with you, but we'll show up for every meeting, so no one will ask any questions."

I grabbed his arm. "Caesar, why would anyone come after me? Why would they bother? I'm just a human girl they got the better of. Why bother?"

"I don't understand everything happening and neither does Griffin. We agree on two things. One, Rowan had no idea what happened to you when he sent you away. I think he thought he was owning the promise he made to you? I don't know, and I can't ask him. I can only go by what he said, and he doesn't lie. That doesn't mean, as you know, that things don't get twisted in what is not said."

Okay. I had to dwell on that. Was it possible Rowan really didn't have ill intent when it came to me? I'd sort of settled into the thought that he was mean, as his father was, and that was all there was to it. Of course he'd absolutely not been mean when he was a human. Maybe he was a little bit tempered in his meanness? Really, I had no idea.

I needed to focus. "And the second thing that you agree about?"

"We need to keep you close, so when things take a turn, you're near enough for us to protect you. This is going to get worse before it gets better. I'm not even sure how it will work out at all, but that's what Griffin and I agree on." He stared at me a long moment, his monster evident in his gaze. They were rare moments, but still I could sometimes absolutely see the duality of these men... they were both man and monster. How did it work in their heads? Did they battle? One step aside, one run things, or was it a combination at all times?

I'd never ask, and as I wasn't going to become a vampire, I'd never know. I also wasn't an idiot. He was telling me to get in the car, so I would. I looked around. "We need the books, and I never got to gather any stuff."

"All of that stuff should be thrown away. We'll buy you more stuff. One thing vampires never worry about is money. You don't have to anymore, either."

I shook my head. It was hard to believe, and I couldn't let myself get used to it. Yes, for the moment I would stay with the vampires, but if things got out of hand, I would run away during the day while they slept. If they decided to chase me, I'd face that problem when it hit. Nothing to do at the moment but live in the present and hope that I could handle what happened when it did. I really had no choice. *I certainly couldn't continue as I had been. Apparently, I'd been really close to death.*

I grabbed some of the books off the table and headed toward the car. Outside was cooler, and a gust of wind blew my hair temporarily in my face. I brushed it away awkwardly with part of my hand while I carried the books. It wasn't really a car waiting; it was a mobile home. I decided not to think too hard about how he obtained it, since I knew he didn't buy it during daylight hours.

Was this what he was arranging—or stealing—when Griffin showed up to save me? I was still standing there open mouthed when he came out, holding Griffin over his shoulder. He nodded toward the vehicle. "I told you to get into it."

Should I argue with him because he'd said car, and it was absolutely not a car? No, I would leave that one alone.

Without comment or argument—which made me feel way mature—I got in behind him.

The inside was big enough that it fit two couches and two coffins. It really looked like they'd torn it up to make it work for their purposes. Right then, Caesar set Griffin down on the coach. He turned to look at me. "Sit back here with him while I drive?"

I pointed at the coffins. "I think we need to discuss these."

The last time I'd seen similar ones had been when they crawled inside them to die. I shuddered. Turned out I had an issue with coffins. I could do without ever seeing one again.

He turned away and walked to the front. "We'll need somewhere to stay during the day. It's about a thirty-five-hour drive. It will take longer because we'll need to stop for gas because we have you with us. I could run this easily in a night. I packed the small fridge with food for you. We'll need to feed, if you don't wish to be the source of that for us. We also need to hide from the sun and sleep. It's not a matter of staying awake and being tired. We can't physically remain up yet. Also, I don't know that we can absolutely find a house with true blackout curtains. I don't want to use vampire friendly hotels. You'd be too evident. This is the best solution, so we'll get in the coffins. They'll protect us."

I swallowed. *Well... okay*. Of course they should be protected. I'd just deal with my feelings. I was good at it. I'd been silently handling the shit that bothered me my whole life.

"There are vampire hotels?"

Caesar didn't answer but instead continued to the driver's seat at the front. "If you aren't able to handle driving it, we'll pull in places for the day. You can let me know. Don't drive it if you can't. I don't want you to have a car accident. The police discovering two dead bodies in the coffins with you will be a difficult, awkward situation that will lead to too much publicity."

"Ah... okay. Then maybe I better sit up there with you to see how you do it."

He turned on the ignition. "After Griffin wakes up. I think he'll want to see you right there when he wakes. He was very nervous about what happened to you. We have many, many hours for you to learn to drive it."

It was hard for me to picture Griffin nervous and even weirder to think Caesar would be concerned about that. None of my time with the vampires revealed them being tender with each other, not even in friendship, at all. Emotions weren't their thing.

What is going on here? It wasn't just my blood making things different, it couldn't be. No other vampires reacted strangely, that much was for sure. A wave of withdrawal hit me, and I sighed. Why did it hit when it hit?

The world rushed by outside even at the staggeringly slow speed Caesar drove the motor home. I swallowed and sat forward to stare closer against the window. It was the furthest I'd ever been from home. I'd dreamed of the moment, saved for it. Back in high school, my whole plan was to get on the road and drive with no direction to some-where else. Anywhere else. The whole idea of *somewhere else* had been so important. *Here I am, somewhere else.* Still moving and it was happening; I was leaving Kentwood.

I touched the window with my fingers as if I could feel the passing scenery, and ingested the experience through the tips of my fingers into my soul. *This was what I wanted.* Well... it was slightly askew. I didn't plan on a motorhome with two vampires, the details were irrelevant. *It is happen-*

ing. I couldn't see a thing, really. It was dark, but it was happening.

"What do you see that's so interesting? If I recall, there's not much to see for a very long time."

I turned at the sound of Griffin's voice. He stared at me from where he'd lain down, not having moved but awake, watching me.

"It's new. I've never left home, not ever. Once I was addicted, I thought I'd live and die my whole life in that place." *And it had felt like an incredible amount of pathetic.* "I'm having a moment."

He tilted his head. "I forgot that about you. It's interesting what stays and what doesn't stay through the transition. Yes, this is your first time leaving. It can't be very exciting, but I'm glad you are getting out."

A feeling moved through me. It wasn't just my withdrawal, it had to do with him specifically. *He is hungry.* I rubbed my arms. *How do I know that?* Well... I wasn't sure I actually did, since it was just a feeling, but when I'd been ten years old, I'd been convinced I could feel ghosts jumping around the room. Turned out I'd just watched something scary on television, because feelings were just that, feelings. They weren't facts.

If I wanted to know, I had to ask. "Hungry?"

He lifted an eyebrow. "Yes, but not so much that it has to matter right now. I've been hungrier than this. It's small."

I rose to my feet, gripping the wall to sit down next to him. As I did, he sat up so we were both upright on the couch together. "You can feed."

He ran a finger down my neck. "This was torn up yesterday. I think you can do without being bit today."

That was remarkably kind of him, for a vampire. I'd never known one before Griffin and Caesar who cared what the human felt about being bitten or what condition they were in afterward. "Well, that's very nice of you to say, but I'm having withdrawal, so the timing might be bad, but I sort of need you to bite me. It's like your hunger and my need match right now."

He stared at me without moving, his gaze all vampire, a red rim that spoke of his monster visible for me to see. Faster than I could have anticipated, he darted closer to me. Still, he made no move to bite my neck. "That's interesting, isn't it? That I need, and so you are in pain."

I'd said it as sort of an off the cuff remark from my train of thought, but did he think it meant something? "Are they connected?"

"Well, the only way to know is to track it. See if that continues to happen. Is it just me or Caesar, too? You were withdrawing before I got to you, before Caesar was, so unless it changed for some reason, then I don't see logically how it can be. Still, I'll think on it." He rubbed his nose against my neck, taking a deep breath. "You should know I hate to feed. I hate the need. It gets in the way of everything. I'm trying to accomplish something, and it all has to stop to feed."

I took his hand in mine and squeezed our fingers together. "You had to eat when you were human, too."

"I did, but I could actually do other things when I ate. Talk. Study. Watch television. I didn't have to be totally consumed by eating, so that I couldn't even think about anything else except that which I was doing." He breathed in again. "But while I hate the need to feed, I love to feed off you. Obviously, the things feeding off you does to my body play a role, but it's more than that. I like how you taste. I don't mind not thinking when my mouth and my teeth and my tongue are on you."

I caught my breath, my body vibrating from his words. "Griffin."

"I think that I won't ever stop hating the need, even if I really like how you smell." With those words, he bit me. I cried out, not in pain, but as pleasure took away all my discomfort. I closed my eyes and leaned into the experience. I didn't have to support my own weight, I just leaned against Griffin.

He didn't feed for very long—maybe just a minute or two—but by the time he finished, I panted with a different need. I wanted him to take me, to push me down on the couch and make love to me until the ache formed between us found release.

As if he could read my mind, when he'd licked my wound closed, he pushed me down on the couch so that I lay beneath him. Griffin stared down at me. "You want this or is it just the chemicals that happen between us?"

"I want you. I always wanted you." Right in that moment, I could have been a vampire in my inability to lie, and yet I left things out. We didn't need to talk about my overall vampire issues right then, not when I wanted Griffin so much. I didn't care what he was.

Caesar wasn't far from us, but I couldn't have cared less. I wanted Griffin, and we were going to have each other. *Right this very second.* I'd sort out other issues later. There was only Griffin. He was all that I wanted in the world.

We tore at each other's clothes, and he stopped, but just so that he could make love to me with his gaze. I'd never thought a vampire could look at me like that, but he didn't look like just a vampire; he was Griffin, and the way that he practically touched me with just his gaze was as intoxicating as his hands.

"Your skin is healed where I fixed you." He grabbed my

pants and tore them in half, throwing them over his shoulder. The car drove steadily, and I was easily able to pretend we weren't moving right then. "And you are very much fucking alive."

I guessed that was a good thing, because it spurred him onward. My underwear was a thing of the past. Gasping, it occurred to me what he was about to do just seconds before he did it. With one hand he pushed my knees aside and the other grabbed my other thigh.

Griffin wasn't gentle. He licked the outside of my pussy with a determination that spoke of the focus he had in both lives. There was nothing gingerly about the velvet stroke of his tongue. I grabbed the top of his head, holding on to his hair, not sure if I wanted more or to push him away. It was very different than my minimal previous experience, almost too much.

Despite my insecurities, I couldn't bring myself to tell him to stop. I *did* want his mouth on me. Griffin went for it, not pausing until he found my clit and sucked on it. Hard.

I cried out. *Yes, I like that.* It was so much, I couldn't even give it any thought. I just had to ride the wave that was my orgasm. It hit out of nowhere, struck me almost instantly, and released all the tension I carried since that monster tore my neck the night before. Griffin had saved me, and now he was giving me what I needed, over and over again.

I dug my hands into the bare skin of his back. I wanted to mark him, to own him in any way I could. He didn't even flinch. Instead, he lifted his head to stare at me. "That didn't take long. I was hoping to have to work at that for a while."

"Guess I was ready for you from the blood sucking."

He ignored my description of it, tilting his head before he scooted us both back a little. Griffin pulled off his own underwear and I almost laughed at the abrupt motion.

Vampires didn't have a lot of finesse, but he was sort of hot in his own, unique way. At least I knew what he wanted.

But he surprised me by smirking. "I'll suck you any time, Maci."

I rolled my eyes but quickly stopped because he pulled me on top of him. "This will go better with you on top."

I didn't mind that idea. I needed to take back some control, if for no other reason than to preserve my own sanity. I rolled on top of him, which was awkward on the couch, but my lack of grace didn't matter.

"I don't have that much experience, so tell me if I do something you don't like."

Griffin shook his head. "I doubt that's possible. Tell me if I hurt you. I forget that you're so fragile."

"I'm not fragile for a human." And I really didn't want to discuss it right then. I wanted his cock deep inside of my body, and from the looks of how hard he was, I'd say he wanted the same thing. I shifted around until I could climb on top of him, straddling his body. The position meant I could control how fast I took him inside me.

He was big, and I needed to stretch to fit him. Inch-by-inch, I did just that. It was staggeringly slow, and by the end, he hissed out a moan that told me he was ready to move. *Looks like the vampire doesn't have more control over this than me.* And I loved that.

Griffin lifted his eyebrows. "Ready?"

"Are you?" I lifted my hips a bit then pushed back down to give us both a jolt of pleasure.

"Oh, Maci. More than ready."

That was all the incentive I needed. Up and down, I moved on his cock, rubbing my clit against him when I wanted and reveling in the noises he made. They told me he was mine in that moment. Griffin belonged to me right then, if only right then, and I would revel in every second of it. The thought made me grind against him harder. He cried out, his hips buckling as he pushed his cock even further inside of me.

Over and over, we found our rhythm until I had to touch my own breasts, had to squeeze them to take away the ache that I couldn't lose. He grabbed my hands, pulling them away. "I do that."

Well, if he insists. Griffin took over, grabbing my breasts in his strong palms pinching my nipples. I cried out. Yes, right then I'd needed the relief that pinch of pain could give me. I couldn't explain it. I just did.

I closed my eyes. The pinch had taken me out of my head enough so I could lose myself in the sensations. I rode him as if we'd danced a million times. I just knew how. It was natural, as if Griffin had been my lover a long time. I loved it.

My orgasm hit me all of a sudden, but not like the earlier explosion to release pressure, more like a release. One second after another, my pleasure seeped out of my soul until tears leaked from my eyes, and I cried my release on the edge of my tears.

Griffin followed me, his loud moans telling me he also skated the edge before following me over.

I collapsed on top of him, breathing heavily. For long seconds, he held me, and I closed my eyes. I forgot that he'd died in a coffin. I forgot he wasn't the Griffin I had known forever. None of that mattered. There was just this Griffin, and he was all that I needed.

We breathed together.

I could completely fall asleep like this. It would be so easy. I could...

Griffin pulled out of me, setting me gently on the couch

and crossing, totally naked to a bag on the other side of the vehicle. He pulled out clothes and dressed himself, not saying a word or looking back.

I winced at the sight. *That's right; he's a vampire.* He wasn't going to give a shit, not really, about what they had just done. *Silly me for forgetting for a long moment.* It was fine to enjoy these guys, but absolutely not okay to start warm sentiments that might turn into love. Sex was sex. Vampires had it all the time with the paramours, and it would never be anything other than that.

Sighing internally, I forced the ball of feelings down into my stomach. *I've gotten good at that over the years.*

I didn't have fresh clothes to wear, so I stretched out my legs and did my best impression of nonchalance. "One of you needs to give me a shirt and a pair of shorts. I'm without a change of clothes right now."

"Grab my bag," Caesar told me. "Take what you want. We'll get you clothes soon."

I looked over at him. *Fuck.* I'd completely forgotten him during my little romp with Griffin. Was he okay with the fact he'd just had to listen to that? Well, yes, he probably was. Again, I had to remind myself vampires didn't have feelings like humans. *He said he and Griffin plan to keep me together. That must mean they're both fine with this.*

I rose, and with confidence I didn't feel, I walked to Caesar's bag. *Fine. I'm naked. That is fine. It is fine. I'm fine. It's all fine. Naked is fine. Sure it is. Fine. Fine. Fine.*

6

Caesar stopped for gas in a town called Ogden, and I learned we were actually in Utah. The realization stunned me—we'd actually crossed states. Griffin took over as driver, and Caesar came back to join me.

The vampire I just had sex with went even quieter than usual afterward. *Did I do something wrong?* I really didn't know if I wanted the answer.

Ignorance really could be bliss sometimes.

Caesar sat next to me on the couch, knocking me out of my musings. "Have you eaten?"

Several hours earlier, I'd had some crackers and cheese, but it was almost morning. "I did."

He nodded. "Good. We'll have to get in the coffins soon. You'll drive to an address I've set up on my phone, an Airbnb Griffin found for you. After you park there, you can head inside for the day. Leave us locked in here, so if there are any video cameras on the house, it just looks like you parked and went inside."

I supposed it made sense. "Better than stopping some

place for the night with this thing? Like a mobile home park?"

"I prefer fewer people around, because this isn't how we normally travel. There are hotels that cater to our kind and keep specific rooms for vampires entirely dark. That's how both Griffin and I got here. We also travel faster than this in regular cars, but we needed to stay out of those hotels. I don't want any other vampires spotting you, so this was my best solution. Given more time, I might come up with better ideas, but this works for now. I think."

"It's a good solution," Griffin supplied from the front seat.

"So, your voice does work? I wasn't sure." I called out to him, and Caesar's mouth twitched into a grin.

"What should I be saying?" Griffin asked after a long moment.

I held up my hand, not that he'd see it. "Nothing. Please, don't say a word."

Caesar laced our fingers together, lowering my hand from where I'd lifted it to hold it up. "The town is called Rock Springs. I don't think you need anything, but if you do, it's big enough for you to get it. Might be kind of awkward to move this around town with us in the coffins but do what you must. We'll never know."

A sadness wafted over me. Yeah, they'd never know, because they'd be dead to the world in coffins. "Does it bother you to get in those things?"

"No." He blinked as if the question surprised him. "Not at all. Does it bother you to think of us inside them?"

"Seeing you go into them was the worst day of my life. Every minute knowing you were dying was an hour to me. It went on and on. I imagine it's nothing in comparison to what you went through. Anyway, my feelings on the subject don't really matter. I... Never mind. We don't have to stop; I can keep driving for a long stretch until you guys wake up. I can gas this thing up, and..."

He shook his head. "That's too much. You have to rest, and you have to eat. Otherwise, we'll likely drain you too much when we need to feed. Granted, for me, my needs seem to be very minimal currently. Still, *no*. You can't drive all day while we can't help you."

I supposed it made sense. "Okay."

"Good. Thanks for not arguing."

"Tanner has lost his voice. Griffin called out from the front again and both Caesar and I turned to look at him. "You know that, right? Not that you're going to see him, but did you know?"

It took me a long moment to answer him. *Was he still on my comment from before? About him not being able to use his voice?*

"I did know, yes. I think that's particularly awful considering he sang and played music." He asked me to remember their birthday week, too. I had, in my own head, the year before, though it had been hard to really care about anything when it felt like death greeted me personally every day. *Okay, this year I'll do better*. I'd light a candle or something. Maybe these two would actually like to celebrate?

The whole thing confused me.

"Maci, if I hurt your feelings because I was quiet, I'm sorry. I'm trying to sort things out in my head. It's how I work on problems," Griffin said.

I swallowed. "Not speaking to a person right after you have sex with them is harsh and feels like a rejection. Going forward with me, or with anyone else you have sex with after I'm dead or gone from your life, just know it's really best if you communicate afterward for at least a period of time."

Caesar frowned and squeezed my hand again. "That won't be any time soon, Maci. Our entire focus at this point is on keeping you alive and well."

"Right, so you can figure all of this out. I get it." I rubbed my eyes. "How long do you have until you get into the coffins?"

"Maci..." He didn't continue until I made eye contact with him. "It's more than figuring things out. I don't know what it is exactly, but it's not that." He dropped my hand and rose. "In a few more minutes, we'll trade, and you can drive. We'll get in once you're on the road. It's best to be settled before the need for it pulls you under. Otherwise, we stumble around and eventually we can even fall over. Early Vampire issues—happened to me once in the very beginning."

Griffin snorted. "Once?"

"Maybe more than once, actually. But he shouldn't be laughing at me. I remember it happening to Griffin, too."

"All right, me, too. Yes," Griffin confirmed. "All of us. Except for Ace. Never happened to Ace, which always confused me. How does he *do* that? He's just so constantly in control. Even Rowan struggled with the daytime problem. Not Ace. Why was that?"

Caesar rose and walked back to the front to sit in the passenger seat. "It's just one of those things. We'll never understand it."

"Seems like you all get unique abilities. Caesar, you said you can tell when a woman is ovulating. Can anyone else do that?"

Griffin shook his head. "Not me. I can see farther than others can. If I focus, it's like my eyes are binoculars. I don't think others can do that. Rowan can strategize six steps ahead of everyone else in an instant. He holds hundreds of pieces of information in his head at once. Ace is brutal, but I don't know his particular talent. Tanner can't talk, so if he can do one thing or another, I don't know about it."

"Maybe Ace's gift is not being stumbly before he has to go to sleep." I didn't really know anything, but it could fit into what they described. "I used to stare at the cabin you were in, trying to catch sight of you. I saw you once, Caesar. You and Rowan."

He rubbed his eyes. "I'm glad I didn't know. It was hard enough to keep me in there."

"It really was." Griffin laughed. "You were like the nightmare scenario. Rabidly hungry, strong, and determined to get out the fucking door every day. Yeah... better you didn't know."

Eventually, it was time to let me drive. I hadn't worried about the mechanics of handling the vehicle—*driving is driving right?* Well... it wasn't quite so simple. There were things to consider that I never had before, like spacing. With no past experiences to draw from, I held on tight as the sun rose. I found myself so preoccupied with trying to handle the driving that I didn't give them a second thought as they got into their coffins and presumably went to sleep for the day.

Somehow, I managed to find the destination from the navigation. Parking was tricky, and I twice almost ended up on the curb, but the street was wide. Fortunately, that width also meant we didn't stick out too far onto the street for anyone to complain. The plan hinged on no one finding me remarkable or being interested in the vehicle, so no one noticed the coffins inside.

After I parked, and before I went inside the rented

house, I did look back into the motor home. Goosebumps broke out on my arms, so I rubbed them. *Caesar and Griffin are inside of those boxes.* I'd seen them there before. I walked over to them slowly and touched the wood on the tops. *Okay, I have to get control of myself. They aren't dead this time. They are already vampires.*

What is done is done.

With shaking hands, I locked the vehicle behind me then walked toward the front door. I had to look really strange on the cameras I was sure were watching me. Homeowners would be silly not to have devices recording their properties while they had guests. The code worked, so I stepped inside the empty home. Once I closed and locked it behind me, I took a deep breath.

The house, which I hadn't focused on when I'd gone inside, was pretty nondescript. Two bedrooms, one bath, and a wide-open space that served as both kitchen and living room—basically, a mansion compared to my apartment. I forgot all the food back in the motorhome, but I would have to go out for it later.

Right then, I needed to lie down.

On laden feet, I made my way into the bedroom and face planted on the bed. The guys were outside. Anyone could hurt them in that moment, but not even that anxiety kept my eyes open. *They're closing whether I want them to or not.*

A touch on my shoulder made me rear up, a scream caught in my throat, and my heart beat so fast that I could've been running, not sleeping.

"Easy," Caesar sat on the edge of my bed. "You were deeply asleep, and didn't hear me come in. It's time to get going."

I looked around. Sure enough, darkness filtered through the window. "I slept all day."

"That's good. You needed it." He rubbed my hair away from my forehead. "Griffin will sleep a while yet, but I thought we should get going. Come on. Let's lock up here. We've paid for it through tomorrow, so there should be no trouble, and go from here."

A thought dawned on my still muddled brain. "Cameras! They'd see you walk inside."

"Sure. They'll think I spent the day in the motorhome. Maybe they'll think we had a fight and you made me stay out there. Whatever reasons they come up with, it doesn't matter now. My only concern was getting you to rest in a place where there would be no questions. We'll do this from now on."

I let him lead me from the house. "You're not hungry. I don't sense your need to feed, am I right?"

"I'm not. It's incredible how long it has been. Something to do with you, your blood, and its effect on me."

We walked together inside the motor home. It looked as I left it. Even though I was practically dead on my feet, I made my way to the small fridge to pull out some food—a cheese sandwich would be all I could handle at the moment.

"Is it possible to stop for coffee? I don't usually drink it, but I think it might be pivotal right now."

He nodded. "Absolutely, we can."

Caesar drove the car better than me. I sank into the seat up front with him, kicked off my shoes, and proceeded to eat my cheese sandwich. The next place we stopped, I intended to shower. If I'd guessed I would sleep the whole day away, I would've found the energy to do it before I went to sleep.

"So... do you feel like a reincarnated vampire? Some-where in there, do you carry memories from hundreds of years ago or whatever you guys were supposed to be?"

He frowned when he answered me. "I can't speak for the others, because we don't discuss it, but I'm not. I suppose I'm a huge disappointment in that way, but I must admit... I don't give a shit. They certainly treat Rowan as if he has all the answers from the universe. Maybe they're right and he does. I don't know."

I took his hand. He said he didn't give a shit, but it had to matter. *Even vampires have to live up to expectations.* His entire human life had been about him being some important reincarnation, and if he wasn't that, it had to suck.

He stared at our joined hands. Sometimes he could seem so human, but in that second, I could tell he absolutely *wasn't*. I took my hand away. The gesture was a total waste. Caesar wasn't hurting inside. He said he didn't give a shit, and I had to believe him.

"So, you and Rowan don't talk much? I feel like... and maybe I'm misreading it, but you guys aren't really with him anymore. Ace is, but not you."

He shook his head. "Not much. In the beginning, we remained together, but they pulled Rowan away, then eventually Ace, too. The rest of us were put with the general population, sent to war, or left to mull around."

"They should give you jobs. Imagine what vampires could do for the economy if you all worked. I mean... *someone* is making money. You're all loaded." I finished my cheese sandwich and put my feet on the dashboard.

He nodded. "I'd love a job, so long as it didn't take me away from making sure you were fine. They can't put us to work. How would we disappear for battles?"

Only the car lights banging down the highway in the opposite direction broke the darkness, but it hit my eyes like an assault every time. *Maybe I'm getting a headache?* They almost had an aura. "I'd say battle is going to take you away from keeping me safe."

"True, but Griffin doesn't fight. They leave him to read and read. I'm not sure and he's not even sure what they want from that, but he'll never leave you. I'll come and go. They do like how I fight."

I didn't want to think about it. Vampires fighting vampires seemed a myth too ridiculous to consider. Where did they have their epic battles away from human eyes? Satellites never picked up the action? It seemed nonsensical. However, I was seated next to someone who had done it, so I had to believe it happened. He didn't lie.

"And, Tanner? How do you guys handle him? Griffin came looking for you, so you two must still be in each other's lives. How do you deal with someone not talking?"

He tilted his head. "Tanner is very good in battle, but you're right. We don't have a real relationship anymore. I do understand him in the sense that my vampire understands his. We communicate about blood and other things that way." He was quiet for a second. "I think you're overthinking how we handle friendships as vampires. We don't really care about things the same way anymore."

"Really?" I lifted my eyebrows. "Because you seem to care about Griffin, and he cares about you. I may be over-thinking it, but it's possible you're underthinking it, too."

"Maybe."

It felt like a win, so I smiled.

He took my hand in his "I can take care of myself, if it comes to that. I have before, and I'm sure I will again, although I appreciate you wanting to. That seems like friendship, too."

There he goes again, seeming human. It was so easy to forget and so completely devastating to my heart.

Griffin's coffin lid creaked behind me as he pushed it open and I forced myself to continue looking forward; I didn't need that imagery. *Not ever again.*

I ALWAYS WANTED to see the country, and I suppose I did, just at night from a mobile home. From gas stations and houses they rented for me to spend my days. They all blurred into one place after another, but I saw signs on the highway, indications of my progress toward my new home with the vampires—not just driving endlessly nowhere, from one highway to another. *Cheyenne. Lincoln. St. Louis. Nashville.* They were avoiding detection with me so we went a way that Caesar thought was best. Beyond those were a million other places that I didn't recognize the names of but were part of my strange road trip with them.

We fell into a routine. Caesar drove the first part of the night, until we stopped for gas; Griffin took the second part. Neither of them had to feed, and I wasn't in withdrawal. After the second night, it started to feel really companionable. On a journey with two gorgeous vampires who occasionally told fascinating stories about finding people to bite and making them forget it ever happened to them—that was a vampire gift they all had, but no one had ever used on me. They all wanted me to know that I had been their prey.

Eventually, we pulled into a home fifty miles outside of Asheville, North Carolina. Aside from fighting off exhaustion, I didn't want to wear their clothes anymore, and my overall mood shifted to cranky. Still, the idea of being on the east coast of the country filled me up, so I bounded out of the vehicle with energy.

Caesar nodded toward Griffin. "Get her set up. I'll bring

in the coffins. Last night in them. Tomorrow, we'll darken the place up so we can sleep in beds. I'm going to get rid of this thing before dawn. It draws too much attention. We'll have cars soon, too."

Griffin nodded and escorted me inside the house. They'd bought it for me, sight unseen. It didn't feel like mine, and I didn't think it ever would. It was their house, and for the moment, I would stay in it. Caesar proclaimed it mine, but him saying it didn't make it so. *What would I even do with something like this?* It was too much. I could argue but the futility of that was beyond me. They'd win the argument. If I just kept my thoughts to myself and knew the truth, it was good enough.

"If you look out that window in the morning, you'll see a creek. I thought you might like to have a view. I thought the woods would remind you of some of the nicer places in Kentwood. Well, there's a creek there now, but you can't see it. Four bedrooms. Two baths. It's fifteen minutes from the rest of the vampires. Just far enough, they never come over here. They won't find you, but we can come and go easily to be with you."

I touched his arm. No matter how much I tried to make myself stop doing those things, I couldn't help it. I needed to touch, I expressed myself that way. "Griffin, this is lovely."

"Good. Take a look around. Pick a room. We're going to install real darkening curtains tomorrow that will allow us to stay here during the day. The decorations are from when the rental company owned it, but we thought it would be easier to have the basic furniture already here. Obviously, if you hate the stuff, we'll get new things."

I laughed, walking toward the kitchen. "You think I have taste in furniture? I never thought to have anything like this in my life, not even to visit. I'm grateful for anything and this is gorgeous."

In the white kitchen, all of the appliances looked new. The table was laid out with plates and silverware like someone staged the place. All of the bedrooms offered the same king sized beds and white comforters. But the best part was a clawfoot bathtub I discovered in one of the bathrooms. They said to pick a room; I wanted the one connected to that bathtub.

"This one, if that's okay." I called out to Griffin who grunted his ascent.

A few minutes later, they installed the coffins into two other bedrooms, which I guessed now belonged to them. Caesar left. All of it happened so fast, I wasn't sure what to do with myself at all. Everything had been about getting to this place. *I'm here... now what?*

I sank to the floor in the bedroom and pulled my knees to my chest. Griffin found me there minutes later.

"What's the matter?" He sat down next to me.

"Now what? What do I do now? I'm here, so do I just hide in this beautiful house forever? What do I do?"

He tugged on the edge of my hair. "No one knows you're here. If I have my way, no one will ever know. You can make a life here during daytime hours. The daywalking vampires don't go shopping or to school. They don't have jobs. They only did those things when they had to because of us. Now, if they wander around, it's inside the compound. Most of them prefer to sleep. Do whatever you want. What did you want to do when this all went to hell for you? Remind me. Did I know?"

I swallowed. "I wanted to get out of town."

"Okay. Well check that off. You did it. What else?"

That's a very good question. "I wanted to graduate high school."

"Ah yes, okay. Do that. Graduate high school." He rose as if he just solved all my problems right then and there. "I'll leave my credit card on the counter. Use it tomorrow. Get whatever you need, sign up for whatever you want. Make a life." He looked over his shoulder. "But spend your evenings here with us."

Could it be that simple? *Make a life.* How did someone go about doing that?

My stomach grumbled. *Well, first things first.* I'd eat, unless Caesar had taken all of the food with him.

As it turned out, he hadn't. It was all on the counter. I stared at the various foods we had purchased on the road. It looked a little bit like I was a twelve-year-old boy trying to eat as much junk food as I could. Chips. Dip. Popcorn. At some point we abandoned all pretense of nutrition for me. *I need to do something about that.*

"I need to go to the grocery store tomorrow."

Griffin nodded. "Caesar will come back with a car. Use it. My credit card. Get whatever you need. Anything at all."

"Thank you."

He couldn't answer my *now what.* No one could do that but me, but I wasn't going to be locked in this house. I should go try and have a life.

What was a life?

"Do you remember that hypothetical you sent me that one time? About the miners and needing to kill someone or not?"

He nodded. "Sure."

"How would you answer it?"

"Now?" I nodded—yes, that was what I wanted. I didn't

want to know how the dead Griffin would have handled it. I wanted to know how this one would.

"I'd kill the injured miner. Why would anyone do anything else?"

It's just what I thought he'd say. Life had a simplicity for the vampire in some ways, and it was in those ways that I envied them.

7

How does a person make a life? In my borrowed clothes, I sat down to make a list. I managed to sleep for about four hours, so it was almost ten o'clock as I ate my sugar cereal and stared at the list. Mismatched stuff filled the kitchen. None of the plates were the same. The previous owners obviously didn't care about that when it came to their guests. I didn't really care either, but maybe if we stayed for a long time, at some point I'd do something about that. I wasn't some kid who was about to go on a spending spree just because I could because of Griffin's credit card in my wallet.

I will use it sparingly until I get a job.

Well, there's something to write down... a job. I need one of those. I added to *finish high school* and to stock this place with food that wouldn't make me sick if I ate too much of it. I needed clothes. A glance out the window told me Caesar had brought a car. The keys on the counter probably belonged to it.

So the first thing I have to do is figure out how to get my GED. A quick search told me, in North Carolina, if I took the test in-person, I didn't need to complete any mandatory prep. *That's good.* I might still buy a book just to see what to do. I tapped my pen on the counter. I was starting to have a plan. *Maybe Griffin was right after all.*

With that in my heart, I got busy getting busy. After another search showed me nearby shopping, I got down to it. By the end of the day, I successfully bought clothes, groceries, and applied for a job in the store where I had done both of those things. Finally dressed in clothes that fit, I spent the rest of the afternoon wandering around the town to see where I lived. It was small but beautiful and the mountains in the distance were stunning to look at.

Maybe I would've loved anywhere new, but it really seemed the absolutely most breathtaking place I could've imagined. The house was really beautiful, too. I spent time walking around the creek, trying to make sure I didn't accidentally end up on someone else's property. It was hard to tell where theirs began and Griffin and Caesar's ended. I had to guess. In any case, it was also stunning.

I cooked myself some dinner, a chicken that also included salad this time, and I'd cleaned up when the feeling of withdrawal hit me. I stopped and leaned against the wall. Goosebumps broke out on my arms, and I rubbed them away. Caesar's face passed through my vision like he was with me, even though he was in the other room. He was hungry. When he woke up, he would need to feed. *There it is.* If I still doubted whether I could tell when they were in need, I found my answer. *I'd known Griffin needed it, and now Caesar.* It had been almost a week since Caesar needed to do it, an incredibly long stretch. I didn't think even the elders went that long without.

He'd taken the bedroom closest to mine and Griffin was in the room next to his. On quiet feet, although I supposed it didn't matter, I made my way there. I kicked off my shoes and got into the bed next to him. The sun had just gone down in the sky. I'd never paid such attention to the shifting from day to night as I had the last week. It was like I had two days in one, when the sun was out and I was alone and what happened after the vampires got up.

I didn't mind being alone, but I did like it better when they were awake. Caesar moved on the bed, a pained look coming over his face. He really didn't like waking up. Being hungry probably made it worse.

"Hey," I whispered to him. "You're hungry. It's okay. You can feed. It's fine."

"Maci," he whispered my name. "How did you know?"

That was the question, but not one I had an answer for right then. The immediate problem was his hunger. The why of how I had managed to connect to him so closely that I knew he needed to feed before he did was something for later, if it was ever solved.

Caesar scooted closer then bit my neck. I closed my eyes, pleasure rushing through me. I'd never get used to this part, never take it for granted. If I was lucky in the past, numbness was the best I could hope for. This was a little piece of heaven. My nipples hardened, and I reached out to grab his shirt, aching to hold onto him.

Caesar adjusted, one arm sliding under to give me support and the other drawing me closer as he fed. He wasn't starving but he needed. I wanted to provide. Heat creeped up my spine, engulfing my body, and settling in my pussy. I pressed my lower region against his hardening length. We were both dressed. Nothing was going to happen here while he fed, yet I needed the connection, something to anchor these feelings to.

I sighed. I'd always wanted Caesar, even back when he

was the teenager who didn't sleep well without me. There had been an ache for him then, too.

The hand that held me close dropped lower then he pushed his fingertips beneath the elastic waist of my pants. I moaned in anticipation. Yes, that was what I needed. Maybe I'd been wrong? Maybe it *could* happen while he fed. I didn't have to guess what he found when he pushed my panties to the side and slipped two fingers into my wet heat. I wanted him. There would be no question about that.

"Please," I whispered to him.

Against me, his body seemed to vibrate. Maybe he'd liked that. Caesar found my clit and, in a circular motion, started to stroke me. My breathing sped up, my breasts tightening in anticipation. I didn't want to do this alone. Yes, he was feeding, but he was hard, too.

I did as he'd done and slipped my hand beneath his pants waistband, finally finding his cock and stroking him, long and hard.

Against my neck, he moaned, eventually pulling off to lick the wound closed.

"You didn't have to stop feeding." I don't know I found the words. I could barely speak. It was more like I panted them out.

He kissed the edge of my chin, then the end of my nose. "I was done. Full. At some point it's just indulgence because I love how you taste." He closed his eyes. "Thank you for the wakeup like that."

"Inside of me." What he was doing felt awesome, but it wasn't the same as having him deep within my core.

He grinned against my mouth. "Yes, incredible. Yes."

We fumbled around, ridding ourselves of clothing until, in a swift move, he pulled me beneath him. "I want to feel you come around me."

"Can't think of anything I want more." In fact, it was *exactly* what I hoped would happen.

He kissed the edge of my neck and then down to my breasts, taking one of my nipples between his teeth. When he nipped me, I cried out. *Well, that was unexpected.* I thought he'd just get down to it, but clearly Caesar had other plans. We were both beyond ready, yet he took his time. Caesar made love to my breasts. The more that he sucked, the louder he moaned. *Or maybe that's me?* It was hard to tell which one of us was more turned on as he sucked and I squirmed.

"Caesar," I begged, not sure I could take any more of his sweet torture.

He lifted his head. "Going to build up your tolerance for this. I intend to spend entire nights doing nothing but sucking on your tits. Hours of it, until you're begging to come. But not tonight. Tonight? I'm going to give you what you want, because it suits me to do so."

He was such a vampire right then, I almost rolled my eyes. Spoiling the moment seemed like a bad idea when I was getting exactly what I wanted. *If he wants to think he can order me around, we'll just go with that.* At least until it didn't *suit* me.

We shifted only slightly until he pushed inside of me. I cried out at the wanted invasion. He wasn't gentle, but that was fine by me. It was just what I needed right then. Over and over, we came together, me lifting my hips to meet his thrusts. I ground myself where I needed to feel him until we were both moaned again. The bed creaked and bumped.

I hung on for dear life until I exploded around him. He grinned for a second before following me into the moment.

I panted as he pulled me against his chest. It was nice,

and I forced my eyes closed before I could ruin anything by overthinking.

Outside, thunder grumbled across the sky. I lifted my head, pulling back a bit, and he rolled to the side. "It was blue skies all day."

"It upset you when Griffin went silent after you had sex, but with me, you want to talk about the weather?" He smirked. "Yes, it's thundering, which sucks, because I have to go. As soon as Griffin wakes, we have to make an appearance at the compound."

I leaned up on my elbow. "Do vampires hate the rain? Do you melt in the rain?"

"Everyone hates the rain, even vampires." He kissed my cheek. "That was fun. And thank you for using your magic powers to know that I needed to feed. It was awesome to wake up like that, again. Much, much better than the ache that settles on me when I wake up hungry and have to seek a human to fool into feeding me. Or bothering with a servant. Or someone who is hanging around just hoping they can be one."

I ran my fingertip down his chest. "How are the servants? They were my friends for all those months, or close to it. My bunkmates. How are they?"

He winced. "Can I admit I have no idea? I've never given them any thought. I suppose that makes me as bad as the others."

"Not unless you're trying to hurt them as some kind of game. But, yes, you should know who they are, ask what they're doing or feeling, because that's polite. They're waiting on you." A thought dawned on me. "Do you know the names of the paramours?"

"Not at all, and I don't need to know them. Parading

around in expensive clothes and carrying on like they've won an award? It's eye roll worthy."

I wondered if he understood what he'd just said. "Listen, I didn't like them either when I was there. They're not great people, but you're essentially keeping me like a paramour. Paying for me. Fucking me. What's the difference?"

"A world of difference. We have known each other since before I was a vampire. I think if I couldn't buy you anything, you'd still be hanging around, or at least I hope you would."

I kissed his chest, feeling his bare skin against my lips. "I would. Maybe some of those women would, too. We don't really know them. I don't know that I can make grandiose statements about what they would or wouldn't do."

"You're being too kind to them." He rolled over. "Griffin's up. We need to go, but we'll be back later. Then you can tell me about your day. I'm curious about what you did."

I nodded. "Sounds good. Oh, I noticed there is no television here, if you want to get one. I would have bought one today, but I didn't realize it earlier."

"Yes, television. We'll come back with one. It won't be terribly long."

I wrapped myself in the new bathrobe I found while shopping— white and soft, slightly too big on me, and I'd always dreamed of having one just like it. Griffin stepped next to me as I exited the bedroom, coming out of the bathroom. He smelled like he'd just showered.

"You look cozy."

"Thanks," I kissed his cheek then froze. *Should I not have done that?* He squeezed my arm in response, so I supposed it wasn't too much of a misstep. "Have a good meeting or whatever you're doing."

He rolled his eyes. "It'll be dull. Full of battle plans and a discussion about getting rid of the Betrayer. It's always that. This war has waged forever. Rowan is doing a great job with new plans, but really... even if we do beat him, what will we do with ourselves then? I'm going to sneak away and grab books to bring back here. They won't notice I've left once they've noted that I'm there."

Whatever worked for him. I wasn't sure I'd ever really understand their society. When it had been Fredrick running things alone, there weren't meetings. Or if there were, I'd been unaware they were having them.

On that note, they left. I stretched my arms over my head. I'd wanted them awake, and now they were already gone. I did get a heck of a roll around in the sheets with Caesar, so I guessed I didn't get to complain.

After a while, there really wasn't anything else for me to straighten or make look nicer. I'd never lived in such a beautiful space, so for as long as I was there, it would be kept up really well. I wouldn't take it for granted, that just wasn't in my nature.

The rain let up a little bit outside, still coming down but not heavily. The previous owners had placed three rocking chairs on the porch under an overhang. I flipped on an outside light and thought it looked like the perfect place to sit, rock, read and watch the rain. Sure, I might seem like I was ninety years old, but what else did I have going on right then? My phone wasn't great on a good day, and if I spent too much more time searching on the internet it might just totally die and have to charge, which one day it just wasn't going to do anymore.

I didn't get it from a reputable store, but one I was pretty sure had sold it to me on some sort of black market for phones. It wasn't like I could get it fixed. I needed it not to die for as long as I could. Which meant that with no television and no company, I would instead read a book like someone's grandmother and pretend that was absolutely something a person my age should be doing.

I could go out and find a social life. What did people do in this town for fun? Maybe I'd find out as I met people at work, assuming I got that job.

With all of it heavy on my mind, I sat down to read another vampire book Griffin had left behind. That was pretty much my reading material at the moment, if I didn't want to study for the GED, which I had decided I would spend part of the next day doing. I would also buy some fiction. That was on the agenda big time. Or maybe I could look up some things online—when I had the phone officially charged—and see what some people were reading in college level classes.

That could be fun. If I managed to pass the GED test, maybe I'd enroll in community college. Work. Put myself through, maybe eventually even make it to a four-year college. Sure, it might take me decades, but clearly I would have time to fill in between vampire visits.

If I stick around that long.

In the meantime, I read my book and tried not to yawn. The really thick, dense material basically charted how vampires moved from season to season during the Middle Ages. *Why did anyone write this crap down?*

Thunder boomed again; seconds later, the rain picked up. How much time had passed? I yawned again and checked my phone. A strong sense of withdrawal hit me, and I grabbed my now-pounding head. *Okay. I have to focus on something else.* There was nothing I could do about the fact that, for some reason, I needed to be bit again, even though I had Caesar bite me earlier that night. Previously, I needed to be bit up to four times a night. It wasn't so weird I needed them to feed again. No, it had been odd that it slowed down. *I have to keep my head about this.* Did one of the guys need to be fed? My sense of someone needing didn't come. If either Caesar or Griffin needed me, I didn't know which one. *Maybe they are just too far away for whatever this weirdness is?* If it was that at all.

I needed to think about something else. Anything else. *Okay. What was I doing before the need hit?* Time. *Yes. How much time has passed?* I looked back at my phone, rubbing my head. Surprisingly, several hours. I wasn't sure I could give a report of what I'd read if I had to, but I understood the gist of it. *They moved around because...*

Lightning flashed again and movement caught my eye. *Is someone there?* It was dark except for the lights over my porch and the distant flicker of my neighbors' homes, but no one was close. Certainly, no one came to greet us, and I really doubted they'd show up at almost nine o'clock at night.

The blurred image moved forward, fully visible for the first time to me as he got soaked in the rain, staring at me from about six feet away.

Tanner. It was Tanner.

I gasped. With my phone in my hand, I tried to think past my terror. *This is bad.* What is he doing here? How did he find me? Had something happened to Griffin and Caesar? I shot out a text to them. Two words: *Tanner here.*

He hadn't moved, but I would have to soon. I stumbled to my feet, the pain of withdrawal making it hard for me to even do that, and I had to grip the chair.

"Hi." It was probably a stupid thing to say, but I had no idea how to greet Tanner after so much time, knowing he couldn't talk. "I know I shouldn't be here. I know. It's a long story. But listen... I'm not okay. That's probably obvious. If you're going to do something to me, I'm not sure... I guess, I don't know what to say to you. Are you here to hurt me?"

That last question is really the most important.

He hadn't moved. Rain pounded down on him, showing just how intimidating Tanner was in that moment. Somehow, being a vampire made him bigger, or maybe that was just in my mind.

I swallowed. He couldn't answer me. Why had I asked?

My knees gave out. One second, I could stand. The next, I couldn't, but I never hit the floor. Tanner was suddenly there, holding me up, my breasts pressed against his hard chest.

He stared at me, his eyes tinged vampiric red. Still, his hold wasn't painful, gentle but firm.

Tanner carried me into the house, putting me on the counter so we were eye to eye. He let go of my waist so that he could take my hands in his. In a swift move, he flipped my hands over and examined my wrists, a frown forming on his face. He ran one finger over one of my scars.

"I know. It looks bad."

If he heard me, he made no acknowledgment of any kind. Instead, he proceeded to check my arms and my neck. Finally, he lifted his gaze to meet my own. I swallowed.

"Tanner, I know this is weird. I know it is, and I know you're breaking rules by being around me, but could you bite me? Please? It hurts until I'm bit. It used to be constant, but now I can't tell when or if I'll need it. Please. I don't know if..."

Whatever I would have said, stopped because he tilted my head back just a little. In a smooth move, he placed his mouth against my neck. I thought he would bite me—in fact I craved his bite—but he kissed me there instead. A deep press of his mouth against my skin. It was such a sweet gesture.

A second later, he bit where he'd kissed me. I sighed. Pleasure took over the pain, pushing it away. I knew this feeling. It was the same one as with Griffin and Caesar. This was what happened with them. Tanner was somehow the same and it was such a gift.

He caught his breath, letting go of where he sucked on me.

"Maci," he whispered my name. I jolted.

Had he just spoken or was I losing my mind? "You can talk?"

He didn't answer, going back to drinking my blood. I leaned against him. Maybe I imagined the whole thing. I smiled. *This is heaven.* My body was liquid pleasure. *Have I ever felt better than this?*

It occurred to me I was getting a little bit loopy. "I fed someone today. Don't accidentally take too much, please."

After a few more blissful moments, he pulled back, licking my wound closed. "I would never take too much from you, Maci." His voice was low, gruff, as if he hadn't used it in a long time. "I can hear your heartbeat when I feed. I could tell if you were in danger." He pulled me into his arms. "And I haven't been able to say a word since I woke up a vampire. Completely unable. You gave me back my voice. Other things, too. How did you do that?"

I wished I could give him answers. "I don't know. Truly. It's a different experience for me, too. What you're likely feeling, I am, too, and that's not normal. Or at least, it wasn't."

He visibly swallowed before he picked up my wrist. "Did Caesar and Griffin do this to you? Because if they did, I'll tear off their fucking heads and burn their bodies while their brains are still alive, so they can see it happen."

Well, that's violent. I gawked at him. "No, it wasn't them. Caesar saved me, actually. How did you know about them? Did they send you here?"

"I could smell you on them." He tilted his head in that vampire way. "I can't talk, but my other senses are very intense most of the time. So, I stole Caesar's phone, paired it, and tracked where he had been. I had to find you. Every single bit of me had to be here."

8

I let his words move through my woozy brain. He couldn't talk, but he had extra sharp senses, and he'd stolen and paired Caesar's phone. *After* he smelled me on them, which was sort of gross. I had to keep getting used to things being yucky over and over. Just when I'd get used to one thing, something else happened, and I'd have to not focus on the grossness of it again.

Okay. I pushed the thoughts away. He could smell me on them. *Fine. I'll process that later.* Just then, the sound of screeching tires sounded outside. I'd no sooner heard it than Caesar and Griffin were through the door.

Tanner turned his head slowly to regard them. It was almost more threatening that he took so long to acknowledge them than if he'd turned right away, almost like he was letting them know they posed no threat to him.

"If either of you thinks to take her from me in this moment, think again."

In unison, both Caesar and Griffin gasped.

"You can talk?" Caesar practically shouted while Griffin rocked back on his feet.

His reaction was slightly more tempered. "She gave you that back. Her blood. Like it's returned other things to us, unless you've been pretending this whole time."

Tanner ran a finger down the side of my cheek. "There has been no pretending, I can assure you of that. I'm not certain I could pretend if I wanted to. We don't lie. I couldn't have avoided my voice for so long. No, the part of me that is vampire doesn't want to talk, so I don't. That's all there is to it, until now."

He picked me off the counter and carried me to the couch. "She's a little dizzy from the feeding, I think. Do you have any juice in the house?"

Griffin crossed to the fridge. "I'll get it."

"Probably because she fed me this morning, too. It's amazing how she handles all the blood loss. It's really incredible, and just another of the many things we can't explain. She's getting stronger every time. Still, she's human. Better if we can avoid two major feedings in one day."

"Oh, but I love it." I curled against Tanner. He was here. That was just so incredible. I didn't even care about the yuck factor from earlier. It was so much better he was here.

Caesar sat on the edge of the couch while Tanner stroked a hand down my arm. It was slow, methodical. He was obviously hard, but making no moves to do anything about it.

"Tell me how this happened." Tanner stared at Caesar. While they weren't being overtly hostile, I detected no warmth between them, not like there was with Griffin. *They used to be close when they were humans. Did their vampire sides not care for each other? And how did having a side work anyway? Someone should do a study.*

Caesar squeezed my foot. "I couldn't stay away from her. I knew it broke the rules, but I haven't been able to think about anything other than her once I could think, not since waking up a vampire."

Tanner frowned. "I remember you yelling about getting to her in the beginning but not afterward. I couldn't talk, or I would've told you I had similar thoughts. It was hard to get under control."

"Well, you and Griffin are stronger than me. I never did get it under control. One rising, I woke up, and that was it. I had to see her. Just *see* her is what I told myself. I left, crossed the country, and found her near death. She didn't know she was that sick, but she was."

Griffin set an orange juice in front of me, with a straw poking out of the glass. I didn't usually buy straws, as they were a luxury I couldn't afford. But with Griffin's credit card, that had been my small splurge. Seeing it made me smile.

Tanner smoothed his hand up and down my arm. "Why is that? What happened? Who did this to her?"

His movements were so soothing. My four hours of sleep must not have been enough. I cuddled against him, and when my eyes threatened to close, I didn't stop them. I'd heard the story several times and lived it myself, so it was fine. *I'll just sleep for a little while.*

"Maci." A low voice interrupted my rest. "Okay if I stay here next to you?"

It took me a second to recognize Tanner. My mind was shut off, already drifting back to dreamland. I was in my bed but had no memory of getting there. Morning must be coming soon if he was getting in next to me. "Of course."

I think I said that. It must have been something close, because the bed dipped. "If you get out of bed, try to be careful with the sunlight. I don't know what you know about it. The sun won't kill or scald me, but it burns like hell."

I rolled toward him. "I won't."

His next words were whispers. "Sleep well and long. Have good dreams. And if I can never speak again, thank you for this miracle of my voice for even a little while. You have three protectors now."

That thought followed me into my dreams.

"How did it go?" I watched Tanner from across the room as he stared at the crystal lake in front of us. He jumped and I tried not to smile. When he got lost in his thoughts, he really got lost in them. Swept away like he wasn't there at all.

He held out his hand, and I walked toward him, taking it. "How do you think it went? Badly. No one wants war. I think they might just give Fredrick what he wants to avoid it. I can't even blame them. They have children to protect. It's bad enough the humans could one day find out about us. They don't want to put them at risk fighting other vampires. He's being more aggressive. I spoke to them, assured them that we had no intention of putting anyone's children in danger, but... you can imagine."

I wrapped my arms around him, drawing him close. "Thank you for trying. My fear is that with Fredrick, there will be almost no children born. He'll only be converting people he can control. Over and over again. Killing the women. Using human women to birth vampire babies because they're easier to get rid of afterward."

"I fear the same thing." He drew back to look at me. "The first person he'll want to kill is you. He hates you."

Well, I did publicly humiliate him once, when he'd been advocating to eliminate the rules that kept humans safe from us and us away from the humans. In retrospect, not well done on my part, but the man was a jackass and I never had tolerance for selfish ignorance. It wasn't that we disagreed—he was cruel for the point of being cruel, power hungry, and too young to be such a megalomaniac.

Or maybe there was no age limit on that.

"Don't worry about me. You have enough to do with this happening." I sighed. I didn't want any of them killed. "I love you, Tanner."

He tipped up my chin until I looked him in the eye. "I'd destroy the world for you. Any vampires who tried to hurt you would be dead in a second. Any human, too. The entire world will get out of your way, because you are the most important person in the universe."

It wasn't actually in his nature to be violent, but when it happened, he proved the most lethal of all of us. I wrapped my arms around his neck. "If anything were to happen to me, I need to know that you're going to be okay. That you're all going to be okay."

He shook his head. "My darling, there is nowhere you could go that I won't follow you. That includes death. If anything happens to you, I absolutely will not be okay. Not until I'm with you again."

I kissed his bottom lip, biting down on it lightly. "I need to feed. Is it a good time for you?"

He twirled me around until my back pressed against a nearby tree. "It's always a good time. It always will be."

I WAS HAVING such strange dreams lately, casting the guys in fantasy vampire roles when they were clearly not the same men. I didn't know who I was in the dreams, either. Couldn't I just dream about flying or something, like normal people? Or be on a boat? Or any number of things?

I contemplated the weird dreams as I drank orange juice

and ate eggs at three in the afternoon. I stared at my phone, which really was on its last legs. The screen sort of wiggled sometimes, but I had a text that I got the job. It made me smile, even though I had no one to share the news with currently. It would be hours, and even then, we might not get around to discussing it. I hadn't gotten to tell them a thing the night before.

It didn't really matter, since vampires were incredibly self-centered. I knew it firsthand and better than most. Mine wanted to protect me, and they were taking care of me. If we couldn't have daily round-up conversations, it was going to have to somehow be okay. I sighed. There were a lot of things I would need to learn to be fine about. *That word again.* I was thinking it all the time. *Fine.*

I stared at my wrists. They were a good reminder of the full situation. *Fine* was a lot better than my life just over a week ago. *Who knows where I'll be this time next week?* I needed to get out of my funk. *Somehow.* Everything was so much better with Tanner there. Since he'd arrived, it was as if a hole I didn't realize I had filled in a bit. Not entirely, but a little bit—significant enough that I could feel it.

With the hours remaining until they woke up, I studied for my GED. I also responded to the email offering me the part time job telling them I would take it and be there the next day. I'd already filled out the forms they needed online. My phone made replying and working online challenging— maybe I'd also purchase a laptop after I got paid.

I was grateful the vampires were taking care of my necessities, but I wouldn't be using them to buy frivolous things for myself, even if I requested a television. Speaking of which, the new one likely filled the large box in the middle of the living room, but it was too big for me to handle, so I had to leave it. *They must have brought it in after I conked out on Tanner as though I've never slept before.*

Forcing my mind into the zone where I could actually study proved challenging, as though doing so was a muscle I needed to flex but hadn't used in too long. I shivered and rubbed my arms. It wasn't cold, so I wasn't sure why I felt chilled. Still, I rose, leaving the book and all thoughts of anything else as I turned and walked from the house. I wasn't even sure what I was doing. My mind went blank.

I blinked. I found myself in the woods and staring at a man—*no, a vampire, because his eyes are red*—who regarded me quietly. "This is going very well. Things are finally moving in the right direction. Although I wouldn't have planned the detour that the last year was on you, daughter, I will say that we may finally get where we need to go."

The sun blazed down, the trees offering some shade, but it was still absolutely daylight out. *Did he say daughter?* "Daughter?"

"We do this every time. It's unfortunate. If I could let you remember, I would. There is very little I would enjoy more."

Well, that told me nothing. I wasn't frightened, so maybe that meant something. "You can walk in daylight."

"I'm very old. It's time to feed you. We do this frequently. There's nothing to be concerned about, because it gives you the ability to handle your current situation, and means, if you were to die, you'd change into the vampire you were always meant to be."

The vampire I was always meant to be? "What?"

"Drink this." I stepped forward and took the glass he offered me.

Right before I would have drank it, I paused. *Something is just so off about this.* "Are you doing something to me? I have no questions, no fear, and I'm doing what you're telling me to do, yet I can't even remember getting here."

"It's called compulsion, something we can do with humans. We can all make humans forget, which is how we feed openly. I think you already know that, but, yes, I'm making you do things. Stay inside tonight. There will be a battle. Rowan only thinks he's winning. For now, it suits me. Soon, things will change. You'll make it all better."

His words should make me afraid, but instead, I drank down the offering. *I've done this before.*

The memory was right there, but it slipped away.

I STOOD IN THE KITCHEN, and the sun was going down. *What am I doing here?* When had I gotten in the kitchen, and why had I gone in there? I just wasn't sure. I rubbed my head. Maybe I needed a doctor.

Need hit me—the withdrawal big—and Tanner's face flashed in my mind. He hadn't taken enough the night before and he needed more. I spun around, nearly colliding with Caesar.

"Hi," I smiled at him. "You okay?"

He tilted his head. "Hi. Yes. Were you just outside?"

"No, I was in the kitchen." I shook my head. "Why?"

"Your hair is wet. It's raining." He touched my shoulder. "Your shirt and pants, too. Are you okay?"

I swallowed. "I don't know, honestly. I can't remember how I got to the kitchen or what I was doing. It's like there's a gap, as if I was sleepwalking or something. I used to do that. I must have dozed off and walked around? Maybe outside? And then I woke up in the kitchen."

Caesar tapped my chin, so I'd look at him, making me

raise my gaze from the floor. "You do sleepwalk. I hate that. During the night, I can prevent it, but if you're doing it during the day, I have no idea how to make it stop. Are Griffin or Tanner hungry? Is that where you're headed?"

"Tanner, yes, Griffin no. Long stretch for him. Maybe tomorrow?"

He sighed. "We have to start monitoring how much you feed and when. I would love to get to the point where it's spread out for you. We can find other people to feed from and space out how much you feed us."

I grabbed his arm. "Actually, I hate that idea." They were mine to feed. It was a strange but real thought that I had to acknowledge. "And if you ever must, I'd really prefer you only fed from men."

I didn't realize I felt that way until I said it. I looked away. It was foolish of course. They might very well have sexual feelings for men, too. I didn't know how any of it worked, I just hated the idea of another woman and might be able to handle it better if it was a man.

He pulled me against him. "Other people are just food, I assure you. This doesn't happen with them. Whatever this is, it's you, not us." He kissed my cheek, lingering there. "You're magic. You've always been magic."

"Caesar," I whispered, not sure what I would say, but he let me go.

"I have to do my check in. Griffin is going to stay with you tonight, and Tanner didn't think anyone would look for him tonight, either I have to go. What are you doing after you feed Tanner?"

I took his hand and squeezed it. "I'm staying in tonight."

"Good. Then I'll see you when I get back."

Tanner appeared next to us. He didn't speak, tilting his head like he was taking in the scene. Yes, he was hungry, but the utter quietness of his movements told me what I needed to know. He wasn't able to speak again.

I let go of Caesar, who nodded to him, before I tugged Tanner closer to me. "It worked once, maybe it will again. Even if it doesn't, you need to feed. I can feel it. You didn't get enough yesterday."

He didn't move, staring at me again before he leaned over and inhaled me. He lifted his head, only to do it again. *Do I smell bad?* I'd showered and put on deodorant when I got up. *What does he scent that bothers him?*

"Tanner?"

Eventually he stopped, placing a kiss on my neck as he had the day before. With a gentle bite, he took my blood. I closed my eyes, ready for a long feeding to finally make him full, but he pulled back, closing the wound with his tongue.

"Thank you, Maci. Brought my voice right back. Again."

I shook my head. "You're not full. You're not done feeding. Why did you stop?"

"I intend to finish, believe me. But not here. I planned for us a date. Worked on it last night. Let's go. I can feed later."

No, that wouldn't work. "I told Caesar I was staying home."

"Text him. Tell him your plans changed. He doesn't own you. If you want to go out, you'll go out. Griffin's staying here. You aren't bound to the house every night."

As though he'd conjured him by saying his name, Griffin entered the room with a book in hand. "I'm going to get through this monstrosity of vampire history before dawn if I have to literally not look up from the pages."

I walked over to kiss his cheek. Griffin would never ask for affection, but it didn't mean he didn't need it. *Maybe it means he requires it more.*

"We could stay and help Griffin." It seemed really important that I stay home. I wasn't even sure I could explain why.

"No, go." He kissed my cheek. "It'll be better if I'm alone and not distracted."

Well that was no use. Tanner held out his hand. "You'll be glad you went out. Come on. Let's have some fun."

I didn't have an excuse to say no. Tanner just got his voice back. Did I really want to deny him a night out? Vampires never wanted to have fun; they wanted to torment and destroy. *Well...all vampires except these vampires.*

Taking his hand, I smiled. "Okay. But I have to be home by midnight. I'm working tomorrow."

"You're doing what?" Griffin whirled around. "When did this happen? Where are you working?"

Oh that's right. We'd never gotten around to discussing any of it. I shrugged. "You said get a life. I got one."

Tanner squeezed my fingers. "Maci, we're all very rich. You don't have to work."

"We're sleeping together." My cheeks heated up as I said it. I wasn't technically sleeping with Tanner yet. Still, I let the words hang. "It feels really icky to me to spend your money like I have any right to it. I'll use it for food and things like that, but the rest of it, I'll figure out. You've put a roof over my head and stopped my decline thanks to my withdrawals. I'm so grateful."

Griffin and Tanner made eye contact. Truthfully, I had no idea what they silently said to each other, but right then, I wasn't sure I cared. *That's how I feel, so it needs to matter. Period. End of story.*

"We can talk about this later. I'll get you home in time for you to get some sleep for work tomorrow." Tanner sighed. "Even if tomorrow is the only day you go."

"It won't be." I smiled at him. "Sure, take me out. Where are we going?"

His smirk was all vampire. "You'll see."

That doesn't fill me with a lot of confidence. His idea of fun and my idea of fun were probably two *very* different things.

As it turned out, he wanted to go to the movies. I almost couldn't believe it. I never considered vampires as movie-goers, but Tanner had rented out the entire theater for us. An old building, more of a throwback than a current theater, but there were two different stadiums for seating.

A muscle ticked in Tanner's jaw when we entered, and by the time we'd sat in our seats, I'd quit asking him questions.

"What's the matter?" If he wanted to go home, we could leave. I wanted to stay home in the first place.

"I think I underestimated how much smelling the humans would bother me. No one smells as tempting as you do, ever, but as you've noted, I'm hungry, and there are a few of them here. I don't want to feed off them around you."

I leaned closer. "I thought maybe you didn't like how I smelled. You were sniffing me pretty hard and then you didn't feed."

"You did have a scent on you I couldn't identify. I don't know what it was. It's faded. Maybe you encountered some perfume or something? Not sure how to describe it. No, you smell fantastic. You always do, but I don't want our relation-ship to be me just feeding off you. They had you for days during your trip across the country. Griffin saved your life. I'm already at a disadvantage, since apparently you're going to have to give me back my voice every rising. I need to gain footing, and it seems like the smart move to not use you like my feeding tube."

I turned in my seat to regard him. "Tanner, this is my

second date in my whole life. You took me on my only one before this. You're not in competition with them. How I feel about you is unique to you. It's us, and my relationship with them is also that way. You don't have to win. It's not a race where everyone else started ten minutes before you."

"Of course it's a race."

We were absolutely not going to see eye to eye about it.

The lights in the theater went down. I still wasn't sure what they were playing.

"It would make me feel much better about things if you'd feed until you were full. It would certainly win you bonus points."

He stared at me for a long second. "Thought we weren't competing."

"You said you were."

He was quiet for a second as the credits to a movie I'd seen advertised once began. It was a comedy, an older one from a few years earlier. I'd never seen it.

"We're in public."

I smirked. "If anyone came in, they'd just think you were giving me a heck of a hickey."

He laughed. It was an actual joyful sound. *So amazing to hear a vampire do that.* I loved the moment.

"You play dirty, Maci."

I did. That was for certain. "I don't want to feel your hunger overtake me when it gets too bad. Do this for me, won't you?"

Tanner bent over toward the screen. "Guess this is our version of making out in public."

It really was.

9

I tried to watch the movie, I really did. But soon my eyes closed, so I just felt what his mouth did to my neck and what the connection between us was making surge through my body. I squirmed in my chair, and he placed a hand on my knee, stopping me. Tanner didn't want me to move and right then it worked for me to do what he wanted.

Well, it more than worked. Still, I was absolutely not watching the movie.

After a few minutes, he pulled away from my neck, licking the wound closed. He was full. I could feel it in my bones in that way I just could these days.

"Thank you, Maci." He whispered in my ear. "I don't think I've felt this good since I first rose. I didn't know I could. So what can I do for you? How can I make you feel good?"

I had to draw the line at actually doing anything publicly. "We're a little in view for me to do much of anything right now. You sucking on my neck was one thing, but the two of us going at it in the seats seems like a bad cliché I'll live to regret in no short amount of time."

He smirked at me, the movie screen illuminating his face in colors and shadows as the film progressed. Tanner had always been so gorgeous, and nothing had changed in that regard. The lines of his face were a little bit hardened, his shoulders broadened. Like Griffin and Caesar, he was more a predator and less the teenage guy I'd fallen in love with all those months and months ago.

"Understood."

Out of all of them, he seemed the most human when I was around him, yet he was the one who'd lost his voice. He asked me to remember their birthdays, and he'd been the one to hold the gun to his head the longest. For precious seconds, I'd wondered if he considered ending it all before he could become the person in front of me.

What does any of it mean? I didn't have a fucking clue.

"What does it feel like when you can't talk? Why does that happen?"

Tanner frowned. "You don't want to watch the movie?"

"I've missed the beginning. I can try to focus on it, if you want me to." We were enough alone or maybe I was adjusting to the thought, so it wasn't like we were being bad theatergoers. He'd bought out the whole place, which had to be because he didn't want to be seen there, maybe coupled with the idea that he didn't want to go on some kind of killing rampage that ended the lives of every human.

Much as I might be comfortable with the three vampires in my life, I couldn't forget who and what they were.

Some humans never returned home because a vampire ended their life and then disposed of their body. *How many missing persons cases are vampire related?*

"It is like there are two parts of me that make up a single entity that ultimately is me. I don't know if all vampires can feel their dual nature the way I can, but for me, it's as though I have the part of me that can talk to you, talk to others, communicate with humans and the rest of the world, and the part of me that is purely different. It is only interested in feeding, in killing, and not much else, actually. While the part of me that can communicate observed things, made note of life, the other part of me just won. I didn't have balance; I had control, and then I smelled you. Suddenly, the part of me that lay dormant awakened and wanted out. But it's like this part of me slides away sometimes. It's not painful or difficult, just more primal."

He clearly couldn't have gone too far because he'd been able to pair a phone, and he certainly seemed to have a grasp on what happened. I'd never understand it, and that was fine.

"Well, I'm glad my blood helps you to push this part of your consciousness to the front. I like talking to you. Do you have any interest in singing?"

He tilted his head. "Absolutely not. That's a human concern."

Well... that's that, then. Okay. I sat back in my seat to watch the movie, but I didn't really watch it so much as I stared at the screen and tried to absorb everything. I was sure the movie would be funny under other circumstances, I just wasn't in the mood to laugh.

Maybe. Or something.

He wasn't laughing either, but I wasn't sure he would anyway. I'd never seen a vampire actually watch television or a movie.

"This is my second date ever. You brought me on my first one, too." I mentioned it earlier, but I repeated it for something to say. Filling awkward silences was something I was constantly compelled to do.

He crossed his arms over his chest. "That resonates in my memory as a really good night. A happy human memory. There really weren't many of them, and the most prevalent ones include you. And you're obviously making quite an impression on my vampire memories, too."

"Well, I'm glad to be memorable."

He leaned his head against mine. "If we're not going to watch this, and frankly I can't tell if this is a good movie or not, because I can't smell them, and that is really important to me. It's a little bit like watching stick figures running around on screen. I can't seem to really care about this story."

That was interesting. "We can go. You paid for it, though, so I feel bad for wasting your money."

"I took you out. It was what I wanted to do tonight. You feed me. I'll do things for you, too."

I don't know why his words burned the way they did. He hadn't really said anything particularly terrible, just talking about a quid pro quo. Since I fed him, he took me to a movie. It wasn't because he'd been overwhelmed with wanting to take me on a date.

I've had that version of Tanner. He's dead now.

No, this was how vampires treated their paramours. They fed off of them and bought them things. Somehow. I had to remember to treat them like a business transaction and not like people I cared about.

If I couldn't feed them anymore, they'd stop doing nice things for me.

This really isn't going to work in the long run.

They'd died and woken up with a different soul.

The trouble was, I still had mine, and I was still longing for the ones I lost.

Sex was all part of it, too. I got to have it because I let them feed. My blood gave them the ability. If I couldn't do that, I wouldn't get to have the intimacy either. My head started to pound. From one day to the next, I had to readjust my sense of morality and how I defined myself in their world. Once upon a time, the only thing I'd had was who I was. Now I wasn't sure I had that anymore, either.

"Let's go home. I need to get to bed. Work tomorrow."

He nodded. "Yes. It's still much earlier than you indicated, but that's fine. Maci, are you okay? Your entire demeanor changed."

Yeah, it's important to check how your food source is doing. "I'm fine."

My favorite four letter f word has certainly changed over time.

He took my hand, and I let him lead me to the car. Tanner didn't try to drive, although he'd directed me there earlier, he made no move to take the wheel from me. I was glad to have that much control of my life. Small but significant moments mattered to me.

Or maybe I was just fooling myself.

We drove in silence for a while, passing houses until we were back on the one lane highway that took us through a patch of thick woods. We'd eventually get to our creek house from this road. Mountain laurels and oak trees shaded the world from view, and even at night I could see they were beautiful.

A flash of red caught my eye, and I gripped the steering wheel tightly. *Did something just explode in the woods?* "What was that?"

"I don't know." He whirled around, looking left and right and then doing it again, checking all around us.

It happened again, and I caught my breath. "Should I pull over?"

"Yes, but then don't stop. Drive all the way home and don't stop. Lock the doors. Tell Griffin we just stumbled upon a battle. I'm going to see if I can help."

My mouth fell open, fear flooding me. I knew I shouldn't leave the house tonight, as though someone had told me I shouldn't. I shook my head. It didn't matter right then. I slowed the car and pulled over, finally coming to a stop.

"Vampires are fighting right now? This very second?"

He gave me a short nod. "They won't see you. They're busy. Drive home. The last thing they want is for humans to see them. Drive straight home."

"I will. You'll be careful?" Fear was like a wakeup call. The circumstances of my life were currently sucky, but I didn't want them to die. Again. I grabbed his arm. "Don't forget you can't talk. They can't know you can talk. Be careful. Who is in this battle? And what exploded?"

Tanner leaned over to kiss my forehead. "Get yourself home."

That was apparently the extent to which he would answer me. Tanner was out of the car a second later, closing the door behind him and disappearing into the woods, where every so often, something exploded red.

Vampires are fighting in there and not the friendly kind. I shivered. Why did it feel like I had eyes on me right then? I looked all around but nothing stood out. Tanner said to get home, that was what I would do.

I put the pedal to the metal and with a screech of the tires, sped down the road. The battles weren't hypothetical. They were happening right there, close to my new home.

With shaking legs, I practically fell into the house, closing the door behind me. Vampires were dangerous enough when they were just trying to feed off me, so how bad would it be if they were battle enraged? What would happen to the humans who lived nearby and had no idea what the hell headed their way?

"Maci?" Griffin strode toward me. "What's wrong?"

"There's a battle nearby. Tanner told me to come home fast. He went to see if they needed help and he got out of the car by the woods. You know that area?" I wasn't being particularly articulate, and I didn't really care. This was fucking scary, there were no two ways about it.

Griffin sighed. "Leave it to them to pick the one place where I'm trying to hide you and decide to have a battle there. Smart that Tanner got out. He'll lead them in the opposite direction."

Was that why he had done it? He hadn't explained himself, other than he'd decided to go, thereby leaving me alone in the car to be terrified all on my own. Griffin didn't seem the least bit scared.

"I'm frightened." That would have to do for an explanation. Even as a vampire, he should understand why someone like me would be afraid. Too many vampires around, too much risk of being spotted, and I wasn't going to end up their plaything again—not if I could do anything about it.

He extended his hand. "I won't let anything happen to you. They're not coming through this door. The reason they're in the woods is because humans aren't, generally, in them in the middle of the night. It's still a little early in the evening for my taste, but I wasn't consulted, so for now, I'd rather they forget I'm here so I can stay with you. It'll be fine. Come on."

My hand shook, but I let Griffin draw me to him. It might be a business transaction between us, but I'd take the comfort right then. "I can't go back to how it was. I can't. I think maybe I should go. Run far away from here. I'm sure you can all find someone else to feed you. Maybe everyone will be like me now."

"Maci..." He hugged me, which was really surprising. "There is nowhere you could go that the three of us won't follow. We can't let you go, you understand that, right? You're ours."

I shoved him away, stepping out of his arms like they'd scorched me. He couldn't have known the emotional havoc I'd just experienced with Tanner, but I couldn't leave it anymore. This was too much. It just was.

"I'm not going to spend my life being cattle for you. It doesn't work for me. I don't want you all to give me things as if we're involved in some sort of transaction. I know I'm not making sense, but there are vampires fighting *five minutes* from here. Vampires who made my life hell. You guys can't do the same, just hiding it in movies and televisions." Speaking of which, he'd hung the new television up on the wall—*actually, that was hugely nice of him.* "Thank you for that, by the way."

Griffin ran a hand through his hair. "You're not understanding how fundamentally we don't feel things the way that you do. I care about you as much as I am ever going to care about anything. You know I'm going to live a really long time? That you will be dead and buried, dust in the wind. You could have children who are dead and buried, and I won't look much older than I do right now. Maybe because of that, we're made to not really hold on to emotional attachments. Can you imagine a species that lives as long as we do if we really cared that deeply about things emotionally?"

If he had a point, he should make it, because he wasn't improving my mood. If anything, it got worse because he pointed out that, in addition to how I was feeling, I was also being unreasonable because I expected something they physically couldn't give me.

The last thing I needed in that moment was for him to call me on my shit.

"I can love. I can hold onto relationships. I may even be able to mourn who you were for the rest of my life. I may still feel the ache for the guy I knew and loved for one week when I'm eighty years old and still feeding the three of you like it's my job because your fathers made me fucking addicted to the need."

"So it's quid pro quo for both of us, then. You feed me because it makes me feel better than anything else has since I first rose, and I make sure you don't succumb to the addiction I didn't cause in you." He motioned between us, in a back-and-forth action. "Anything else that happens is actually just nice, right? A thing that friends do for each other or whatever."

I rubbed my eyes. "You're never going to understand it, because while you can apparently remember things from when you were a human, you can't feel what you did then, and I'm not being reasonable in thinking you should. Got it. Goodnight. Please don't let the vampires out there kill me. It would be really fucking inconvenient for you to have to go find another constant food source that actually turns you on sexually at this point."

Yep. I was shouting.

"Maci." He shook his head. "You understand that I'm not

trying in any way to upset you or cause you pain. I'm just telling you the truth."

Yes he was. I swallowed, tears flowing from my eyes. I didn't even try to wipe them away. "I'm always expected to change, to adapt to what you all want. I am human. This isn't how I want to live my brief life. You can comprehend that much at least, right?"

He was quiet and I waited for the next emotional blow. "I can, actually."

Well, that's unexpected. "See you tomorrow."

I almost threatened to run again, but we both knew it wouldn't happen. I couldn't live without their venom. If I did manage to escape from them, I'd be back right where I was before.

He grabbed my arm, stopping me when I would have turned toward my bedroom. "You make me wish I was human again, so I could understand you. This is all very new. Tanner only recently arrived, and his arrival threw you for a loop. We found balance with each other—Caesar, you and me. We all have to adjust to the newness of having him with us again. Don't go to bed yet. Stay out here and talk to me about things other than what's making you upset tonight. Let's leave that. Just for now. Tell me about your job tomorrow. Tell me about your GED. Tell me about what you think about the creek. Something."

For someone who only moderately cared about me because I'd be dead very soon in his lifespan, he certainly did want me to sit down and talk. I wiped at my eyes. "We can talk."

"Good." He walked to the couch and patted the seat next to him. I sat a distance away from him, giving us both some space. For my part, I really needed some right then.

"How did your reading go?"

He shook his head. "I want to hear about your waking hours, about your daytimes that I can't be part of. I know you've gotten a job. What is it?"

"You know that big super store on the edge of town? It's where I've gotten most of what I bought in the time since we've been here. I'm going to work there. I guess I'll be helping out wherever they need me. My GED test is in a week. Hopefully I'll pass the first time, and then I'll figure out the next steps. Nothing really exciting, I guess. Just getting started."

He tilted his head. "That was a lot you got done very fast."

"How did it work for you? You rose. You were locked in that building where they brought people in for you to feed from. Presumably, they all died. I don't want to know about that part, but at some point, did it change? Like, all of a sudden Rowan was capable of decision-making, and they assigned you tasks to get done?"

He strung our fingers together. "Your skin is so soft. I'm not sure how to answer your question. Rowan was just always in charge. From the moment he woke up, they treated him like he was the boss. We were just assigned to do things. They never checked to see if we had some kind of knowledge of the dead vampires in our minds. They just sent us out like we knew what we were doing, and it seemed very much like we did."

That was interesting. Why had they risked so much if they weren't going to even see if it worked? Maybe they were just so sure of themselves, they believed it had without even checking? It was just bizarre.

"I'm going to bed." It really was getting late. "I hope the other two make it back before dawn. Where will they go, if they don't?"

"They'll make it back. One thing about vampire battles is they always have a set time limit. Unless you're ancient, you can't be awake during the day, so they always finish at least one or two hours before sunlight. That way, everyone can retreat to safety before they go again. Even the Betrayer seems to honor those rules."

I yawned. "Who did he betray, just out of curiosity? Does anyone know?"

"I don't actually, but since you mentioned it, I'll make it one of those things I learn about shortly. I'm making great headway. There's lots of history I didn't know. It seems like we used to have more culture, more choices. We lived among humans forever and didn't make them venom dependent, so they were our unwilling yet stuck companions."

Despite my bad mood, I grinned at his funny description. "How are all of them? All of those people who picked up and moved because you guys did? Have they all just resettled their lives here?"

He shrugged. "Honestly, I have no idea."

"Caesar has no idea about the servants; you have no idea about the humans around you. Becoming a vampire has made you both snobs, Griffin."

He leaned back, stroking a finger down my cheek. "Snobbery is a human concept we don't give a shit about, but I can try to do better if for no other reason than it would make you happy, and I know there are lots of ways I'll never make you happy. I'll find out about the servants and the people, how's that?"

"Better." I got to my feet. "We can be friends. We can sleep together. Every so often, I'm going to be really mad about life and get pissed off about the whole situation, at least until I'm old enough to not give a shit about anything anymore."

Griffin was quiet, and I wondered if he wasn't going to answer me. Finally, he said, "It's early days for you to know how you're going to feel about anything. Give it a week before you start making proclamations."

Snobbery might be a concept that vampires didn't care about, but assholery translated just fine, that much I knew for sure. He was fully aware of how shitty what he'd just said sounded.

"Thanks for giving me the timeline for when I get to feel things. I'll be sure to make note of the proper moment I get to forecast my feelings. One question, though. Is it mansplaining if it's a vampire doing it? Should I call it vampire-splaining? Or maybe we'll just chalk it all up to you being generally condescending?"

He rose. "I don't know how this will work any better than you do. I found no record of it ever happening before, so I can't explain it, which is driving me nuts. We'll know more when we know it, end of story."

Except I was pretty sure it was the beginning of a story for me, and I wasn't at all sure I would like the ending.

10

I woke up when the bed dipped, as Tanner climbed in next to me. I considered telling him to go elsewhere. The four hours I slept did nothing for my bad mood, but my tired brain quashed the idea. I didn't have the wherewithal to handle the conversation right then, and I'd be over it by the time I opened my eyes in the morning and then it would be a thing that I'd kicked him out when I saw him after his rising.

"How was your battle?"

"We won." His grin surprised me. For a vampire, he seemed almost giddy. "Well, the battle, not the war. I led everyone further away from here. It was great."

Was there ever a more bizarre moment than this? "I'm glad it was great." Were battles *great*? Wasn't that the opposite of what battles inherently meant? Did I even know what was and wasn't anymore? *No, I absolutely don't.* "And you managed not to talk?"

"I didn't say a word. Caesar was amused, but no one else was the least bit the wiser." He rolled over until he was on top of me, then stared at my face. "I should feel badly for waking you, but I don't. I have an hour until the sun comes up. I wanted to see you. I didn't make myself clear earlier, and I want to do so now."

Great, I actually have to wake up for this kind of conversation. "Okay."

"When I put my lips on you and I feed, you give me back a portion of my life that I thought I'd lost forever. I don't know how I'll ever be able to express to you what that means. To be able to talk? That's a gift. I want to give the same to you. You feed me, and I do nice things for you, because it's the only way I can make my gratitude clear."

My cheeks heated up. That was an entirely different take than what I interpreted from what he'd said. "You're trying to say thank you?"

"In my way. Why would you keep giving me this gift if I wasn't doing equally nice things for you?"

It has to be a vampire thing. They didn't believe anyone would do anything for anyone else without a really fucking good reason—like a payment. Like someone doing something nice for them. There would never be a *just because* for a vampire.

I leaned back on my elbows which brought my face closer to his. "So, in the future, why don't you try *thank you* with me and leave it alone? Take me to a movie because you want to spend time with me at a movie and not as part of some demented payment plan? You'll build up more good will that way."

He blinked before he leaned down and kissed my collarbone. I shivered, my body waking up and wanting more, even though I absolutely hadn't fed him. The thing growing between us had nothing to do with blood. "Does this feel like a business transaction to you?" he growled.

I lifted an eyebrow. "Well, I guess it would depend on what kind of business I was in."

"You're not a prostitute or a paramour, since I know you equate the two. You're Maci Green. And, right now, I'm going to show you so much pleasure, you won't know what to do with yourself."

My heart skipped a beat. "That's quite a promise. I think I might know exactly what to do with myself."

Who was this person coming out of my mouth? *A month ago, I wasn't sexually active, and now I'm tempting a vampire into carnal acts like I've done it a million times before?* I didn't recognize myself, but I liked it just the same.

"We'll see about that." He rolled me over. "Put your hands on the headboard."

I swallowed. Maybe I had gotten more than I'd imagined in this situation? *What exactly is Tanner going to do?* I rolled over and grabbed the headboard. He pulled down my pants, slapping me once on both ass cheeks.

I cried out, surprised when I creamed at the contact. *Wow.* I widened my eyes and tried to take a deep, steadying breath. My hands shook. *I really, really liked that.* He'd hit me on the ass, and somehow it made me even more turned on.

"Tanner." I didn't know why I said his name other than because I had to.

He pressed his nose against my shoulder. "You smell so fantastic. I have to remember not to hurt you, that you're fragile." He lifted his head to whisper in my ear, "But I want to take you hard, to claim you. I know I still have to catch up to the other two."

"It's not a..." I never finished what I was going to say, because he pressed his finger inside of me. I closed my eyes. From his vantage point, he had a different way to rub. Or maybe it just felt that way because it was Tanner, and I'd never felt his finger inside of me before.

I reveled in the sensations as he stroked my clit, bringing my nerve endings to life until I squirmed against him. With my back to him, I couldn't have seen his face even if my eyes were open. *Does he like this? Is this doing anything for him, or is this all about me?* How did I feel about the possibility it was? *Fuck.* I had to get out of my own head.

That wasn't a problem, because he pinched me on my clit and my mind went blank. Nothing beyond the movement of his fingers and what he was fucking doing to me. *More.* I wanted more. I ground against his hand, making sure that I kept mine on the headboard, because that's what he told me to do.

Finally, I came. Hard. My back arched, and I almost let go as my whole body tensed, unable to do anything but react to the sizzling waves of pleasure inside of me. I panted, almost fell backwards, and only his cool finger stroking down my spine finally settled me down.

"Easy, Maci." His voice was low. "Come back to me. I want you present in your mind for this. I want you to feel what I'm going to do to you."

I swallowed, trying to catch my breath, but when I finally found my voice, it was scratchy. *Was I shouting?* I didn't even know.

He stroked a finger over my breast, flicking at my nipples. "Don't let go of that headboard. I love your body like this, stretched out so I can see all of you and all you can do is feel."

Tanner slapped my ass again, and I winced before I grinned. I loved the sharp bite of pain. "I wouldn't have thought this of you. I swear, you used to be the sweet one."

"I don't know what I used to be. Different life. Keep

those hands on the headboard, because I told you to, and don't let go."

I had to push back, I just did. "What will you do if I do let go?"

He whacked my behind gently. "That's a taste."

I smiled as I got even wetter. What was going on with me? "And if I didn't want you to do that?"

"Maci," his voice was low and right beside my ear. "My senses are more advanced than yours. I can absolutely tell that you want me to do that." He slipped a finger inside of me and I gasped. "You are just as wet as I knew you were going to be, but if you want me to slap your ass again to prove it, I would be happy to give you what you need."

No one could deflect an answer like a vampire. I dropped it. His hand stroked over my thigh as the other hand pressed against my clit. I cried out, closing my eyes. "Yes, more like that."

"I know what you need." He nipped on my back, but it wasn't to suck my blood.

Tanner really seemed to know. Second after second, he brought me close to completion before he yanked it back, stopping me from getting what I needed. It was the sweetest torture. I squirmed against him, even trying to grind against his hand, but Tanner remained in charge. I had no chance to take what I wanted, so he was going to have to give it to me.

That thought made me finally stop fighting. *Tanner will see to it that I get what I need.*

The realization changed the energy in the room, because Tanner pressed inside of me. Due to the angle, I couldn't see his long, hard cock, but boy could I feel it. He was so deep inside of me, I wasn't sure where he started and I ended.

"Fuck. This is... wow. We should have done this when we were humans. I'll never get enough of this."

I never would've survived the loss if we had, but I didn't need to say the words. I didn't want the pain right then. Not even a little bit. I wanted Tanner to keep doing what he was doing. Each thrust pushed all my thoughts away. There was only the bed as it creaked, the noises we made together, and the way that he made me cry out. The way my body pulsed around his until all that pent up frustration made me explode around his cock.

Seconds later, he found his release with a long groan, his head falling down to rest against my shoulder as I dug my hands deeper into the headboard. I hadn't let go. I smiled. *Yes, I've been very good.* I'd completely taken his directions.

He pulled me back and I had no choice but to release my obedient grip to turn in his arms, holding onto him instead.

"Got you." His voice was low.

Tanner really did have me.

At least until the sun comes up. I closed my eyes. Thoughts were back; they always returned. He was a vampire. I couldn't let my heart do what it wanted, and I couldn't fall into the arrangement with them as though it was something that was good for me. Sex was sex. Griffin had hurt me with his silence after sex. If I wasn't foolish, I didn't have to make the same sort of mistake.

Tanner laid us both flat on the bed. "Stop thinking so hard. What does it take to turn off that mind of yours?"

I laughed, snuggling against him. I'd take the minutes before he disappeared to the daylight. "If I ever figure it out, I'll let you know."

∾

I SLEPT for a few hours before it was time for me to go work. It was weird to lock the door and leave them all there. Each day, it got a little bit harder. Somehow, the same men who were violent and brutal when they had to be proved themselves to be the most vulnerable creatures on the planet during the daytime. *Until they're much older, at least.* I leaned against the front door and slowed my breathing.

I was being ridiculous. Vampires survived for thousands of years; they didn't need me babysitting them while they slept.

And I need this job.

I steeled my spine and got to it.

Luckily, I had worked for long enough to catch on quickly, because I knew how to stock shelves, take inventory, and keep my head down. They didn't know my mother, so maybe they'd put me up front eventually, but I was starting in the back, which was fine by me. *Plenty of time to learn the store.*

"So, what did you do to get stuck back here?" a voice asked, and I looked up at the woman asking me the question. She chewed gum, made a bubble, and then smiled at me. Like me, she wore a blue employee vest. Her short, blue hair stuck out in dandelion tufts of sky, and she wore a ring in her left eyebrow. I decided she had to be my best friend.

I rose from my squat in front of some toilet paper and grinned at her. "Well... I applied. I imagine you did, too." I offered my hand. "I'm Maci."

She shook my hand. "Stella."

We were roughly the same age, but if her footwear was any indication, she was funkier than me. Her feet were covered in black boots that couldn't be comfortable to stand in but made her look tough. My sneakers didn't compare.

"I thought I knew everyone in town around our age. You

must be new." She nodded at me. "Two pieces of advice. One, don't eat the hot dogs they sell in the truck out back. They're practically poison. Also, Stan is a nightmare. Don't let him get you alone. 'Me too' didn't happen here. Just don't find yourself alone."

I swallowed. *Stan? Our boss?* I hadn't been alone with him yet. He'd hired me, but he had someone with him the whole time. Then someone named Kristi had trained me first thing in the morning. Maybe Stella's steel tipped boots made more sense now.

"How bad is it?"

She shrugged. "It is what it is, right? Anyway, we'll get a drink and talk about it. I've got your back."

Did she? Did strangers just do that? The last time I'd had a decent experience with a stranger I'd ended up getting fed on by vampires and in constant fear of withdrawal. Of course, it had been the greatest week of my life.

I smiled at her. "Thanks. I don't drink, but I'll have soda."

She nodded. "Sounds cool. See you later."

Is that how making friends worked for adults? It really can't be that easy.

Stella introduced me to her friend, Kevin. He was tall and funny. So far, all the employees I met were really friendly. Maybe it had to do with them knowing nothing about my past, but they had no reason to hate me on contact. Although I didn't say anything about it, I sat with them during lunch and listened to them talk about their favorite tattoo shop. They even invited me to join them, like I was living in an entirely different world.

After lunch, I met Stan while I put price labels on things. His eyes didn't go immediately to my face but started on my breasts. I swallowed my disgust as he leered at me. I never experienced such creepy behavior at work before, despite my many years in the workforce. Usually, I ran into problems like him with the male friends my mother brought home. Internally, I sighed. *I am so over this and it hasn't even started yet.*

How bad could Stan be that I had to avoid being alone with him?

I tugged at my shirt so it showed less cleavage—not that it had been particularly revealing to begin with—and hoped it might kick him out of stunned staring and we could move on with the conversation.

It worked. He put out his hand. "I'm Stan, and it looks like you are my newest worker bee."

Fuck. I hated him. Really, *really* hated him. He was what, thirty years old? Did he think that sounding like someone's creepy grandfather would work here? Did he just want to look, or would I be forced to endure more? How much would I be forced to tolerate from him?

Things are different now. I'm not desperate for money to eat, and I could find another job.

"Maci Green." I shook his outstretched hand, quickly pulling mine back. "How am I doing so far?"

"Well, you're certainly classing the place up, making it pretty."

Maybe there is an easy way out of this. "I have a boyfriend. Maybe we could just get that out of the way right off?" Technically, it wasn't true, but I wasn't a vampire. I could lie all I wanted, even if I am usually bad at it. What I actually had was three vampires dead to the world at home, but the second the sun went down, it could mean trouble for Stan if he didn't mind his behavior.

Not that I would do that. Would I? Truthfully, right in that second, I didn't know.

He nodded. "Lucky guy, but here, you belong to me, so, yes, you're doing a good job. Keep it up and we won't have problems."

With that statement, he took off to bother someone else. I stared at him, his long brown hair swishing as he went. I wasn't sure he washed it anytime recently, and the smell of his too-strong cologne lingered in his wake. From across the aisle, Stella watched me. I nodded to her, a *thank you* for the warning. I liked to think I would have figured it out on my own, but warned was warned, and that was all there was to it.

I wanted a job, needed some independence, but it didn't have to be this one. If his behavior got worse than him just checking out my body inappropriately and saying quasi-rude things, I'd figure something else out.

I could thank the vampires for the small victory, even if I never intended to tell them anything about the situation. I didn't want Stan's blood drained just because he was a dipshit. If he got worse, I'd reconsider. Apparently, I kept a lot of darkness inside of me that I hadn't known about before. I didn't even mind it.

Somehow, I made it home before sundown, just in time to make myself a chicken sandwich and smile about my day. *What is this feeling? Contentment?* I didn't know that I'd ever felt that way before.

A surge of hunger hit, so I closed my eyes. Both Griffin and Caesar were hungry. *Well, this is a first.* So far it had been like they went out of their way to avoid being hungry at the same time. Tanner would need to feed, too, so he could talk. I finished my chicken and stuck my plate in the sink. *I guess it's time to see just how I will handle this, if I can at all.*

I was just a human girl who could do what human girls

could do, wasn't I? Or was something else happening? I just didn't know.

Caesar would wake up first. I would head to him and then, presuming I could, I would go to Tanner and then to Griffin.

He hadn't moved, so I crawled in next to him, waiting for him to wake up in the darkness. Minutes passed, and he rolled over, pulling me to his side.

"How do you always know?" His voice was low. "It's like a gift, and not one I deserve."

His mouth came down on my neck, kissing me there before he bit me. Pleasure surged, warmth flooding my every cell. I closed my eyes as he fed, his body hardening more with each second we lay pressed together. I could just feel it or I could do something. I'd had a long day and I needed more—not the way that he did, but it didn't mean I couldn't take.

I ground myself against his cock. Both of us were still dressed, me more so than Caesar. His pajama pants weren't much of a guard between us, but it was something. For me right then, it was too much.

Moaning, I gripped his shirt while he fed. The grinding felt great, but it wasn't enough. *This will work better if he's on top of me.* It was awkward, but I managed to roll him over until he was the one on top. By then, he had the idea. One handed and with maybe a smile on his face as he fed, he got his pants off and then my own.

It wasn't the most glamorous joining ever, but in seconds, he'd pushed himself inside of me.

"Yes," I said on a sigh. *This is what I need.* He filled me up, my muscles accommodating him, my body craved sex with Caesar as much as his did my blood. I physically fed him while he fueled my soul.

Whatever. I was overthinking. *Again.*

Fucking him just fucking works.

I clawed at his back, probably leaving marks, and he stopped feeding on me. I hoped he had gotten his fill and I hadn't just put him off. As he smiled down at me, I knew it was the first option. There was a fully fed, really happy to be fucking me vampire inside of me right then.

I stroked the side of his face. "Harder."

"Don't want to hurt you." He tilted his head. "Are you sure? You're human and breakable."

"Easy fix to that. If I tell you to stop, stop. And then we can be sure I'll be just fine." He pushed inside and I moaned. "Yes, more of that. Just harder. Please."

There was no such thing as too much. I had to have it.

Caesar slammed into me, and I groaned. *Yes, that.* Harder and then harder. I loved it. *More.* Maybe this was a new thing for me. Maybe it was just in the moment. I didn't care; I just craved it. The minutes went on and the door opened. We had an audience, but I couldn't open my eyes to even see which one of them it was.

If anything, it drove me harder. I wanted them to watch. Their eyes on me as Caesar and I fucked was just what I needed to send me over the edge. Caesar grabbed my breasts, squeezing them as I came around his cock. On a sigh, I let the world leave me and just felt the pleasure he was giving me. He followed me as I collapsed on top of him.

Caesar kissed me on the neck where he had bitten me earlier. "That was a hell of a way to have a rising."

I grinned at him. "Great way to end my day."

The bed dipped next to me, answering the question of who was in the room with us. *Tanner.* Vampires obviously had no sense of privacy, and I clearly didn't care. He stroked a hand down my hair, so I rolled off Caesar to get closer to him. Tilting my head, I let him get closer to my neck. "Take what you need, Tanner."

I was still naked from fucking the shit out of Caesar, yet I already had Tanner attached to my neck. Griffin appeared in the doorway, and I grinned at him. "If you still have any blood left, I'd love a taste, too."

Actually, I felt great. Remarkably wonderful. *What is this feeling? Is it happiness?*

"I do. Plenty of the red stuff left for you."

His smile was slow. "Good." He pounced on me, and I squealed. *Yes, this is happy.* Griffin whispered in my ear. "I don't like to mix sex and blood, so now I'll feed, but when I get back from this meeting at Rowan's behest, I'm going to fuck you into tomorrow."

I'd just had an incredible orgasm, but I couldn't wait.

11

My stomach growled as they left, which surprised me since I'd already eaten dinner. Regardless, I was in too good of a mood to care, so I hummed my way toward the kitchen to find something to eat. I heard them pull out and I launched into song, performing a decent rendition of a Broadway musical at the fridge while I rummaged to figure out what I wanted.

I had no warning I was about to lose the ability to stand upright.

One second, I considered peanut butter and the next I was on the floor. Pain rendered me speechless and thoughtless. Nothing in the universe beyond the all-consuming horrifying agony that scorched my nerves like fire. *This can only be one thing.* Somewhere in my destroyed mind, I recognized it as extreme hunger, a near death need for a vampire feed. I tried to figure out which one of them was in such pain. *Which one of them sank into the depths of near death so quickly that they assaulted my senses like this?*

I tried to get up off the floor. I had to call, had to text.

Something. What happened? All three of them *just* fed. Was it a car accident? Did they get set on fire? Were they dying?

The door banged open, and although it hurt, I tried to turn my head to see who it was, but I couldn't see as my eyes blurred.

Our visitor hauled me off the floor and shoved me against the wall. It didn't hurt, but I wasn't sure at this point that anything else really could. The face in front of me was recognizable, but not one I had seen in a very long time.

Ace. I wanted to say hello. I missed his face, and even though I knew he wasn't the Ace I had once known, it was so good to see him. *Beyond good. Fantastic.* If only I could think past his pain, past his need. Past the utter nightmare he brought with him right then.

His eyes, red and huge, stared at me where he'd pushed me at the wall. His mouth seemed pale in comparison to his eyes, and he tilted his head.

"I told myself it couldn't be you. The other night, when you drove through the battlefield—it couldn't be. But it was. So easy, in fact, the smallest amount of research managed to get me here. They really should have been more careful about how they betrayed us." He practically snarled as he spoke. "Are you working for the Betrayer? Are they?"

I'd do anything to find my voice, but like Tanner, the pain stole my ability to speak clearly. All I could do was cry out.

"What was the matter, Maci? Were you looking for some revenge because they held you prisoner last year? How did you make them turn on us?" His grip on me was strong. I couldn't have moved even if the other pain wasn't threatening to make me black out. I tried to talk, I really did, but all that came out was a whimper. *How does Ace live like this?*

Why was it so bad?

I'd ask him, if I could. My silence must have made him angrier, because he narrowed his gaze. "Just couldn't stay away from vampires, Maci?"

He bit my wrist. I thought I couldn't feel any more pain, that I'd reached some kind of maximum threshold, but I was wrong. It surged through me like an assault and brought with it my voice from wherever it had retreated into the void of absolute agony.

"Let go. Stop. Please. Let my wrist go." It was shaky and strained, but I was able to understand myself perfectly well. "Feed anywhere else. Please. Just, anywhere else."

Tears wrenched from my eyes and for a second we struggled as I tried and failed to pull my wrist from his mouth. It was a battle of wills and he had paranormal strength I'd never have. He lifted his gaze and met my own. For a second, I didn't know what would happen. In that second, he realized there was something different about my blood. That feeling that happened with the other guys took place with him, too.

I could see it all over his face, almost as if I could hear his thoughts.

"It hurts her." Tanner's voice boomed in the room. "It hurts her. Drop her wrist."

Ace didn't move—not even at the sound of Tanner's voice—but he stared into my eyes. I don't know what he saw there, but he dropped my wrist, licking it once to close it. If he heard Tanner, he didn't acknowledge him, and I couldn't even turn my head to look in his direction. *Are they all back or just Tanner?*

I didn't know.

"What was that?" Ace's voice growled preternaturally

low, different than earlier. I was already his prey, but if I made any sudden moves, it would be worse. Maybe that knowledge remained in the back of my brain somewhere from when a very distant ancestor used to run from wolves to get into her cave. I didn't care how I knew it, though. I just did.

"We don't know," Griffin's voice answered. "But I bet if you bite her somewhere other than her wrist, she'll let you find out more about it, like the three of us have."

Ace lifted one eyebrow; a move I'd never seen him make as a human. Was he always able to do that? Was my brain coming back online? Did it matter? Not at the moment, no.

"She's a human. Taking what I need from her will kill her."

I swallowed. "It won't. Not if you stop before it does. And I think you can. They can. Even though you're hurting so much. It's pain like I didn't know existed and I thought I understood just how bad it could be."

He tilted his head in that vampire way that used to drive me crazy, but I started to realize it translated to mean confusion. They tipped their heads that way when I said something so very off to them, they couldn't make sense of it. Maybe it was too human most of the time, but in this case, I suspected it was just too weird. I couldn't make sense of it and I'd been living it.

"How could you possibly know anything about my pain?"

I swallowed, and I couldn't help but notice his gaze fell to my neck—*probably checking out my pulse*. He hadn't taken his mind off feeding from me, and I was pretty sure it was the best possible thing he could do right then. Loaded with discomfort, I still wanted Ace to feel better. I wanted to see who vampire Ace was when he wasn't in a frenzy from needing to feed.

I missed him.

"She just does, and it turns out we know her pain, too, since all three of us were struck with it in the car. I was pretty sure she was dying, but now I see it's just you." Caesar had to be speaking through clenched teeth from the shortened way his consonants sounded as he spoke. "You can find it out, too. Like why Tanner is speaking. The things that have happened to Griffin and me. I can give you the whole speech about how this happened later, but at the moment, you can either let her down from that wall and behave like something other than an animal, or I'm going to put you down like you are one, history or not."

Was that amusement that crossed Ace's features? It was brief, just a second, so I really couldn't tell for sure.

"As if you actually could." He rubbed a hand over my wrist. "Who did this to you? Who made your wrist scar? Why do you taste the way you do? Why do I feel so... different?"

"Why did you feel so bad to begin with?" As I asked the question, he set me down on the floor. "If you bite my neck, we'll both feel better, then we can talk, okay? We don't have answers, but that's nothing new for me since I met you. Knowing something was happening that I didn't understand. If you're all there with me, then welcome to the party. Please, bite my neck."

He cupped my cheek. "They all bite you like you're their paramour and you like it?"

"If there is some rule book that only paramours can be bit on their neck, I've yet to read it. They bite me there because I like it, but make no mistake, I'm no one's paramour. I'll never be one of those kept women. Never."

He pressed his lips to my neck. "There you are."

I didn't get to ask him what he meant by that because he bit down and I closed my eyes. *Yes, that's so much better.* Any other problems or concerns could be addressed after I'd soothed the ache inside of me—that had to be from him. And now it seemed the others could feel my pain. What was that about? We were all in some kind of codependent blood sharing relationship that none of us could understand but could no longer do without.

Right then, it was fine with me. I melted into Ace, letting him support my weight. My knees didn't want to hold me as adrenaline crashed out as fast as it surged. Pain left with it and my head sagged while he fed.

I was just going to check out for a while, and that was perfectly fine with me.

Awareness trickled back. I was on the couch, lying on Ace, and my feet on Griffin's lap where he rubbed them. Was he really doing that? Griffin didn't seem like the foot rubbing type.

"She can't possibly be feeding all of you and not be dead."

Caesar sat on the floor in front of the couch. "She survived being fed from ten times a day by the elders. Somehow, she's doing what isn't possible. Why does she taste so good? Why can we feel things when it should be hundreds of years until we can feel? Why does her blood give Tanner back his voice? We have a million whys."

I lifted my head. "You're not fully fed."

While I felt much better than earlier, my joints ached. Either one of the others had crashed into hunger or he wasn't done.

He squeezed my shoulder and then seemed to stare at his hand, tilting his head. "I'm more fed. I wasn't taking anything else from you. Despite your assurances about how you can handle it, I'm not going to drain you to death. I'm never full. I haven't felt this fed since I first rose. I live in constant hunger. This is like a vacation from pain."

That was fine and good, but I didn't want to live with his constant ache as if it were my own. "Ace..."

Griffin squeezed my foot. "He can take more tomorrow. You won't feel it until he's almost risen again, if I'm understanding it correctly. And he won't ever terrify you like that, because if he does, I will take off his fucking head."

"Only if I don't do it first." Tanner spoke in a low voice; he was probably about to lose his ability to speak again. It was late for him.

Fine, I supposed they were right. I struggled off of Ace. "I'm going to bed. I have work tomorrow."

Ace shook his head. "Why do you have to work? Have they not explained to you how rich we are?"

"They have, many times. But, as I told you earlier, I'm not a paramour. I'm not living off you as some quid pro quo for taking my blood and having sex."

His eyes widened. "So that's happening with them, too?"

Obviously, they hadn't explained everything yet. "It is." I wasn't embarrassed, and if Ace wanted to have sex, we'd do that, too. I was sleeping with a bunch of vampires despite really hating vampires as a whole. I liked the three I'd been living with and probably would like him a lot, too, once he was better fed and not trying to be scary.

It turned out I didn't have any puritanical feelings about sex at all, and I liked myself for it.

Besides, the three I was sleeping with were really, *really* good at it. Why shouldn't we all indulge?

Ace changed the subject, pointing. "Is that your phone?"

I nodded. "Yeah?"

"We need to get it updated. It's not safe for her to use one so damaged. What if she needed help?"

Like earlier. I walked into my bedroom. "Not a paramour. I'll buy my own phone."

I closed the door.

The next time I woke, it was daylight. I didn't need to see the sun to know it, because my body had officially gotten good at telling. I was living a half-human, half-vampire life and my body clock adjusted accordingly.

Surrounded on both sides, I recognized Caesar and, although it took me a second to really identify the energy, Ace. I sighed. I did love being smooshed in the bed. Safety in company, perhaps, especially after years of being alone in my trailer, wondering if anyone would break in and hurt me.

Not that they could have done much of anything to protect me at the moment, since they were basically dead to the world until sundown.

"Hi," Ace said, and I jumped, nearly coming off the bed. Had I misjudged the time? *What is happening here?*

"How?" I sat up and turned toward him. He did the same. In the pitch blackness, it took a second for my eyes to adjust to the low light enough to focus on Ace.

He didn't pretend to misunderstand. "I can stay awake and resist the pull to sleep. It hurts, but I can. I've made it to about ten o'clock before I can't stand it anymore."

Really? He could? I had a million questions, but he kept speaking. "The others don't know. It's not something I advertise. I actually prefer it if other vampires don't know. It's not something I should be able to do, and it's not like I've been particularly talking to the other three here. I've pretty much been on my own since the change."

His words created more than a million queries but one most importantly. "Why do you do it? Stay up? If it hurts you? It must be contributing to your constant pain. That was the most intense agony I've ever experienced."

He sighed. I would've loved to have been in the light talking to him, but it probably would have hurt him to be touched by it, although I didn't imagine it would bother Caesar if we turned on the lamp. I leaned over him and did just that. The light was bright, and it took me a second to adjust. A quick look at Caesar showed he hadn't moved at all.

"I resist the sleep because it hurts, and I don't want to give into it. I don't like having no say in when and how I sleep. I do it because I can do it. I'm not sure I can explain it any better than that."

I supposed it would have to do then. "You could treat it like pulling off a bandage and just do it."

"That's what happens most nights, but tonight, I wanted to make sure you were okay. I treated you roughly." He took my hand in his, running his finger over my wrist.

I waited, but the obvious apology that should come didn't arrive. I rolled my eyes. *Vampires are frustrating, end of story.* Then again, so were most men, from what I'd heard. I didn't have much experience other than the men my mother brought home, and they were an outright nightmare.

"Okay, so I guess that is your version of I'm sorry. I could make a whole thing out of you not saying the words, but it would be fruitless with you and, frankly, frustrating as hell for me. It's too early for this. Let's just move on."

He nodded as though he agreed. Which part exactly did he find he agreed with? I let it go. There really wasn't a choice.

"Every vampire but my father bit you for months while we were dead. It is hard for me to contemplate that you're here. And I don't understand how what you did to me happened."

We could discuss it over and over for the rest of my life if he wanted. I had no answers. "Ace, why did you come in here like you wanted to kill me? And was it just my blood that made you change your mind?"

"No, I wanted you to go away. To run far away from here. I didn't expect to be around very much longer, since I was feeling so bad. I assumed the next battle would be my last, so I wanted you to go somewhere else before it happened. I thought these three somehow tricked you into staying with them."

That didn't make any sense. "How would they have done that?"

"I don't know. I'm not exactly in my right mind." He looked away for a second. "Somehow, you could feel what I do. It's not normal. I haven't felt full, or anything besides starved, since I woke."

Because he was supposed to be drinking from me. I blinked. It was a sudden thought, full of a sureness and certainty I didn't understand nor could I explain. But I knew it to be true, so I said the words aloud. "You should have been with me. Drinking from me. Maybe your body just understood and couldn't tolerate others."

He blinked. "Do you suppose that's possible?"

"I don't know anything about anything for sure anymore. That's a guess." We were straying away from the point. "If you didn't intend to hurt me, why did you do what you did? Vampires don't lie."

Ace shifted slightly. "I do. I stay up into daylight and I lie. I'm not built correctly."

I opened and closed my mouth several times trying to

come up with a response. "Well, then, I'll just have to figure out when you're lying I guess."

"I won't lie to you again."

Of course he could be lying when he said it, but then that was true with most people. I had to figure all of it out. "We'll just deal with that another time. For now, let's figure out what we're going to do about the sleep problem. I can't imagine that it isn't playing a role in how badly you're feeling and consequently how badly I'm feeling." My bones started to ache again. "You need to go to bed."

"I hate it. The pain. It really hurts when it pulls us under. I can't help but resist it."

I swallowed and then linked my hand with his. "You're making it worse, I bet. The harder you hold it off, the worse it gets. Tell you what? If you go to sleep now, when you open your eyes I'll be back from work. And then you can feed again and finally be full."

"I hate that you're working and that you have that shitty phone." He scowled and a piece of his hair fell into his eyes. Without thinking about it, I brushed it away. It was something I would have done for him when he was a human. If it startled him, I couldn't tell, because he didn't even head tilt.

I took a deep breath. "Ace, we can talk about it when you rise. Okay? Between one breath and the next, give into the pull. Let's turn off this light, lie back down together, and you can close your eyes and rest. Then we'll be together the next thing you know."

"There are still things to talk about. You know that we can't all just hang out in this house like we're in a bubble. The elders are still out there, not to mention Rowan when he finds out, and he will find it out."

No wonder he can't sleep. "None of which we can solve right now."

We both scooted down and I leaned over him to turn off the light. I pressed my forehead to his. "Between one breath and the next, just give in to it."

"Be careful at work. You're on your own during the day without any of us to protect you. There are eyes everywhere. Trust me, I found you just because you drove through the area where we were fighting. It's only a matter of time until you are seen by someone who you don't want to be seen by."

I kissed the end of his nose. "I am warned. I'll be careful. I made it all on my own addicted to vampire venom with no help and managed to get around, but you're right. We can't just stay in this house forever. It's the best place I've ever lived, and I never want to leave it, but I'm fully aware that there will likely be a time that I am running for my whole life, or I'm back with the vampires, or you all leave me, and I'm once again addicted to venom with no one who will help me."

He shook his head. "I've only been back a few hours with you, and even I know that won't happen. I'm amazed I made it this long. I don't know why I didn't do what Caesar did and find you. We all should have done that."

"Rowan told you not to. He abandoned me." I kissed his cheek. "Now close your eyes and go to sleep."

"We didn't discuss it, not once, but I'm pretty sure he thought he was living up to a promise. We didn't know what happened to you, so that's my guess. Rowan is the perfect vampire and part of that is never going back on your word, right or wrong. If you say something, you do it, so he did what he said." He shook his head. "I know, we can talk about it after rising. Fine. See you then."

Ace closed his eyes. "Between one breath and the next."

"Exactly." As I had no experience doing this myself it was hugely hypocritical for me to even act like I knew what I was talking about. Even so, it worked. With a shake that traveled through his whole body, Ace finally gave in to the pull. I didn't move for long moments just to make sure it was real.

I had a whole day ahead of me where I had to pretend this wasn't the way I lived when vampires were awake. The good news was Ace's pain finally fled my body.

12

My co-workers, minus my boss, continued to be delightful on my second day at work. If Stan continued to creep me out by looking down my shirt, I was willing to put up with him for the company the rest of them provided. It might not have been the best call, but after so long of others making decisions for me, it was at least *my* call. *It works for now.*

Stella and I ate lunch together outside, leaning against the back of the building. The warm and lovely sun danced golden on my skin. It was nice to remember I was human—unlike my vampire roommates, I could sit outside without discomfort and see the sun every day if I wanted. It was important for me to remember I still had a human life and not just become part of theirs.

"Do you have a boyfriend? I heard you tell Stan you had one. That was smart, but it won't dissuade him forever. I learned that the hard way."

I looked over at her as she ate her ham sandwich. "Do you want to tell me what he did to you? Or what he's still doing?"

She shook her head then shrugged. "He just annoys me. I don't let him get me alone. Once, he backed me in a corner, but that was just the one time. His uncle is the mayor, so they could get me banned from working anywhere in this town. He told me as much. Anyway, I just wanted to warn you."

I knew the feeling. "My mother had me blacklisted at home. I couldn't work anywhere they could see me out front. It really sucked. I bet something could be done about Stan, if you wanted that." *Maybe vampires could feed on him?* I didn't even wince at the thought. Maybe I was a little bit dark. Somehow, I was fine with that possibility.

"Enough about Stan. What are you doing tonight? I know some fun places to hang out and drink." She smiled broadly. "If you really don't have a boyfriend, there are some cute boys around sometimes. Well, maybe not cute, but good looking enough for one evening."

I swallowed at the thought of the death sentence it would be for any poor one-night stand. The same guys who might handle Stan if I asked them would certainly break all the bones of any human I dated, not that I wanted to hook up with anyone else. I had great sex, a lot of it.

"I'd love to have drinks sometime but maybe just to hang out and get to be friends or whatever. I have almost no experience with that, but my boyfriend is real. And he's a little bit scary, actually. Not to me, but maybe to Stan or anyone else who tried to mess with me."

She took another bite of her sandwich. "I'm jealous. I want a scary boyfriend who could make things hard on people who are mean to me."

"Oh, you don't want anything to do with the baggage this one carries around." I could be speaking about any one of the vampire boys, that much was for sure. "Besides, you'll meet someone. Plus, you should get out of here. I like you. I'd like to be friends, but I'm a big believer in getting out of places that don't make us feel wanted. Life's too short, you know? I spent years trapped in a box of my mother's creation. It's not perfect here, but it's so much better for me."

She nodded. "Someday maybe I'll leave this small town and go to another small town, and for whatever reason, it'll feel better to me, too. For now, how about Friday? Want to hang out Friday if tonight doesn't work?"

I wasn't working tomorrow at all. Then half a day on Thursday and Friday. I could probably make that work if I told the guys I wasn't going to be there when they rose. They were going to have to get used to my coming and going a bit. At some point I'd be in school, too. They might not even mind that much, it would certainly free them up to go back and forth more to their compound. And I'd make sure everyone was fed the day before and get Tanner speaking as soon as I came home.

"I think that should work." I really hoped it would.

I ATE and showered by the time the guys started to rise. My hair was still a little bit damp, but only Ace was hungry. I knew it before any of them even opened their eyes, so my radar clearly extended itself to also cover him.

I sat on the edge of the bed, watching Caesar's eyes flutter open. He blinked, reaching for where I lay when he fell asleep before he realized I wasn't there. A second later, he sat up to pull me to him in a tight hug.

"Hi." I hugged him back. He was always the first awake. With his head pressed against my forehead, I wasn't sure it was even an accurate description. Maybe he just started to come back to consciousness. It was ridiculously adorable, but I was pretty sure as a vampire he would strongly object should I use that word.

Finally, he lifted his head. "Hi," he answered. "Good day?"

"Good day." I nodded. "I worked. Getting the hang of some things, making friends with a coworker. It's good, so far."

He squeezed me again. "That's good. I'm gonna go shower. Then, since Ace is here and likely not to be sending out a text demanding everyone's presence immediately, we could go look at the creek behind the house. I've still yet to see it."

"We can do that, if you have a flashlight. My eyes can't see in the dark like yours do."

He kissed my cheek. "My phone has one. Yours would, too, if you'd let me buy you a new one."

"Nope." I kissed him back.

I'm going to look at a creek with a vampire. Those were not words I could even have imagined thinking a month ago. Griffin stumbled in the room and sat down next to me on the bed. "I'm sleeping next to you tonight. They're all pushy about it, but it's past being my turn. I'm reserving a space."

Griffin picked me up in his arms and I let him squeeze me. They were clearly changing. It wasn't just me and my strange ability to handle blood loss. No way would Griffin seek me out for a hug even days ago. I couldn't say I minded —maybe I was getting used to their vampireness, and maybe they were adapting to me, too.

"Okay, sounds good." I kissed his shoulder. "Sleep okay?"

"Think I had bad dreams, actually, not that I can remember them. Vampires don't remember dreams, but I struggled past a general sense of ugliness when I rose. It's passing. How was your day?"

That sucked. "I hate bad dreams. My day was okay. I'm off tomorrow, so I can actually sleep in. That's something to look forward to. Then I have to study."

His eyes widened. "You could study tonight. I'm good at it. I was as a human, and I carried that trait through transition."

"Not tonight. I worked today, so I just want to, I don't know, do *other* things. Caesar said something about looking at the creek."

Griffin tilted his head. Maybe the idea was just a little bit too human for him. "Is he worried it's going to overflow?"

I nodded. "That must be it." No way would I explain to Griffin that I was pretty sure Caesar thought it would be sort of a nice, romantic way to spend our time together. *Unless I'm wrong, and it's really about the creek overflowing.* Was that possible? It couldn't be, could it?

"Then good idea to check it." He kissed me again before he left the room. I didn't know why he'd exited until Ace started to move on the bed. Griffin must have known he was about to get up and need to feed. They could probably hear the rising before I knew it was happening, although they had no idea when the others were hungry. That was my own private, strange superpower.

I crawled over to him, fitting myself next to his body. As quietly as I could, even knowing the others might hear and wouldn't understand, I whispered in his ear, "I told you I'd be here."

He rolled toward me, taking a long breath next to my neck. "You made it through the day."

Ace really worried about my safety. We were only back in each other's lives—*or after-lives?*—less than a day. Why was he so convinced everything would go astray? "I did. Feed. You're hungry." A lot less than he had been, but the ache was there.

Instead of biting me, he ran a hand down my side. "When I woke up the first time, I thought you were there. I searched for you all over the room, convinced you were supposed to be there."

"I was nearby. Maybe you could sense that or smell me or something."

He lifted his head. "I'm always hungry. You can't fix that. There's no way."

"Yes, I can." I tilted my neck. "Trust me."

Ace seemed reluctant to try anything good for him. He didn't want to feed, and he hadn't wanted to sleep. It was like he got used to pain and refused the idea there could ever be anything else.

He bit down, and I settled in next to him, my body pressed so tightly against him, he had to feel it when my nipples hardened like pellets of small pain that turned into pleasure with any movement against them. I moaned and closed my eyes.

Ace squeezed my waist as he hardened with each passing moment. The minutes passed, and we did nothing but hold on to each other while he fed. The ache in my bones from his hunger passed until it vanished entirely. He wasn't hungry anymore, and I knew it before he did. His sucking tapered off, and with a swipe of his tongue, he finished feeding from me.

But neither of us moved. Finally, with a big squeeze on my arm, he raised his head. "How are you such a miracle?"

I kissed him, hard, and right on the mouth. I had no answers, but I really wanted him right then. He kissed me back, over and over again. Ace took possession of my mouth like he had every right, and I loved it.

When I would have hurried us along, he slowed me. The man seemed to be in no rush, each kiss becoming a slow, prolonged dive into heaven. I smiled against his mouth and let my mind float away so I could actually, for once, be present in the moment.

We moved like we'd done it before, even though it was our first time. Everything with Ace felt that way, as though it was remembered and not new. *Add that to my ever-growing list of what the fuck.*

"Do you know what I'd like to do someday?" he whispered in my ear.

"No. I have no idea." I discarded my shirt impatiently. He wasn't dressed from the waist up, so I wouldn't be either.

He stared down at my breasts and seemed to lose his train of thought, because he didn't tell me what he wanted to do.

I bit my lip. *That is stupid cute.* I flicked my own nipple, and his eyes glowed red for a second.

"Like that?" He flicked my other one and I grinned.

"Right now I do. It changes. I guess I'm just an enigma."

He sucked on the end of my nipple and then lifted his eyes as I moaned. "The best kind of enigma."

Are there other kinds? I might ask another time. Right then, I couldn't think, because we were pulling each other out of the rest of our clothes. His gaze traveled downward, taking in what I looked like naked, and I lifted my eyebrows. The way his breathing sped up told me he liked what he saw. Maybe I shouldn't care but I really did. I wanted Ace to think I was sexy. *End of story.*

"I remember thinking you were the most beautiful girl

I'd ever seen. I thought so before you ever spoke to me, back when I was also human."

That was pretty much the vampire way of telling me he'd thought I was pretty back when he used to think such things. I winked at him. "Thanks, Ace. I remember thinking you would be a douchebag, and then being pretty excited because you weren't."

He laughed, which seemed to surprise him, because then he rapidly blinked. I didn't let him overthink his joy, grinding myself against him before I took control of his mouth again. We both moaned. I'd never be as strong as he was out of the bedroom, but damn if I wouldn't be in control right then. I wanted him and he was going to give me what I wanted.

Ace rolled over on top of me. His grin was slow. "I think you like being on top. So do I, it would seem. We'll have to fight over it."

That sounded perfect, and just what I wanted with Ace. He surged into me, and I cried out, but not before I wrapped my legs around him and lifted my hips to challenge his control. He was on top, but I could still win our war of pleasure. Maybe we could both win, and that was the point.

Over and over, we moved. At some points, he was on top, only to find himself again beneath me. We rolled, we pushed, we groaned, and clawed at each other. In the end, when I came around his hard cock, I cried out his name and maybe blacked out for a second.

I needed Ace. Where had he been and how had I existed without his hard cock dragging every last inch of pleasure from my pussy until I might never see straight again? We pressed and pulled until he shouted my name, coming inside of me.

When it was over, we panted together, wrapped up and tangled in both arms, legs, and the sheets on the bed.

He rubbed his thumb down the side of my face. "Where have you been all these months?"

We both knew the answer, so instead I pointed out, "This is about the time when you call a meeting then everyone disappears for the night."

He smirked then rolled away, grabbing his phone. For a second, he scanned through it. "The usual bullshit. The war. Blah blah blah. The elders can't text. Hell, they can barely handle using the phone to make calls, so instead they have someone else text for them. Every night, it's the same message. Every night, I have to send a message to let everyone know when to meet." He rolled onto his back. "I'm thinking tonight we don't have a meeting."

I leaned onto my elbow to watch him. Ace was beautiful, but I knew better than to expect any sweet words post-coitus. "Don't you think canceling your meeting will draw unwanted attention? Shouldn't you act as normal as you can?"

He shook his head. "Those three weren't exactly acting normal. Besides, I'm just not having a meeting tonight; it won't make waves. But make no mistake, this won't stay hidden. Not for very long, anyway. We'll be in the public eye soon, and Rowan will know before that."

Truthfully, I missed him. With the other four back—well, sort of their vampire versions, anyway—it really didn't feel right to be without Rowan.

But these guys knew him as a vampire, and I didn't.

"How bad will it be?"

He raised an eyebrow. "Depends on which Rowan shows up. I told you, he is the perfect vampire."

I took his hand. "Funny, I'm pretty sure they would have said that about you, too."

Ace tilted his head. "Yet I'm the poorest made vampire ever." He got out of bed and dressed while I watched.

I could just go to bed right then. It would be easy—I'd lie down and let the whole day go. I was human—or at least I assumed I was, despite my ability to feed four vampires with no issue—so I was supposed to sleep at night. But if I did, I'd never get to see the guys. *Somehow, I have to make this work, even if it means sleeping at odd hours and always being a little bit tired.*

Or maybe the blood loss made me tire. *I bet I'm really anemic.*

I gave myself a minute to reset before I dressed and followed him out to the main room. They stood in a circle, and all glanced my way when I entered. "Did I catch you in a private conversation?"

"I was just telling them what I told you—that Rowan will know about this." He looked over his shoulder at me. "Pretending he won't is ridiculous. The elders hurt you, they abused you."

Caesar crossed his arms over his chest. "Not your father, but the rest of them, yes."

I walked toward them, the blow of the air conditioning bringing a chill to my skin. Or maybe it was the memories of which he spoke? Not long ago, I'd been at the mercy of those vampires. I could be again. I needed to remember that, even as the trauma started to fade from my mind. It was as though every feed I got from these four took me further and further from that time.

"Why is that?" Ace looked at me. "Why did my father not feed from you?"

"Maybe he prefers something in an AB negative?" I

made a bad joke, but it seemed like someone had to say something about blood type. Tanner rolled his eyes but smiled at me. I walked over to him and extended my neck toward him. He pressed his nose to the curve of my skin for a second before he took what he needed. It was always almost nothing. Seconds later, he pulled away, visibly swallowing before his voice must have returned.

"That's a myth you know. We can't actually taste the difference between blood types."

Griffin rocked back on his feet. "Speak for yourself. I can taste differences. I can tell blood types."

Ace ran a hand through his hair. "Really? I can't."

"Me either." Caesar sighed. "We all have our strengths. Listen, I agree. Rowan will eventually find out, but I don't trust him to not take her to the elders and have her executed. Not to mention all of us. I'm more concerned about Maci, but we'll die, too. The question is why the elders were so intent on harming her in the first place. She was a human girl we made friends with for one week before we died. We held guns to our heads and insisted she be around to be brought to us when we came back. They didn't have to do *this*. And they certainly never acted like they were taken with her blood like we all are. I think our first and foremost concern isn't Rowan, but the elders. She can't be taken to the elders."

I walked away from them, looking for cookies. *Do we have cookies?* I was pretty sure I'd bought some. After a second, I located some gingerbread cookies—perfect. I took a bite and the sugar rushed to my mouth. I never wanted to give up the chance to eat these kinds of things. They'd been a total treat for me growing up. I basically got to eat them if someone sent them in for birthdays at school. Someone else's birthday, not mine, since my mother hardly ever remembered, not that we would've had the money to send snacks for the whole class anyway.

When the school eliminated people bringing in birthday snacks because of food allergies, my gingerbread cookies disappeared. Cupcakes, too. I closed my eyes and chewed. With my eyes still closed, I spoke to the room. "Do you ever miss eating?"

I opened my eyes to see why no one answered and found them all staring at me. Ace shook his head. "We're talking about your possible death, and you want to talk about food?"

I rolled my eyes. "Yes, that's exactly what I want to talk about. One hundred percent."

Griffin walked over then put his arm around me. "It depends on the food. Cooking food smells like death to me. I don't like the scent. It's nauseating, actually, but something like that cookie smells like nothing. I miss the concept of eating. I never tasted anything as delicious as your blood, so, no, I don't miss eating. Do any of you?"

After their resounding *no,* I smiled. It was sweet, in a vampire way. I was basically their personal feeding bag. At some point, I'd clearly become okay with the concept, even sort of flattered over the whole thing.

"Speaking of death..." I set down the cookie bag. "Griffin killed a vampire to save my life, and that was just damned amazing." I kissed his cheek. "But I need to be able to save myself from vampires. I don't want to be the feeding tube for other vampires, just you guys." *And maybe Rowan, if he doesn't try to kill me.* "How can I defend myself? Can someone teach me?"

They stared at me as if I grew two heads, but finally Ace spoke. "I need to hear about this vampire you killed, Griffin.

I've really been left out of doing anything for you, Maci. That being said, I'll teach you. We can start tonight."

"Great." The cookie made me thirsty. *Water is the name of the game now.* "It isn't that I don't worry about the elders. Trust me, I do. But they've already destroyed me. I don't have a death wish, but that's all they have left to do to me, so if I spend too much time worrying, they win. You know what I mean?"

Tanner sighed. "I don't but maybe it's a vampire thing."

"Maybe it's a Maci thing." Griffin squeezed me. "Since we don't have a meeting tonight, thank you Ace, let's go look at the creek. We have a house with a creek. We should at least go look at it."

That sounded like a plan.

13

It turned out looking at a creek in the dark wasn't very exciting, even with the help of Tanner's flashlight from his phone. The guys could all see just fine, but I didn't know if they were overly moved by it, either. We sort of stared at the creek for long moments before we walked back inside my little house.

I touched the side of it when I entered. When Caesar and Griffin arranged the place, I believed I could leave if I wanted. I'd run, if I had to. At present, I wasn't so sure I *could*. I loved the house. I'd never in my life had so much company, so many people who cared about me—even if that was because I fed them and made them feel better. Whatever their reasons, it worked for me.

I loved the building.

It might be the first place that ever resembled a home for me.

"I'm going to update your phone tomorrow, and I'm going to pay for it." Griffin walked past me into the house. "I'm letting you know before I do it, but I can't stand that your phone won't even run the flashlight. You can be annoyed with me for a few days, but you can do it with your new phone that works, so I'm not worried it's about to fall apart. Money is meaningless to me. I'm spending it on you."

I opened and closed my mouth. "I thought you understood how I felt about this."

"I tried to understand. I've obviously failed. I need to be able to reach you because safety is an issue. You said it yourself. I had to kill a vampire who wanted to kill you. Now you want to be taught to protect yourself in case we're not around. The key to keeping you alive might be for your ability to use your phone in an emergency."

I sighed. "Griffin..."

"You're not our paramour. We get it. That's not what you want to do, and I'm not trying to force the issue." He tilted his head. "But you have to let us take care of you or this isn't going to work. Not because you give us blood and sleep with you, but because we're friends, right? That's what we are and what we once were?"

Oh, Griffin was so manipulative. He really was. I scowled at him. "Fine. Thank you for the phone. I am aware of what you just did there, and I want you to know that. I wasn't fooled or stupid about it. I'm saying yes because you're right and it's going to be a good long while before I can afford to replace it myself."

His smile was huge, which took some of the sting out of giving him his way. "Great."

"How did you kill the vampire?" Ace leaned against the wall watching us. "Also I'm more than a little jealous that you got to do that. I'd kill a vampire for you any day, Maci."

Tanner nodded. "Me too. Give me a vampire to kill and I'll do it."

They weren't even hungry, but their bloodlust was there just the same. Caesar watched me, not saying a word. It was funny, even Griffin didn't have the same experience as

Caesar and me in the beginning. Only he really saw me with the other vampires. Only he understood what my life was like.

Did he know what it meant that I was asking for help to never be put in that position again? Even if I had to beg a vampire to feed, I wouldn't have to worry they could hurt me anytime they wanted.

"You guys are so anxious to kill each other."

Ace nodded. "We're not really naturally group oriented. It's sort of evolved that way, I suppose, but I'd rather just be with all of you and fuck the rest of them. I wonder if we could read an actual history that hasn't been doctored if we'd see that we used to be more like small clan groups or something. Not this large vampire gathering that we're doing. I swear it's why things always go bad. There's too many of us."

I blinked. "They're all doctored?"

"All of them." He nodded. "It was one of the first things I noticed when I was changed and finally let out of the holding house. The books they gave us to read were different than the ones the elders have in their private library, not that I've particularly gotten to peruse them all. They still guard their stuff like it's a state secret."

Maybe those were exactly the right words. "Ace, do you think it might be worth it to, I don't know, *find out* why your dad never bit me? Like, maybe he isn't exactly on the same page with the others."

"It might be." He cupped my face. "But you asked me to teach you how to kill a vampire, so I'm going to do just that." With a nod at Griffin, he stepped toward one of the chairs. "How did you make the stake I assume you used?"

"First the stake, and then the burn. I broke the chair, and made a stake out of it fast. I don't think she can do that. She might be able to break the chair, but probably not tear off a piece of wood. She'd never have the strength. Don't be mad." He held up his hand. "It just is what it is."

Tanner nodded. "She can't be expected to do that."

Apparently vampire killing class is going to be a group activity. "There might not be a chair around the next time I need to defend myself against a vampire. I could just bump into one on the street."

Ace rocked back on his feet. "Okay. We need to make her stakes, and we need her to carry them at all times. The actual staking is something we can teach her to do, but humans have been driving them through our hearts forever. It shouldn't be impossibly hard."

"The humans who do it are usually huge men." Caesar sighed. "That's why they end up as legends. In books. They're not usually tiny human girls. Buffy, aside."

I do love that show. I used to watch it on reruns. "She was supposed to have special powers. The Slayer thing, but I'm just a human girl, so I think we can state definitively that I don't have her ability."

"You're not *just* a human girl." Ace cupped my cheek. "You're *our* human girl. I'm going to break that chair. We'll make some stakes out of it."

I grabbed his arm. "Not that chair."

I could never have predicted I'd have that reaction, but I didn't want him to break the chair. "It goes with the set. See? They all match. This is… stupid, I know. Only I love every-thing here. Every single piece of furniture. Please don't break it, even if we need to make a stake. I'm being…"

Caesar moved to me, crossing the room faster than I could track. I so rarely saw them use their vampire powers, but there it was, on display. "It's okay. You don't want him to break the chair, so he won't break it. This is your home. We bought it for you. Everything in it is yours. We will buy some things tonight to break. Ace and I will go do it now. Come on."

Tanner took my hand. "You can burn us, too. It's doubly effective. First stake and then you burn, just like it sounds, and just like Griffin did. That's the way to handle it. And, on that subject, if Griffin and Caesar got to buy you a house, I would like to buy you something."

"If you come up with something, let me know. I'm already compromising on the phone. Perhaps I have no morals left at all. No self-respect. I'll just be your paramour and only be interested in what you could all buy me."

His smile was slow. "I'd love to be able to pamper you all the days of your life. Don't knock it until you try it. Why do we need rules, especially when it comes to gifts? We make our own, right? You could be our version of a paramour— one where you're more likely to tell me to fuck off than to let me order you around. Think about it."

"I don't think at this point we need labels." Griffin shrugged. "We're working. We'll leave it at that. I'm texting Caesar to get you a lighter, too. One of those little torch ones. Anyway, if we're not going to break furniture, let's go ahead and watch a movie." He pointed at the television. "We never have a chance to just sit and watch a movie."

He was right.

It turned out the two vampires who stayed with me couldn't have more different tastes in movies. Griffin wanted to watch something dark and spooky, while Tanner preferred watching things blow up. I yawned as we settled on a comedy that I was sure none of us really wanted to see. I didn't really care one way or the other what we chose; I just liked being in between the two of them with nothing dire going down.

Griffin ran a hand through my hair. "Everyone goes running and I get to stay here. They don't know how foolish they are to always be bounding about. The best stuff is just getting to be here with you."

Tanner smiled. "I may have to reconsider things."

"Nope, don't. I get to be here with her alone. That's the key." He stared at the screen. "You deciding to not go running around to fight defeats the purpose."

"Then I suppose you shouldn't have brought it up."

I rolled my eyes. "Maybe I'll start working nights."

"No," they both said at the same time, suddenly in unison.

That was what I'd wanted. "Then I think you should stop arguing like petulant children. The only person here entitled to still act like a petulant child is me. I'm the only one here still human and maybe allowed to be." I grinned. "I'm only eighteen. I can still have tantrums and act ridiculously, right?"

Griffin took my hand in his and kissed it. "My memories of humanity fade quickly, but if I remember correctly, I'm pretty sure you were born an adult, at least in your soul. I think they gave you no choice, Right?"

He was absolutely on point with that. I'd never gotten to be any kind of wild teen and I never would. Maybe if I lived to be fifty, I'd have some kind of mid-life crisis and do it then. *Wouldn't that be ridiculous but somehow apropos at the same time?*

Old when I was young, young when I'm older? I grinned at the image. Maybe I'd get my first tattoo. That brought up a memory and I pulled my legs under me. "How do you like your ink? The tattoos you got before you changed?"

Tanner shrugged. "I never think about it. I know it was

meant to be a sort of fuck you from that me to this me. I can appreciate the effort."

Griffin played with the end of my hair. "I don't care about it one way or another. Here, stretch out. You can't be comfortable like that."

They were being too nice. Yes, things had changed between us a bit, but these were still vampires. "What's going on?"

Tanner leaned back, taking my legs and placing them on his lap. "Griffin has something he needs to tell you."

"Something that I need to have my legs in your lap to hear?"

"No, but it certainly can't hurt." Griffin squeezed my shoulders. "And, it gives us the benefit of getting to touch you more. We seem to like that. Very unusual for vampires."

There was always going to be a part of me that was something Griffin wanted to study. It should bother me more, but like most of our strange situation, the more time that passed, the less it bothered me. I might be good with just being a food bank altogether in a week. Hell, I wasn't complaining about it at the moment, considering how good it made me feel, and not just the sex. I liked that it was me making them feel better.

That was a realization that should rock me, but it looked like I was unrockable at the moment. "So you're buttering me up?"

"We need you to drive an hour to meet another human and get a book from him. I would go myself, but he won't meet with vampires. He's hiding from them, so he only does business during the day."

Well, that's unexpected. "You need a book from him?"

"That's right, and I can't get it from him at night. Well,"

Griffin sighed, "I *could*. I mean I could rob him. I could go in there and take it from him. We have a vampire hacker. He's very good. I could ask him to find this guy's home, and I could go take what I wanted from him, but I'm trying to consider your feelings about my behavior. Am I wrong in assuming you wouldn't like it if I found him, drained him, and took his books?"

I blinked. "Griffin, I think there has to be a middle ground, but you're correct, I wouldn't appreciate that behavior at all. No, I'll go get the book." In fact, I would keep him away from any human beings until we sorted out all the steps he could have taken before he drained this book man to steal his stuff. As human as they could seem, parts of them were probably never going to change.

If for no other reason than to save everyone around us from being sucked dry of their blood, I needed to remember that.

"I think we can assume this man is afraid of vampires." Tanner shifted slightly on the couch, squeezing the top of my foot. "He has all the vampire books, but he doesn't deal with vampires? There's gotta be a story there. He's not hiding, but he's careful. Griffin said his name was Justin, and you were his girlfriend Maci, in case you needed to show identification."

This is getting stranger and stranger. "Why Justin?" It didn't really matter but I was curious enough to ask.

"I don't know, actually. The name came to me, and I went with it. Anyway, I've made up this whole story about how we need the book because I'm being harassed by a vampire, and that you need to come get the book."

This must be some kind of book. "Why do you want that book?"

Maybe I should have started with that question? That

would have made more sense, but then again, when did I ever make sense these days?

"It's a complete version of one of the ones the elders have edited. I don't know why this guy has it, but he spoke about it on a public forum for people who believe in vampires a while back. The hacker we use doesn't bother to monitor it, because it's mostly filled with crazies who are looking for vampires in a romantic sense."

Tanner laughed, interrupting Griffin. "They just need to speak to Maci. She could tell them how fucked up a romance with vampires can be."

Romance? I really hadn't thought of our situation as romantic, but the idea made me smile. "Does that make you my boyfriends? Never mind. No, don't answer that. Too much for right now. Go on. Okay, he doesn't monitor the vampire erotic roleplaying chat, but you do."

"Well, I scanned it. I stopped when I saw the title of the book because it's a real title. I don't even know that this dude knows what he has, except he knows that he has *something*, and enough real history to make him scared, so we need to grab that book and see if it has the missing pages. The easiest option would be for you to do it, if you're comfortable. I see no danger in you meeting with him, as it's a daytime thing, so there won't likely be any vampires there. I mean, unless for some reason he's hanging out with the elders."

"Unlikely, since he's alive," I pointed out then I nodded. "Sure, I'll do it. I'm studying tomorrow for my GED, but I can fit in a drive to meet him, too. That's not a problem."

Tanner took my hand in his before he squeezed our linked fingers. "I'll be your boyfriend. I wanted to be in both my human life and now."

That was sweet. "If only there was any part of my life that could have a boyfriend."

"Better to have lovers." Griffin lowered his voice. "Granted, I am benefiting from that arrangement."

The door flew open and the other two vampires strode inside carrying dilapidated wooden chairs. Caesar grinned at me when he spoke. "We were on our way to buy them when we saw these sitting outside someone's house. Seemed better to break old ones people were throwing out than to waste new ones."

"Out here." Ace went back outside before he threw the chair against the porch floor with such a force it shattered in two. Griffin had done the same when he saved me. It was amazing they were that strong. I could throw that chair around, and I wouldn't be able to break it. I was pretty sure they couldn't have done it as humans as easily, either.

It's a good thing the neighbors never seem to notice what we're doing.

If they did, at least they hadn't been able to get in touch with us about it yet.

With a piece of wood in hand, Ace struck the ground again, splintering it until it looked like a pretty ugly stake. I supposed it would work.

He stared at it for a second. "This will work for tonight, but tomorrow we'll make some better ones you can carry on your person. They won't even set off metal detectors."

"Good call." Tanner nodded.

I blinked. *They have to be kidding.* "Where exactly am I supposed to keep this stake on my person? I mean I could put it in a purse, but..."

Caesar shook his head. "No, that'll be too hard to get to, so we'll tape it to you."

We are absolutely not.

Nope. Not going to happen. "Sorry, that won't work."

I'd never been yelled at by four vampires at the same time before, but I was then.

～

"*WHAT ARE YOU DOING?*" *I approached Ace, slowly. The hard line of his face, the slight tic in his jaw—he was mad—and I didn't want to make it worse by breaking his attention too quickly. He concentrated on whatever he stared at, even though I couldn't see the object of his rapt attention. Ace always seemed to be the most intense of us, the most powerful. He'd deny it, but it was true. I was immensely grateful he loved me and was always on our side. If it had gone any other way, Ace would be a powerful enemy.*

Without looking in my direction, he extended his hand, so I laced our fingers together. On another night, in another time, we'd go hunt together. Not to kill the humans, as there was no need for that—not when we could easily feed each other with our human companions generously providing when we needed it and not dying for their trouble. No, we sometimes liked to stalk for the fun of it.

Our prey never even knew, making the activity harmless. It gave Ace what he needed when instinct rode him hard.

But things were different at the moment. We weren't hiding, per se but we also weren't running around like nothing was happening. They might strike at any time, and I wasn't entirely sure we would win. We were in the right, but there were more of them. The lure of power—not something that Fredrick or any of his cronies could really understand—was too strong for young vampires. They didn't know those instincts that controlled them were actually gifts if they were turned the right way.

Ace could teach them, if only they would listen.

"*Ace?*" *I asked again.*

"What's going on?"

He tilted his head. "They're coming. Closer every rising. They're in bloodlust, and they're listening to him."

I swallowed. "What do we do?"

"We fight." He kissed my hand. "I love you. Whatever happens, I will always love you, even if I have to burn every one of them to the ground."

He really would, if it came to that. I leaned on his shoulder. "This is all about me, you know? If I stepped back and let you or Rowan lead, they'd accept that."

"Then they really do deserve to die."

It was that simple for Ace.

I YAWNED over my coffee the next morning. If I intended to pick up the book Griffin wanted and make it back in time to study for my GED, I needed to leave soon. I hadn't brought up the errand in front of Caesar or Ace, and I'd noticed neither had Tanner or Griffin. Were there alliances that I didn't really understand between them? Ace and Tanner shared a bed—Ace was actually asleep, I'd checked. Caesar and Griffin always did recently, too.

Maybe I was overthinking the entire situation. Maybe they did all know what was happening, and I just wasn't privy to the discussion. *That's the most likely scenario, isn't it?*

I drummed my fingers on the counter. I doubted that Caesar and Ace would be particularly happy with me traveling so far away from them, but it didn't matter. I was doing it. I just had to wonder if I would ever understand the ins and outs of these guys since I wasn't a vampire myself.

Finally, as I finished my coffee, I resolved to get more sleep every night. If I wanted to keep up the unusual amount of feeding I was somehow able to do, I had to take better care of myself.

The car they got for me was fun to drive, and using the GPS on the new phone waiting on the counter for me when I'd gotten up—already set up for me, thanks to the vamps— I easily navigated to the highway and headed into the mountains.

They must have gotten—perhaps stolen?—the phone when they went out to get chairs. The stake sitting next to the phone made me smile. I still wasn't going to strap it to my body, despite the duct tape they'd also left helpfully on the counter for me to find. *Did they actually think I would duct tape a stake to my body?* I rolled my eyes. It was ridiculous, and I bet it would itch if I even attempted it.

I'd keep the stake in my purse, which would have to be good enough. We still hadn't discussed how I was supposed to stake a vampire anywhere. I didn't imagine they'd let me stand still and guess exactly the location of their heart, so unless I found one sleeping and decided to stake it, I would be really shit out of luck.

I shook my head. It was time to go for a drive, even if everything in me wanted to never leave the house again. *What is that all about?* I pushed my worries away. I'd lived my whole life with an element of fear chasing me, so the drive wasn't any different.

14

With the radio blasting in a car that I was pretty sure wasn't about to fall apart at any second, I felt freer than ever before. The drive proved beautiful—was this how other people got to live? They could just *be*? No worries because their mother might not come back and then they'd starve to death because there wasn't an adult in a hundred mile radius who would care. No worries because vampires might make them so addicted to their venom they couldn't survive another day. No worries that the vampires they were falling for might someday just up and leave them because they got old, and then venom addiction would just rush back and kill you.

I blinked. *Okay.* Apparently, *I* worried about that. Thank goodness for my stream of consciousness or I'd never know what I really thought about anything.

With a song I didn't recognize blaring on the radio, I pulled into the driveway of the address. As described, it looked like a cabin in the woods in the middle of nowhere, but weirdly, all of the trees around the cabin were gone. Not even a single shadow slanted over the house. I pulled the car to a stop and stared at it, trying to decide why I found it unsettling. I might not even notice the lack of shadows, except the ones around our house were deep. They'd never seen the house before they bought it, so it was pure coincidence, but it crossed my mind that, should the guys ever be able to stay up in daylight, they might be able to stand in the shadows to hide from the sun for a second or two. *Or maybe they wouldn't.*

Regardless of my ruminations, the cabin gleamed in bright sunshine. Even on a rainy day, there'd be no hiding near this home, not until about a quarter of the way down the driveway.

Considering what Griffin told me about this man's feelings regarding vampires, I couldn't imagine the lack of cover was coincidental. I got out of the car and locked it with a beep and then did it again just to be sure.

It was a super expensive car. My vampires might not care about money, but I did.

I grabbed my purse—which contained my wallet, my phone, and the stake—to head for the front door. One of my vampires had put cash in my purse, too, I noticed upon inspection. My guess was Griffin or Tanner, since I was still pretty sure the others didn't know I planned the trip.

Walking toward the door, I stopped when it flung open before I made it to the first step. "Stop."

A balding man in his thirties stepped onto the porch. Like me, he had a stake. Unlike me, his was visible.

I stared at the wooden device. Okay, I wasn't a vampire, but if he shoved it in my chest, it would kill me just the same. At the very least, it would do serious damage.

I held up my hands in the universal sign of surrender. "I'm not a vampire. It's the middle of the day. The sun is shining, and I'm here for a book."

He stared at me but didn't move. Apparently just saying I wasn't undead didn't mean he was going to believe me. *Smart.* I wouldn't necessarily believe me, either. For all he knew, I might be the most ancient vampire ever, so I could just drive cars and skip around in daylight if I wanted.

I took a step toward him and dropped my arms so I could pull my sleeves up. I'd gotten good at wearing long sleeves no matter the weather. I didn't bother with the vampires but otherwise I didn't need the whole world seeing my wrists. I did, however, need this guy to see them or this whole drive would be for fucking nothing.

I held them up. Hopefully he had good enough eyesight to see my scars. "They hurt me. The vampires? Over and over. My boyfriend is in hiding because he tried to stop them." Okay, so I lied a little bit. Truth and lies mixed together. Whatever, maybe he'd believe me. "We need that book."

He dropped his stake, and his stance relaxed a little. "I have to be careful. They come looking for me sometimes. Not lately. I've given most of the stuff they want to people who wanted to defeat them. Or did." He ran a hand through what was left of his brown hair. "They had my girlfriend for a long time, too. Then she escaped. Or they let her go? I'm not sure. She took off with a lot of their stuff, most of which they wanted back. What you want, they don't seem to care about." He shrugged. "Probably because no one can read it. It's written in an old language we don't understand."

Griffin would understand it. He was amazing like that. "Okay. Well, my boyfriend wants it, so I'll take it and go." I paused. "What happened to your girlfriend?"

I don't know why I asked. Maybe it didn't matter, or maybe it was one of those questions where I didn't want to know the answer.

He visibly swallowed. "She's dead. Not because of them. She just wasn't the same when they let her go. She couldn't survive how she felt afterward, because it was almost like she still needed them to bite her. The doctors thought we were crazy. The one guy who would finally see her was no help."

Should I tell him she probably was addicted and *had* needed them? That they did that to her? "What was the name of the doctor who saw her?"

I had a feeling that I already knew, but I wanted him to confirm it.

"Lamar." He looked away. "I never liked the man."

No, I bet he hadn't. Lamar worked for the vampires. Whatever he did for his girlfriend, it wasn't to save her. I almost told him so, but I closed my mouth to say nothing instead. I didn't want to show my hand. Too much was at stake with keeping our secret.

"I'm sorry that happened to you. If I were you, I'd get out of this area of the country. Why stay close to them? Why not go far, far away?"

"Sometimes staying in their backyard, where I can keep an eye on them, is the best thing." He shrugged. "Also, she died here. I like being close."

I could certainly understand the sentiment and actually agreed. We were obviously staying close, too. I took the book from his hand and handed him the money Griffin gave me. A crawling sensation strode up my back, and I spun to look around. *Is someone staring at me?* I rubbed my arms.

"Maybe don't stay here too long." I didn't owe this man anything except the money I'd just paid him, but the vampires already took so much from him. In a sense, we were in this together. Vampires had taken from both of us.

The difference is I have four of them on my side and this man is alone.

Besides, my fate was always determined in this fight. I blinked. Where had that thought come from? Was I doomed already?

I wasn't particularly fatalistic. Or maybe I was.

Those thoughts plagued me, sucking the joy out of the drive back. A few hours remained until sunset, and I really did need to study, so once I was officially home and showered, I resisted the urge to look through the book Griffin sent me to fetch and instead studied for my GED. The book was vampire business. Although I might be wrapped up in their world, I was determined to have a human life, too, which meant I had to pass my GED. Well, at least I wanted to. That had to amount to something.

I was about three quarters of the way through the review when I started to feel them waking up. None of them were hungry, not particularly, but my subconscious remained fully aware of them. Ace first, then Caesar, Tanner, and then finally Griffin. They stumbled out of their rooms like they'd all been on a bender the night before and I had to smile. Waking up wasn't easy for vampires, akin to coming back to life in its own sick way.

When Tanner entered, I spun in my chair to extend my neck to him. Whether he was hungry or not, he needed a fix of my blood to get his voice back. It was a daily need, and I could at least count on having a small amount of venom as well as the pleasure surge he gave me.

He bit down and I smiled. *I never would've believed I'd love it this much.*

Griffin leaned against the wall. "How did it go?"

"How did what go?" Caesar rubbed his knuckles on my

cheek gently. I smiled at him as Tanner pulled away from my neck.

"I went and got a book Griffin wanted." It seemed an easy enough explanation.

Ace stopped walking on his way into the living room, his eyes flushing garnet. "A book he didn't want us to know he sent you for or he would've told us about it. Why? Was it dangerous?"

His voice lowered to the point that I shivered from the intonation of darkness in it, and I wasn't even the one Ace was mad at right that second. I thought of his point, too, though, and preferred not to again. "It's fine. I'm here. Nothing happened, other than me getting the book." I pointed to it on the counter. "It's there."

Overwhelming pain struck me, and I fell backwards off the stool where I'd perched. Strong arms caught me before I could hit the floor. "Whoa, Tanner, what did you do to her?" I threw my arm around Caesar's neck, since he was the one to catch me, and tried to hold on through the waves of pain.

"Someone is angry with me." I could barely speak through the chattering of my teeth.

He whirled around, pointing his finger at Ace. "Knock it off."

"I'm not mad at her," he yelled before he rounded on Griffin. "I'm ticked at him. This is not on her."

"Not him." I shook. The sensation was external to us, like Ace with his hunger. Whoever's emotions I picked up was hungry, yes, but that wasn't his primary complaint right then.

"It's Rowan." Tanner spoke in a low voice, placing his hand on my leg. "I can feel him, like I could you. He's here."

As if he'd conjured him, the door flung open and Rowan stared at us. Caesar squeezed me tighter for a second before he set me down on the ground. "Stay there. This is going to get ugly."

"You're damned right it's going to get ugly." Rowan spoke through clenched teeth, stepping inside. The door slammed behind him, but he never touched it. For about three seconds, I didn't understand before it occurred to me Rowan had closed that door with his mind. *What the fuck was that?*

I pulled myself to my feet. He could be angry with me and direct it straight at me if he wanted, but I wasn't going to face him from the floor. Caesar moved until he stood directly in front of me and in a blink Tanner was to Rowan's right. I didn't see where Ace had gone until he stood directly in Rowan's face.

I didn't see Griffin anywhere, but I could feel him nearby in the room. Why couldn't I find him?

Ace wasn't in Rowan's face very long. After a long stare, Ace was thrown to the side and then through the window, where he must have crashed outside. Again, Rowan hadn't touched him.

I wondered why they all followed him, and there was my answer. When the universe doled out vamp gifts, Rowan apparently got more than his fair share of them.

Caesar darted forward only to be slammed back into the wall for his trouble. Pinned there, a roar sounded from his thoughts, more animal than human right then. It was like I could hear his monster directly.

"Tanner, Griffin, don't move." I had no idea if Ace was okay, but Caesar clearly wasn't. Rowan's fury seemed clearly focused on me, and I didn't want anyone else getting hurt on my behalf.

I held up my hands in what I hoped he still understood as the universal sign for surrender. "No one has to get hurt."

I no more than blinked before Rowan moved into my

personal space, staring down at me. "They're betrayers. They are going to get more than hurt."

His words struck and I shivered, swallowing away my fear. Vampires got off on terror, or at least the ones who hurt me had. At the moment, Rowan was in league with them. He'd stay that way until I moved his category in my mind.

"They'd *never* betray you. They hid me to keep me safe. I was dying. But no one betrayed you, Rowan."

"Leave her alone," Ace shouted from the doorway as Griffin appeared behind Rowan. He grabbed their leader's arm for one second before he ended up pinned next to Caesar on the wall. I breathed hard, but Rowan remained so still, I'd think him a statue... if his anger wasn't surging at me like a palpable entity in the room with us.

Tanner hadn't moved, but I had no expectation he'd stay that way very long.

"How did they betray you?" If I could get him talking it might help.

He didn't answer, so I just let myself stare at him. If I took the power out of this, the discrepancy between us, and the fact that he might tear out my throat before I could convince him to think differently—then it was just me staring at Rowan, the boy who made sure I had lunch to eat. The boy who stopped me from vanishing in the woods. The boy who had held a gun to his head and told his father to not kill me or he'd shoot himself. They'd all done that for me, but it had been Rowan who spoke the words. *It had been Rowan, but now he is this other being.* An angry creature who could pin my guys to the walls with his thoughts and throw them through windows.

"Do you know how hard it was to keep my promise to you? A promise that I never should have made in the first place, because there wasn't a chance in hell I should've been able to keep it as a vampire? We die as a human, and I had to carry part of that with me to keep my promise to you. And I did it. Despite that, you've all betrayed me. I let her go, and you're all here with her when it was expressly forbidden."

With a shaking hand that absolutely betrayed the image of bravery I tried to project, I touched the side of his cheek. He didn't stop me. He was angry but there was something else that he was trying to keep from me—pain.

But not from hunger. *From loss.*

"They saved me. You didn't know it, but the other vampires bit me while you slept. Bit and bit and bit me." I turned my wrist over so he could see. "Sometimes up to ten times a day. I was dying. Slowly. Painfully. You wanted me to live a life. That's why you made that promise when you were a human. Maybe it feels foreign to you, but I remember you said you wanted me to be safe and happy. You protected me."

His gaze dropped to my wrist, and he stared at it like he'd never seen one before. Was he counting the scars? Imagining just how many teeth bit into me without closing the wounds to make it look like that?

I let him stare and I kept talking. "They *saved* me. And they've been keeping me here in this house just a few short days. Barely a week. They did it so they'd be here for you, to do what you needed from them, to fight the Betrayer, and to keep me away from the Elders. Because if I don't get venom now, I'll die. The things I had to do to stay alive? It was awful. So bad, I'll never be able to really talk about all of it."

"Go on." His voice was low. "Explain to me how betrayal isn't betrayal."

I dropped my hand but only so that I could take his in mine. This was all instinct. I really had no idea what I was doing. It was more likely that he'd tear out my throat than actually listen to me. Still, I had to try before everything ended in bloodshed.

Besides, I missed him. This was Rowan. He'd have denied it, but he was absolutely our center in a lot of ways. We weren't whole without him. If I could have him back, I wanted him.

Whoever this version of him is now, we have to fit together.

"Because maybe your intentions behind sending me off, behind letting me go the way you did, were good. You were keeping a promise. Without knowing the things you should have known, they made it impossible for your intentions to happen." Although I improvised, since Caesar and Griffin never said they saved me to keep Rowan's promise, I didn't think I lied to him exactly.

"Rowan," Tanner's voice was low. "Taste her blood then tell me you wouldn't have done the same as we have."

The vampire in front of me jumped. "You're talking. How?"

Tanner walked toward me and placed his hand gently on my arm. He stroked my skin in a long movement of his thumb. "She made it happen. I don't know if you believe in fate, Rowan. I don't know if you're the reincarnated soul of a long dead vampire. I know I'm not. I have nothing in my mind but my own thoughts and my monster. But if you believe in there being a rhyme or a reason of anything, a fate, then let's say this woman in front of us was meant to meet us when she did. Take a drink. You'll see what I mean. She gave me back my voice. I can't talk after risings each day until she gives me her neck." His eyes seemed to glow red as he spoke to Rowan. "Or don't. Then you can wonder for the remainder of your very long existence if you should have. We *didn't* betray you, I can promise you that, but if you hurt her in any way, we will."

Rowan glared at him, nostrils flaring in fury. "If anyone else besides one of you said that to me, they'd be dead."

"Drink. Threaten murder later." He shrugged. "Or don't. I can promise you, it will be your loss."

The room was so silent, I could have heard a pin drop, but even an inanimate object wouldn't dare make a sound in that second. Right then, everything had to be utterly silent. Rowan could hold them against walls with the force of his brain. I'd bet he could crush me into nothing if he desired it. Or he could bite my neck, and we could all be one again.

Tanner had challenged him. I swallowed, knowing it would bring attention to my throat. It wasn't why I'd done it, but I didn't mind the result. *That's good.* I had his attention. Maybe it was time to ask for a little bit of truth.

The answer would tell me a lot.

"Isn't there any part of you, deep inside, that misses me?" I barely whispered the words. "We had one week together, but it shaped the rest of my life. I'll never understand it, but I hear it's like looking at someone else from a distance, your human self, but you can still see him. Doesn't that view, the small one, make you want to take a bite?"

In a million years, I never would've imagined enticing a vampire to bite me. *This is lunacy.* But it made total sense to me. I wanted it, and he had to be convinced.

He moved so fast, I never saw his mouth move until he bit down on my neck. My whole body sighed at the gentleness he used. I almost lost my footing and would've fallen over, but he placed a hand on my back, keeping me upright. His body tightened. Yes, he was feeling what they all did. My blood was different, and it woke him up in a way that shouldn't be possible. By my fifth time, I could recognize the signs.

For me, yes, he turned me on, but it was more like the

sweetest relief from missing an essential organ that had been denied to me for too long. Yes, I needed Rowan. I missed him. I closed my eyes and leaned against him while he fed.

He wasn't very hungry, so soon he pulled off me. *Rowan must not be an overfeeder.* He stopped when he was full, and although he pulled his head away from my neck, he didn't let me go.

"How?"

All of the others stood nearby, like they were ready to take him on as a group if the need arose.

Griffin shook his head. "No idea. I've been searching for the answer."

Rowan growled, "Is that why you sent her to that man to buy his stupid book?"

Well, that answered that question. I thought someone had spotted me. "Was that you at his house today?"

"No, it was one of the servants. They'll have to be handled now. She told me as soon as she saw you."

I caught my breath. "Which servant?"

He waved his hand. "Who knows what their names are? A servant. She'll have to be handled."

I stared at him. *He is such a vampire.* "There was a time you knew their names."

"Do you want to talk about servant names, or do you want to talk about what we are going to do about this? Griffin, that book won't tell you jack shit. The good books that might explain things are in my office."

"Locked away where I can't get to them." He rolled his eyes. "Because you can't know she's here."

As they bickered back and forth, I stared at my broken window. My house had gotten beaten up. I stepped toward the mess and out of Rowan's arms. *I supposed it's just a good reminder that all things could be shattered.* The question was *can they actually be fixed?*

"Her name is Claudine," Rowan said, interrupting my thoughts.

I barely knew her. She wasn't part of my group when I'd been there. "Thanks. I think you guys are going to have to go home with Rowan and sleep elsewhere."

Caesar crossed to me fast. "Why is that?"

"We have to get the window fixed. Someone has to come and do the work. I won't risk your daytime exposure. Go home tonight. I'll take care of it. Oh, and I'm going out Friday. I'm making friends that have nothing to do with any of this."

Rowan was back but the good feelings from him feeding on me were nowhere to be found. They'd flown out my broken window.

15

I imagine if any of them had a clue how to fix a window, they would've argued with me, but they didn't. Caesar grumbled, but at the end of the night, they left me alone in my house. It was the first time I've been really alone since Caesar found me. I didn't know what to do about Rowan. He hadn't said a word since our re-introduction. He watched all of us, but I wasn't sure what he was thinking, and I didn't have it in me to force it out of him.

Not when he'd broken my house.

I slept for a few hours then got up for work. I yawned and recorded the numbers of several people who might be able to fix the window in my phone. I'd call them during lunch. I touched the wall on my way out. Caesar gave me the house to keep me safe, and Rowan had hurt it within minutes of showing up.

Was that just what I should expect to happen? That it would just constantly get beat down? I gritted my teeth. No, it wasn't. I was going to keep this dang house safe if it was the last thing I did.

I knew I wasn't being reasonable. I also didn't care.

Finally, I found someone who would come while I was at work and fix the window. I sent him some money over an app and hoped he'd actually show up and not cheat me. I didn't really have a choice unless I wanted to miss work, which I absolutely didn't. It was my third day. I needed to work there longer before I started missing shifts if I didn't want to get fired.

But leaving the house with the window broken made my stomach hurt, like an unfinished project, and I'd never let that happen in school. I sighed. There was nothing I could do. I hadn't broken the window. The vampires did, and I needed to remember they were capable of breaking more than just windows. Yesterday, I met a man hiding in the mountains because vampires were so brutal. They still tormented him, even after his girlfriend was gone.

What would happen to me if these guys grew tired of me? Would they? Was it just the blood that kept them with me?

Why was I obsessing?

I'd finally decided it was Rowan's fault when I got to work. Things were a mess in the store, so who had created the mess in my house mattered less than helping to get the shelves restocked. Everyone had a different story about why things were so askew, but I'd worked enough places to know that it really didn't matter. We had to get things right or the whole day would go badly. With Stella's help, we got it done fast. Everything was back where it belonged.

If Stan stood in the corner and stared at my breasts while I worked, I pretended not to notice. I had enough troubles for one day.

At least, I thought that was how it would go until my shift ended. Tired with an achy back, all I wanted was to go home and shower. A text showed a picture of my fixed window—which reaffirmed my belief in humanity, since I'd found a trustworthy person to do the job—and I looked forward to seeing it for myself. *My poor house*. We only owned it for such a short period, and already it had been damaged.

I had to stop obsessing about it. Or maybe I didn't. Wasn't it normal for regular folks to worry about their homes?

"Hold on a second, Maci," Stan called, making me pause. Stella, who had been really quiet most of the day, stopped next to me, squeezing my shoulder before moving toward the door. We were supposed to go out the next night, and I hoped she still wanted to. There was always a risk where I was concerned that I'd just been really off putting and hadn't known it. That might be because I spent so much time on my own as a kid.

I tried to smile at him, even though he spent most of his time staring at my breasts. I liked to behave well, even if the people around me didn't. I couldn't control their behavior, just my own. If I remained better than I was raised to be, it seemed like a pretty good *fuck you* to my mother's low opinion of me.

So low, in fact, she'd been willing to give me to a man she brought home one night. *Or maybe that was the drugs. Maybe I wasn't being fair enough to her.*

"Maci, stop." I turned at the sound of my name being called again. Stan charged toward me like a man on a mission. Had I done something wrong or was he just going to be obnoxious because he hadn't gotten enough looks at my bra strap that day?

I was really in a foul mood, and there wasn't anything I could do about it. My equilibrium still lay smashed in my kitchen, my mood as shattered as the glass. I could lay all of my grumpiness at the feet of Rowan for now. At some point, I'd have to own my shit, but I wasn't there yet.

And, Stan really wasn't helping my already shitty mood.

"Yes?" I turned back to him.

"Who said you could leave?" I blinked. *Is he serious?* I looked down at my phone. It was seven o'clock at night. The sun was going down, and I didn't have any shifts far after sunset—for obvious reasons. In fact, it was half-an-hour past when I was supposed to be done.

I tilted my head, doing my best impression of a vampire. They were intimidating when they did it. Maybe I could be, too.

It didn't stop Stan. He glanced at my breasts before he looked back up at my face. "Who said you could leave?"

I took a deep breath and dug for hard-to-find patience. How did anyone handle dealing with the odious man long term? I needed and wanted the job, but I might have to rethink things and soon. I'd get the GED and then... find something else.

He was going to be tiresome.

I blinked. *Such a strange word for me to think.* I would say assholish or exhausting or something. Oh well, I needed to stay present. What did he want? *Oh yes, I'm leaving.*

"The schedule said I could leave." I pointed toward the clock. "I signed out on the tablet, and it's ten minutes past when I'm supposed to be here."

He shook his head. "You need to check with me first."

That had absolutely *not* been part of the orientation, but I'd only been at the job for several days. It might really be part of it. My last job I'd been entirely on my own most of the time. Truth was that I wasn't used to having to check in with people. It wasn't unreasonable to think that I had to tell him before I left. Of course, I was leaving whether he liked it or not. The sun was setting around me and I needed to get home before the vampires came back to roost, so to speak.

"Sorry about that. I'll remember that tomorrow."

Chills rushed up my back as he regarded me. Maybe it was one of those things leftover in women's genes from all eternity, but I sensed the presence of a predator in him, one that wanted to hurt me. Maybe my own instincts were heightened from my year of being an unpaid servant to the vampires who fed off of me completely without my consent, but I knew Stan wished me harm. I hadn't done anything to him, certainly nothing to warrant the evil that his seemingly bland gaze threw my way, which meant something was wrong with him, something that made him want to hurt, regardless of the person.

He put out his arms. "Give me a hug to apologize."

Give him a hug? I might be frightened, but not enough to do whatever someone wanted just to try to avoid making things worse.

I absolutely did not need the job that much.

"I'm not going to give you a hug." I shook my head. "Whatever it is that you think you're doing here, you can knock it off. I'm not interested, and I'm not going to kowtow to you because you're my boss. You can just fuck off."

His eyes flared. "How dare you speak to me like that? You're..."

"Maci," Rowan's voice stopped the conversation. He walked toward us, dressed like he was just any other young human man that happened to want to discount shop at the store. He was beautiful and, for a second, relief flooded me. He had been my protector for the few weeks we'd known each other, made sure I ate, and taken care of not just me but every one of his friends. Maybe it was cognitive dissonance, but I forgot what he was now for just seconds, and they were beautiful, blissful moments that I wanted to roll around in. But then the truth flooded in fast.

Rowan was the leader of the vampires, set up to take over for the elders, and it appeared he slid into the role with ease. He'd banned me from getting what I'd needed, but it didn't seem he'd really understood what he was doing.

In this case, his gaze was focused, Rowan knew exactly what he was about to do.

I swallowed. "Rowan..." I hated Stan because he fit into the box I'd been warned about—just another man who wanted to take what he could that I didn't want to give. It was different with my vampires—I actually wanted to give them blood. Maybe it was a chemical thing, and I was being manipulated by my own body, but fuck it, I really loved it.

I didn't want it to go away because they got caught by humans who would talk too much—like Stan.

I stepped forward but it didn't seem to stop Rowan at all.

"What's your name?" Rowan's voice was low, predatory, and Stan didn't miss the threat. His body visibly vibrated. I wouldn't have been surprised if he pissed himself in a second. The image made me smile inside. *Just how sick in the head am I?* I forced my attention back to the moment. Rowan really might hurt him.

"Stanley," my boss whispered, all of his gumption gone.

"Stanley," Rowan touched his shoulder. "You're working with Maci?" Rowan's voice took on a seductive purr, something I'd seen other vampires do in the year I lived as a servant. The compulsion of their tone could convince someone to let them feed despite their actual desire to not be food. They liked to act as if humans ran to them, always ready and willing to serve as food, but that wasn't always the case. It certainly hadn't been for me during that time, although no one ever bothered to seduce me by using voice tricks.

"I'm her boss." Stanley sounded downright zoned out.

I crossed my arms over my chest and walked closer to Rowan.

"Anyone could see you." I didn't try to lower my voice. "We're in public."

He didn't look at me, keeping his gaze locked on Stan's. "And there's nothing to see but a conversation. I'm not floating him in the air or even drinking from his neck. Stanley and I are just talking, aren't we, Stanley?"

"Yes," the other man visibly swallowed. He might sound calm, but behind his eyes, I saw fear. He didn't know what was happening and I'd seen—and felt—that myself many times. The man was a problem, but I didn't want him harmed. Truthfully, I didn't want anyone to ever be hurt because of me. While this might fall under the *he did it to himself* category, I couldn't let Rowan hurt him just because Stan aggravated me. I'd quit. There were human alternatives to solve the problem of Stan.

The guys got rid of a teacher who had been mean when they'd still been human by having the vampires take her on. I didn't need a repeat.

"Rowan, enough." I hoped he would listen, because pulling on his arm would be fruitless and frustrating. I had no idea what my next move would be after that.

"You're going to treat this woman with respect at work, do you understand, Stan? Say yes if you do and no if you don't, so I can make myself even more clear should your answer be no."

Stan nodded slowly. "I understand."

"Good." Rowan stepped away from him. Finally, he regarded me. "Let's go."

I nodded, sparing a glance at Stan as we left him standing there. Experience told me he'd be like that for another ten minutes before he snapped back to his senses. He'd do what Rowan told him to do for a few days at least. I wished it lasted longer, but that wasn't likely unless Rowan bit him, which he hadn't done.

Well... it would buy me a little time.

Without speaking, we walked together to my car. I didn't know how Rowan got to the store so fast, but he apparently intended to come back to the house in my car with me, since he slid into the passenger seat.

Or at least that's what I thought until I pulled onto the road. "Turn left instead of right."

He didn't ask or even explain where he wanted to go. The old Rowan would have. He would have explained and explained—what he wanted to do, where we were going, why we were doing it—and then he would've squeamishly told me that he couldn't explain the big gaping hole of whatever had to do with the vampire world.

I was so desperate for friendship and understanding, I'd gladly put up with not knowing, as though it was all I deserved from him.

Sometime during the last year or so, I figured out I sort of hated him—all of them—for that. But I only had myself to blame for accepting so little as my due, and I had to live with that, too.

What was it about Rowan—alive or as a vampire—that always made me do so much self-reflection? Being in his presence just made me want to be a better version of myself, and I had no time for that sort of undertaking.

"Where are we going?" I'd start small by asserting myself, and we'd go from there. If he didn't want me to go home, he needed to at least tell me where we were going.

That hardly seemed like too much to ask.

"I want to show you something."

Well, that tells me nothing. "Rowan, I'm not just going somewhere with you. That's too vague. Please, tell me where we're going or I'm driving home."

He turned to me. "You trust the others but not me."

He didn't phrase it as a question, so I didn't take it as one. "You left me to die. I would be dead, if it wasn't for Ace's father sending help for me, and I still don't know why he did it, so, no, I don't trust you."

"Stop the car." He paused for a second. "I would like to have a conversation without you crashing this car and ending your brief human life. I'd survive it. You wouldn't."

Well, harsh... but true. I pulled the car to the side of the road and parked it. The streets were quiet, and it wasn't that busy around us, but if he really thought his words might devastate me to the point that I would accidentally kill myself driving, then I would take him seriously.

"We're going to look at something I think could be illuminating to you, and then we're going to speak truth to one another." He looked away. "If you're going to refuse, there are ways for me to force you to comply. Obviously, I'd rather not do that."

I almost argued. I could point out the threat alone was enough to force me to do it. I could even turn the car around and drive home, calling his bluff. I didn't know if Rowan really intended to force me or if he was just testing me. Hell, I didn't know if vampires bluffed at all. *Did they?* That was a good question. They said they didn't lie, but I found that to be sort of bullshit. It depended on how long you stretched the word.

Even knowing all of those things, I did nothing. First off, I found it pointless to argue with vampires. Also, I didn't know at this point if Rowan was really one of mine or if he was still too connected to the ones who had hurt me.

But I also wanted to know what he wanted to show me.

I might regret it later, but better to know what drove him out to my work so soon after sunset. I needed to hear what he had to say.

With a nod, I pulled my car back onto the street. "I don't know why you thought that would make me have an accident."

"Humans are unpredictable. They make big things out of small things. I had no idea how you would react."

I shook my head. "Do you see humans just driving off the road all the time? Every conversation pushing them off the road? That was ridiculous. You said nothing of significance, so there was no reason I couldn't have kept driving."

He titled his head and looked up toward the sky through the front window. Was that the equivalent of a vampire rolling his eyes?

I was pretty sure the others just outright did it, but Rowan was different, more powerful than the others. I supposed he had been born to be great. *Or reborn. Whatever.*

He pointed in the direction he wanted me to go, and I drummed my fingers on the steering wheel as we traveled. The slight ping on my fingers was a distraction but not enough to stop me from speaking the first real thought that crossed my mind. "I could have *died*. You left me to die."

"Yes, you could have." He stared straight ahead. "But you didn't. That's curious, but not the most interesting thing about you at this point. I'm sure the human I was would be horrified with what you went through, but since he did, in fact, perish in a box, there isn't anything he can do for you now. I'm afraid you're stuck with me. I see you as very much alive, and I'm not going to apologize for events I didn't even know about."

Well... I suppose that is that. I opened and closed my mouth. What was there really to say? He wasn't sorry.

"That being said..." he continued, drawing me back to the present. "I think if I had known what happened to you, what condition you were in, I would have kept you around. That in itself, though, is a problem. Turn left here."

I obeyed, and we drove in silence while I stewed on his words. "What would you have done differently?"

"I would've made you one of them."

One of who? I came to a stop at the side of the road, and it took me a moment to understand where he indicated. In the distance, nondescript houses surrounded mansions in the center of the town. If I hadn't known I was in North Carolina, I might have sworn I was back home. The vampires pretty much recreated their previous compound in a different location. I blinked.

What did he mean, he would have made me one of them? *One of who?* Then it dawned on me. *The servants.* They ran around, some carrying brooms, all in a hurry to go wherever their masters ordered them to be. I knew exactly what was happening in the scene in front of me. The vampires were finally awake, so their servants had a lot of tasks to perform. I lived as a servant during the year when Rowan and the others had been reawakening.

"I *was* a servant."

He shook his head. "You were temporarily a servant. People don't get to be temporary servants. You've figured that out, right? They're either servants or they're dead. No one really gets changed. No one moves on. You would've lived the rest of your life as a servant if I'd been aware you were addicted to vampire venom. I would've done it to keep you alive. Permanently. No Caesar coming to check on you. No little house in the country to make you comfortable. Your blood would have been interesting, and we might've been curious about how your blood was different from others, but you would've been a servant. You can still be one, if you want, but I suspect you don't. I'm not making light of your pain, Maci. It's real and it's significant, but maybe things worked out for the better in the long run."

I never wanted to kill anyone more than I wanted to kill Rowan in that moment.

16

Months of pent-up emotions crashed out of me in a surge of adrenaline I wouldn't have known was possible up until then. I raised my hand and struck Rowan. A hard, fast slap. He could've stopped me. Maybe I had magical blood or whatever, but no super speed—vampires were way faster than me. Rowan *let* me hit him as hard as I could across his cheek.

We stared at each other, breathing hard. "You don't get to tell me how to feel or what would have been better or worse. None of us know exactly what would've happened, so stop pretending to be logical when you're spinning a fantasy. You want to talk about facts? Your father kept me prisoner and addicted me to fuck with you, and that's a fact. He did it to prove you never got one over on him that day when you all pulled out guns. He kept to your agreement, but he didn't give you what you really wanted. Also you don't know what the servants' lives are like, really, because you've never given a shit about them. None of you do. If they can never be vampires, you should stop telling them that maybe they can be. You know, because you never lie, but that's a total lie."

First, I hit him, and now I yelled in his face, but my heart raced like I'd been running a race. "Sometimes? I hate you. All of you."

When Rowan raised his hand, I wasn't sure what he intended to do. I hit him, after all, so he might do worse to me. He wasn't human, and his reactions couldn't be counted on to be empathetic. I simply didn't know this version of him yet.

So when he smoothed my hair off my face and cupped my cheek, my heart stuttered for a second. "You're so beautiful when you're angry. No, that's wrong. You're *always* beautiful. What I mean to say is that even anger is beautiful on you."

"Did you listen to a single word I just said?" I lowered my voice. Screaming and pounding on Rowan wasn't getting me anywhere. Maybe talking to him would prove to be fruitless in general.

"Every word you said and those that you are not saying." He kissed my cheek, roughly in the same place where I'd struck his. "You're right about the servants. I'm afraid that's out of my purview. My father still controls that, but I'll see what I can do. They didn't create me for my managerial skills at home, rather to win a war. As for the rest of it, yes, you're right. That's why my father did everything he did. He is conniving and petty. I know better, but my human self believed in fruitless things. I cannot change the past and what was done."

Why was he being so reasonable in the face of my completely nonsensical temper? "You broke my house," I sulked.

He nodded once. "For that, I am truly sorry. I could've done better than that. I don't usually lose my temper, so I doubt you'll see that side of me again... unless I have to kill your boss." Rowan smirked at me. "I wanted to today. Badly."

"We aren't going to come to consensus about what happened when you let me go, because all of it was awful, and none of it was actually either of our faults." I tried to make peace with the situation, but it was a struggle.

He smoothed my hair again, and this time, shivers of pleasure traveled up my spine. "We don't have to ever agree about it. You can hate me and be angry at me for the whole of your very short human life. I'm still going to let you pound on me all you want because I don't want this to be the last time I see what fury looks like on you. I pretty much want to drink in how raw, stunning and human you are right now."

All of the vampires were condescending with Rowan as the worst of them. *So why did I have to find him so fucking sexy?* I took off my seatbelt with shaking hands and crawled over the center console to straddle his lap. He pushed his seat back, giving us both more room just seconds before our lips met. I didn't know who ultimately kissed who. It didn't matter.

We practically fused together. He liked my anger? *Fine. He can have all of it.* I would push it right into him. Against me in just those seconds, he hardened. We'd had no blood exchange since he'd risen, so that was a very good sign that things were working just fine.

I pulled back to stare at him. His red-rimmed vampire eyes stared back at me with longing that would probably make him horrified. I sort of loved that thought. He opened his mouth, but I pressed my hand over it. I didn't want to hear what he had to say right then.

If he could be a condescending asshole, then so could I.

"Quiet. No talking right now."

His nod told me that I could move my hand away, and so I did, which revealed his smirk. I waited for him to say something, to prove he didn't have to listen to me regardless of what I wanted, but he didn't. Instead, he grabbed the back of my head and pulled it toward him, so our mouths danced together again. I closed my eyes.

It was nice of Rowan to take charge of that moment. The thought warred directly with my need to control him, to be the one to bend him to my needs and desires. *Oh fuck it.* I really didn't care. I just wanted to kiss and kiss him for a little bit until we lost our clothes.

As if he'd read my mind, he pulled my shirt off and discarded it. We were so close to the vampire compound, they could see us if they looked, yet right then, I didn't give two shits. *Let them watch me fuck their reborn leader. Let them see me take Rowan inside of my body, and just for those minutes, let me make him mine.*

I tugged at his clothes. I didn't want to be naked while he was basically still dressed. If I was getting vulnerable, so help me, so was the big, strong vampire. He might not see it that way, but I would pretend for a second that I understood him.

He didn't stop me, and soon, even though we had to bang our arms and legs on the window and side of the car to do it, we were both naked enough for me to admire the gloriousness of his naked form. Rowan had filled out since becoming a vampire, part of his change. I knew it but still, it took my breath away to stare at him like that.

I ran my hand down his chest, toward his stomach and his abs jumped beneath my touch. Lifting my gaze to his own, I breathed, "You're beautiful, Rowan."

He shook his head. "That's my line."

Rowan squeezed my nipple and I gasped. "Do that

again."

"In due time."

Okay, so he wanted to play with me. That was fine. "I have to wait until you want to?"

"Yes. I have many plans for you, Maci. Trust me."

Right then, I would. I couldn't promise I would under other circumstances. He pressed a finger inside of me and I moaned. My body was alive, every nerve ending wanting more. His touch. His tongue. His body. Whatever. I just wanted it. *Right now.*

"I thought my interest in sex died with my human body, but you make me burn, Maci. The way you smell, the way you move? Maybe your blood triggered it, but this is more than blood. It's you, damn it. And I'm going to be addicted to you every day until the day you depart this earth."

I shook my head. "No death talk during sex."

His smile grew huge. "Okay. That's a deal."

I loved the electrical shocks of pleasure emanating from his finger circling my clit until I ground against him, but it wasn't how I wanted to come. Not at all.

"Just fuck me." I used the dirty word on purpose. Maybe I wanted to shock the leader of the vampires, to make him think I was a very bad girl. After all, he wasn't the only one who'd been reborn lately.

I didn't give him enough time to answer, just climbed on top of him until I could fit his cock inside of me. He groaned, throwing his head back, his nostrils flaring. Yes, I had him right where I wanted him. For the next few moments, his pleasure would be mine, and I'd have my own, too. I'd never been so lucky.

Riding him was hard in the car, because we could hardly move, but I managed to grind my clit against him with a desperation I'd never felt before. I didn't just *want* to come, I *craved* it. Fuck, I needed it. *Right now.*

He pulled on my hair hard, and I smiled through the bite of pain. I wanted to hurt him a little bit, too. Since he'd given me permission, I dug my fingernails into his chest.

"Yes," his voice was low. "This is just how I need you."

We didn't speak more than that, not in any discernible language. My body throbbed, it begged, and finally it exploded around him. His fangs extended, and we stared at each other. Was he going to feed?

Rowan didn't move. Finally, I said something. "Fuck. Did you want to?"

"Only if it's okay with you." The red flared in his eye. Vampires, particularly powerful ones, didn't ask permission to feed. It must have taken a lot out of him to say those words.

I nodded. "You always have my permission."

"Good to know." He bit down on my neck, lower than where Caesar usually bit me, as though they all claimed their spaces on my body without needing to discuss it. I closed my eyes. His cock, which had already been hard inside of me, somehow became more so as he sucked.

I moaned, and he squeezed me tighter against him. The anger of our joining fled and what was left was only tenderness. Or at least that's how it felt to me. His hands stroked up and down my back, slow motions, as the feeding progressed. I hadn't felt his hunger, not like I did the others usually, but now I could. He was starved.

His hips jerked, bringing us both back to where we had been before. We weren't finished and I loved it. This time, the pump of our hips moved slow and fluid, almost in time with how his mouth sucked on my neck. Warmth stole my thoughts, and I floated toward pleasure that his body easily brought to my own once again.

Finally, he let go, licking my wound closed. I'd been so solely focused on Rowan, there hadn't even been room for anything else, but as we sat in the fogged up car, with my head pressed against his chest because I just couldn't hold it up anymore, with my eyes slitted to only let a little bit of reality in... I could feel the others.

Their needs floated toward me. I usually couldn't block them out. Did they all just wake up or had Rowan's presence and the tension between us somehow blocked them out temporarily? *So many questions and never any answers.*

Rowan nuzzled where he'd bit me. "You okay? I didn't take too much, right?"

I ran my hand through his hair, more instinctively than with any conscious thought. "Doesn't seem to be a problem anymore. It's as though, with every feeding, I get better at it."

"Makes so little sense." He kissed my shoulder. "Can we stay like this?"

"Naked in the car? No. For one thing, I have work tomorrow. The next thing is that..."

I never got to finish my thought, because a knock on the window made me jump. Rowan didn't react at all. He must have known Tanner was about to arrive. I laughed. "It's like he read my mind. I need to feed Tanner. He can't talk until I do every day."

Rowan lifted an eyebrow, skepticism all over his face. "How convenient for him."

"You think he's lying?" I grabbed my shirt from the back-seat. *No more naked in this car. What were we thinking?* We were too close to the vampire compound to be rolling around in the car. What would happen if Rowan's father happened upon us?

This was stupid.

Hot, but stupid.

"Vampires don't lie. I'm sure he's telling the truth. It just seems awful convenient that he must be fed *every* day."

I waved my hand at him. "You were just inside of my body. Let's not be jealous now."

"But vampires do jealousy *so* well." His smile told me he was joking... sort of.

I opened the window and managed to step out of the car with one leg in my pants and the other out. It took me a second to adjust. It wasn't just Tanner there. The others stood around the car, too.

"Did I take too long getting home?" I stepped toward Tanner and extended my hand. His familiar, clean scent washed over me. There was a minty smell to his shampoo. They were all starting to leave their things at my little house. His soap had the hint of sandalwood, too. The combination of the scents was heady and all Tanner.

My nipples hardened as he bit down on me to take what he needed. *How could I be turned on again so fast?* There was going to come a time when I wasn't going to be able to walk from all of the sex I wanted.

Caesar looked at Griffin and then at me. "We'll always find you."

"You were distressed. I sensed it as I woke." Ace took my hand as Tanner fed. "I couldn't leave the house, but I could feel it."

"Right, well, that's my fault." Rowan leaned against the car. "Did I need to check her out? Like a library book? Do I say I get to have alone time with her and that means you stay away?"

Tanner released me, licking his lips before he closed the wound. "She decides what she wants and doesn't want.

That's how it works. If you want alone time, don't make her so upset the rest of us can feel it."

"I'll send a text."

I laughed. Rowan couldn't promise not to make me upset. At least he was honest.

Caesar looked around. "Why did you bring her here?"

"To make a point I'm not sure I made." He nodded toward the houses. "I'm going to go give my nightly orders. I'll meet you back at the house." Rowan passed Griffin the keys. "Take care of your girl. Caesar, you'll be up for fighting tomorrow."

He shrugged. "Figured as much."

He had? "Why didn't anyone tell me?"

"It's not new. I fought just recently. I didn't think you'd need to know."

Maybe he was right. *All of this is so new.* How much did I need to be told about their vampire lives? What were we doing anyway?

"Let's go home." I didn't want to be there anymore. Sure, I just found enormous pleasure and come to some sort of understanding with Rowan, but in the distance, right in front of my eyes, servants worked for the creatures who made my life hell for such a long time. It was too close for comfort. They'd taken too much from me. Even though I knew the guys around me would try to prevent that from happening again, should those vampires try, I also understood what only a person who lived alone most of her life could.

In the end, it is always me versus the world.

I didn't like my chances in the vampire compound.

Griffin nodded. "Sure. Let's go."

I was glad no one argued, not that I thought they would.

None of them seemed to want to hang around there very much anyway.

"TELL me again why you have to go?" Griffin tilted his head as he regarded me eating my salad. I needed to do better about what I put in my body. If I intended to keep up a life with them, I had to stay healthy.

Or at least I thought I did.

"Because I want friends. I want to have a life during the day." I'd explained a few times already, but they didn't seem to care. The general consensus was they didn't want me going to a bar without them, and there was simply no way they could go.

He scowled at me. "Then have friends during the day. This is a nighttime event."

"And the nights belong to you?" I lifted an eyebrow. "I don't remember making that deal. I'll be gone for a few hours. Then I'll come home, feed Tanner, and any of the rest of you who need it."

Tanner rubbed my shoulder, drawing my attention to him. "It isn't just that we want to be fed. We're... very invested in where you are and how you are doing. I think you understand because you seem to be about us, too. I have this general feeling that is very contradictory. It's like I need you to be safe and healthy, while also sensing all the time that something is wrong. I can't explain it."

I tugged on his shirt. "The only thing wrong is that I don't yet know what my waking life will be. With you guys, it always sort of feels like I'm in a dream, a fog, that's not quite real and yet somehow is."

From the couch, Ace laughed. "Look how poetic you're being."

"Bite me." I rolled my eyes and took a bite of my lettuce.

"Don't tempt me, beautiful."

The door opened and Rowan strode inside. "We won tonight's battle."

He didn't sound enthusiastic, just bored. "Isn't that a good thing? You guys are winning against the Betrayer, who's betrayal somehow no one knows, but you keep fighting anyway. In fact, it all seems a little bit like dystopia? But, anyway, why aren't you happy?"

He slid into the stool next to me, stared at my salad as though it was a foreign object, then finally answered. "Because he never really goes *away*. We win, yet they come again. It feels like fake wins. Like he lets us have the little skirmishes for some reason I can't comprehend."

"Yet, when you suggested that to the elders, they scoffed." Ace shrugged. "They want you to win. They like that you're winning. They don't care that it doesn't make sense."

Caesar shook his head. "Thank the universe I don't have to speak to the elders. Ever."

"Watch out. I might make you." Rowan grinned. "What are we doing tonight?"

"This is what we're doing," Griffin nudged me. "Watching her eat and convincing her she doesn't want to go to a bar with her new friends tomorrow night."

"You're not convincing me." I finished eating and rose to clear my plate. Tanner stopped me with a kiss then took the plate from me to wash it. "You don't have to do that. I ate it; I'll clean it."

He glanced over his shoulder. "Pretty sure I would have done this when I was a human, so I'm doing it now."

"Why? Don't you like this better?" Griffin walked to the window to stare out at it.

Tanner shook his head. "No, I don't care for being stuck and not able to talk. I don't like that at all. You prefer it?"

"Worlds better. I couldn't go back. Caesar?"

He shrugged. "I don't really give a shit, truly. Why think about things that don't matter? We're vampires. Who cares what we prefer?"

Ace lifted his head. "Going to ask me?"

Caesar shook his head. "I'm not."

I turned to Ace. "Which do you prefer?"

"This. Being human wasn't fun for us. We lived in terror and fear. Why do that again?" He lay back down on the couch. "Rowan? Which do you prefer?"

"That was someone else's life. I can vaguely remember it, but not in a real way. I don't know how to compare the two when one doesn't feel real to me." He looked at me. "When is the bar?"

"Tomorrow night. And I'm going."

He smirked at me. "Sure. Sounds good. Have a great time. We'll see you when you get home."

"Number one, I didn't ask for your permission. But, secondly... I feel like you're saying something that I don't understand, now that I heard what you said."

He patted my shoulder. "Paranoia is sexy on you, Maci."

"Movie?" Griffin strode to the couch. "Let's watch a movie."

So I ended up watching a lightweight comedy with all of them. None of them laughed at the funny parts, which was funny unto itself. The sound of my laughter alone in the room jarred me, though, as if I was doing something wrong, laughing at something inappropriately funny. I'd never realized that my own laughter sounded so strange... so wrong.

Caesar squeezed my knee. "I think it's hot."

How did he always know what I was thinking? I went back to watching the movie, laughing a little bit less loudly, but some of it was just too funny not to really have a good belly laugh after. Apparently, I had the sense of humor of a five-year-old boy. *I'll just own it.*

After the movie, Griffin put on a television show with subtitles, and I closed my eyes despite myself. I woke up when Rowan picked me up to carry me to the bedroom.

"You know you can't stay here." Ace's voice roused me as Rowan tucked me into my bed.

Rowan sighed. "This is where I want to be. All of you stay. I'm going to stay, too."

"They'll notice if you're not there. No one is going to take note that we're not, but you just can't sleep here, Rowan."

He made a sound close to a growl. "She's here. This is where I want to be."

"I know."

I lifted my arm, stretching it toward Rowan. "Lie down with me for a little bit and go home before dawn, how's that?"

"See?" He crawled into bed next to me, still addressing Ace. "You woke her."

I smiled as I fell asleep.

My alarm woke me, and I rolled over to turn it off. It was morning, and I had to be at work too soon. *I need to give myself more time in the morning.* Ace sat on the edge of the bed, so I grabbed his leg. He should absolutely not be up. "Why are you awake? It's not okay when you do this. It has to hurt you. I can feel it."

He leaned over to kiss me. "I like to have a moment alone with you. Just you and me, just for a moment, so I wait for you to rise, and I get to kiss you. Now I'll go to bed. Don't worry about my pain."

I kissed him back. "Do you need to feed?"

"No, love. I'm fine. Go about your day. I'll see you later. Have fun at the bar."

I was going to have fun. Whether they liked it or not.

17

I hadn't been in the bar for more than ten minutes when I wanted to leave. I never had friends in high school before the guys. Well... one friend, who I used to watch television with, but she moved and I never saw her again. *Wait... did that happen?* Or had she been vampired and killed or something? I groaned. Why hadn't it occurred to me before then that she might have been harmed? *Damn it.*

Happy noise filled the bar, but I only knew Stella, and she was flirting with a bunch of goth guys who surrounded her. Practically holding court. I was happy for her, but I didn't know anyone else, and since I got carded, I sat drinking a ginger ale in the corner. I could leave, but going home so early would be too much of a win for the guys, who didn't want me to be there.

My boss entered, pale-faced, then proceeded to leave really quickly. I didn't know what was going on with him. No way he still remembered what happened with Rowan, but he remembered to leave me alone. That was how it worked, unless the vampire wanted you to remember, and I didn't think Rowan would've risked being remembered.

Okay, I would go see what Stan was up to, since it wasn't abandoning ship altogether to keep an eye on him and my curiosity was piqued.

It wasn't just because I was bored.

I stopped to say goodbye to Stella, but she was in a zone, and I didn't want to mess with that. Since I knew she actively pursued a relationship, I didn't want to risk disturbing her and making them all leave. I really knew nothing about men, or rather not living ones, anyway.

I delayed just enough that I probably missed following my boss, but that was fine. He really just provided an excuse to leave. If I couldn't find him, I'd go home. Sure, it would mean a lot of *I told you so* from the people I wanted to hear it from the least, but I'd rather face them in my pajamas so I could forget how I really couldn't function like other people my age.

Maybe I really wouldn't have a life in the daytime or nighttime, either. Maybe I was just some kind of vampire hanger-on-er and I'd have to be happy with that.

Or at least glad not to be dead or going through withdrawal.

The night air was cooler—it bit my skin and I wished I'd thought to bring a sweater. Sometimes it struck me as weird, how the weather continued to change, and life continued to go on despite whatever chaos struck my life. Above my head, the light flickered.

"Not having fun?" Caesar asked from where he leaned against my car.

I stopped to stare at him. "I've been here *forty* minutes. You just woke up for the day. You can't possibly miss me already."

"I think you might be underestimating how much we all miss you *every* second of every day. You're not with us when we wake, at least not all of the time." He put out his hand and I let him tug me toward him. "It would be better if you could sleep when we do and wake with us. Not possible, but I'd like it better."

"Me too," Griffin said as he appeared at my side. I jolted and then laughed. Maybe we needed to get him a bell. Actually, that would be a great gift for all of them.

I patted them both on their arms. "The thing is, guys, it's not like you could wake up to protect me then, anyway. Besides, humans have to live in the daytime."

"Do they?" Ace rubbed my back. *I need bells, damn it.* "Who says?"

"I do." I sighed. "What would you all have done if I'd been in there for hours and come out drunk?"

"Waited." Rowan spoke across the parking lot as he strode toward me. "Just like we did, but I predicted you wouldn't be in there long. You're not the bar type."

What was it about Rowan? I either wanted to fuck him or smack him, and the two feelings were not mutually exclusive. "You're an expert on bars, now?"

Griffin interrupted us. "Hey guys, before you start bickering, Tanner's in the car. Could you give him his voice back?"

I nodded. "Sure. But you're right. I'm not a bar person. Feel free to be smug."

"Oh," Ace laughed. "We don't need permission for that."

No, they really didn't.

I sort of liked it, just the same.

IT WAS funny how happiness snuck in and took over my life. I couldn't remember a time I had been as content and pleased with things as I was for the next couple of weeks. It was so all-encompassing to feel settled and okay. With Rowan on our side, I stopped worrying about the elders.

Days moved into routine. I worked, or I had days off, but I spent my evenings with them. Sometimes we watched movies, went for walks, or they bought me things they thought I would like. At least I thought they bought the stuff. Maybe they just stole it? I learned to not ask some questions if I didn't want the answers.

If that made me a hypocrite, I supposed I could live with it. Besides, I was having way too much sex to be concerned with much other than eating, fucking, sleeping, working, and, for a change, laughing.

They didn't need very much blood. It seemed like maybe one of them, once a day, outside of Tanner's daily sips.

I lay on the floor with my head in Griffin's lap while he rubbed my back. "You need to be careful how you're lifting boxes."

Since I made the mistake of telling him my shoulder hurt, he seemed convinced I would perish from my strenuous life. I rolled my eyes but let him rub my back just the same. "I'm okay."

"You don't have to work."

I lifted my head. "Yeah, I do, and, yeah, we've had this fight already. I'm not having it again. I need my own job. I feel too much like your paramour otherwise."

He sat me up so I faced him. "Would it be so terrible to be my paramour? I'd take such good care of you. For your whole life, I'd never let anything happen to you. You would never have another worry."

Caesar scooted over next to us. "Why do you get to be his paramour? I found you first. You could be mine?"

"No paramours. Nope. No thank you." I got up. "What

are we doing tonight? Anything?" I was good with the idea of not doing anything, content to stay there, in my happy house that became more and more a home to me every day.

I blinked. It wasn't just the house that felt like home to me. *The guys are my home.* What was happening? It had been... what? Weeks since I'd hated vampires more than anything?

"I found some things in the book." Griffin lifted the book I'd retrieved for him from the guy hiding from the vampires. "It seems some of our history is wrong. Or the book is wrong. What I mean is there's a conflict of stories. Maybe we had a more profound history than we've known? Art. Music. I'm... I'm looking into it."

I stroked his face. "That would be amazing."

"It would be." He kissed my cheek. "I'll know more soon. Finally, I feel like I'm getting somewhere."

Ace tugged on the end of my hair. "Maybe tonight we could go into Asheville. I found some late-night clubs we could try out, because I'd like to dance with you. I'll even try not to kill anyone who bumps into you."

The door opened and closed as Rowan entered. He couldn't sleep there—a continued bone of contention that kept him constantly disgruntled. He smiled when he saw me, which always seemed to lighten his face up.

"Caesar's on the field tonight. Ace you're on tomorrow. Tanner, you're the day after that. I'll be the day after that. Griffin, keep up the research."

With Rowan in on everything, they weren't all called out on the same night anymore. I only worried about one of them every night, except Griffin, who never got called to fight. He was fine with that, finding the whole thing ridiculous. He could kill as easily as the rest of them, but there were better uses for his time.

"We were just talking about going to Asheville."

Rowan leaned against the counter. "You look pretty, Maci. I could go to Asheville."

"Thank you." I stood up. "So, should we go?"

I didn't have to work the next day, or I would've said no to Asheville. We'd probably get home just before sunrise.

"Did you eat anything?" Rowan walked toward the fridge and opened it. "Or am I making you something?"

Rowan hated the smell of food cooking. They all did, but Rowan seemed to dislike it the most. Ace hated the smell of orange juice. Tanner never complained, but the scent of coffee made him gag. If Griffin and Caesar had complaints, they didn't voice them, although Caesar had hated it in the beginning, too.

"I ate already."

My whole body suddenly went cold, as though I'd stepped into a freezer completely naked and been locked inside. I doubled over, my hands going to my head as my ears rang and my vision blurred.

"What is it?" Ace had me in his arms and against his chest. "Talk to me. What's wrong?"

"Her pain." Tanner gasped. "It's awful."

I couldn't answer him for a long second. I had to think, had to make it through the awful so that I could even explain the horror that suddenly dawned on me. "Caesar," I managed to choke out. "He's hurt."

"He's what?" Rowan's voice boomed around me. I closed my eyes. I had to center, to push through his pain so I could make some kind of decisions about what to do. The door slammed open and shut—Rowan headed out to find Caesar.

I gripped Ace's shirt, my hands shaking. "Take me to him. To the battle, right now."

"No," Griffin snapped, answering for Ace. "That's too

risky. Humans will give him blood. He can feed from you later. You on the battlefield is not going to happen, and Caesar would say the same."

Fuck that noise. I pushed off Ace. I wasn't losing Caesar. There was nothing that was going to take away my happy, not as long as there was strength left in my body. Pain wouldn't take me down, and these vampires weren't going to dictate things. They just weren't.

I stumbled backward, pushing Ace back with a shove when I did. "Then I'll walk to him, and so help me, if any of you try to stop me, I'll never speak to you again." The likelihood of that was small, but in that moment, I meant it—I fucking *meant* it. Caesar didn't need random blood; he needed *my* blood. Damn it. He did.

"Okay." Ace nodded. "Come on. I'll take you. In the car. You'll stay in the car. We'll find a way to bring Caesar to you. Okay? That will have to do. I'm not parading you around for the elders to see. Especially not any of those fuckers who fed from you before."

Griffin shoved Ace's shoulder. "Why do you think you get to decide this? I just said no. You don't outrank me, and despite what others think, I'm absolutely as capable of fighting as you."

"Boys." I put myself between them. "I don't give a shit about your bickering right now. Griffin, he's not in charge, but neither are you. I run my life. That's how this works. And I'm going to Caesar, the same way I'd go to any of you. Time isn't on my side." I could feel the cold surrounding me. It was going to consume me, take me under, and I'd never come out the other side. *Like drowning in cold.*

"I'm going."

A muscle ticked in Griffin's jaw, but he backed off. I walked outside and was hustled into the car by Tanner, who scooted in to sit practically on top of me. We took off with a screech, the car practically coming off its wheels with how fast Ace drove it.

Griffin tugged on my hair. "He wouldn't want this. You know that, right? I wouldn't want it, either. You anywhere near this is not on our agenda. I don't even think Ace would want this."

Hearing his name, he pounded on the steering wheel. "No, of course not, but if she's going to do it anyway, then I'm going to help her, so she doesn't get fucking killed. How is that?"

I didn't answer, drowning in ice. Tanner sighed. "We'll figure out a paradigm after this. For now, she helps Caesar, and then we'll know how we'll proceed in the future. She was so pale when she felt his pain. I don't want that again. She's not better yet. Everyone, just calm down."

We finally arrived at the location of the current battle. It felt like hours passed, but it probably took ten minutes. Sometimes time physically hurts in its passage; I don't think I understood it before then. There was pain to the way time moved fast or slowly.

I didn't have to get out of the car. Tanner jumped out before Ace even really slowed down, and Caesar was placed inside by Rowan. He nodded at me and then at Ace. "Get them out of here. Fast. Attention is turned elsewhere."

The car jerked forward, but I hardly noticed it, all of my attention on Caesar. I'd never seen an injured vampire before. They hurt me, but I'd never seen any of them as anything but powerful and healthy.

Caesar looked like he would die... any second. Pale skin, with blue veins tracking jagged lines all over his face—even right under his eyes. His lips were pale, void of any blush of redness at all, and his eyes, barely squints, were pure black.

He shook his head slightly but I understood the movement. "No." His voice was a whisper. "This is too close to the others."

I groaned. "You can yell at me after you're healed."

He would never be able to reach my neck, so I placed it right against his mouth. Caesar wasn't getting a damned choice. I closed my eyes as he bit my neck. This was going to be a brutal feed, which I could tell before his mouth even met my skin.

Against my body, his shook.

I WAS ALREADY DRINKING orange juice by the time I was conscious enough to really understand what was happening. At some point, I must have sat up on the couch? Orange juice meant they'd been taking care of me, but only Ace was by my side at that moment. I was grateful for him but it was unusual. Then it dawned on me—the sun was shining.

Ace shouldn't be up, either. But he was. That was when the door slammed open. I spun around. We were in so much trouble.

FLAME

For Carol Meijers...one of the best people ever. I am privileged to know you and call you my friend.

PREFACE

Rowan's father threw me to the floor of his office. My shoulder jarred, taking the brunt of the blow as my body vibrated from the force the vampire used to shove me down. I groaned as cage doors clanged shut behind me.

Maybe cage isn't the right word? More like an enclosure. As I tried to pull myself up, my palm flattened on the floor, but heavy metal bars surrounded me, and he'd locked me inside, so it sure looked like a cage.

Shouts sounded from outside. Fredrick—who took way too much joy in shoving me around—headed to the hallway to check out the source of the noise, shutting the door behind him. They had Ace with them, and he likely wasn't coming as easily as I had. I knew better than to struggle too much against vampires, but Ace was a vampire, too. If it wasn't daytime, he might have even been able to take them on. As it was, the fact that he was awake was a minor miracle he'd rather the others not learn about. *So much for that.*

I got onto my knees and wrapped my fingers around the cool steel of the bars. For just a second, I tried to breathe. *Okay. This is happening.* The elders found out about me, and it was probably somehow my fault. Maybe someone saw me at work in the store? Maybe it was the bar— *I knew I shouldn't have gone to the bar*. Was it the time I got the book for Rowan? Or when I saved Caesar? Or maybe it was when I'd been in the car with Rowan. *Hell, every time I left the house, I basically asked for this to happen.*

Letting go of the bars, I leaned my head against them instead. I never wanted to be back under the control of these people, but they addicted me to vampire venom, so what did I do instead of running as far from the blood suckers as I could? Instead of doing the smart thing, I fell in love with five of them and ended up locked in a cage.

Or an enclosure. I groaned. As usual when I'm scared, my brain focused on ridiculous little details like editing my own thoughts, but it wasn't like I knew what else to do, other than scream until my throat bled. *They'd get too much pleasure out of that. I won't scream for them. Fuck them.*

The guys could feel my pain as well as I could theirs lately. Maybe they had more opportunities to be distressed, but I knew they'd sense me as easily as I could them. They'd know I wasn't okay. Bad things might happen then. I didn't want them hurt regardless of what would happen to me. As human teenagers, I'd loved them, and they might have technically been dead for a long time, but I somehow managed to fall in love with the five people they became, too. Even though I hated vampires, I absolutely and unequivocally *didn't* hate them.

With a thunk, the door swung open, and Fredrick dragged Ace into the room, where almost all of the other elders waited. He hardly moved. By this time of day—*it has to be noon or even later now*—he wasn't even supposed to be awake.

Vampires acquired day-walking as they aged. It was

unheard of for someone like Ace to even be able to do it all, but he'd risen from death with the ability. We didn't know why.

Typical. There are so many things about our situation that we still don't even understand.

As Fredrick closed the door, Ace hissed at him. It wasn't a sound I'd heard him make before. Other vampires, yes, but not Ace. My guys had been as close to human as you could be without actually being one.

Well, they'd been very human since they came back into my life, anyway.

Right then, Ace looked like a wounded monster, all traces of his humanity erased as if they were never there in the first place. His eyes gleamed red, jewel bright with blood. Even his skin was tinged rosy and his hands shook. Pain hit me fast. He needed to feed. I'd do it, if he wanted me, but it would expose what happened when we fed—and the way it turned us on—in front of their fathers.

Still, I'd do it. *Anything for Ace.*

"Explain how you're awake!" Fredrick shouted at Ace. "Explain it to me."

My guy lifted his head just a touch to regard Frederick before scooting himself as close to the edge of my enclosure as he could get. "I don't have to explain anything to you. Not ever again. You're nothing compared to me. I'm one of the reborn, remember? You worked your whole life to make sure I existed. You created us. I'd love to know how something as small as you thinks it has the right to ask a question of me."

I lifted an eyebrow. The words were downright hostile for Ace, the "good" vampire so far as I could tell. Sure, he'd been filled with rage and quasi-delusional from his inner turmoil, but he'd also been Rowan's best helper, willing to obey any command.

Frederick reared back as if he'd been struck. I tried and failed not to smirk. Okay, he also hadn't been expecting that from Ace.

All of the elders in the room had fed on me at some point or another, I realized as I scanned their faces. Well, except for Ace's father, and we still didn't know why he hadn't. It hadn't been top of my list to find out, what with everything *else* going on at the time.

In retrospect, maybe it should have been.

I reached through the bars and took Ace's hand in mine. A slight tremor shivered from his fingers, so I squeezed back. *This has to be hell for him.*

"It's going to be okay." I don't know why I would promise him that when nothing about the situation seemed anywhere near okay. Maybe it was because he would've done the same for me—once upon a time, back when he'd been human—and even though vampires didn't generally *need* reassurance, they still deserved it.

He nodded. "It is, because I'll tear them to pieces if they come anywhere near you again."

The sentiment was sweet, but I doubted he could tear anything apart in that moment. I got to my knees and dropped his hand, grabbing onto the bars so I could see the men who featured in my nightmares—back when I used to have them. My nightmares stopped one day; maybe that was when I officially gave up my hope for having a better life, since there was nothing left to frighten me.

Well, except for this very scenario. I did *not* want their mouths back on my wrist. I had to say something. Sometimes I actually could talk myself out of trouble. "So what is the problem? Is it that I'm in the state of North Carolina? I'm not bothering any of you. Why do you care that I'm here at all?"

Frederick snarled. "Rowan gave an order, and it's been broken."

I held up my hands in the universal signal for surrender. "Okay. Solid point. Let's ask Rowan how he feels about it when he wakes up, shall we?"

"I can tell you how he'll feel." Ace panted between words. "He'll want to tear you apart for touching her. Rowan changed his ruling on Maci. If he didn't tell you, that's your fucking problem, not hers. Get her out of this cage immediately."

A muscle ticked in Frederick's jaw. "If that is true, then we have a bigger problem than we realized." He looked over his shoulder. "Take your son away from here. I'll handle this as it always should have been handled. I tried it your way. Now we'll try mine."

Ace's father stared at me for a second longer. Although I only knew him as a monster who failed to protect his son from death and didn't torture me— for whatever reasons— for just a second, I could have sworn I saw pity on his face.

He nodded. "Come on, Ace."

"I'm not leaving her." Any façade of humanity vanished from Ace right then. His voice rumbled low, sounding animalistic and not at all like I was used to hearing from him.

I squeezed his fingers again. "There is nothing you can do for me right now. I know you want to, okay? I know that. I love you. I told you guys that, I think?" It was a bit of a blur. "Even if that isn't something you feel. Despite that, what you're doing right now? That feels like love to me. I need you to go with your father, and I need you to rest so you can help me tonight, okay?" I said more than I intended in front of our audience, but wanted to make sure I reached him. What he needed was to feed from me; it would make him strong. But feeding would showcase more than my words revealed, and I didn't want to go that far.

Of course, his father would make sure his needs were met by some random human. The thought burned, but I had no time for my emotional mess. Ace nodded once then rose. "Maci is Rowan's paramour. If you hurt her, there will be hell to pay."

Quite a statement, if not an outright lie. *Sort of.* I was almost all of their paramours. In fact, I was pretty sure they all would've given me that role, if I would've accepted it. But that was as close to an outright lie as I'd ever heard Ace say aloud. Technically, vampires couldn't lie—except for Ace, apparently. *Yet another way he's different.* But as far as this particular lie was concerned, if he didn't speak to Rowan before Rowan spoke to Frederick, the bad guys would know he could lie. Then he was really screwed. They'd already clued into the fact that he was still awake. If he could outright lie, it certainly wouldn't make things better for him.

He did an impressive job following his father from the room without shaking in weakness, though I knew it had to be hard for him. With a final glance back to me, he disappeared from my view. Maybe in some alternate reality he stayed and fought off every vampire in the room so we could escape together unscathed, but that wasn't my reality. In my world, Ace was a young vampire, practically unable to function past sunrise, even though he somehow could stay awake. There was nothing he could do for me right then.

Frederick's smile defined unkindness. He bent to address me. "I let you live because they backed me into a corner, but I am no longer bound by those constrictions. Now, you're mine to handle as I see fit. There is no rule protecting paramours and, besides, Rowan is too young to have a paramour. I don't know what they do with you, but it can't happen anymore. I knew who you were the second I spotted you, and I won't let you win."

He knew me? Of course he did... "You've always known me. I was just a normal teenage girl minding my business when I got sucked into your world and this nonsense. I never wanted anything to do with any of you bloodsuckers."

The click of the cage door opening was my only warning before Caesar's father hauled me out of the cell. He swung me around like a rag doll then shoved me at Frederick. "If we're doing this, let's get it done. You all might be comfortable daywalking, but I hate it, and I always have. Get rid of whatever you think she is and be done with it."

"You can't just kill me. Your son will never forgive you. None of them will. They'll destroy you for this."

Frederick shook his head and grabbed my arm. "By the time they're old enough to even attempt such a thing, they'll have long since forgotten everything about you."

Oh, I doubt that very much. It gave me little comfort, but I knew the guys were a lot more powerful than he would ever believe. *Rowan could take him down right now.*

I struggled against Fredrick's restraining grip, but it was futile. Eventually, my struggles must have annoyed him, because he whacked me right over the head. My ears rang before everything went black.

Then, I died.

1

ROWAN

I t was harder to wake up than it should have been. The last waking had been rough, and I'd given up the pretense of going home. Maci was in the house, awake but struggling, when I finally gave in to the dawn. I wasn't leaving the space where she resided until I put eyes on her the next waking. Hopefully asleep. Somehow, Ace could stay up. I didn't understand it. I was more powerful than him, yet he could do things I couldn't do.

Caesar moaned from his position in the bed across the room from me. We all struggled to get up. *Why?* I rubbed my arms. *What makes this night different from every other waking?*

Everything was wrong.

I threw myself out of bed and made my way to Caesar. He'd almost died in battle—*would* have died, if Maci wasn't such a fucking miracle. *Now I have to send Ace tonight to fight.* I hated it. They were my family. I didn't want to fight a meaningless war, and I didn't want them to, either.

I want this to end.

Where was Maci? Usually, I felt her the second I woke

up. Like a beacon calling me to her side, whether I needed to feed or not, she called to me. Tonight, unfortunately, I would need to feed. It would be better if Caesar could have had her alone, but we would all be hungry after what happened. Could she really handle that? She was just a human.

There was nothing "just" about Maci or our situation.

Caesar stared up at me. "Somethings wrong. I can't...feel her."

"Me neither. I'm hoping that just means she's out cold." We'd check her room. Tanner and Ace intended to stay with her. Griffin had the room to himself, and I'd bunked with Caesar in case he needed something—not that I could rouse if he did. The pretty-much-being-dead every day thing was getting old, fast.

Griffin rushed through the door as if I'd conjured him while Caesar swung his legs off the edge of the bed.

Griffin burst out, "They're not here."

"What?" His words didn't make sense. "Who's not here?"

"Ace and Maci. Tanner can't talk. I'm not sure they were here at all."

I tore into the other room, finding Tanner staring at the bed. He couldn't speak verbally, but I understood his expression completely. He was scared. *She isn't here.*

I ran a hand through my hair. "Where could Ace have taken her? The hospital? Check your phones." If she was at the hospital, I was going to freak the fuck out.

"I told her not to give me so much blood," Caesar yelled, his frantic tone matching the dull thud of my heart.

There were no messages. No way would Ace have forgotten to reach out to us. *What does it mean?* I took a deep breath. I was a vampire, a tracker. *If somehow someone came here...*

The door swung abruptly open, hitting the wall with a bang seconds before Ace's father dragged him into the room. Ace's eyes shined pure red and he raved, throwing his body onto the floor with a howl. I'd seen someone act like that once before—a vampire who needed to sleep and hadn't.

"What's going on?" I dropped to the floor to check Ace, my friend in this life and the one before. Griffin joined me soundlessly. Caesar and Tanner hadn't moved. They stared at us as if they'd been turned into statues. *What are they sensing that I'm not?*

"She's *dead*." Ace pounded on the floor, his hands fisted. Over and over again, punching as if he intended to break through the floor itself.

The sound of his thuds filled the void where my heartbeat and breath should be until I realized I wasn't breathing and gasped in enough air to speak. "What?" I rasped, still barely accomplishing sound. It couldn't be true. *No*. The only "she" he could mean would be Maci, and there was no fucking way. *No. Absolutely not.* Anger burned through me, and my vampire surged to the top of my consciousness. *Things need to break; they need to tear. We need to destroy.* To answer the impulse, I lifted the table from the floor and ripped it to pieces with my mind as if it were made of cardboard.

Everything must be destroyed. The world is demolished. It will be over today. Everything. No, Maci, no world left to give a shit about. "Let's destroy everything," I said, giving voice to the only thing my vampire would accept as suitable in the circumstances.

"On it." Griffin backed up. "Lemme grab my flame thrower. We'll start with the main house."

"Stop." Ace's father's voice rang out loud, commanding.

"It's my fault," Ace cried . "I tried, but I'm not strong enough. I tried."

Some fracture of my mind noted it was amazing he was awake at all. If there was blame to be meted out, it had little to do with Ace.

Not that it mattered. Everyone would die.

"She's coming back," his father yelled, capturing my attention. "Her father has been systematically feeding her vampire blood for years. I don't know where they dumped her, but she'll be back in a matter of months. How many? Again, I don't know, but I know she'll be back."

I tried to slow my heart rate to listen past the rushing in my ears—easier desired than done. "What?"

"You *had* to know she wasn't normal. She's like you. She was born to be reborn. It's a long story, but for now, you need to get your stuff together and run from here. Go see Warren, her father. I'll tell you how to get there, then he can explain the rest. Maci *is* coming back. She'll be different, like us, but she'll be here."

Ace hit the floor again, his rage unwavering. "He *killed* her."

Yes, he had. Our little human was fragile, and she was gone. I failed her. I tried to picture her in my mind's eye as she had been just the day before. We'd rushed her back after Caesar practically drained her dry. She'd been loopy but happy. I handed her orange juice.

"I love you." She'd smiled at the room. "Oh, I know you don't do love, but I love you. All of you."

I didn't utter a word, like my mouth was glued shut. My hands started to shake. *Vampires don't love.* But...Maci. *Oh, fuck me, I love Maci.*

And she is gone. She was coming back. That was important, and I needed to remember it so my vampire didn't slip my tethers and rain blood on the earth. But *my* Maci—the one I had known, the one I fell in love with—she was gone forever.

Regardless of whatever happened later, things would have to burn.

2

MACI

In the end, everyone dies.

Eventually.

Hopefully not too soon.

Cuz then it's tragic or something.

I have no memory of my own death.

I remember one last shot to the head by a scared man, one whose fear of losing power left him with no choice but to kill me.

So he did.

I only barely remember that happening, though. More like still frames from a movie than something that happened to me.

My guys woke up in coffins, reborn vampires with ceremony and excitement. Not that I remembered that fact particularly when I opened my eyes during my own rising. No, as I clawed through dirt and bodies, pulling my way toward the surface, I was fueled only by the aching hunger that called on me to feed. Later, I'd learn they'd thrown me in the pit where Frederick disposed of female bodies of servants he promised to change but never would. When they died, he dumped them there.

He'd thought I couldn't become a vampire, so that's where he put me, too. Just another body.

I smiled to myself. *He didn't know about the feedings.* All those years of vampire blood coursed through my veins just *waiting* to change me the moment Frederick dumped me in the fucking pit earlier than expected. But I didn't remember that then, either. I didn't know anything. Or even think that I should. All of that dulled; it fled like it didn't exist. There was nothing to think about left in my mind.

I didn't care about any of it, not really. All I wanted was blood.

So that was what I went looking for—blood.

3

The campfire crackled and spit flames. I bent over it, warming my hands while the scent of woodsmoke made me a little nostalgic. But for what? I wasn't sure.

The dead bodies were starting to cool all around me, yet I was still hungry. Then again, I was always hungry. I could put out the campfire with a bucket of water, but the fire burning a hole inside of me couldn't be quenched—not that I was sure I wanted it to ever stop. Why should I bother, when so many people just sat around the woods at night waiting to give me what I wanted?

I clenched my fists. *It isn't enough.* I frowned. But *why* was it never enough?

A noise, the cracking of a branch, caught my attention. I whirled around, ready to strike again. Were more humans just waiting to help me get through the night? I hoped so. My stomach gurgled in agreement. Hiding in their camper would be so much nicer when the sun came out if I could, for once, have a full stomach when I rested.

Five men stared at me from the other side of the fire,

appearing soundlessly from the forest near where I'd discarded two of the bodies. None of them spoke, silent in the way they regarded me and unmoving, utterly still. I wasn't fooled. They might strike at any time; they were just like me.

I bared my teeth. *This is my hunting ground*, the gesture should tell them. *I found it, and it is mine.*

The one in the center of their group nodded, as though he'd understood what I didn't say aloud. "For five nights, we've been looking for you."

Why? I didn't know them. I'd only been awake and starving for five nights. In that time, I'd done nothing to deserve their attention. They could only want the territory, and I wouldn't give it up.

"You're hungry," said the one all the way to the left. His voice resonated lower than the first one. "We're so sorry you've had to wake up alone. We had no idea where you would rise or when. We waited until we could sense you, and then we came looking. I'll *always* find you."

Nonsense. They needed to go. "Mine." It was all I could manage past the territorial spirit rising in my chest. I would make them leave if I had to, and my muscles coiled, readying for the fight.

"She has no idea who we are at all." The one all the way to the right sighed. "I hoped he would be wrong about that."

The one who they all stared at periodically—he must be their leader—appeared suddenly in my face. I reacted, shoving roughly at his meaty body. He could burn in the flames if he didn't get away from me. I'd put him in there myself, face first.

Except...he didn't budge.

"You're hungry, and we can all feel it. We can make this easier for you. Just come with us. You don't remember us now, but you're very important to us. We've waited a long time to find you. I'm Rowan—do you remember me at all?"

His words didn't make sense, especially not with the hunger making my jaw and veins practically ache with a need that the sound of his rumbly voice wasn't helping. What did he mean when he said I was important to them? *That can't be.*

I was starving. If I meant something to him, or any of them, I wouldn't ache constantly from hunger. Anyone who mattered to him shouldn't have been left in a hole to claw their way through the dirt just to feed like an animal.

The more I thought about his words, the angrier I got. The flame inside of me rose, curling white hot, far more dangerous than the nostalgic crackle of campfire. *I don't want his nonsense. Or his...untruths.* I wanted none of it. No. The hunger blinded me, leaving me panting like a dog. Finally, I found one word to speak, and I would repeat it until they understood. I pointed at the ground. *He has to understand.* "Mine."

Rowan nodded, as if I answered his question. He brushed the hair away from my forehead, and for a second, something stirred inside of me that wasn't the pangs of the need to feed that rode me constantly.

But just as quickly as it arrived, it fled, grated away by the never-ending hunger. I shoved at him once more, yet again, Rowan didn't move. "In a few weeks, when you're properly fed, you'll be stronger than me for a while, but you're not yet. Come with us, Maci. There will be plenty of blood for you where we're taking you."

No. I didn't believe them. There would be nothing there; he just wanted to take me from my place where the humans came. Besides, the sun would be out soon to burn me and force me to sleep. *Absolutely not.*

"Tanner," he said as he looked over his shoulder. "She's not coming willingly. Get her there whether she wants it or not. *Without* hurting her. The rest of us will clean up the site, like we have the others for the last five nights. Remember, we knew this would be hard."

I blinked, and the one he called Tanner appeared before me. Tanner was the only one who hadn't spoken yet. He stared at me for a long, still moment, and my monster shifted inside of me. His beast was close to the surface, like mine. I could see it there, writhing just below the edge of his steady gaze. Rowan hadn't released me, but Tanner put his hands on my arms, holding me steady for another long second before he pulled me against him. I yanked backward, trying to escape his hold, but I didn't move an inch. Through Tanner's eyes, I could see what rode me gazing back, and I stopped tugging. *He has trouble being here, too.* Like a caress, his monster touched my own. I couldn't explain the sensation if I'd been asked to, but I don't know if anyone else ever experienced such intimate knowledge.

My stomach turned, a harsh reminder of the need raking razors down my throat. I needed blood. More of it. *Now.*

Rowan dropped his hold and Tanner took over, walking as if he didn't for a moment doubt I would follow. What choice did I have? *They're taking my food away.* He was stronger than me.

Yet, as starved as I was...right in that moment, as they all stared at me quietly, I realized I'd never felt safer, not in any other moment of the five days of my memory.

Like a blip, the sensation passed. "Hungry," I repeated, trying to speak past the dryness of my aching throat.

"We know," the first one who spoke to me answered. "But not for much longer."

Pain rocketed through me, the need for more blood my only thought. Instead of giving me blood, Tanner stubbornly dragged me wherever they were taking me. I struggled, but it didn't matter.

AFTER THEY DRAGGED me through a house, my heels thudded on each step of the stairs to the basement where they promptly locked us inside. No buffet of humans fat as ticks with pulsing blood waited for me in the basement where they took me. The loud click of the lock moments before echoed through me like a death knell. Understanding flooded me. *They lied. There is no food here.*

"Liars," I hissed, scanning for a possible escape route.

Instead of being a proper, spooky dungeon, the vampires had brought me to what looked like a normal living room, despite it being downstairs. Couches and chairs decorated the space, as well as some clean, crisp-looking art. No people, though. No blood. No windows to escape. Way more of them and only one of me. Would they leave me here with no food? *Liars,* I thought again.

Rowan spoke past the terrified thudding of my pulse. "Never. Vampires don't do that. Well, *most* vampires don't." He shot a look toward the one who first spoke to me. "Some of us have the extraordinary ability to do so. But not me. I might deflect, but I'll never lie to you, Maci. There *is* food here." He turned and offered me his neck. "Take it."

I blinked. His words made no sense. *He isn't what I eat.* "Not right," I managed, shaking my head and trying to understand past the jarring dissonance of my thoughts.

"It is for us." His voice was low, a growling caress in my ear. "I know you think you need to feed from humans. I understand, and you're right. We do that, and you still will, I promise. But when vampires share a strong relationship—a soul- mated relationship—they can sustain one another this way. It's actually more filling and better for you. Plus, you can't kill us, not by drinking from us. Although the dead humans might not bother you now, because it never bothers any of us when we first rise, I can promise you it will eventually. Let me feed you, Maci."

He kept calling me that name. *Is it mine?*

It could be my name.

Not that I cared, I reminded myself, focusing on the neck he still offered so invitingly. I had to admit, I found his words intriguing. *Could I?* My stomach cramped. I had no choice but to try. I needed something, anything, before I died from the need.

My fangs elongated, preparing to sink into his flesh. Next to me, one of them sucked in a breath—*if they stick around, I'll eventually need names just to tell them apart.* "That is so fucking sexy," he growled.

"Ace," another one said, his tone full of censure. "We don't want to scare her."

I wasn't scared—not of them, at least. I needed to feed, but my only anxiety stemmed from the continued pain from my hunger.

Without further delay, and because I couldn't take the pain a moment longer, I closed my eyes and bit Rowan's neck. The only joy I could remember came from these moments, from feeding. I loved the way it felt to pierce the skin, the anticipation of what came next. Usually, whatever human I found screamed their head off at this point, but not Rowan. He shuddered against me, almost like...he *enjoyed* the feel of my teeth breaking his skin? His blood hit my tongue and it was my turn to gasp.

His didn't taste like a human's, that was for damn sure. This taste seemed thicker, more metallic, and it was oh-so-very warm. I sucked harder, and he shook against me. I didn't know if his knees gave out or if we both just sank to the ground.

"More," Rowan's voice rasped scratchily. "Please. Take more. All of it. I *need* you to."

I lay against him, him beneath me, and as I sucked, his body hardened. What was that? I should know. Only, I didn't, because there was just the need to feed. That was all there could be.

A hand smoothed against my back, rubbing gently. "He means it, take all of it." That was the voice of one of the guys whose name I didn't know yet. "You can't kill him. He'll pass out, wake up, feed, and then you can feed off him again. Take everything you need."

Pounding sounded in the distance, and the person talking sighed loudly. "Ace, go deal with him."

"Already on it, Griffin."

I appreciated when they used their names—helped me figure out who was who without asking. Footsteps sounded, but I decided I didn't care what was happening. Nothing mattered more in that moment than the rich pulse of blood over my tongue from this other vampire—Rowan—who I intended to feast from for as long as I could. His movements, the way he ground slightly against me, slowed, making me wonder if I truly might be about to drain him dry.

"I want to see her."

"No." I could hear the heat of Ace's anger from where I straddled Rowan on the floor. "We told you—you'll see her when we say and not before. Go away, or I'll take her so far from here that you'll never see her again. Remember, you need us more than we need you."

Idly, I wondered what was going on. Not that I particularly cared one way or the other, if I was being entirely honest. Rowan was done, not a drop left to take. I lifted my head and stared down at his calm face, his unmoving body. Would he be okay, I wondered, since I'd taken all of the blood he offered me? Would he really wake up?

Griffin touched my cheek. "He's fine."

His touch felt nice, as did the heat of the blood coursing just beneath the surface of that caress. "More."

He tilted his neck, offering me exactly what I wanted. "My turn," he said, managing somehow to sound exceptionally dominant while his pose screamed vulnerability I was only too happy to exploit.

4

I bit into Griffin's neck, eager for more. I didn't expect variation, yet I found his taste distinctly different from Rowan's. Sweeter, sort of, but darker, too. Like the bite of dark chocolate as it glides down your throat and coats your very soul in sticky goodness. *Why do I know that taste?* I wasn't sure. I couldn't have explained it; I just needed *feed*, *more*, and *now*.

One of the other ones—Ace?—still argued with a male at the top of the stairs.

"She's my daughter," the unseen voice said.

A hissing sound replied before Ace said, "You made her a pawn. You made all of us pawns, but Maci had it the worst. I don't even know where she woke up," he shouted.

I closed my eyes. *Let them argue.* The blood ran hot and wet down my throat, cool waves of peace easing the snarling pain of starvation as I swallowed more and more.

Like Rowan, this vampire also sagged, knees going soft, so I rolled Griffin beneath me, and he moaned. The low sound resonated through me, sparking nerves and swirling blissful sensations through my blood-drunk mind. As a

Once I finished, I gently laid the husk of Tanner onto the floor.

"Ace," Caesar spoke low. "Your turn."

He sighed. "I'm not sure I deserve it. You know what happened. This whole fucking thing is my fault."

"This whole thing is her father's fault—Frederick's fault, not yours. We've discussed this. I go last, and you agreed, let her suck you, because she's ravenous, and she will be for weeks. Hurry it up, before the sun rises. I want her as close to fully fed as possible before she goes to sleep for the night."

Did he say weeks? I got up on all fours. "This won't stop?"

Ace crossed the space between us then knelt in front of me. "Eventually it lessens, but we're always hungry. Except when...well, enough questions for now. Come on, because he's right. I don't have time to obsess, but there's always later."

I caught a movement nearby out of the corner of my eye, so I shot a look in that direction. Rowan started to roll to his side, proving they'd been right. I hadn't killed them. *That is...good.*

With a wrench of my head, I looked away. There were more pressing things than Rowan waking up. When I couldn't find the words to explain myself—my brain just didn't want to help me right then—I pounded on my chest. Finally, I managed to say, "I don't want to feel like this forever."

"I know." Ace took my hand. I was a little ashamed to see my fingers tremble in his. "But you'll get used to it. Maybe after this initial awakening, we'll be able to feed from you like you do us."

"Ace," Caesar shouted. "Too much, too soon."

Ace winced. "I'm sorry. I wasn't thinking."

"Obviously." Caesar practically groaned. He knelt to join us. "Come on, Ace is waiting. You're hungry. Deal with that, and the rest will be explained later, I promise."

I wanted answers but not more than I wanted blood. I dove at Ace, my mouth making contact with his skin as I took him down to the floor, my body on top of his. He cried out, the sound quickly changing to a sigh. He liked feeding me; they all did. The idea should be strange, but it wasn't. Mostly because I liked it, too.

His blood was warm, and it flowed easily down my throat. I almost choked on it, taking too much in a single gulp. Forcing myself to slow was hard, but I managed. His heart beat in my ears. I could hear the sound of it, so full of life and hope. Thinking back, I realized I could hear all of them, but I hadn't cared.

This was different. He was different. Awareness seemed to wash over me in a wave.

Rowan stopped to regard us as he passed us, heading for the stairs, but I didn't look up to meet his gaze. Eventually, he said something to Caesar, who only grunted in response before Rowan headed upstairs. I lifted my head. Ace was done. He had been the fastest yet. A door opened and closed. I looked in the direction of the noise to realize Rowan was gone. Where had he gone?

Caesar didn't move toward me. We weren't done. I was still hungry. I set Ace down on the ground, surprised to see a smile on his face.

The awake vampire shook his head when I glanced his way. "Not yet."

"Why?" I demanded. I couldn't take him in a fight, but they promised me I'd be fed.

"Because Rowan needs to come back before I can let you feed. I don't trust the people upstairs as far as I can throw them. I'm not sure they'll do the right thing, so one of us has to be awake at all times. Rowan can manage to stay up for ten, maybe fifteen minutes after the sun rises. So, we give him five minutes to feed and come back, then you can feed." Caesar rose and walked toward the stairs. "You can wait that long."

I thumped my hand against the floor. "It hurts."

"A temporary pain, and you should remember that. Breathe. You're strong; you always have been. You live through things that kill other people, so I know you can handle your hunger, Maci. I promise you can...and I'm sorry."

I got to my feet—they were wobbly, but I managed. "Sorry because I'm hungry but you won't feed me? Or are you sorry because of whoever it is upstairs that you don't like? My father? That's what he called the man who came down, I think. You don't like him, I can tell."

He lifted an eyebrow. "I *hate* him with a passion I rarely feel, actually. But, although I suppose I am sorry that you're hungry, that isn't why I'm apologizing."

Nothing made any sense. I had a father, and I couldn't give two shits that he existed. I only wanted what Caesar had and wasn't giving me. "Maybe he'll feed me. My father?" I paused when he frowned and shook his head in a swift, definitive movement. "Why are you sorry, then, and why not?"

"He can't feed you because only we feed you, period. End of story. And I'm sorry because I didn't find you before you rose. You awoke alone, and for that, I am sorry. I *will* always find you...only this time I was late. I felt you rise, but then it took days to pinpoint where."

He felt me rise? There was so little I understood about being a vampire. I walked toward him. "I was in a hole.

There were dead bodies everywhere. I clawed my way up, through them and through the earth." My hands were still dirty from the pulling and grabbing, actually. I stared at them as if they were foreign objects. I only needed them to grab on while I fed, so what other purpose could they serve?

I thought about the hole again. "Why *were* there so many bodies in there?"

Caesar shook his head, his lips thin before he explained. "Frederick kills women. He doesn't let them turn—major power move. He dumped you in with his victims, I guess. It makes sense, since to him, you were no different than them. I do owe your father thanks for one thing, even if it never needed to happen the way it did."

Rowan slammed the door as he entered, and I could see he stood at the top of the stairs. "Back."

Caesar needed no further invitation, and he pulled me against him. "Come on. It's almost daylight. I don't know if you know yet, but you'll be aware that it's daytime whether you're inside or out. We can feel it. You'll feed us both to sleep now. I think we have roughly ten minutes left together."

Rowan came down the stairs two at a time. "More like eight." He touched my back. "You'll get the hang of this."

I didn't want to get the hang of it. "Why?"

I hoped he knew what I meant. I didn't need an explanation of why I'd get the hang of it, not really. It was all too much.

Caesar lay down, drawing me against him, putting my mouth right where he wanted it. "Rebirth is hard. It does get easier, but no one is going to fuck with you ever again."

I bit down.

~

CONSCIOUSNESS FLOODED INTO MY MIND, the sound of low voices buzzing nearby. I wanted to bat the sound away, but the hunger forced me awake. I had to find food. *Blood. Now.*

Rowan stared down at me. "Welcome back. You're starving, I know, but you should shower first. You're covered in blood. That's normal, by the way, so not judging. We're not monsters, though, and we don't have to live like that."

Are you fucking kidding? "I need to eat first."

"It won't help. Only time will fill the ache in your stomach enough that you can otherwise function. You need the blood. We're here to give it to you as we did last night, forever. I know you, Maci. Or, at least, I did. In several manifestations of my lives, I have known you, and at no time would you be comfortable like this. You'll be glad for the shower, and then you can drain me until I'm senseless again."

I let him lead me to the bathroom, even if I was grumpy from the pain. He was right, I was a mess. A big one. And the aching inside me couldn't get worse, while I could get cleaner.

Stripping off the clothes I obviously died in felt ridiculously good. I dropped them on the floor, and only then realized I was completely naked in front of Rowan. I turned to find Rowan wasn't the only one getting a show. Ace stood next to him, and they both stared at me with obvious interest.

I turned on the water with one hand while I maintained eye contact with them. "Humans don't like to be naked."

Ace visibly swallowed then arched one brow. "Sometimes they do."

"You knew me before I was a vampire." That much had been obvious, but I found myself mildly curious. "Did I—she—like to be naked?"

Rowan's mouth twitched. "Sometimes."

I looked down at my body. I hadn't considered my appearance up until that point, not in the least. What did it matter, really? I was a vampire, and my sole purpose was to feed until I was sated. Then feed again. It seemed a wasted existence, since humans did other things.

"What is the point of any of this?"

Ace moved around me to touch the water. "Right now, the purpose is to get clean. Afterward, the only thing I'm interested in is getting you fed. Someday, not too far in the near future, you'll have other needs, other things you want to think about and do. I promise you, Maci."

Once again, I stared at my body. I had curves, breasts, hips, shapely arms and muscular legs. My stomach was flat, my abdominal muscles apparent. I was strong, and my hair was long, falling past my breasts.

"Did she look like this or has the body changed?"

They were both silent until Rowan finally answered. "In some ways, yes, in some ways, no. Mostly yes. Nothing drastic changed, but, yes, we alter physically when we are reborn."

Ace crossed his arms over his chest. "You can't remember yourself before the change?"

"Personal memories come back last for the females. It's why they're so at risk during this part. That's the excuse my father uses for what he does. Her memories will return, and she'll just know everything again suddenly. For now, get clean, Maci. You were a beautiful human and you're a stunning vampire. I could look at you naked for the rest of my life and never get bored, but we're on a deadline. Looming sun and all that, so time to get clean."

He was right, and the faster I cleaned, the faster I could eat.

"I'll stay with her," Ace said to Rowan as I stepped under the spray and pulled the curtain closed to separate myself from them. "You deal with Warren. He isn't going to stop, because he thinks he has rights. We knew he could be this kind of problem, and only you can deal with him long term."

Rowan audibly sighed. "If I let Griffin handle him, we'll have an incident. We're only here because he has the knowledge we need. I'm not convinced any of us are what they want us to be, not even Maci. In the meantime, I'm not facing Frederick blind, not while Maci is vulnerable. Until she's not, we'll stay. Afterward, as far as I'm concerned, the whole world can fuck itself and get out of our way."

Ace laughed. "Same page."

"Good. I need you, all of you. Always have. She needs blood as soon as she's out, obviously." I heard the door close, meaning he'd left, so I closed my eyes. There was so much information, and all of it confusing. *Vulnerable.*

Is that what I am? I didn't feel that vulnerable. *What a nasty word.* I was capable of doing harm to anyone and anything. I ran a hand over my body with the soap. Shampoo. I knew what that was. I used it, too. Conditioner. Dirt flowed down all around me until it stopped and finally the water ran clear. I could understand why they wanted me clean—I wouldn't have wanted to smell me either, and the thought made me smile.

I was funny. That was something I could know about myself. Maybe not much else.

I am funny.

And not *vulnerable.*

I turned off the water and flung open the shower curtain. Ace stared at me for a hot second, then dropped his gaze. He started at my feet and his gaze slowly traveled up my body, investigating every nook and cranny along the way. *Is he checking to see if I washed properly?*

As I let the water drip down me, I didn't even look for a towel. It was sort of nice to be wet. The room was warm. The yellow wallpaper might be peeling in places, but the water pressure in the shower was amazing, and the tile beneath my feet was cool, a nice contrast to the warmth of the room.

"I'm not," I finally said, since he still just looked at me.

He cleared his throat. "What?"

"I'm not vulnerable."

Ace leaned against the wall. "Would you like a towel?"

I didn't care for his non-answer. *Why does he think he can speak to me like that?* I grabbed him, ripping him off the wall, and he just smirked at me.

"Already feeling strong? I'll need to watch myself now so I don't let you take me by surprise."

He halted my pulling on him. So, he didn't want to make this easy. That was fine. I could grab him and take control, if I wanted to. It would help if he didn't expect me to do it. I kissed his neck a second before I bit it. He gasped, his arms coming around my wet body to hold on. We both slid backward with the momentum into the sink. His body hardened, particularly his cock, which pressed against me, hard. I reached out to cup it instinctively, and he groaned.

That certainly didn't happen with the humans, not in my memory anyway.

I lifted my head, licking his wound closed to save every drop of his precious blood. Ace was spicy, and I hadn't really noticed last night. I was definitely more awake at the moment.

"Normal?" I squeezed him so he'd know what I meant, and he gripped the sink on a gasp.

"With you, yes. Not with anyone else."

"Why?" I licked my lips. The answer seemed important.

He let go of the sink to cup my cheeks. "Because we belong to each other. We always have. That's why we can feed you. You'll never want anyone else now. Sure, you can still feed from humans. It's how I stayed alive the last ten months, all of us have. But we're yours and you are ours. We were always supposed to be together. And when we feed, we want more than just blood. We want sex. Because we belong to each other. When you're not so needy, you'll want it, too. Then it'll be..."

He didn't finish what he was going to say. I knew the answer anyway. "Perfect."

Ace nodded once. "Perfect. You are incredibly coherent right now. Much more than you should be."

I gripped his shirt. "I told you I'm not fucking vulnerable."

I bit down again.

When his body jerked against my own this time, I gripped him hard through his pants. If this had happened with all of them the night before, I hadn't noticed, but I was fully aware now. I stroked him. It wasn't close enough. His pants were in the way. There was only one thing to do. I tore his pants off.

Ace laughed—not the response I was going for. His blood was what I needed, but it wasn't *all* I needed in that moment. No. His underwear was in the way. It went, too. I squeezed again, this time feeling his warm skin against my fingers. He wasn't laughing anymore.

I fed, bringing his blood inside of me as I stroked him from his tip downward. One movement then another. He pulled me against him, reaching for my pussy. I stopped his hand. Another time. I didn't want it, not yet. I only wanted him to come. That was what I craved.

We stayed like that, me stroking him as I drank him down inside of myself. Minutes passed. There was just Ace and the noises he made in the bathroom. Maybe we were the only two people in existence? Right then, it seemed possible, even though I knew better.

His body jerked as he came in my hand. I smiled as I finished feeding. His body sagged against me and I held him in my arms, knowing that had been so different than it had been before.

I smiled. *Guess I actually needed that shower.*

The sound of footsteps in the hallway caught my attention. Griffin and Tanner entered the room from the bathroom, then Griffin took Ace from my arms. "I've got him."

His gaze traveled my body and shivers broke out on my skin. His neck was inviting. I almost grabbed him and bit, but I resisted...just to prove that I could.

He winked at me. "Guess we don't have to worry about your human sensibilities anymore."

I turned toward Tanner as Griffin left the room with an unconscious Ace. Tanner was once again silent. His monster was close and mine squirmed to join him. I shoved her back down. It was hard enough when she mostly left me alone. I didn't need her asserting herself more than was natural.

"Not talking again." That much was obvious.

He stared at me, so I did the same, letting myself see who he was. Danger stood in front of me, yet I wasn't afraid. I was either foolish or brave, but what did it matter when I was so fucking hungry, too?

"After I bit him—you—he could talk." I ran my hand down Tanner's neck, right over his pulse, the place I would make mine shortly. "Why?"

He wasn't going to answer me, just to let me see how far down he controlled the vampire in front of him. There was no separating them right now. I leaned over to whisper in his ear. "Is it because you know that I can protect him?"

Tanner's monster found that funny. I didn't know how I knew it exactly, but I did. A quick ripple of amusement fluttered through me. No, he didn't need me to protect him. They were perfectly strong and scary all on their own. It was something else, though. He just needed me. Tanner didn't want to be present if I wasn't. And the only way to be sure that I was there, that I was real, that I wasn't going anywhere was the feeding.

Did he want my neck? Yes, he did. For now, though, he'd wait. I blinked. We'd just had a conversation, the voiceless monster that was responsible for our rebirth and walked with us always. I smiled at him, slowly.

"Maybe someday. If I feel like it."

I grabbed his neck and bit down. *Best not to let the males think they could always have what they wanted.* It wasn't time for him to have my blood. With Tanner's pushy monster, I might have to make him earn it.

How did I know that? I wasn't sure.

He sighed when I bit. "Maci." The sound of his voice was low, like music. *He should sing sometime.* Not that very second but maybe when I wasn't so hungry. "Thank you, Maci. I need this."

I lifted my head. "You don't need it, per se. You're fine down there with him. You want it. And I want you to have it. There's a difference. Don't mistake the two."

"True." His body hardened, pressed against mine. "You should have been with us the whole time."

"I don't even know what that means." And right then, I didn't care. My moments of clarity had passed. I'd done too much thinking and not enough feeding. I was done with the bathroom.

I dragged Tanner from the room. I'd fed on the floor the whole night before and that had been great. I wasn't picky, but the beds in the other room caught my attention. I'd given no thought to my surroundings. There was a large bedroom with multiple beds. That was going to work much better than the floor.

I threw Tanner down beneath me. He wasn't fighting me at all. Would he ever? That was something we were going to have to figure out eventually if they planned to keep me here with them. Those were questions for another night. I bit down.

5

I stared down at Tanner. "Do you want me like Ace wanted me?"

"He still wants you, I can guarantee that. No past tense there. And, yes, you don't remember this, but when we were human, I took you on your first date." He took a deep breath against my neck as if he wanted to draw me inside of him. I liked that. I got wet. I loved the sensation, but I needed his blood more than sex right then. The haze of hunger threatened to overtake me again. I didn't want that. I certainly didn't know anything about when I'd been human, not even a glimmer of a memory available when I tried to find them.

I bit down on him again. His body jerked against me and, unlike the night before, I had a complete sense of what that meant. It made me smile against him. Tanner more than liked me feeding off of him. There was power to this and also a sense that I could have what I wanted when I desired it. Right then, what I wanted was his blood. It was warm, spicy, and there was an essence to it that I could now taste as Tanner. I'd never mix his blood up with Ace's; I'd always be able to tell them apart.

He dug his hands into my back, his fingers cutting me. I snarled, drinking deeper. I wasn't upset, since I liked the pain. It meant power. It was nice to have other vampires around who could dish out that kind of feeling. Allies were important and Tanner was mine. *No, that's not right, because he's more than that.* What had they said? *Soul mate.* What did it mean? I had no idea, really, but I understood blood, and I had to have that.

I sucked and sucked.

When it was over, his hands lay limp on my back. I lifted my head, licking my lips. A smile still shadowed across his face. I'd sucked him dry, and he liked it.

I wiped my mouth. Maybe it was time to find some clothes. Did I have any besides the ones I'd risen in? Someone would know. I stepped into the hallway, leaving Tanner unconscious on the bed. My stomach clenched, reminding me I wasn't done.

"Hey," Griffin said from where he leaned against the wall. "Still hungry."

He didn't ask it as a question, but he had to know I still needed to feed. Presumably, he'd been through the transition himself. I stepped toward him.

In a swift move, he touched my back, right on the cut that Tanner made. As I watched, pretty much transfixed, he brought my blood to his mouth and sucked the red drop right off his finger. I caught my breath. There was something about the intimacy of the act that I liked. I took a step closer then bit down on his neck. If he got my blood, I wanted his. His finger was still in his mouth as I got the first dose of his blood in my throat.

His body stiffened and I gasped, the world graying out for just a second.

I tensed. What was happening? Griffin was gone. In his stead, a dark landscape spread before me, the moon high in the sky, and land as far as I could see. I looked down. I wasn't naked anymore. Instead, I wore a long dress with a swooping neckline that showed off my cleavage and left my neck vulnerable. I rubbed my hand over my neck, relieved not to feel blood.

My hands...

I stared down at them. They weren't my own. They were older. Despite the darkness around me, I could see clearly that my skin was different. Usually, I was slightly olive skinned, but my hand seemed strikingly pale. Even my hair was longer, falling nearly to my waist and blonder than it should have been. I caught my breath.

I wasn't myself. Yet...I somehow was?

"Darling?"

I turned around to see Griffin, except he absolutely wasn't Griffin. He was taller, broader shouldered, and his hair fell past his shoulders. Gnawing my lip, I tried to make sense of things. Like me, he wasn't quite right, and yet, he was absolutely the vampire I knew. A sense of déjà vu overwhelmed me, almost bringing me to my knees. I'd seen this before? But when? I wasn't human, so it wasn't me remembering my human life.

I spoke, not knowing what I would say, as if the words came from my mouth because I'd already said them rather than it being a choice in the present. As though I was only along for the ride rather than steering myself, which made for a very uncomfortable sensation. "Are you okay?" I asked Not-Griffin.

"No, I'm not okay." He shook his head. "I don't know

where the others are, and we know the battle isn't going well."

It absolutely isn't. In my mind, I could picture a battle I'd never seen with my own eyes—but this version of me had. I pulled on Griffin's shirt gently, hoping to ease his worry.

"They'll be back. They're all still alive. I'd know it if they weren't." *Of course, the question was what would happen next. Warren betrayed Frederick and the others. We only knew what was going to happen because Warren had been caught. We would all have to go into hiding.*

Every vampire who wanted to continue to live in harmony with the humans, to have lives that were filled with love and not power, would have to run away. Everything inside of me abhorred the idea, but I would not lose my guys. We'd go on our next rising.

"I know." He kissed my cheek. "I wish you wouldn't step outside. It's not safe."

"Nothing is safe, but I need to be outdoors. I can't possibly be locked inside all of the time."

He sighed. "My love…"

Heat started, flames covering my body. For a second, I didn't scream. Shock flooded my system. I was on fire, and so was Griffin.

I screamed.

Rushing back into my body, I was on the floor of the house where I had been since the vampires came for me. I screamed, still feeling the bite of fire even though I absolutely wasn't on fire. Griffin did, too, apparently, writhing in agony. And just as suddenly as I ceased, so did he. He sank to the floor next to the wall, holding his head. "Damn."

Caesar picked me up off the floor and held me against him. "What the fuck happened? What's wrong?"

Rowan rushed over, squatting between Griffin and me. "Explain."

I didn't have the slightest idea what happened, so I couldn't answer him. Instead, I just trembled in Caesar's arms. I'd been on fire, my skin burned from my body. I shuddered remembering it, and how it felt.

"It happened." Griffin still hadn't moved from where he was on the—floor, and his voice sounded rough, as if someone put his voice through a cheese grater. He probably felt the skin flay from his body as well. We shared that, assuming he had been there too. I didn't really know for sure how any of it worked.

"I need blood." I managed to crack out my request before I started to shake violently. My head clouded over. There was only the need to feed. Everything else had been too much.

"Here." Caesar gave me his neck. "Take it. Whatever you need, Maci." He petted my hair as he extended his neck lower. "Take it. Always."

I bit down. Their voices drifted over me while I closed my eyes. I'd done too much. I just needed to feed, nothing else.

"I took her blood," Griffin explained to Rowan. "And then she drank from me. Suddenly, I was in his body—you know, the one I'm supposed to be reincarnated from or whatever. The guy they kept expecting me to be, but I wasn't when I rose—like all of us, but I *was* him. And she was there, too. She was that woman, the one her father wants back. It worked. We really are who they think we are. *Fuck*."

I closed my eyes, still feeling the bite of flame. I didn't want to be her. It hurt too much.

"Maci," Griffin's voice called, and I lifted my head. Truthfully, I had no idea how long Caesar had been unconscious beneath me, but he was. I drained him a while ago.

Only Griffin might understand me. "It hurt."

"I know it did. It mostly hurt to watch that version of me burn." He pulled me off Caesar. Ace came up the stairs, his pallor grayer than usual, and he shot us a look I couldn't understand. "Come on. Let's get you in some clothes, then you can feed from me. You must still be hungry, and Rowan wants to go last before bed."

Griffin didn't strike me as cuddly, but he held me in his arms like I was important to him. "You felt it, too? The burning."

He nodded once. "I did, but the rest of it was great. It really was. I'm not him, but I feel better for knowing him."

I lifted my head. "The rest of it? The two-minute conversation we shared? That wasn't so fantastic. It was mostly stressful."

Griffin's mouth fell open like a landed fish. "That's all you saw? At the very end, I saw their whole relationship."

"Why would you see more than I did?"

"I don't know." Rowan paced the room. "But we didn't know that you two sharing blood at the same time would trigger anything either, so obviously we're all in the dark, and no one knows jack shit."

Dark amusement had me smiling. "Does he curse a lot?"

"No," Griffin replied with a laugh. "I'd say the circumstances we're all in warrant the words though. Like I said, I saw the whole relationship, and the burning still sucked. Must be awful for you."

I shuddered at the memory. "Not doing it again."

"Only he was with you when you burned. You won't see that again, I don't think. Come on, Maci, feed. You need it."

Griffin didn't understand, so I tried to explain. "If that's how we die, if that's what happens to us, then why are we doing this at all? Why even be vampires? Why do we bother with any of it, if it all just ends up like that? We'll end up screaming as we die no matter what."

Griffin shrugged. "That's the nature of life for all beings, I think. I don't believe most living creatures enjoy their eventual end. We all had a terrible first death. Maybe you don't remember yours, but I remember mine. It sucked. The good news is we all got a second chance—maybe a better chance. I wouldn't be human again. I prefer being a vampire."

Rowan stopped pacing to point out, "It's not just flames. We could be beheaded. We could be staked. There's lots of ways to die."

Griffin groaned. "I don't think you're helping."

"I'm not trying to help, I'm trying to explain. She doesn't know everything about our lives yet. I want to make sure she's fully informed. We all need to see like you did, Griffin. We have to. Otherwise, Warren will use us the way that Frederick used them."

That name rang a bell for me. "I heard that name in the vision. Warren betrayed them or something."

"Yes, he did." Rowan approached me slowly, squatting down. "And Warren is upstairs right now. He's not supposed to be. He's supposed to be in his own house, but he refuses to leave. He's your father, Maci."

That makes no sense. "He was absolutely not my father in that...memory or whatever it was."

"No, he wasn't." Griffin sighed. "It's complicated. How about we agree to talk about it tomorrow? Answers tomorrow, and tonight, you need to feed."

He was right, and truthfully, right then, I really didn't care that much. I didn't give two shits about the person whose memories I had. What happened to her? Not my problem. I knew just how to solve my problems...

I bit down on Griffin's neck. He sighed and leaned back as if he'd been waiting for my bite.

This is all that matters. Only blood counted for anything.

Sometime later, Rowan lifted me from Griffin. "Come on. Feed us both to sleep. Tomorrow is soon enough to figure things out."

"I don't want to do that. I don't care. I'm not sharing blood if I have to go through that again."

He sighed. "You don't have a choice, Maci. We were born without a lot of choices and reborn that way, too. But we also have certain things, certain people, that others don't have. For that, I am actually enormously grateful. You're not supposed to be cognizant enough to even discuss any of this right now, but you always defied expectations. Some of it, I understand. Some of it, I don't, but I'm glad to be here with you while we figure it all out. If I could go back and answer something your human-self said to me, I would, if I could."

I swallowed and blinked fast, not sure why tears threatened to fall. Why was I upset? I hardly understood a word he said to me. Still, I pressed on the thread I could follow. "What did she say to you?"

"That she loved me. All of us. She said it."

I dwelled on that for a second as I turned over to reach Rowan's neck. "How lovely for her to have loved."

"I suppose that's one way to look at it." He tilted his neck to give me better access. "Bite me. Put us both to sleep. Can you feel the sun coming?"

Maybe. His pulse called to me, so I bit down instead of answering him.

~

I WAS ONCE AGAIN the last to wake. *How do they all get up so much earlier?* I had no idea the world existed until my eyes flew open every rising. What got them up so much faster?

Ace sat on the floor next to me and explained. "It comes with age. I can stay up past sunrise when I'm not drained of blood." He winked at me. "Your question was written all over your face. Come on. Go take a shower, put on some clothes. I left some for you in the bathroom. If you're up for it, we'll try to talk about things with you that aren't about blood. We haven't gotten to do that with all five of us awake at the same time as you."

It was an interesting thought. My monster paced impatiently inside of me—she didn't want to talk about anything. She just wanted to feed. Tanner stepped forward, taking my hand. He wasn't talking again, but I could understand him just fine. His monster was present, too, and if I wanted, we could be purely animalistic together. The thought was appealing.

Still, I walked to the bathroom, letting my hatred of existence show all over my face. What was the point, if I had to feel like this every time I woke up? I washed quickly. The shower was less exhilarating, but maybe simply because I didn't have to wash off death, dirt and blood. Instead, my muscles ached. I felt stronger killing the humans than I did feeding from other vampires—although that hadn't been the case before I'd been thrust into those memories, so maybe that was the problem, since the guys tasted so much better than the humans. My mouth watered at the memory.

Turning off the shower, I dried off and got dressed. Ace left me some soft black pants and a black t-shirt that didn't quite cover my belly button, so part of my stomach showed. They didn't leave me socks or shoes, but I was mostly dressed.

The heat from the steam of the shower followed me when I walked back into the main part of the basement.

They all waited and turned to regard me when I entered, but not one of them spoke. They were worried about whatever it was that they had to say, I realized. How did I know that? Had my human-self known them so well that part of what she knew passed onto me? *Maybe.*

"Say it." I didn't pretend I couldn't read them, calling them out on their silence.

Rowan rocked back on his feet. "I promised you answers, and you're going to get them. The vampires alive today are warring. Warren, your father, and his friends—which also includes Ace's father—are against my father and some of the others. A prophecy was discovered some time ago, back when some part of you was alive in another vampire. It said that those particular vampires—the one you saw, Griffin's, the rest are ours, I presume—would reincarnate, and that we would help win a war for whichever side controlled us."

My head pounded. They hadn't fed me yet, so it was a lot to digest on an empty stomach. I tried to concentrate despite that, but it was a struggle to remain focused.

Rowan kept talking, seemingly unaware of my struggle. "My father was convinced that leaving you out of it was the way to go. He didn't like you when they were all alive at the same time, so he mastered things—and he killed any woman who was pregnant with a girl. Your father took advantage of his surety that a girl child would be his undoing. On his end, he made sure his human got pregnant with a girl—you. But we weren't raised together, and you didn't know anything about vampires or any of it. He didn't raise you himself, and instead he sent you away so you'd eventually find us. And you did."

Ace finally interrupted. "But your asshole father didn't

leave things alone even at that point. He kept feeding you vampire blood, so if you died, you would change. He kept us all in the dark in regard to his plan, of course. He had his reasons, and he doesn't elaborate on that part. So now you're here with us as a vampire, and none of us had our extra memories until yesterday."

The fire. I shuddered. "I don't want to burn again."

"I don't think you will, because only Griffin saw you burn. Any blood you exchange with me can't show you something I wasn't there to witness," Ace supplied, rocking back on his feet. "It's too much to ask you. You don't even have your human memories yet. We aren't going to be used by either side. Right now, we're here with your father because he has what we need—information. It doesn't have to be that way, but for now, we have to know what he knows."

"To keep you safe," Caesar explained in a low voice. "I'm not running anyone else's war, but we have to know how we can best control our own lives. Fuck all of the rest of them."

I understood finally what they were saying. "You need me to share blood and to go through all of that again. Maybe not burning, but who knows what I'll remember, so I have to go through that again whether or not I want to. I have to do it so that you can all have the information you need to keep going."

Silence hung heavy in the room for long moments, no one answering me, until finally Griffin did. "You need the information, too. Frederick killed you, by the way. With no intention of you being reborn, he just killed the human who bothered him because he hated that woman. Why? We don't know. I'm not even sure that I know, and I have all of that guy's memories. I only have the sense that he absolutely hated her. What did she do to him? We need to know that."

I lifted my chin. I wouldn't be threatened. "You'll deny me blood if I say no?"

Tanner jolted. He couldn't speak, but he grabbed my hand and put it over his heart. His monster met my gaze. No, he wouldn't deny me blood. He'd *never* do that.

Why? It would be the logical way to make me comply.

Caesar strode over and placed his hand on my cheek, cupping my face gently. "It needs to be your choice. We can't make you do anything, and we won't starve you. We'll feed you forever. You're ours. I'm hoping when you gain clarity, you'll remember that. You can think about it in the meantime. Nothing has to be done today, or at least not all of it. Whatever way you want to do it, we'll do it. I can't pretend to understand what you went through in that memory. I do know my own death, and I know I wouldn't relive that on purpose. We'll take our cues from you, but we're all in agreement, it would be best for this to happen."

"Well then, let's not put it off." I didn't need it hanging over my head. "Let's get the pain over with, since that's all my life is anyway."

Rowan held up his hand. "Hold on. That isn't all your life is, and if you feel that way, then that's the first thing we can fix. Come on, enough of this basement." He took my hand in his. "We're going upstairs."

"Is that safe for her?" Ace was quick to follow when Rowan pulled me up the stairs. "We've locked the world out for a reason."

"She's a vampire. Maci can defend herself pretty well, I would imagine. Besides, I don't think Warren wants to hurt her. He wants to *use* her. Griffin, I charge you with doing something about that tonight."

He laughed. "I love fucking with Warren."

"I know you do." Rowan's grip was strong in mine while

he keyed in a code to open the door at the top of the stairs. I pulled my hand free, stopping him from moving onward. "What's wrong?"

I pointed at my feet. "I don't have shoes."

"That's okay. We're only going to step outside for a second. You have strong, vampire feet. They won't get hurt from a moment shoeless." He kicked off his own shoes. "There, we'll do it together."

The sound of the others kicking off their shoes made me smile. They were sort of...cute. "I need to feed," I reminded him.

"I know." Rowan squeezed my hand and pulled me into the hallway. I hadn't really made note of the house when we arrived, so I scanned the building. The doorway opened onto a huge front hall, with massively tall and oppressive ceilings. To the left, the hallway opened into a living room that looked comfortably situated. The right opened into a large, industrial sized kitchen—which was funny in a vampire household. It wasn't like they ate.

That was when I smelled them...*humans.* I caught my breath. I preferred feeding off the guys, but there were humans nearby, and they smelled so edible. My stomach clenched, a painful cramp grumbling through me in a wave.

Ace put his arm around my shoulders. "Ignore them. You don't need them."

"Why are there humans here, and why couldn't I smell them from downstairs?"

He shrugged, the movement jostling both of us. "Maybe you can only smell us, babe."

Griffin groaned. "And Ace dives into the cheese this early into the reintroduction."

Rowan opened a porch door and gestured for me to follow him through it. The wind blew through the opening, cooling off the room significantly. Rowan held my hand as we stepped into the night, and the breeze pushed away the scent of the humans. Instead, all I could smell was the wild and trees. I closed my eyes. I hadn't loved the smell of the earth when I'd been running around trying to survive, but tonight, it was breathtaking.

And alive.

The world was filled with sounds. Crickets. Birds. A car horn in the distance. The wind looped around my head—a gentle breeze, but it felt like so much more. And the colors everywhere. Everything seemed more vibrant and detailed than I remembered.

I lifted my head. "This is...so much better."

"We're not meant to be locked inside." Rowan's voice was low. "It's necessary right now, but that isn't how we live. This is how we exist. Our lives aren't pain; they're filled with purpose. I didn't understand that myself, not until there was you. Caesar knew. He woke up knowing that you were our reason. It took so much longer for us. I'm grateful to him for finding you. I'm elated that you're here with us, even if how it happened was hell for you. I just need your buy in, Maci. Can you trust us to get through this with you?"

My skin tingled. There was life out there, and my heart clenched at the thought of leaving the five of them. He didn't need my buy in. He'd had it from moment one, even if I hadn't understood why and still didn't, really. "You need to feed from me. If we're going to do this, let's not keep hiding."

6

"Come on." Rowan gestured with his hand. "You need to feed, and there's absolutely no reason you can't do it out here in the night, with only the moon watching."

I lifted my gaze to stare at the celestial body he mentioned—partially hidden by clouds and not full, but still lovely. I smiled at it. "Well..."

I never got to finish whatever I was going to say. Tanner rushed to me, stopping in front of me. We stared at each other for a moment, our monsters greeting the night. We weren't just humans in another form; we were predators. I could see it right there in Tanner's gaze, the needs that would always be there. I didn't have to hunt humans—but that didn't mean I didn't want to. Perhaps not craving humans was another skill I'd slowly get a handle on, but I didn't have it yet.

Tanner grabbed my arm. What did he want from me? But then it dawned on me. He wanted me to catch him, to find him. I yanked out of his grip on my arm and nodded.

We could do that. He rounded on Rowan—Tanner couldn't talk, but Rowan must have understood him. Their leader— and that was clearly what Rowan was—stepped back, putting his hands in front of him. "I won't interfere."

With that, Tanner ran past me faster than I could believe was possible. *Oh wow.* My body tingled with anticipation. My bare feet forgotten, I took off running. I'd never been to this place before, but I felt like I knew it because I tracked Tanner. It wasn't about where we were going anyway, just about what I chased. My mouth watered, and my head buzzed.

Yes, I'd been made to do this. I needed it.

Tanner was fast. I'd catch a glimpse of his dark shirt, and then it would be gone. I couldn't go by sight, not with prey so much better at running than me. He'd been living with his monster a lot longer than me, so they were more in sync.

That was the answer. I had to stop thinking like a human and just, for a few minutes, trust my vampire self. It was the only way I could use my beautiful monstrous strength to catch Tanner and give us both what we needed. My thoughts fled, my mind only interested in the smells, the noises, and the ease with which my body moved when I wasn't fucking thinking about it. I ran, not sure if I was doing the right thing or not. It didn't matter. I knew I could catch him. I was just that good.

Time had ceased to matter when I finally spotted him. He made the wrong turn and, for just a second, was clearly in view. I rushed forward and took him straight to the ground. He went down with a thud, my mouth on his neck before I let my brain turn back on. I wasn't gentle, but he didn't seem to mind. The sound of his sigh, filled with pleasure, made me smile as I sucked down his blood. I needed it and what was clear was that he wanted it.

"Maci. " He sounded like he was smiling . "Thank you. For catching me. For this. For all of it. We're vampires. We live at night, but our lives are not dark. Now that you're here, there isn't any more bleak. Feel that, too."

I did right then.

I took what I needed.

CAESAR RUBBED blood off my chin. We both sat with Tanner while he slept off what I'd done to him. We weren't in the basement, and he couldn't just be left outside, where anything could happen to him. Particularly not since I was fully aware of the fire issue—one match and he was gone.

I wouldn't lose him. Not any of them. Whatever else I didn't know, I understood that fact perfectly. They were mine, and a surge of protectiveness rippled through me. I couldn't lose them, not again.

"You're all torn up," Caesar said as he picked up my foot. "I'll get you some shoes."

I shrugged. "It didn't hurt."

"Honestly, it looked exhilarating. I'd ask you to chase me, but I can't have you out of my sight long enough to disappear from my view."

He swept his finger over my bleeding foot. "May I?"

I tilted my head. "Are you actually asking?"

"If I take your blood and then you feed from me later, you'll get zapped back into that other person's memories so, yes, I'm asking. Griffin fell into it by mistake, but now that we know it can happen, you'll get a say before you are forced into experiencing that again."

Caesar seemed very focused on keeping me safe, so I figured it might be left over from his feelings for my human-self. I couldn't think of any other reason he'd want that journey, not unless he really thought it was the best way to prevent something from going wrong.

"Go ahead. As soon as Tanner's up, we'll jump in, so to speak."

"Tanner's up," the vampire himself said, and I noticed he leaned on his elbows. "I'm good. I'm going to go find a human to take care of my hunger, then we'll move forward. Caesar doesn't have to babysit me another minute."

I laughed. "It was actually my idea."

"Nonsense. He might have let you think that, but Caesar is our watcher. He's good at it, takes care of everyone. He went along with it being your idea, but I promise, if you didn't think of it, he would've."

He stood, brushing off his jeans. "That was fun. You caught me fair and square. I didn't let you do it."

What a ridiculous notion. "Of course I did."

"Is that my daughter?" I didn't recognize the voice, so I turned in time to see Griffin blocking another man's entrance. *Warren*...that had to be him. I stood, brushing off debris from my own legs. If I was meeting this person, I wasn't doing so from a position of submission. Caesar stuck his finger, the one dotted with my blood, in his mouth. For a second, he closed his eyes. I guessed he liked the taste.

Griffin shook his head. "Not until we say yes. In fact, pack your stuff and get out of our house. Go home. When we're ready for you to see her, you can see her, but not a moment before."

Warren pointed at me. "She's right there! At least let her see her mother. The woman has waited almost two decades to see her."

They hadn't said anything about a mother. I never thought about having one of those, although I suppose everyone did. I didn't just pop out of nowhere into existence with only a father. At some point, I'd been human, which required a father *and* a mother.

"She's not her mother. None of you behaved as actual parents and, you know what? That's fine. Vampires make terrible parents. We all had the worst of parents as humans, but what you two did to that human girl was deplorable. Even if she's fine now—strong and beautiful—what you did to her when she was a baby is irredeemable." Griffin practically snarled, "*You* wanted this. *You* wanted us to be here. *You* betrayed and hurt people to ensure we showed up. Well, here I am. Think you can take me? Want to try?"

I could actually smell his anger in the air. It tasted bitter, acidic on my tongue. Strong emotions had different scents, some of which smelled or tasted different, even though it was the first time I encountered it.

Caesar smiled, but no mirth glinted behind his eyes. "When Griffin gets like this, it's incredible. He doesn't usually fight, because he's more of a thinker than a brawler. But when it comes to you? All bets are off. Rowan was smart to sic him on Warren. When you're only willing to kill for one person, you're willing to go to extremes. We're the same that way, and we're all devoted to you. Know that."

Warren met my gaze, despite the distance separating us. "I'm your father, Maci."

I turned my back on him. I didn't have all the information I needed to deal with him just yet. I wasn't ready. If Griffin and the others didn't want me talking to him right then, I'd trust them, so I wasn't going to do it. Why fight for the purpose of fighting when I was sure there were more meaningful battles to come?

"Remind me not to piss you off," Tanner said as he walked away, presumably to go feed. My stomach panged. I really didn't want him feeding from someone else, but what was I supposed to do about that? I needed to spend some time actually focused on the problem—they couldn't keep feeding from humans. They were mine, but we'd be in a constant circle of feeding, with one of us always draining the others, wouldn't we?

Warren left as well. The air moved better without Warren there, but without Tanner, it felt emptier. Caesar pulled me to him. "Would you be okay if we went inside to feed? I don't like how exposed we are out here."

Griffin laughed. "I wouldn't let anyone get to you, Caesar, but that's fine by me. Go inside. Have some private time with our girl. We need to move upstairs and figure out what to do about the humans in the house. We need them to feed but...yeah, I don't want to keep her in the basement forever."

Regardless of who I might have been before I awoke as a vampire, I awoke as someone who didn't give a shit about planning or logistics. They could work the details out any way they wanted, since I didn't care where I passed out for the night.

I threw a final glance over my shoulder. It was probably best if I couldn't see Tanner feeding off a human. I might snap the person's neck, unable to resist the urge.

Caesar led us into the quiet house. The smell of the humans had dissipated, which meant someone moved them outside. Obviously, the guys needed food nearby to keep up with my waking hunger, but I hadn't considered the logistics at all. Not that I had answers as to what to do about it.

"What's the matter?" Caesar led me to a bedroom on the second floor. Fortunately, it didn't have the scent of having been recently occupied, which I found I desired. I lived basically in the dirt surrounded by dead bodies just days ago, so why did it bother me? Had I been suddenly domesticated?

I tried to find the words to explain something I didn't fully understand myself yet. "I don't like you guys feeding from humans. I understand the need, I'm just explaining what's bothering me."

He brushed my hair away from my face. "You are days from changing. At this point, I was raving, either trying to eat all the time or thinking about you. I was incoherent, a lunatic, starved. You're having *conversations*. It won't be forever that you can't feed us. We'll actually be constantly feeding each other, because we don't need as much when we're with you. Just a bit, then you'll feed off someone different. None of us will be starved. You'll be full all the time, that's how we'll work this. For now, yes, we have these humans. They want to be here, because they want to be vampires. Unlike Frederick, Warren'll actually make them vampires afterward."

Very interesting, but his explanation did nothing to soothe my jealousy nor my desire to destroy whoever Tanner touched. I smiled at Caesar, but I imagine the expression held about as much happiness as his earlier baring of teeth. "If you're expecting reason from me, you're going to be immensely disappointed," I finally replied.

"I'm not expecting anything from you except for you to be yourself."

They acted like they all cared for me, but none of them knew me, not really. I didn't even know myself yet. "Who was she? The human that wore my body that you all liked so much."

He sat down on the bed, kicked off his shoes, then leaned against the headboard. "I didn't just *like* her. I was obsessed with her. I needed her more than anything in the universe. Although I made the error of my vampire life by not telling her, I loved her very much."

His words made me catch my breath. I wasn't sure why, but my face felt hot, and my heart beat a little harder. "What was your reasoning for not telling her, if she mattered that much to you?"

He offered his hand, and I easily linked my fingers in his, allowing him to draw me closer. "Because I thought vampires didn't love, so I didn't believe what I felt for her could possibly be love."

I snorted. "Yet somehow you've learned differently in the time since she died?"

We were so close, practically mouth-to-mouth, so I took the initiative and kissed him. I needed to feed, but I wanted to know what his lips felt like touching mine. He closed his eyes and didn't press for more when I moved away, missing the warm embrace of our linked lips the second it passed.

"I did." He answered my previous question. "First of all, I didn't know vampires had soul mates until her. Once I understood why I couldn't do without her, why I needed her to feed from, that I loved her? And then to experience the nine, almost ten, long months she was dead, and you weren't here yet? It was hell. So, yes, I learned a lot about my feelings since she died. They're lessons I won't readily forget." He lifted his lids. "You need to feed. I can feel your hunger. Feed, Maci. I know you, even though you're about to tell me I don't. I do, so feed and don't argue for now."

I couldn't help but smirk. "Don't you want to have sex with me, Caesar?"

"So much, Maci." He bit my lower lip. "After you feed."

I rubbed against him, but I said, "You're going to travel if I feed. We both will."

Caesar leaned over to kiss my cheek, lingering there.

"Then we'll have sex afterward. You'll bite me, feed a bit. You'll travel, come back, feed until you're almost full...but stop before I'm knocked out. We'll have sex, then you'll finish feeding."

My smile was slow this time. "You like to be in charge."

"Only when it comes to you and how I want things to be. I don't give a shit what happens otherwise."

I had similar thoughts myself earlier. "Okay."

"Thank you."

I bit his neck, and not gently. He groaned, which turned out to be the last noise I heard before I was thrown backward into the memories of the other person who apparently lived in my head. I hadn't asked for any of it, I didn't want it, and there wasn't a thing I could do to stop any of the things happening to me.

If there was someone to complain to, I would complain about the absolute lack of control life gave me, but sadly, even vampire life apparently came without anyone who gave a shit.

"What are you doing?" the man who was Caesar but wasn't asked.

I extended my arms toward him, and he crawled into them, nuzzling against my neck. He was the most affectionate out of all my guys and would like what I had to say the least. "I think this is the end."

"Why? Why now?" He lifted his head. "Frederick isn't garnering *that* much support."

He hadn't seen what I had the day before. He didn't know. "He is. They like the idea of power, of living on their own terms, of owning humans. They don't want to search for soul mates, and they don't want to follow the rules. I heard people chanting their support of him. And then he said anyone who disagreed needed to be killed." I sighed.

"He looked directly at me. I thought about killing him right there."

"I would have, and I wish you had." He closed his eyes. "I won't let them hurt you."

I shook my head. "We have to talk. Seriously, sit up."

With a grumble, he lifted his head and raised an eyebrow. "What?"

"I think this is ending. I also think the prophecy is very concerning. They say those people will die, but then they'll be somehow reborn at the same time? Do you think it could be us?"

He took my cheeks in his hands and smoothed his thumbs under my eyes. "You need to feed. You'll feel less filled with doom if you do."

He might be right, but I growled at how easily he dismissed my words as a need to feed. I shoved at him. "You're not listening to me, and I'm not to be dismissed. Out of everyone here, I'm the most intuitive. I might not see prophecies, but I'm strong in our powers. Due to that, you should listen when I tell you we're in big trouble."

They liked to baby me, to make sure that I was happy, that I had everything I wanted. Most of the time, I even felt like they listened to me and valued me. On this subject, though, they couldn't seem to see the threat Frederick posed.

"If we don't take this seriously, we'll all regret it."

I jerked back into my body at the same time as Caesar, because he grabbed his head the same way Griffin did after he saw those other vampires. My head didn't hurt, thankfully, but both of my men showed signs of pain after the vision.

He pulled me against him roughly until we panted

together, not once allowing me to look away from him. "I saw his entire life. How much did you get?"

"Just a long moment." I swallowed, my mouth going dry when I smelled a familiar scent. Blood leaked slowly from the wound on his neck. We hadn't been under for very long.

He rubbed my hair from my forehead. "Which moment? They shared so many."

"The one where she begged him to listen to her and he didn't."

Caesar frowned. "Not his finest moment, that's for sure. Trust me, she was right, and he regretted it. They arrived home just in time to see you and the one I think was Griffin burn. It was absolute hell, but none of that matters right now. Let's assume you're seeing the things that you need to see in this whole fucked up situation. If that's true, you saw how we didn't listen to her. Because of it, she burned to death with the one who wasn't Griffin. The rest of us saw them die, and then we died terribly afterward. I'll admit, you seeing that moment feels like a big warning sign, and I'm not an idiot."

I hoped that was true. If not, and if our history was just bound to repeat, then what was the point?

"Look, I'm not dismissing the topic or the conversation, but you must be fucking starving."

He wasn't wrong, but it wasn't what I wanted just then. I licked the blood off his neck, reveling when Caesar shuddered beneath me. I kissed his chin and then his mouth. "I'm going out of order, but I want to fuck you now, Caesar. I want to feel alive in this body, like it's not just hers. And I don't like being chained to my stomach. I'll feed when I want and not otherwise. That's what I got from that experience—I'm not going to waste time feeding when I should be doing other things."

Beneath me, he caught his breath. "Whatever you want, Maci. Feel alive in your beautiful vampire body."

I tugged off his shirt, revealing his muscled skin beneath. I had questions for them later. There were so many things about being a vampire I didn't understand. Were we this strong when we were humans? Did it matter? Caesar's body attracted me, but not as much as his self-confidence and the way that he looked at me—as though the world moved because I was in it. Those things were the real turn on.

Or as much of one as I apparently needed. I wasn't particularly concerned with physical beauty—I preferred strength—but Caesar was a gorgeous man. I traced along the smooth skin over the bumps of his abdominal muscles with a fingertip. I wanted to bite him there... *Maybe another time.*

He tugged at my shirt, pulling it over my head. "I liked it when you were walking around naked. That was the best, but we wouldn't want other people to see you that way. Your nakedness belongs to us."

I grinned at him. "That seems very human of you, Caesar."

"Well, we can blame you for that."

He flipped me over. I caught my breath. I guessed I wasn't going to be in charge all the time, which was more than fine by me. Caesar—*hell, all of them*—were strong males. I could tell by watching them, taste it on my tongue in their presence, it practically took up its own separate sense. They let me be in charge, but that's all it was—them letting me.

I need to remember that.

Maybe I shouldn't have found their superior strength so sexy?

"Fast." I didn't want to wait. I was wet and achy. I needed

to be fed, but another part of my body felt neglected since my rebirth and proved just as anxious to find completion.

"Tsk tsk." His smile was slow and all-consuming. "This is my show. You don't tell me how it will go."

I bit down on my lip, thinking about making him bleed, and not because I wanted to feed. There was power in blood. I could take it back. Maybe.

"But it is my pleasure to give you what you want." Caesar grinned, and his toothy smile spoke of ownership. That was okay. I already knew, in the brief time we'd been together, that the opposite was also true. I owned him as much as he did me.

And he was more than fine with that.

He tore my clothes from my body. I wanted him as naked as me, so if he could tear, so could I. With a yank, I removed his clothing with a satisfying ripping noise.

I might not remember being human, but I must have been weak, because I reveled in my strength. He flipped me over easily, so I grabbed onto the headboard. I wanted the moment, and I wanted to share it with him.

He rose up behind me, the sheets pulling up against my skin with his movement. Caesar palmed my breasts in his big hands, and I gasped. My nerve endings sparked to brilliant life, leaving me wanting more touch, as much as I could possibly get.

"More," I demanded as the thoughts slammed around in my head.

"Plenty more to come," he whispered in my ear. One of his palms streaked down my body while the other one squeezed, applying slow even pressure to my breast in his hand. I sighed. Yes, gentle slow movement, the best sensation in the world.

Caesar pressed a finger inside of me. I clenched my

muscles around him writhing, into his touch. "More," I whispered again, my voice practically wobbling in my need.

He leaned over and pressed his nose against my neck. "I know what you need, Maci," he promised as he pushed his cock inside of me.

7

I gasped. Yes, I wanted more. As much as I could have. Needy heat rippled down my body, an ache between my legs building with each slide of his skin against mine. Caesar couldn't hurt me. There was just so much pleasure in the bites of pain where his fingertips pulled me closer. I closed my eyes and rode the waves as they hit me. I moaned and yelled, I even screamed, begging him for more. Nonsense words, but I had to give sound to the sensations flooding my body. His grunt in my ear, as he thrust balls deep inside of me, was the best sound I'd ever heard.

I came around him, all the tension of the day releasing in one instant of pleasure I knew I'd never forget. He came with me—with a hard jerk, Caesar was, in that second, entirely mine. After a moment, he pulled out of my body and flipped me over.

I groaned. I liked how full I felt with him inside of me. My body still throbbed where he'd been only moments ago.

He kissed my mouth, grinning against me. "That was insane."

"Not the word I would've used, but I suppose it'll do." I

wrapped my arms around his neck, surprised by how much I wanted to just snuggle against him. I didn't think I was a clingy person, but it seemed right then, I absolutely was.

"What word would you have used?" He kissed my cheek. "Amazing?"

I smiled, slowly. "I guess I can't use one word. I'd say it was just what I needed."

He nodded. "Absolutely." He fell quiet for a moment and then stroked a hand over my hair. "What was it like? I want to know what waking up was like for you."

He wants to discuss that now? "Why?"

"I searched. For the ten months you were gone, I never stopped looking for you. I'd rise, feed, and seek you. I thought, if I could figure out where he put you, then I could be there when you woke. You wouldn't have to be alone. We all looked. Eventually, the others decided we should wait to feel you when you woke. I couldn't. I had to know where you were, but I failed anyway. Ace's father told us you would rise, or I would've died when you did. Somehow. I can't be without you, Maci. I've known it since my own rising."

I sighed because thinking of my earliest memories wasn't comfortable. For him, I'd try. "It was dark. Cold. Dirty." I lifted one of my hands to look at my clean, even fingernails. "There were bodies everywhere. I shoved them aside as I pulled myself out of the earth. It took a long time because I had to rest often."

"We felt you rise. All of us did, like a pulse of light in the darkest night. We darted out, but it was imprecise, so I couldn't find you. Then you were moving. I think? If I had to guess, you were in the pit, wherever you awoke, for two risings."

That would make sense. I shivered. "I didn't know how much time, just that it took a long time. I was so hungry, and there was nothing to do but dig, climb, and push bodies." I'd rather never think of that time again, I realized with a shudder. "No more of this."

His lips brushed mine, and they felt warm and alive and nothing like the bodies in the dirt. "I think of it as the second time I failed you. I just needed to know how bad the failure was."

I lifted an eyebrow, wishing he would kiss me again instead of talking. "So that you can keep some sort of running tab of how much you owe me?"

"Yes. Exactly."

I groaned. "It would be better if you kissed me."

Caesar pulled us both up to sit, and I swatted at him. "What are you doing?"

"Feed," he said as he tilted his neck. "Come on, finish. You're hungry."

I was, there was no doubt about that. But I was always hungry, and there were things I wanted to say, so I said, "I don't like you feeding from humans. Not any of you. I fucking hate it."

He lifted an eyebrow. "You should still be too much in a haze to notice any of it, and yet you're incredibly cognizant, more and more so every day. You shouldn't be able to care enough to notice who we feed from, but I get it. I wouldn't want you feeding from anyone other than us, either. For now, though, while your need for food is still so extreme, we don't have a choice. There will come a time when we can feed solely from each other, because none of us will need to do it every day. For now, that's just not possible."

"Fuck you for being reasonable," I growled, then I threw him down beneath me. A second later, I bit back down right where I had earlier. I fed deeply. *If this is how it has to be, then so be it.*

Caesar moaned, the same sound he'd made when he was buried deep inside of me. I shivered with desire, a pulse of remembered pleasure making me rock against him. I reached for his cock as I sucked, and I stroked him. He shuddered, and I closed my eyes. We would both get what we needed.

He came in my hand about a second before I finished feeding from him. I lifted my head to find the beautiful man completely unconscious.

Sitting back, I sighed. I had to stop feeding before they conked out. It would be nice to have more conversations similar to the one Caesar and I shared.

Okay, it turns out I'm a talker. Who could have guessed?

I stood up, the remains of our fun dripping down my leg. *Whoops.* It looked like I needed another shower. At least I was starting to remember personal hygiene again. I made my way into the bathroom then stepped under the steaming water. It was instantly warm. Was that usual for showers? I didn't think so.

The door to the bathroom flung open, and I peeked around the shower curtain to see Rowan in the doorway. "Tanner and Caesar should never have left you by yourself."

I shrugged then let the hot water run down my body. I loved this feeling. *Did I used to scald myself under the spray when I was human?* "Caesar got drained and Tanner did, too, but he's up and feeding."

I heard the footsteps as Rowan strolled the rest of the way into the bathroom. "We're supposed to be making sure you are watched."

I pulled back the curtain again despite the water that flowed past me and onto the floor. "I'm a vampire, Rowan. I think I could defend myself from most things. Just not fire, apparently."

"There are many things you're not equipped to handle, although you soon will be, no doubt." He stepped closer, his gaze concerned. "Your father is very worked up."

"Well, it's not a picnic for me, either, so he can wait his turn."

My statement earned me a smile from Rowan. I had a feeling those weren't given out all the time, and a flush of heat warmed my cheeks with pleasure. He sighed and then stepped into the shower and under the water with me, fully dressed. I smirked at him. "You're going to get your pretty clothes wet."

"I couldn't care less." He tilted my neck back. "When you let someone bite you, it's submitting to them. I can't let that happen except with us. No one gets to bite you but us. Never."

I lifted an eyebrow but didn't wrench my neck away. Rowan could bite me if he wanted. In fact, I'd love it. I reached around him to grab the body wash then squeezed out a dollop of sweet-smelling soap into my hand. As he held me, I washed my pussy with the soap. He watched my hands, not letting go of my neck.

"What did you see today?" His words, seemingly so disinterested, contrasted the way he watched me and the bulge growing in his wet pants.

I didn't pretend to misunderstand him. "I saw all of them not listening to her, which meant that they all died."

"I suppose the lesson there is that we need to do a better job of listening to you." He bent over to kiss at my neck, his lips and breath warm against my already hot flesh. "I want to feed from you more than anything, but I don't want you to keep having to travel through memories."

I shook my head. "I'd have to feed from you, too, for it to work."

He kissed me again. "If you keep cleaning yourself like that, I'm going to come in my pants."

I hadn't even been thinking about it since I'd started doing it. Certainly, I hadn't been touching myself enough to elicit any kind of real pleasurable response. "Would you like to do that for me, Rowan? Then you can drink my blood, I'll drink yours, and we'll see what it is that we see together?"

"One thing at a time." He dropped his hand from my neck but only so he could push me against the wall by my shoulders. Rowan pressed a finger inside of me. "I think you're clean now, Maci. I wish you could remember what I remember. I know you will, but I have spent the better part of the last few years either wishing I could do this to you, remembering how we briefly did it, or remembering how it felt to sink into your heat. At this point, you might say I'm obsessed with you."

I spread my legs slightly to give him better access. He used the space to find and press against my clit, so I moaned. Pleasure surged through me, a resonating ripple of bliss. I closed my eyes. *Yes, I want more than that. So much more.* He found a rhythm I liked and he kept to it as I rocked my hips into his palm. I opened my eyes to watch him as he pleasured me. *Yes.* With eye contact, it was so much better. I caught my breath, my muscles starting to clench from his ministrations. *More.* This time I might have spoken the word aloud, but I wasn't sure. *What is even happening between us?* It didn't matter. But it did because I could feel something profound growing between us. The water, the quiet, his hand as it massaged my clit until my knees buckled. I exploded around him, my head hitting his shoulder until he supported my entire weight as I shuddered against him.

"Maci." He was hard, but he made no move to do anything about it, instead, stroking his hands down my skin in long, soothing strokes. I should do something with his cock. I wanted to. Badly. I just couldn't seem to bring myself to move right then. "I am so tired of you having pain. When you were a human, things were so hard for you. We can blame your father for that, since he put you in an untenable situation and left you to deal with it like you were nothing more than a board piece in a game to be played. It didn't get better when you were under our care, sadly. You died. Now, here you are, and you have to keep traveling back to some other life that wasn't even your own."

I managed to lift my head to meet his gorgeous eyes. "I think I'm strong. I think I was born in both lives to be that way. I don't think I break easily. Frederick had to burn her alive, that person whose memory I carry. It was the only way he could stop her. I don't think you have to be worried about me being in pain. I think I can conquer it time and again."

He kissed my forehead. "But you shouldn't have to. You captured our souls when we were just humans. We didn't understand then, but I do now. We're just souls when it comes down to it, and our souls love your soul. When you're done with this transition, I'm hoping you'll remember that."

I put my arms around his neck then tilted my head as a pounding started in my brain that I couldn't possibly ignore. "Speaking of pain..."

"What's wrong?"

I wasn't sure. It felt as if pressure built up in my head and wanted to rush out, wanted to force me to pay attention. Rowan reached around me to turn off the water. It was quiet, we were both wet, and in that second the pain exploded. My head felt like it was under water while the rest of my body remained in a frozen block of ice. I couldn't move, couldn't save myself from drowning, couldn't even scream.

Rowan tugged me against him even tighter. "What's wrong?" he repeated.

If I could have spoken, I would have told him. Despite the blinding pain, and in the midst of the most painful moment of my vampire life, I could suddenly remember her.

The human-Maci, the one who died so I could be born.

I gasped for air, wondering if I'd ever breathe properly again.

"I've got you. We'll get through whatever it is." He offered his neck to me. "Feed. Whatever it is, the blood will help."

Right then I couldn't, not while I was frozen in the block of ice. All that existed was memory.

And this time, at least, it was mine.

"You haven't spoken a word in hours." Ace ran a hand through my hair. "We can't help you if you don't tell us what happened."

I tilted my head to regard him. They all wanted an explanation I didn't feel like giving yet. I swallowed. I would need to feed again, but I doubted they'd feed me if I didn't explain. There was no way they would let the sunrise come without me telling them something.

"I can remember her," I finally said.

Tanner nodded. "Yes, we know. Griffin and Caesar traveled with you, remember?"

Did he think I lost my mind? I scowled at him then said, "Not those memories. Those belong to someone else. I'm not even sure why we have to carry them, other than to reiterate we may be truly fucked going forward. No, *my* memories. Maci's memories. The human version of me."

Caesar leaned forward, steepling his fingers as his brow cocked. "Really? So fast, I thought it took females months or years."

"Well, I think it's fair to say our Maci is rather exceptional." Ace sighed. "And maybe it's a good thing. You should know the whole history of who you are. Or were. How does it feel?"

"She froze in the shower like she was turned to stone and couldn't move." Rowan stared out the window. He didn't turn to face us, which would have intimidated my human-self. Not me. Human-Maci thought he was mean, cold, distant. By contrast, I could see he burned so hot, he had no choice but to shut it all down around him. Rowan went still for the benefit of other people, not for himself.

Ace pretended to feel more human than he did, hence him touching my hair the way humans did. Caesar didn't pretend anything, always entirely in the moment just as he was. Tanner never missed a thing, and Griffin was constantly lost in his own head, trying to solve problems. The human version of Maci only understood part of them.

But she had loved them, and they didn't love her—not in the way she could understand it anyway.

I wasn't going to answer Ace's question, since he didn't really care how I felt about having my memories back. He'd humor me, and the rest of them would stand by while he did. I was obviously fine. They weren't going to want more information than that. No, what Ace actually wanted to know had probably bashed at his vampire brain until he could hardly function from needing answers. So I answered those questions instead, the ones I knew he wanted to know but wouldn't ask.

"There wasn't anything you could have done to save her. Frederick meant for her to die. He always wondered if Maci would carry the memories he didn't want her to have. Once he became aware of her existence, that was that. It was delayed, but it was always going to happen. You should never have been able to stay awake in the daytime like that at all, and she didn't die blaming you."

He bent forward as if I struck him, and then he closed his eyes. "She should have."

"I'll say again, you shouldn't have even been awake. There was no way that you could save her from much more advanced and capable vampires just based on their age alone. I mean...it's honestly remarkable that you were awake at all." I shrugged. "Besides, if she didn't die, I wouldn't be here."

That, of course, begged a question. "Would you rather have her? Your human that you all adopted as your own? Or would you rather the vampire she was always meant to be?"

I didn't know exactly what I'd do if they said they wanted the human version of me. We didn't lie as vampires. It meant I needed to learn what questions to ask and what was better left unspoken.

Maybe. Or maybe we'd fight all the time because I couldn't keep my mouth shut. I already accepted that fact about myself.

"No." Ace shook his head. "How could you even suggest that? The second we found out you were coming, we've wanted nothing but you here. I don't know about the rest of them, but I'm blown away by you. I don't place much value on prophecies. Why bother? But I can see why they were afraid of having you back. Why they thought that, if they could control it, then they could stop what's going to happen."

I swallowed. "What *is* going to happen?"

"You're going to destroy them."

I closed my eyes. That sounded exhausting. "I don't know if I have it in me."

"You do." Tanner rose and crossed to me. "It's just too close to sunrise to contemplate right now. Come on. Time to lie down."

It was an idea I could get behind, but I had something else to say. "I don't want you guys feeding from humans anymore. Surely if I could handle your needs when I was human, I can do it now. I don't want you to eat from any more humans or I might kill them. All of them."

Caesar met Griffin's gaze before they both looked toward Rowan who still hadn't turned around. Their leader wasn't answering them. "Is there a problem, fearless leader, or are you just not talking anymore?"

"Something's wrong," he finally said, still looking out the window. "I've been feeling it all night."

Tanner frowned while Caesar and Ace jumped to their feet to join him. Griffin looked between us all. "It's not night anymore. It's practically daytime."

"They're day walkers, or most of them are. I'm not sure they'll stay away from us just because it's daytime, not if they know she's here." Rowan shook his head. "I can stay up awhile. We know Ace can."

Caesar sighed. "I can't. It's already pulling me under. Fuck."

"Me too." Griffin frowned. "And I don't understand how you two can stay awake. Tanner?"

"I'm not being taken under right this second, but that doesn't mean I won't be suddenly. I haven't tested it. I go to bed at sunrise. It just feels like the right thing to do."

I got to my feet. "I'm not the least bit tired."

I'd been exhausted moments earlier, but I found an unexpected surge of energy. "If someone is coming here, then I'll be ready."

"They're not.' Rowan walked over to me. "Not this morning, but *something* is coming. I can feel it on the back of my neck, like it's crawling toward us. I've always had these kinds of senses, ever since I was reborn. They know you're alive, and they're coming."

I didn't know much yet, but I was sure I didn't want to be burned alive. *Not again.* "I need to know how to battle."

"There are a few things we can show you." Caesar placed a hand on my back. His movements were sluggish. "But most of it will be instinctual."

I hoped he was right, because I didn't want to be killed before I even lived in this body. "She had a pointless life."

I didn't know I'd spoken aloud until they all stared at me with such stillness, it might have sliced through the room.

"I hope she didn't feel that way," Griffin said in a low voice. "She was absolutely pivotal to us in human and vampire life. There was so much about her that was important. When I look back at my human life, I feel like he was that way, too, but I think that might just be how we feel about the time before we become vampires. Perhaps it's natural to feel the fruitlessness of a non-vampire life as not having a point, but it did. I don't think we start from nothing as vampires. I think who they were shapes who we become greatly."

Was he right? Did that girl—the one who spent too much time just trying to survive—help to make me who I was somehow? "I want to speak to my father tomorrow," I said. I had questions for him.

"If we aren't attacked immediately upon waking, I'll take you to see him myself. As for the feeding request, yes, okay.

We'll try it. If it doesn't destroy you too much to feed all of us, then that's what we'll do. I don't want to touch a human when you're around anyway, I can assure you of that." Rowan shrugged. "And I don't need to be the leader if one of you would like to take the wheel. Until then, I suggest Ace and I stay up past sunrise to get used to it. The rest of you, get some sleep."

Tanner crossed to the windows and started to close the blinds. I blinked then shook my head. He really shouldn't be doing it alone, so I crossed to help him, and he smiled at me. His monster was always close, and mine liked that so much.

"How did you find out I was coming back?" I hadn't realized how much I wanted to know the answer until I asked. "Did you know I was dead before you found out or after?"

He visibly swallowed. "A few minutes afterward. We were told you were dead by Ace and his father—but that you'd be coming back. Frederick called to taunt Rowan about it, in fact. We...reacted badly. We intended to go out in a blaze of glory, so to speak, while we waited for you to rise, not that I could contribute to the plan. I can't talk without you, but I was happy to go along. Ace's father became more and more frantic. He had to run before he was caught. Quickly, he filled us in about you rising at some point and where we should go to wait for you—here, with your father. We haven't seen him since. Truthfully, we have no idea what happened to him. If your father knows, he's not telling us."

It was a mystery. How was Ace's father connected to mine? And Wanda, the woman who saved me when I was human–she was connected to Ace's father also, but I never saw her again after she made sure I was okay. Was she involved in this, too? I helped him close all the windows to keep the sun out while I contemplated the issues.

When I turned back around, Caesar was asleep sitting

up on the couch. Tanner grinned at me. "He can't stay awake at all when it's time to sleep."

It was sort of cute. I smiled at him. Was that a vampire thought? It seemed a lot like something my human-self would have found amusing. I walked over to Caesar and laid him down so at least he would be more comfortable.

Tanner leaned over to kiss me on the cheek. "I never wanted to be a vampire when I was human. I didn't love it when I woke up and couldn't talk, but now that you're here with us, part of us, among us, it's so much better. I think they know that. I think they understand there is something about you that will cause them problems. That's why they hate you and want you dead. We won't let them kill you again. They made us to fight their wars, and now they're going to get one the likes of which they couldn't possibly have imagined."

I kissed him back, right on the lips. "Maybe. But don't forget, it's really always about power. They're not afraid of me because I make things better. They're afraid of me because they're afraid I'll prove they really never had any to begin with."

8

I couldn't sleep. It was strange. As a vampire, I never experienced sleeplessness before. Insomnia was more of a human problem. Tanner was out cold next to me on the bed, and Griffin was across the room. I left an unconscious Caesar on the couch, but I could hear footsteps moving around in the living room area.

Ace and Rowan.

They were staying up, as promised. Rowan's ability to stay awake during the daytime must have been a newish thing since he wasn't able to ignore sleep when I was human. I rose from the bed and headed to the living room. Ace wasn't anywhere to be seen, but Rowan sat on a loveseat near Caesar. His head was in his hands, and he didn't look up when I came out.

Okay, he could be awake, but it wasn't going well for him. I didn't have any pain at all. I wondered why, but it was just another question to add to my ever-growing tally. I walked over to him and bent down to put my hands over his.

He jumped, like he had no idea I was there. Rowan's eyes were red, bloodshot. He was all vampire in that moment.

Even non-believing humans would change their minds if they could see him right then.

"How are you awake?" he asked, and his voice was low.

"Can't sleep, but you should. I know you're pushing through, but it's not good for you. You won't be able to help any of us in a fight like this."

Rowan furrowed his brow. "I agree, but I can't sleep. It's like I pushed too far."

"Come on." I took his hand and drew him from the chair. It was doubtful he could have stopped me if he'd wanted to right then.

I drew him back to the bed where I tried to unsuccessfully sleep before. He lay down next to me, but his eyes didn't close. If anything, the act of moving around made him seem even more in pain. I lifted my neck. "Feed."

"I'm not particularly hungry."

We'd been through the same song and dance when I was human, as if he had blinders on when it came to what he needed. Rowan looked out for everyone else but himself. "Feed yourself to sleep. You know it'll work. You'll even like it."

He sighed. "I don't want to take blood from you yet. Despite whatever miraculous abilities you may have, you're still a recently awakened vampire. A female vampire, at that, which is almost unheard of these days. I want to cherish and protect you until you're one hundred percent ready."

It was a sweet thought, but also not okay considering the circumstances. He would have to take blood from me one way or another if we ever wanted to recover the memories from the dead vampires.

"Rowan," I said as I drew his mouth toward my neck. "You need this, and I'll be fine. You won't take too much." I wasn't sure he could, even if he wanted to. "I was made to feed you even when I was human."

He ran his hand down the side of my body, stopping at my hip. "You're so beautiful. In every version of my existence, you fill me up inside, make me more than I was supposed to be. I would stay awake forever to keep you safe."

We were both sounding less our vampire selves and more like the humans we used to be. "Sweet sentiments, but I need you strong, and I'm not weak anymore, so let's be strong together. Feed. Sleep."

He shuddered against me. "I get hard when I feed from you."

That I knew, but he continued. "I like it. A lot."

"Okay." I lifted my neck again. "You're rambling."

He bit down, a low moan rumbling from his throat when he did. I was between him and Tanner on the bed, and it made a warm and comfortable cocoon to be between their two bodies. I expected Rowan to conk out almost immediately upon biting me, but he didn't. His body hardened against mine, and for long moments he drank down my blood. I ran my hand up and down his back, keeping him close to me. His pain moved through me. As human-Maci, I'd been acutely aware when they weren't okay, but the sense of their needs basically eluded me since I'd reawakened. I could feel it then, in the early light of morning. Slowly, his body softened, loosening as he fed, until his hand slipped off my hip, falling gently on the bed.

Rowan was out. Small breaths touched my skin where he'd been feeding as my blood dripped slowly down my neck. I pulled his mouth from where he'd latched onto me, his teeth receding from their fang state as he slept. I'd stop bleeding eventually, and my human propensity to not like mess wasn't with me anymore. *Let the blood drip until it stops on its own.*

Ace watched from the doorway. "He so wants to be able to do daytime for all of us, particularly for you. Yet here you are, awake, like it's not a big deal when just hours ago you were going to fall over."

I sat up, shrugging as I did. "That was before I realized we could be attacked during the day. Maybe it's what the humans call adrenaline?"

"Adrenaline doesn't make a difference for most of us. You think Caesar isn't loaded with that, thinking of you at risk? Tanner? They couldn't wake up if their life depended on it right now." Ace surged forward. "And it's still not exactly easy for me, although it's better than when you were killed. That was the kick in the ass to get better at being awake. I needed to be stronger."

He acted as if it was a choice he'd made, not something he battled against. "So maybe it just depends on the vampire?" I scooted off the bed. "You and I can react to adrenaline and circumstances, but for the others, it's just going to take time."

Ace's eyes trailed the dripping blood down my neck. After a moment, I lifted an eyebrow. "Want a bite, so to speak?"

His eyes flared red. "You know I do, but I'm not going to be okay with just a bite, and I'm supposed to be staying up to guard you."

I shoved gently at his chest. "I can guard myself. That's one of the beautiful things about going through this process. I'm not weak anymore."

He smirked at me. "There is being strong and then there is being me. Do you remember my power from when you were human? I'm tougher than the rest of them, even if they'd never admit it."

"Oh, the ego." I shook my head. "Same in human men as vampires. I take that back; maybe you're worse." I slid my hand up his shirt and yanked him to me. "Take the blood. You want it, and I want you to drink from me."

He licked my neck—everywhere *but* the bleeding part. *Fuck, he is being such a tease.*

"I won't fail you. When you know that, I'll feed from you. Not before," he promised.

His alpha-male tendencies were hot, but they did nothing for me right then. I sighed, as if I surrendered to his will, but instead, I grabbed his neck. "If you won't feed, I will."

He nodded, drawing me even closer. "Please feed. Please do."

I bit down on his neck, drinking his blood down into me. He was warm, cinnamon-y and strong. It didn't take long until I was full, so I licked his wound closed as he shuddered against me. Ace really liked it when I fed from him.

"You can't be finished." Was that a plea I heard as much as a statement? He wanted me to keep feeding.

I ignored his question. "Do you know how you feel right now? How you're aching for my mouth on your body? That's how I feel right now. I'm not trying to be cruel. I'm actually full—but you are trying to be cruel, I think."

Ace made a sound that was more like a growl than a groan before he spoke against my ear. "I never want to leave you lacking, Maci, even if you're being a manipulative vampire right now. Congratulations, by the way. You fit right in."

He bit down on my neck. I knew we would both travel into other people's memories, yet still, the jerk backward

took me by surprise. It was rougher than my first walk
through her memories, and that had only been so painful
because I hadn't known it was coming.

Then again, this was Ace. Everything with him was
always a little rougher. It just seemed to be how he was
made.

I sighed and looked around the memory landscape. The
version of him from this reality stared back at me. "He left
here in a fury. What did Frederick want from you?" He
closed our front door and walked over to take my hands.
"You look...shaky."

I supposed that was a good word for how I felt. The body
I currently inhabited burned with a fury not my own but
intense just the same. "He wanted me."

"Wanted you to do what?" He tapped my chin and
grinned at me. "Everyone wants something from you. It's the
nature of you being our fearless leader."

He didn't understand, and I couldn't blame him. In one
hundred years, no one had ever tried to insert himself into
my life the way Frederick just had. "He wanted me, darling.
He wanted to have sex with me. He wanted me to leave all of
you and be with him. When I declined his *gracious* offer, he
attempted to get violent with me."

"Where did he just go?"

Ace's mouth fell open the second I began, and when he
answered me, his vampire was in his voice. If I let him, he'd
go full on eruption and drain Frederick's blood along with
every young vampire in the next two counties. I couldn't
blame him, since I'd do the same if someone touched him
without his consent.

I grabbed his arm, pressing my fingertips hard into his
skin to ensure he heard me. "He's not stable. I think he may
have to be put down. He couldn't have thought my response

would be any different. I'm in committed soul- mate relationships."

"He's out there telling people we need to change the way we do things. To control women. To use them for one thing and one thing only, which is breeding. He wants to make a mockery of everything we've always represented."

I blinked, remembering the present. So far, I moved through time in my memories of these people. I started with her death, and it seemed I traveled chronologically backward. They were just discovering what they already knew in the previous memories–that Frederick was fucked up. I knew it in my real life, too, considering he'd killed me.

I owed him payback for that poor human girl, the one I had been who felt both far away and close to me at the same time.

"He isn't going to live to see another day," the not-Ace man promised.

She patted him on the arm. "I don't know that it's worth it."

Boy, was she wrong. I caught my breath just in time to be thrust back into my own body and timeline. Blood still dripped down my neck and Ace bent over to lick it. I shuddered, his touch giving me a shiver of pleasure while being almost too much in my sensitized state. "Well, that sucked, but your tongue is heaven," I admitted aloud.

He made a sound that might have been an affirmation or might have just been a grunt because he wanted to feed from me some more. I offered him more of my throat, and he bit down hard. I closed my eyes. Yes, it felt fantastic. My body trembled with need, my hands skimming his body impatiently. I wanted Ace to take more, to get what he needed from me.

We were both awake. These moments belonged just to us, which made them more precious somehow.

He yanked away from me, licking the remainder of my blood from his lip with a quick swipe of his clever tongue. Ace winked at me before his face fell.

What was wrong? I looked around as a noise caught my attention. It was the slightest buzzing, but it was getting louder.

This was a new phenomenon since I'd woken up a vampire. "What is that noise?"

"Danger. Not all of us can sense it, but seems you can. I have it, too. There are people coming to hurt us, kill us." He backed up and looked around. "We have to protect them. No, scratch that. I have to protect all of you."

I grabbed his arm. "We're the only ones awake. I'm strong, okay? I woke up a vampire. I'm like you. That woman I keep seeing, they hurt her. A lot. That's not me. I have no intention of dying like that. I'm fighting with you, Ace, by your side. If this is what we think it is—all of us together—then I'm here with you."

He wanted to argue, I could see it in the glare in his eyes. Instead, he nodded. "Okay. You and I are up. We have to keep this house safe. Your father and others can daywalk. We need them to wake up. If they've already gone to sleep, they may not wake up. Otherwise, it's just you and me. Go house to house in this area. You can't get confused. There is nothing around us except your father's group. See who is up. In the meantime, I'll hold them off."

I frowned. "Can you do that alone?"

"I can. Don't forget how incredibly strong I am. There aren't that many of them. Maybe ten? I can manage."

I had to believe him. Much as I was sure that I could handle myself, I'd never battled before. Ace had—a lot. I had to trust him. He needed experienced vampires by his side, so I'd do my best to find them for him.

I ran out the front door. The smell of humans assaulted my nose, and I ignored the sense. I didn't want to feed from them. It didn't mean they weren't the equivalent of a cookie to my old human-self; they could be a snack, but I would control myself. There were more pressing things to do than drinking human blood.

My ears buzzed louder. They were getting close. Whoever Frederick sent to attack us. I knew Frederick would never come himself, not when he could send someone else to do it. He'd be too cowardly to do anything besides light a match and watch it burn.

I didn't know where my father lived versus the others, but I didn't need to worry. The doors started to fly open as I approached, and vampires I didn't know appeared on their doorsteps. Maybe they were all getting buzzed like me, or maybe some of them just told the others. It wasn't a huge crowd, maybe eight vampires, but I was glad to see them.

My father appeared before me. "They let you outside alone?"

I wasn't going to respond. It really wasn't the time. Instead, I nodded to him in greeting and asked, "Is anyone else up?"

"These are the daywalkers among us. Don't worry, daughter. They don't have more than we do. We will beat them back, and then we will move so they can't find us again."

We would run? That didn't sound right to me. What was the point? I didn't ask, though, because there was too much to do. When he would have left my side, he turned around instead. "Our family always has daywalkers. I'm not surprised you are one of them."

I wasn't his family, not really. I was just a girl he'd brought to life so that he could have the memories I carried with me. He didn't even raise the human-me himself. No, he left her with a drug addicted human who completely neglected her. He was lucky I was there at all.

But I'd save those words for when we weren't under attack.

I followed behind him, since he seemed to know where he was going. In the distance, I saw nothing but darkness. My nose twitched. The scent of the approaching vampires rode the wind, as if their ill intent for me carried an actual scent. It made me want to growl in the back of my throat. *Am I a vampire or a werewolf?* The thought made me smile.

Yanked backward abruptly, I knew it was Ace who had me before I could even see him. I recognized his scent. He was mine. I'd find him anywhere.

"I was hoping you'd stay back there a little longer."

I lifted an eyebrow, not that he could see it with my back pressed to his chest. "I didn't have to find them. They all heard the same signal we did."

He nodded and kissed the back of my neck. "That's wonderful."

Excitement moved through me, like a buzz of electricity. Only it wasn't my own. It was Ace's. "You're looking forward to this," I accused, tilting my head to try to see him behind me.

"We ran from them so we could be separate when you rose. I have pain to dish out to these fuckers," he admitted with a bloodthirsty grin.

And then they were there. A dozen daywalking vampires faced us, their fangs visible and all in battle mode. My vision tunneled. I'd never fought before, and so far, I didn't have any memories that included fighting from the visions I had from that other woman's life. Despite that, I felt absolutely confident I could battle just as well as the other vampires present. If I'd been in the mood to laugh, I would have, because it was as though the will to battle surged in my blood.

I launched forward alongside Ace, who took down a vampire who once fed on the human version of me. He'd hurt her, I remembered, so I was glad Ace was about to tear out his throat. I hoped his death hurt, and I hoped he died slowly from the assault, since no one would be around to close his wound and feed him blood.

I was sure that Ace could be counted on to take care of it.

As for me, I leaped onto the back of the nearest enemy and drove him to the ground. I recognized the vampire I pinned, also. He'd fed on her a lot—at least once a day, and he caused her pain and humiliation while he fed.

His eyes widened as he stared back at me. "You! How?"

I didn't know if his question was about how I was alive or how I was awake. Either way, I didn't care to answer. No, my job right then was to cause him pain before I killed him. I wasn't a woman who would be burned alive. I was one who would do the burning. Each and every one of them, if I had to, and if they begged me for mercy, they'd find I had none left to give.

"You're going to wish you'd never been changed," I promised him. I didn't know how I knew he wasn't a born vampire, but I did. They'd made him one of their own as a reward for something, but maybe my predecessor had known that.

I didn't care. He tried to roll me over, but I was tougher than him. I was young but I wasn't weak. I tore out his throat then roared with delight.

It couldn't be all there was to life, but if I had to endure war, then I was glad that there was pleasure to be taken from it. Damn it, I would not lose to these monsters. They would get out of *my* way this time.

I WAS COVERED in blood when I limped back toward our home. Ace was, too. The sun hung lower in the sky. We'd fought all day, and not slept at all. I'd been elated—thrilled, even—every second of the day, but with the fighting over, the lack of sleep started to weigh on me.

The twelve vampires who came for us were dead. None of us were. I smiled at that. I didn't know the names of any of the vampires who were with us except my father and Ace, yet I felt connected to them. We survived together.

"We'll get packed up to go," my father said to the group. "Before the end of the night."

I shook my head, wishing he'd just kept quiet. "That isn't the answer."

"We're not ready to take them all on," my father replied, exhaustion heavy in his tone. All of us looked more haggard, though, and ready to sleep.

"Seems like we did," Ace spoke up, squeezing my hand. "They know where we are, and we know where they are. We could come at them, too." He held up his hand. "Let's wait for Rowan. You're going to want to talk to him. Trust me."

My father stopped walking. "I'd like to talk to you two, since you were here today."

"He would have been, if such a thing were possible," I said through clenched teeth. "And I won't allow you to even attempt to create discord within my family. Whatever else we are, we are solid, is that clear? Ace wants you to wait for Rowan, so that's what you're going to do."

He sighed. "Daughter, you and I need to talk."

"Not now. We need to sleep. I'll speak to you in the next rising." I paused. "With Rowan."

He nodded, which was the best I would get under the circumstances. We turned toward the house that was, at least for the moment, ours. We might be running from it soon, I thought with a sigh. Doors opened and closed around us. Some of the older vampires who didn't daywalk but could rise relatively early stepped onto the porches.

The sun burned my skin as I stared at them, watching them as they stared back at me. I guessed I was a bit of a novelty, as the vampire they all waited for since my father set the whole mess in motion. *Whatever.* The sun didn't trouble me during battle, but it was now. I had to get inside.

One woman covered her mouth with her hand, and I could see tears in her eyes. She wasn't the one they'd called my mother, so I didn't know why she would be so worked up over seeing me.

"Ace?" Her voice was low. "I've waited..."

He stared at her. "You."

That told me nothing. I squeezed his hand. "Who is she?"

"My mother." He scrunched up his face. "How are you here? Frederick killed all the women."

"Your father saved me." She put out her hand. "I..."

He held up his to stop her. "I can't... Soon, okay? There's too much for this. Just too much. How long have you been here?"

Her chin quivered. "I was told to stay away from you. He told me to wait until things were settled."

Ace shot my father a look that could have burned him to the ground. As my human-self had once been held against a wall by the force of his power alone, I knew just how powerful his gaze could be. My father should consider himself lucky Ace wasn't as angry anymore as he once had been. Also, that he was tired as fuck right then.

"Come on." I tugged on his arm. "You can talk to her when I talk to him."

He nodded. "Sounds like a plan."

We absolutely didn't have a plan, but one was forming in my head. Soon, we'd have some answers.

9

"What the fuck?" Rowan leaped from his bed, staring at Ace and me as if we stepped in from another dimension. He must have just woken up. The others weren't stirring yet.

I looked down at my blood-soaked arms. My whole body was covered in sticky redness, but none of it was mine. Rowan wouldn't know that, so I grinned at him, my head hazing over a little bit. I'd never been drunk as a human, not once, but my exhaustion felt something like the descriptions I heard from others.

"I do look a little bit like a crime scene, don't I?"

Ace kissed my cheek, but he was as covered in blood as me. He explained, "We were attacked. Fought all day, but we won."

Rowan's mouth fell open. "What?"

I patted his arm. "We fought…"

"I heard him," he interrupted me. I was too warped in the head right that second to care. Instead, I walked past him and headed toward the bathroom. I would shower, get the blood off, and go to bed for as long as I could sleep. If I could at all. I didn't know how that worked in the middle of the night for vampires. Could we sleep when the night had fallen?

"Are you okay?" Rowan grabbed my arm. "Are you hurt? Do you need blood?"

I kissed his cheek. "Feeling a little bit drunk, but not injured."

"It's the lack of sleep." He cupped my cheek. "None of that is yours? I can't smell through it. My senses have gone haywire."

Ace leaned against the wall. "You should have seen her. She was fucking amazing. At first, I was nervous but not now. She's tough. Maybe even tougher than you."

"I'm getting a shower. You two can compare dick sizes while I do. I don't need the 'who is the strongest' thing you're heading toward."

Ace laughed but Rowan didn't. "Tell me what happened, Ace. Don't leave out a single detail."

I tuned them out as I walked into the bathroom and turned on the spray. Stepping under the water, I hummed to myself. Usually, being exhausted would be painful. I understood that in my gut. It was something all vampires knew. But I felt better than I ever had. Was it the adrenaline from the fight? Or was it because I managed to deal some revenge against people that hurt her?

The door opened and closed. I breathed in, and a familiar scent tickled my nose—Ace. "Can you share that water?" he asked.

I moved, and he joined me under the spray. The blood sluiced away from both of us, coating the floor of the shower before it rushed down the drain. Ace ran his hands through my hair, lathering shampoo into my locks as he did. I hadn't even noticed him grabbing the bottle. It was the drunk feeling, making me less than totally focused. I took the bottle from his hands and began to lather his body as he'd done mine.

"More?" he asked, and I had the good sense to know he wasn't talking about the shampoo.

I smiled. "Against the wall?"

"Yes, my love. Whatever you want, however you want it."

Ace took my directions really well, pushing me against the wall. We stared at each other. "Why did I like that so much?"

He nipped at my chin. "Because you're a vampire, Maci, and we can be civilized with the best of them, but sometimes we really want to be the monsters."

"Dish out pain to our enemies," I added before I kissed him roughly.

Ace didn't wait. He lifted me up, and before I could even think about it, he was inside of me. His cock drove all the way inside, balls deep, as I cried out. Pleasure and pain warred, just as I liked it. "Pin me," I whispered in his ear. "Like you did when I was a human. Or are you too tired?" My question was both a taunt and a legitimate concern. The two sides of me forever warred with each other.

I did love their shower. I closed my eyes and let him drive my back into the cool tiles on the wall. I moaned, each thrust sending a new cascade of shivers through my body. *Yes, I want more like that. So much more.* I dug my fingers into his back. Ace wouldn't break from the pain—in fact the noises he made in my ear told me just how much he liked it. A human would be frightened of him—she had been—but I wasn't. I loved his darkness, because it matched my own soul. Our monsters understood each other.

I saw it on the battlefield when he looked up at me, drenched in a coat of blood. We matched. As he fucked me into the wall so hard we might break it, I couldn't help but grin at the thought.

"Hey," he said, then tugged on my hair, turning my face toward him so our eyes met. "Here, with me."

I nodded, lifting my neck to offer it. If he wanted to feed while he was buried deep inside me, he was more than welcome. But he shook his head once. No, Ace didn't want my blood. He only wanted my pleasure. I understood him, because I wanted the same thing for him.

I squeezed myself tighter around him until he pumped harder. *Harder. And more.* I could hardly think. I ran my hands down his chest, feeling his strong muscles bunch under my touch. Ace exuded power, and it was sexy as hell. The spiral of tension built within me, climbing ever higher as we gasped out our shared pleasure. Finally, and all too soon, I cried out, coming around him again and again.

He wasn't done, and I loved the feel of him finishing inside of me while I quaked in tremors from the high he gave me. I leaned my head on his shoulder. "Wasn't sure if I could sleep at night," I said with a jaw popping yawn.

Ace kissed my cheek. "I think tonight we both can."

"Okay." That sounded just fine to me. I snuggled closer to him, enjoying the feel of his warmth and the cool sheets.

"I'm sorry I got your human-self killed. I'll always be sorry, but I'm very glad you're here as you are, Maci."

I kissed his shoulder with my eyes still closed. "You didn't get her killed. But we *are* going to kill the fucker who killed her."

I really couldn't remember if I said anything else because sleep stole me away.

                                  ~

I ONLY SLEPT A FEW HOURS—OR that's what it felt like— curled against Ace, who was still next to me, when the bed dipped. My eyes were heavy but I forced them open. Tanner stared at me, but it wasn't the Tanner I knew. His monster regarded me from his quiet gaze, but it wasn't anger I saw there or the need to feed. No, he was worried.

I sat up and stroked the side of his face, blinking hard to try to focus my eyes. "You okay?"

He scooted closer to me. I could sense Caesar pacing around in the hallway like I was out there with him. Griffin slammed a book down across the house. Rowan wasn't inside. He'd gone somewhere. It was harder to get a read on him. Ace was out cold, as if daylight had pulled him under. But much as I'd passed out hard, I was surprisingly awake now.

I got onto my knees. "You don't like that you slept through the battle?"

He couldn't talk to me, but I could understand Tanner just fine. We always managed to speak the same language without using words. Even when she'd been human, and I hadn't been there yet, we understood him.

I explained. "It isn't your fault. Some vampires can't rise during the day ever. You're still newly made. I don't know why I can, but I'm sure someday you will. They knew that. That's why they came when they did. It's a good thing Ace and I are weird. You'll get there. That's all. We fought to keep all of you safe."

I might as well have struck him. Tanner's expression said he didn't like it at all. I frowned. "It's not your job to keep me safe. It's our job to keep *each other* safe. You'll take care of me, and I'll take care of you. I'm not going to argue about that, either." I grinned at him, and he rolled his eyes at me.

"I'm pretty kick ass, Tanner. I kept up with Ace. They didn't get to me, not once."

He tilted his neck. Okay. He had something to say, and I couldn't blame him for that. Much as I could understand him, it still had to be frustrating for him. I bit his neck and shuddered with pleasure as the warm essence of Tanner filled me. I usually only took a little bit from him because he needed his voice but suddenly I was starving, and not for just any blood. I really needed *his*.

I crawled onto his lap and drank until I was full. After closing his wound, I lifted my head. Had I taken too much? No, his eyes were clear. He was still fine.

"Don't get cocky, Maci. They sent vampires that died. Next time, they'll send better ones."

I licked my lips because I liked how he watched me do it. "Maybe we'll take the fight to them?"

Tanner smoothed my hair off my forehead. "Not until we've all memory traveled. Only me and Rowan left, right? I think it's important or you couldn't do it. Frederick wanted us without you for some reason…"

I put my hand on his arm. "Because he tried to rape her. Maybe he doesn't want me to remember that and tell others."

Tanner growled, his monster tearing through his gaze. He'd burn the frickin' world for me.

I shook my head, stroking his arm. "It wasn't me. It was her. In this persona of me, I've never dealt with Frederick. I know what he did to her. He killed her. Tried to rape her. Hurt her. Took from her. I know that he killed the human that was me, but I'm okay. I don't intend to let him get anywhere near me again. Third time will be the charm."

He blinked, some of his anger lessening. "I like that idea. Let's do the time travel, then I'll let you rest again. If Caesar knew I was in here, he'd kill me. I was supposed to be letting you sleep. He's in a rage because you were in danger without him. We all are, but Caesar is losing his shit. The rest of us are just quieter."

I lifted an eyebrow. "How did you get in here, then?"

He smiled. "I'm the trickiest of all of us. No one realizes it, but I am. He turned to look at a noise I caused, and I walked right inside." Tanner shrugged. "At some point, he'll cue into the fact that I'm in here, so let's do this before I have to wrestle him to stay with you."

I'd seen such bad stories from this woman's life. The last thing I wanted was more of that, but I'd agreed to it, and at this point it was like the humans ripping off a bandage. I just needed to get it the heck done.

I turned my neck. "Bite away."

Tanner nodded. "I look forward to the day we can just leisurely lie in bed. We'll both wake up together, and I'll just roll over or you will. We can feed at the same time, with nothing to do but start the day like that."

Actually, it sounded like heaven. "Is that possible?"

"Someday." He nodded. "I'm sure of it."

I hoped he was right. "I had an incredible time battling. I felt better afterward than I have since I woke up a vampire. Still, I don't think I could do it every day. I think I might go mad. Lose my mind. Be a shell of what I'm supposed to be."

I was basically incoherent to rational thought until Tanner woke me up. The thought worried me. I didn't want to be more monster than woman. I needed to be both.

"I won't let that happen," he promised, his voice low. Ace still slept next to us despite the fact we weren't quiet. Tanner laid me back down then cuddled up to my other side, sandwiching me between him and Ace. He breathed me in for a long second and the sound moved through me. Ace must have dressed me, because I wore a nightgown and undies. The latter were instantly soaked. Would there ever be a time when I wasn't wet and ready for these guys? I hoped not.

He bit down on my neck gently. Tanner was the most tender of all of them, taking such care with me—which was funny, since his monster shimmered the closest to the surface. He could be violent, yet he never was around me.

I sighed as pleasure flooded me a second before I landed back in the memories of a woman I'd never know but who I spent a lot of time with lately, despite never having met her. I literally ran around in her mind, and she had apparently been lodged somewhere in mine the whole time. Did she influence my human-self in some ways? I'd never know for sure, but it was interesting to think about.

She laughed, distracting me from my wandering thoughts. I watched through her eyes as she touched her version of Tanner. "Read it again," she asked him.

He dropped the book he held. "I won't do it if you're going to laugh at me."

I smiled. "Oh, come on. You love it when I tease you." She got on her knees and crawled to his side then snuggled against him. "I love it when you do all the voices."

"I'm sure the Bard himself would have been thrilled with my performance voices. He'd hire me on the spot."

I rolled over to stare at his handsome face. "Do you think he was a vampire?"

He shook his head. "Not that I've ever heard," he replied as he touched the end of my nose. "I think about writing."

"You should." He smiled at me. When he looked at me like that, it did funny things to my insides. It was so easy to love him.

He leaned on his elbow, playing with a strand of my hair. "You make everything better."

I blinked and I was back in my body. The memory seemed so different from the others. For one thing, it hadn't featured Frederick. It also wasn't dire. No, I simply remembered a quiet moment shared between the two of them. I smiled, realizing for the first time that there *had* been more to her life than just constant pain. She had fun while she was alive, found peaceful moments, and she loved. My smile faded as a pang hit my heart. She really lost quite a lot in the fire Frederick started. Her existence included joy. I might not have experienced much joy in this life or the last, but after experiencing it from her memories, I was willing to fight for it.

Tanner licked at my neck. "I won't lose you like he did." He shuddered and I stroked a gentle caress along the back of his neck. While I was only seeing moments, the rest of them saw the full picture, knew their entire lives.

"I have no intention of dying like that."

He nodded then continued to drink from me. The soft press of his lips, the gentle stroking of his tongue, his hands on me—all of it combined to be soothing, yet it lit up my body with alertness. I had to protect them as much as they did me, and I felt the push to do so like a visceral need. "Do you think that we like each other the way we do because of them?"

It felt like a reasonable question. Why else would we all have agreed to just fall into a relationship together instead of taking time to get to know each other, and time to decide?

He closed my wound then propped himself on an elbow to regard me. "No."

Well, that was a definitive answer. "Why not?"

"Because how he felt isn't how I feel. I mean, he seemed like a nice guy but also a bit of a dumbass."

I snorted and covered my mouth to stop another giggle

from escaping as he kept talking, albeit with a grin on his face because he mirrored my humor.

"I think what happened, Maci, is that we all fell for each other as humans. I think my human-self considered the guys as his friends. You were the girl he so wanted to love, it carried over into the now, into becoming a vampire. I loved the human you were when I was a vampire, and there was no question in my mind I'd love you now. I didn't know how cool you would be, how strong, or how you'd do things vampires shouldn't be able to do so quickly after waking. We should still be deep in the realm of you draining us dry every hour, not to mention you shouldn't be able to talk yet. But here you are..." His voice trailed off. "I bet if we ever see the whole prophecy—the one that is hidden away, the one that made them all rush to have children that carry the memories—we'd finally find out why he was so desperate to keep you away. I bet he knew you'd kick ass."

Tanner didn't talk much, but when he did, he said all the right things. I smoothed my finger down his nose. "I don't see everything you guys do."

"This is playing out the way it's supposed to, I'm sure of that." His monster echoed his certainty. I could feel it in the way I always could with him.

"Why, Tanner, you're a romantic!" I mocked, fanning myself just to see the dimple appear in his grin again. If every day could be like those fleeting moments, I would be glad to rise at sunset and never give anything but those moments my attention.

But I knew better than that. There were things to do. I rubbed my eyes, wishing I had time to rest or, hahaha, take a vacation. "Take me to see my father," I requested instead.

I was more than capable of going by myself, but I sensed he'd feel better if he escorted me. In fact, if Caesar's energy was any indication, I'd probably be bringing an entourage. I glanced over at Ace to find him still dead asleep. I kissed his cheek, and he didn't stir, so I decided to let him rest.

"How are you up when he's still so out of it?"

I shrugged. "You tell me. You've been a vampire longer than me, Tanner."

He shook his head. "Doesn't feel that way, gorgeous. More like I finally came alive when you were reborn."

Now that is something to think about.

CAESAR GRUMBLED the entire way over to my father's house. Apparently, Rowan was already there. Caesar filled me in through clenched teeth as he shot daggers at Tanner with his gaze. He didn't like that Tanner had woken me up.

I kissed Caesar's cheek, which cheered him up. Not enough for him to stop grumbling, but a little bit. Griffin remained quiet as he walked next to me, and we all followed Tanner. I was right—all of my vampires who were awake wanted to come to see my father, even though Rowan waited for me there.

Tanner stopped abruptly, and I almost plowed into his back. The reason for his sudden stop—it wasn't just Rowan waiting for us at my father's house. In fact, a whole circle of vampires stood with my dad. I recognized one of them from the fight, but the others were all new to me. They all turned to stare like monsters in a horror flick while we approached.

Rowan lifted a questioning eyebrow, but otherwise didn't comment on their presence. He held out his hand toward me, palm up. "Darling?" I recognized his invitation for me to join him, or at least I thought I was who he called. I've never heard him call Tanner *darling*.

I stepped around Tanner, although Caesar growled when I left his side.

"Out," my father said to the rest of the assembled vampires. The man I recognized but whose name I didn't know nodded at me. The rest stared at me as if I was a brand new and strange creature they'd never seen before.

I'd noticed they considered me a spectacle last night. I was apparently the new shiny object they all waited for and they couldn't believe they were finally seeing me in person.

I was dressed, but my interest in primping in front of a mirror for the meeting was zero. I just didn't do it.

Rowan tugged me against him. "She's here, so say what you wanted to say to her."

My father shook his head. "I have things to say, and they're not going like that, Rowan."

"I'd like to hear what you have to say. Shall we go inside?" I indicated his house.

He nodded. "Yes, let's go."

Rowan smirked at me. "You're so formal."

"I've been spending too much time in her head. I'm starting to pick up her language."

He sighed. "Guess that just leaves me?"

"Yes, we need you. Otherwise, we're all done."

His body stiffened. "Okay."

Apparently, Rowan wasn't looking forward to his time traveling experience with me. Maybe the others told him horror stories? I really didn't know at this point. They all died eventually in the memories, and at least I only remembered dying once. It wasn't an experience I was sure my mind could stand reliving for each of them, but I supposed remembering was better than not living through it.

I stepped into my father's home. If he thought my guys were going to leave me alone with him, he had another think coming. They remained so close behind me, if I stopped moving, they would've collided like a row of dominoes falling over. Their unspoken message came across clearly, though—they weren't being separated from me.

"Where is Ace?" My father scanned across the faces filling his living room.

I shrugged. I could tell he wasn't a fan of disrespect, and it was just irreverent enough to amuse me. "He had something to do," I answered vaguely.

My father didn't need to know Ace still slept. It might make him look vulnerable in some way. Of course, worrying about seeming vulnerable to them was lunacy. We all awoke with abilities far beyond the normal. Ace could stay awake during the day, which practically made him superhuman compared to other vampires.

But my father would still see weakness in us, I was sure of it. Whatever his motives were, he was part of Frederick's generation.

And none of them were to be trusted. Ever.

My temper was rising, and I knew I had to keep my cool, so I looked around his house to give myself time to breathe. It was decorated as though he'd lived there a long time. Framed art decorated his walls, varying from animals to abstract in nature. *I bet my human-self would have understood what the artwork meant. She was smart.*

I blinked. Toward the end of her life, she forgot about that, but she *had* been quite intelligent. Anger surged through my veins. The man in front of me, despite his eclectic taste in art, caused the shit that poor human girl didn't survive.

Screw calming my anger, I decided. "Talk," I snapped. I didn't particularly feel like being polite right then.

He sighed and gestured to his blue couch. "Would you like to sit?"

"Nope." I snapped off the end of the word with a puff of noise even I found slightly annoying.

Griffin threw himself down on the couch and grinned at me. No one invited him to sit, but he was going to anyway. I grinned back at him. Whatever circumstances made them all mine, I was so glad that they were. Sometimes irreverent, sometimes difficult, sometimes funny...they were so many things. And if we could survive Frederick—as I was determined we would—I'd have a lifetime to know them inside and out.

I was counting on us being wildly successful.

My father had information. *Enough is enough, already.* "All right, Dad. Talk." I crossed my arms over my chest. I was done waiting.

10

"After Frederick killed off all the elders..." He looked away for a second. "I was wracked with guilt."

That was interesting. Not his guilt per se—although, fine, good to know—but that Frederick had killed *all* the elders. Not just the ones whose memories we held, then. That choice made the guys who she thought of as the young ones the actual elders themselves, thereby determining what was and wasn't truth for the vampires. *There was no one left to contradict him.* I blinked and forced myself to concentrate.

He got to pick his truth.

My father sat down on the couch. "Things went badly very quickly. He killed off most of the females. The ones who survived went into hiding. Some of them are here. Eventually, they found their way to us, but most of them were lost. He *hated* women, and I have suspicions as to why. He loved one who didn't love him back. Someone maybe you know, Maci."

I wasn't going to deny it, but he was wrong all the same.

"That wasn't love. If you love someone, you'd never try to force them to do things physically with you that they don't want to do. That's *power*. He tried to exert his power over her, and he wasn't able to do it. I haven't seen all of her memories, but I can guess they beat the crap out of him for it. They probably humiliated him. Make no mistake, you can say what you will, but none of this was about love. His ego got crushed after he didn't get away with doing something atrocious."

We were monsters. We could kill to feed, yet even vampires had lines they didn't cross.

"True," my father agreed with a nod. "Before he killed them, he became obsessed with a prophecy regarding what basically sounded like vampire souls reincarnating. They come back, embedded with memories similar to what we've seen in some animals. Genetic memories, you could say. He thought he could have the best of the ones who passed without having to deal with the rest of it." He stared at me. "I was against the idea. I mean, you can't just go around messing with destiny and things like that. If people are meant to come back from the dead, sort of, then they'll do it on their own."

He held his hands out at the end, as if pleading for me to understand his position. My father was such a mixture of confidence and confusion. He still hadn't entirely made up his mind about where he stood on the events, yet he'd lived through them. They called him the betrayer. He'd clearly done something that had triggered the war we were now in. I was shocked so many chose to follow him. I'd much rather listen to Rowan or Ace, since he wasn't inspiring a huge amount of confidence in me.

Yet I'm alive because of him.

He continued speaking, enthusiastic now that he'd

gotten started. "I thought he was just spouting off at the mouth. I never trusted him, no, but he considered me a friend, and I let him. It seemed...safer. Anyone else who could have helped me was gone at that point. I hung around. I wasn't the only one uncomfortable with the situation. I asked about Ace earlier, because his father was also uneasy. We just kept to ourselves. Finally, after many years, Frederick adopted the policy of making humans our servants by telling them he'd make them vampires. Only he never changed the females. Ever. He hasn't made one single human female a vampire. Not one! The men, sure, if they were stupid. They stay easy to manipulate when they're reborn, and they become his lackeys." He sighed. "It was awful. He'd have the lackeys kill the human women and tell the female servants still working how they were being made into vampires. After a few people started to see through him, he decided it was time we had kids."

The guys stayed remarkably quiet while he spoke. I didn't know how much of the story they knew from their retrieved memories or the books they'd read. It certainly involved them currently as much as it did me. I sat down next to Griffin, sliding my hand onto his thigh. My refusal to sit to annoy my father was beginning to feel ridiculous. Caesar scooted over to sandwich me, but Rowan didn't move. He stood, arms crossed, and Tanner moved to stand behind me.

I was glad they were there. I knew I could fight—as I proved and then some—but their company made me more secure. My father proved a different kind of battle.

"So, then what did you do?"

He'd stopped talking. We weren't going to leave the story unfinished.

Frederick sighed. "They picked women. I'm told he acts

like it all just worked the first time we tried it. It didn't. I refused to participate, so they wrote me off as ridiculous. Even Ace's dad got into it at that point. They impregnated five different women, and they didn't produce the right babies. They had some girls. They were just vampire babies —not the ones he wanted—so he killed them. I don't know how many cycles of trials they did. He finally came up with the idea of using ultrasounds. If one of the babies was a girl, he slaughtered all five mothers, over and over. There had to be *five* boys, end of story. Anything else meant death to the mother."

Imagining them planning and then executing, literally, the plan—it was so horrific, I almost couldn't stand listening, but he continued. "And then the unthinkable happened. It actually *worked*. Five boy babies. There was a twist, too. Ace's dad fell in love with the woman he'd impregnated. He might have had some compunctions about what they did to begin with, and they finally blossomed into true horror when he saw what was being done, what he'd willingly participated in doing. It was like he came back to his senses. Right around that same time, I got really scared. Honestly, boys, I didn't want you back here without her. She made the five of them tolerable."

Griffin snorted. "That is probably still true, but I need you to understand—we aren't the six of them. We're ourselves. Yes, we have memories of a random person embedded in us and we have since we awoke. It's strange, but he doesn't influence me. I don't really care what he did, because he did everything all wrong."

"Maybe that's the point." Rowan shrugged. "To know what *not* to do."

"You haven't seen it yet." Tanner spoke low. "You'll feel differently. I mean, I'm glad to know just how bad Frederick and the others are. I really am, but I already knew. My human-self grew up with them. I would've killed them anyway just for that shit, not to mention the fact they killed Maci."

Rowan nodded. "I'm sure you're right."

I considered Rowan for a long second after he spoke. It must be exhausting, having to lead all of us and be questioned all the time. Although it seemed like a conversation we should have, it wasn't the right time. Some time, though, we'd sit down to discuss some Rowan self-care. Maybe he'd like to try to hunt me? I shoved those thoughts aside and asked, "What did you do when you decided you couldn't put up with it anymore?"

"Ace's Dad came to me first because he knew I'd made a decision. I intended to thwart their plans. I was going to have you, and I knew what steps to take to make it happen. I met your mother, but then...she changed things for me. She was everything. Together we had this place, and we had you."

He said it so nonchalantly, but I saw through him. "How many babies and their mothers did you have to get rid of to have me?"

My blunt question made him scowl. "None. You came right away, which is particularly amazing because your mother is a vampire. Vampire women statistically take longer to conceive than humans, which was why Frederick used them in the first place. But you came to us right away."

Gak, I did not want to think about my parents making me right then or ever, but then a memory hit me, or rather the feeling of one. My human-self dealt with a lot of things she found completely disgusting. I smiled at the sense of it, of her. It was the first time I thought of her and didn't really feel sadness or disappointment on her behalf.

Griffin put a hand on my knee. "As we all know, she didn't grow up with a vampire mother and father. You left her with a human to raise her. A bad human, at that."

He winced. "Yes, I chose poorly, I agree. But we needed someone who could be enthralled enough that they wouldn't notice if we took you periodically. We wanted someone who wouldn't care if you started living with one of your men. We expected it to happen a lot faster than it did, honestly. I was convinced they would bond with you as children, but it was like you all went out of your way to avoid her." The last was said to the guys, not me.

Rowan shook his head. "I can assure you, the human who once inhabited this body would have loved to have found Maci earlier. He only got to know her for a few weeks before he bit the dust."

A flood of memories hit me as Rowan continued to come down on my father for his very flawed plan. *What if we'd never met at all?* I didn't care for the idea of that. Most of my memories of human-Maci's life were a bit of a blur. I could call them up, but it was as if I watched them through a viewfinder from a distance away. I could see the memories, but I couldn't quite touch them, and I didn't care that much about them. I had a general sense of things, but Rowan said *bit the dust. That wasn't what his human-self did. He died in a coffin, slowly, while I died inside watching it.*

These memories didn't feel like someone else lived them. They were right there for me to access, as though I'd been there when it happened. All of that pain. The guys lived it, too. Abuse. Witnessing horror. Her human life hadn't been the only one to be wrapped up in a bed of nails she had to constantly roll around in.

I lifted my head to regard my father. "Well, it worked."

Rowan had been in the middle of saying something, and

I interrupted. My tolerance for the conversation was at about a zero, and I wasn't sure I could take any more.

"What worked?" My father blinked.

"You and my mother and all of the others, you went ahead and made us. That's what you wanted. We carry the memories that, for some reason, you all felt it was important that we have. I'm not exactly sure why you thought it would matter. To be honest with you, they seem to be the memories of a pretty normal woman. A vampire. She had loves, and she wanted to live her life the best way she knew how. Instead, Frederick wanted her, and he couldn't have her, so she was burned alive until she wasn't anything anymore." My hands shook as I spoke. "We're all just ordinary, aren't we? Sure, Rowan probably has some battle knowledge or maybe Ace does, but what does it matter? With all the fighting you've been doing, you probably have it, too." I held up my hand. I was on a rant, and I knew it. "So, congratulations! We're here. We're pretty normal, but I'm not going to live like this. I'm *absolutely* not going to. Rowan and I are going to do what we have to do, and then I'm going to go kill Frederick and the others. Thanks for all the effort you put into having me, but we're never going to have a relationship. As far as I'm concerned, it's just the six of us. The rest of the world doesn't matter to me anymore."

My father sighed. "Maci…"

I didn't want to hear it. "I would've died a human—and never been me—if you hadn't snuck me blood for years. Thanks for that," I called over my shoulder. Human-Maci had no idea what was happening to her, but I could remember those moments quite well. *It must be the vampire in me.* The only thing I knew for sure was I had to be away from my father acting like he hadn't played as much of a role in the situation as Frederick and the others. Manipulation was everywhere.

Caesar ran after me, catching up to be right by my side. Tanner was quickly on the other side. I'd been rude, and I supposed we were guests. The realization didn't bother me. If we had to leave, it might be better. We were predators, and I was pretty sure we could figure out how to survive without him.

"What you said was true," Tanner said quickly. "I don't have any particularly helpful skills that can add to anything."

Griffin caught up to Caesar's side. "Maybe we should just ask Frederick. I mean, I don't want to, because I hate the guy as much as any of you, but, fuck. He knows what the prophecy said, and he knows what he wanted from us. Your father, Maci, has no idea. He just wanted to thwart Frederick. He doesn't even know what he betrayed, which seems odd for a person being called the Betrayer."

Rowan suddenly joined us. They were faster than me, that much I was sure of. I needed to remember that in case anyone ever had to run for help, since it would be better if it wasn't me.

"Maci," Rowan grabbed my arm. "Come on. Let's do what we need to do to finish this whole process. Then we can all meet up and discuss what to do next. If we're attacking Frederick, we can't just knock on the front door and shoot him."

He had a point. We might be chosen or gifted or whatever, but we didn't even know how or what our supposed gifts did.

I squeezed Caesar's arm. "I'll be okay with Rowan."

"I'll be nearby anyway." He kissed my cheek. It was a

gentle move for him. "I'm never waking up again to find you've battled other vampires while I snored."

I smirked at him. "You weren't snoring, if that helps."

"It doesn't. It really doesn't, Maci." He rolled his eyes. "Take my point."

"There's nothing we can do about the sun, Caesar. You won't be able to stay up during daylight until you're able. That's just how it's going to go. No need to beat yourself up about it. Ace can. I can. We're it for right now. Frederick lost. I doubt he'll try a daytime attack again. No, the next time will be nighttime with his entire force behind him. It's either that or we attack him." I shook my head. "It doesn't matter which currently. I was pretty tough."

"Of course you were. You shouldn't have to be, though." He sighed. "We've never, not once, been able to keep you safe or keep you happy. It's always pain and running around. I can't imagine you'll want to stay if this keeps up."

Was that what he was worried about? I leaned in close to whisper in his ear. "Just try to get rid of me."

He smiled slowly. "I'd never do that."

I moved back but Griffin tugged on my sleeve. "I'm going to find out that prophecy tonight."

That was an abrupt shift I hadn't seen coming. "How are you going to do that?"

By way of an answer, Griffin lifted his eyebrows. "Trust me?"

A question for a question. That was never good. But I realized that I did trust Griffin as though I'd known and done so for many lives. I nodded. "Be careful. The prophecy isn't worth your life. I honestly don't give a shit what it says."

"I do." He kissed my other cheek then the one that Caesar had pressed his lips against. "And you know this about me. I can't leave this."

That was true. Tanner didn't kiss me, but his gaze traveled with me when I walked over to Rowan until I left his sight. He was less predictable than the others. I wasn't entirely sure what Tanner would do right then. He might sit down and do nothing or the entire battle could be over when I reemerged, with every possibility in between as well. Caesar would wait for me. He wouldn't move until I returned to him. If Ace was awake, he'd be rip roaring ready to go battle Frederick.

But he needed to speak with his mother. I would push him on that. I'd speak to mine too, eventually, if for no other reason than to tell them to leave us alone. They hadn't raised us, not even the ones who had been present. They barely kept the guys alive. We owed them nothing. The part of me that liked to cause pain—and that part definitely existed since I awoke—wanted to find them just to tell them to fuck off.

I'd see how much I felt like controlling myself.

It would depend. Maybe on the day. Or the minute.

I followed Rowan into one of the smaller bedrooms. He closed the door and, without a word, drew all the shades closed.

Rowan wasn't overly sentimental, so I didn't think he intentionally cocooned us in a silent world where only we existed. "You okay?" I asked as I walked toward him, stopping before I touched him.

He visibly swallowed. "I don't like feeding in front of others. I don't even like them knowing that I'm feeding particularly from you. What happens when I feed from you feels like it should be private. I know I have to get over it, and I've obviously gotten past my hang-ups in the past, but if I have a choice, I'd like to keep what happens between us private. Even if they know about it, they don't have to be privy to every detail. I would like some intimacy."

I was pretty sure I understood. "The things that happen to you when you feed from me? That's what you don't want to share?"

He nodded. "Maybe I brought some issues with me from being a human. Vampires don't care about privacy at all."

"There's no one voice for their vampires. I don't feel the same way about things that Caesar does. Or that Griffin does. He's trying to find a prophecy that I don't think is particularly useful, but it matters to him. If you prefer to feel sexual when we're alone, then so be it. I don't think you need to place judgment on your own feelings. I think they are just what they are, and that's all there is to it. Period, end of story, but that's just my opinion. As I said, there's no one right answer. Feel as you want to feel."

He quirked his mouth into an almost smile. "Did you really just give me permission to feel how I wanted to feel?"

"Well, you seemed to need it." I grabbed him and let him tug me against him. "Is that all that's bothering you?"

He shook his head. "No, but you really don't want to hear more."

"Yes, I do." I meant it. I offered him my neck. If he wanted to feed first and talk later, that was fine, too.

He ran his nose over my neck, right where my pulse would be. I closed my eyes, and he breathed me in, his soft exhale lifting the small hairs near my nape and making me shiver. "I don't want to lead. I know I was born for it, placed in my pre-determined role because of Frederick and also because of whoever this guy is that I'm carrying around. But I don't want it. I never did, not as a human or now. Ace would be better at the job." He sighed. "*You'd* be much better at it than any of us."

I opened my eyes to stare at him. "If I led, would you have my back? Every step of the way?"

"You think Caesar is attentive? You have no idea how fucking there I can be for you if I don't have to figure out how to lead us here there and everywhere. I'll be so there for you, no one will get near you if you don't want them around. They'll find themselves without their heads before they make it to you."

This was an entirely new side to Rowan. I grinned at him. "I think they can keep their heads. Well...maybe they can."

"Give me back your neck, Maci."

He might not want to lead, but he clearly didn't mind ordering me around. I obeyed him happily, and he didn't wait, he bit down on me. I shuddered against him, nearly coming in my pants. I was worked up, and his bite was the relief I needed. Rowan's mouth on my skin, his teeth digging into me. Fuck, it was so hot. It wasn't supposed to be. We were on a mission to travel through memories or whatever, but I couldn't help how he made me feel.

I ran my hands over his chest and held onto his shirt. He finally let go, licking my wound closed. "There's something else I don't like."

My eyes had closed as he sucked on me, and I hadn't even realized it. I opened them. "What's that?"

"I don't like you not being naked right this second."

I let him push me down on the bed roughly and grinned up at him. "So demanding tonight, Rowan, with all your preferences. Want to know one of mine?"

His smile was huge. "Absolutely."

"I'd like you to also be completely naked."

His smile fell. The moment became heavy, weighted with tension. It was serious. It meant something, what we were saying to each other, even if I wasn't entirely sure what any of it meant. I just knew that it would be *something*. Like I could feel the tingling in the room, speaking to the moment, almost like the very bell of fate rang in my ear.

Or maybe I was just a lunatic vampire who had no idea what was going on.

We both stripped quickly. Our gazes remained locked, and I didn't let myself look away. He held my gaze as intently as I did his. When I would have taken off my bra, he stopped me by catching my hands. "I want to do that."

I didn't respond because he undid the center clasp of my bra before I could. Rowan was completely exposed to me. If I looked down, his cock would stand proudly waiting for me, but I still couldn't drop my gaze from his.

"You wanted something from me when you were a human. I didn't understand it then, didn't think I could give you what you wanted. I was wrong. I will not let you down as a vampire."

I wasn't sure what he was talking about, and I didn't want to think about any of the human-Maci's disappointments right then. "Let's be here right now. We're predators. We live in the moment, right?"

He took my cheeks in his hands. "Not true and you know it."

I didn't know what I would have said in response, because his mouth touched my own and I exploded in heat, like I'd stepped into a fire.

Rowan was right. That wasn't true. Yes, I was a predator, but I was also a lover. I could be both.

And with Rowan, I really was both.

He wanted me to be in charge except for in his bed. "Maci." His voice rumbled low and deep, matching the way his mouth caressed mine. "Grab onto the headboard and don't let go. Before you bite me, I'm going to own you. You'll love every second of it."

I smiled at him. "Not that I'm complaining, but I thought that we were just getting our memories worked out. Have we both fallen off track?"

"Once I have you alone, I lose track of everything outside of what is between us. And tonight, I plan to take advantage of that weakness in myself as much as I possibly can."

It was such a different Rowan. It was as if, since he'd been given the freedom to express himself, and I'd listened to him, he became suddenly ravenously affectionate.

I couldn't say I minded. And it turned out that, like Rowan, I didn't want to think of anything outside of what was between us, either.

11

My senses were consumed by Rowan. He pushed my legs apart and met my pussy with his tongue in one eager swipe. I moaned, pleasure surging through me in a rush that stole my breath away. I clawed at my own arms, wanting pain to counteract the sheer bliss that rolled through me. Rowan grabbed my hand and placed it on his back. My monster moved inside of me. Yes, he knew what I wanted. I needed to administer pain, and he wanted to take it.

I loved Rowan so fucking much. Digging my fingers into his back, I wasn't gentle. He raised his mouth and lifted his head to look at me, his eyes gone a bloody red. Our monsters regarded each other easily. His was stronger, but he loved me. He wanted to give me what I wanted...to a point.

"Take me. *Now*." I lifted an eyebrow. Would he comply?

Rowan flipped me over. He was going to do as I instructed, but he'd do it his way. I gripped the headboard. He touched me one more time before he pressed inside of me. "You are so wet for me."

"I think... " I began, then caught my breath as my body adjusted to him. " ...under the circumstances, that's a very good thing, don't you?"

He pushed in and out of me, one stroke after another, over and over. Each delicious slide urged my senses higher until I felt drunk on lust. Rowan didn't answer me, and that was fine. The time for talking was done. We moved as a single unit. He pushed; I pressed. I'd no sooner think I understood what was happening, that I could anticipate what was next, than he'd adjust his hips and it would all start over. I panted, small grunts of noise coming helplessly out of my throat, when he finally jerked hard against my spot, making me shudder and finally come around him. I leaned forward, unable to stop myself and would have hit the headboard if his hand hadn't been right there to stop me from colliding.

I had a second to smile, wondering how quickly I could get better from a head injury as a vampire, when he bit down on my neck. *Yes.* I loved that, but it wasn't what we needed. Somewhere in my pleasure-hazed brain I remembered that. I had to feed from him. I wrenched my neck back. Confusion warred over his gaze for just a second before I bit his neck and fed. *Yes, I fucking love this.* My muscles clenched and pleasure flooded me before I drifted back into the memories of a woman I'd been born to know. I wouldn't have chosen our connection, and I doubted she had known anything about it, but we were linked, regardless.

She turned around, and I caught a glimpse of her in the mirror. She was younger than when I saw her before. Quickly, she walked to the door, and like the observer-slash-parasite I was in these moments, I went along while she swung it open. Rowan—the version of him there—leaned against the outdoor frame, staring at me.

His face spread in a big grin of greeting. "Hi."

She sighed, and her joy moved through me. "You came."

"Well, of course I did." He walked past me into the house. "The others would never have forgiven me if I didn't. Before we met you, I swear we all used to be reasonable, but now that we've met, we're all lunatics to be around you all of the time."

I smiled back at him. It wasn't the first time I'd heard them describe how they felt about me. *Her.* I blinked. It was harder than it should have been to keep my head separated in Rowan's memory. Most of the other times had all been so angst-filled, but she was so happy in that moment. Real happiness, not even tempered by any of the vampire sourness that rode me most of the time. She was truly happy in that second—like, human levels of happy.

They took it for granted, I realized. They expected to have the ability to feel things acutely and purely without having to navigate around the monster inside of them. Or at least they could feel that way sometimes. It wasn't always, because they could experience the full range of emotions, but it stunned me that they could feel unbridled joy. It was the only description I could even begin to explain how she felt right then.

She tugged on her Rowan's shirt. "I feel it, too. The connection. The way vampires can feel if they're lucky? I feel it with you. With all of you." I wanted him to kiss me right then more than I'd ever desired anything in my whole life.

He took my cheeks in his hands, a gentle caress of warmth and strength. "If you let me, I'll make you feel like this forever. Nothing will ever happen to you."

She didn't know it, but I was sure, because I knew the future—he wouldn't be able to keep that promise.

But oh how happy she'd been right then.

I was flung back into my body, and Rowan's arms came around me. He held me close, rocking me gently. I liked him better than I liked his counterpart. He didn't make promises that were impossible to keep. I actually appreciated that he saw how hard life could be and walked that road anyway instead of pretending to be upbeat all the time. That wasn't real. Whatever kind of vampire I was, it wasn't the optimistic, shiny magical-thinking kind.

I was the *I need to blow those fuckers up* variety of vampire.

Rowan helped me to lift my head. I blinked, my vision finally clearing enough to really look at him. "I'm so glad that's over."

"What did you see?"

"A moment they shared in the hall. He professed his love for her and promised he'd keep her safe forever."

Rowan nodded. "Interesting. I got the entire picture of his life. While he was a nice guy, he was completely blind-sided by what life threw at him. I won't be that way, but I've come to believe it won't be me keeping us all safe. I think that's going to be you. You're just too powerful for it to be otherwise. Maci, you should barely be conscious in a need for blood, and I can see that your brain is plotting. You stayed up all day and barely slept, yet you look perfectly fine. It isn't normal. I think...I think if there is part of her in you, then she came back because she's got serious unfinished business, and she's not willing to wait to finish things up."

I kissed the end of his nose. "That's me, not her. She's there, but I'm the one in charge here."

I wanted to be perfectly clear about that. This was my show, not the ghosts of the past. What happened with her? It just made me madder.

DAYTIME MUST HAVE COME, because I woke up when the sun set. I yawned and lifted my head. Rowan still slept beside me. The sunrise took us both down, and I'd done nothing to stop it. Ace stared down at me from the end of the bed.

He rocked back on his feet. "I guess I slept through the whole day."

"You did." I nodded. "And that's fine."

He smirked at me, a familiar Ace expression that said he knew I wasn't saying everything I should. My monster roared to life, awakening to greet his. Usually, that was saved for Tanner, but she liked the way Ace challenged us. My nipples hardened. I'd love to have the time to just pounce on him, but it wasn't going to happen today. There were things to do.

Even if he has really nice cheekbones and abs under his shirt that would be fun to stroke.

I got up on my knees. "I'm going to shower and feed Tanner and then we should talk about stuff that happened yesterday. Maybe we can make some time to see your mother before we figure out how to end this mess. Sound good?"

Rowan groaned. "You don't really ease into the day, do you? It's like up and at it."

I shook my head. "Why bother with baby steps?"

"That could be your whole motto as a vampire: *nothing in small doses*." He lifted himself up on his elbows. "Ace, how did you get in here? I thought I locked the door."

Ace held up his hand, showing them both the door handle he held in his long, elegant fingers. "I removed the barrier. I refuse to be locked away from her. Caesar either. You had one night, so I've been informed. It's a new one. See you later, Maci." He looked over his shoulder as he exited. "I'm not the least bit interested in meeting my mother."

I stood up, stretching. "You're eventually going to have to meet her, you know that, right? If you don't want to now, that's fine, but you're going to have to deal with her at some point. She lives right over there." I pointed in what I was pretty sure was the general direction of her house. "I dealt with my father, so you can do the same."

"I'd rather move. Or burn down the entire house."

That was so dramatic, it might be funny...if only I wasn't absolutely certain he was serious. Griffin rushed through the door before I could say more. His eyes were huge, and he darted from one foot to the next, the most animated I had seen him with my vampire eyes. "Did you get it?"

He held up the book. "I did." As he spoke, Tanner joined us. They all clearly were tired of waiting around. He snuggled up next to me, and I bit down on his neck. His sigh moved through me while I drank and listened to Griffin speak. "I spent my daylight hours in a random trailer in the woods, even though I've never done that before. It was so exciting. I stole from the elders, and then I was practically exposed to the sun. It was...*exhilarating*. Anyway, here." He held up the book. "I've read it."

I grinned as I released Tanner's neck. *Of course he finished reading it already*. In every lifetime, Griffin succeeded in whatever he attempted.

He asked, "Is everyone ready to hear about the prophecy?"

"If we have to." Caesar leaned against the doorway. "I'd rather talk about Maci's tits, but yeah, sure, we can talk about prophecy, if that's what floats your boat."

Tanner groaned. "You're going to want to talk about it, Caesar. I have a feeling it'll be what sets Maci in motion, burning all those fuckers to the ground." His monster flew to the surface of his eyes as he spoke. Tanner liked that idea, and his monster loved it.

So the fuck do I.

I licked his wound closed. "I want to hear about the prophecy."

"Well, it's not our prophecy. You heard that, about us returning in new bodies or some shit to be great leaders. Honestly, feels like bullshit to me. I haven't seen that one, and why would that be, I wonder? I can't deny we're all carrying these memories, and it's not like that's typical. No other vampires are resurrected from the past, so I guess that prophecy came true or whatever."

Rowan cleared his throat. "First of all, we don't know what other vampires are and are not carrying. We activated each other's memories with blood. We're also soul mates. Well, all of us with her, not necessarily with each other. Vampires aren't doing that anymore, so who knows what the norm is? I certainly don't. Secondly, get out of my bedroom, let Maci take a shower, and then we'll do this. She might also like to feed. And that is my last order, because she's in charge from now on."

They all turned to stare at me. "Unless someone wants to object," Rowan added.

"You're in charge, fine." Caesar met my gaze. "But I'm still going to keep you safe whether you like it or not, even if you tell me not to."

I stretched my arms over my head. "I get to keep you safe, too, Caesar. All of you. Yes, let me shower, then we'll talk prophecy. I'm not the least bit hungry. I can't make sense of why I am sometimes and why I'm not other times."

"It's because you're miraculous." Tanner winked at me. "Trust me on that."

In that moment, his monster was nowhere to be found. Just Tanner—practically the human Tanner I'd once known —and in that second, I was Maci from then, too. We stared at each other, familiarity so strong, I could practically curl into it. It wasn't so obvious with the others. Did they notice it? That my human-self had just temporarily asserted herself into my person? Why had that happened?

And what does that mean that it did?

I headed for the bathroom, the questions I had no answers for riding me the whole way.

THE SHOWER RINSED AWAY my sweat but not my worries. The human side receded some, which let me think clearly again. She wasn't riding my brain, and that was a good thing. Too much pain and sentimentality weren't called for in these moments. I dressed in a pair of yoga pants and a t-shirt, preferring comfort and the ability to move over anything sexy or alluring. Other women might want to look lovely.

That had never been me.

The guys were in the living area. Caesar leaned against the doorway closest to me. I wrapped my hand around his bicep for a second as I passed by him. He was strong, his skin warm and smooth, and I loved that. Eventually, I flopped down on the couch. I could feel all of them watching me, their gazes heavy enough to carry actual weight. In any other circumstance, I'd be thrilled to just spread my legs and let each one of them come at me.

In fact, I hadn't really gotten to have sex with Griffin since my rising. We would have to do something about that. He was so sexy. I shook my head. I had to focus. I might be a sex addict, but if I wanted to burn down Frederick's world, I needed to pay attention to Griffin's brain, not his biceps.

For a little bit, anyway.

He held up the book. "This book claims to be able to break the history of vampires into sections. Beginnings and endings, and they call them prophecies. I guess that is what they are . I haven't had a lot of spare time in my life to worry about things like mumbo jumbo, but if we believe it, the book says there will be a great war. The ones who have embraced the vampires who hold onto the past will win it."

I waited for more. When Griffin didn't say anything else, I leaned forward. "What else does it say?"

"It goes on to talk about the reincarnation. Holding the memories of those who lived in the past. It's not necessarily that we *are* them so much as we were born carrying their understandings like a road map. Those people are dead, long dead. The feeling we have where we're not them? Yes, that's absolutely accurate. We're not them, and we never were them. We've seen their stories now, but they're not our memories, and we may never be able to access them again." He shook his head. "But we're supposed to be able to win the war for them, even though it isn't our war. Regardless of the winner, the war sets a new era of vampirism in motion. That's what it says. Frederick wants to be the leader of that era. He's even made notes in the book." Griffin held it up again, gesturing to the page to prove his point. "He thinks he's started that with the changes he made, like there is no way that it can be undone or something. He thinks he thwarted the whole thing."

I rose. "Okay, so what I'm hearing is there is no great revelation in the prophecy. We knew this stuff already, or at least most of it. There is no huge information dump. Here's what I want to know, Ace, are your parents soul mates? Go over there and find out if they share memories with dead people. Maybe it's common and just no one talks about it, like sex or something like that."

"Do we not talk about sex?" Griffin scrunched up his face.

"Humans don't." Tanner shrugged. "I'm happy to talk about it if the subject ever comes up."

Ace groaned. "That was a dirty trick right there, Maci. Now I have no choice but to go talk to the woman."

I shook my head. "I wish I could say that I planned it, but I didn't. It's just my good luck that it worked out."

"Damn it." He walked toward the door. "No one make battle plans until I get back."

"So what do you want to do?" Caesar kissed my cheek. "What is our next move?"

"Tanner," I took his hand. "Go, see my Dad. I want to know how many people we have who would be willing to fight. I want numbers, then we'll plot." I walked to the window to look outside. I needed to access the memories of one very ordinary vampire woman so I could win some kind of war. If Ace's parents weren't also getting those memories, then the difference had to be in that ability. Why did it matter? Or had it never mattered, and only started to because Frederick had made a thing out of it?

He nodded. "Sure. I'm not usually the one sent to talk. I love it. I'll do it." My sometimes-silent soul mate tore from the room.

I pointed at the book. "Griff, are there other prophecies? I mean things that people have thrown out because they were meaningless, or they didn't come true?"

He blinked. "Yes, actually. We had to study all of those books before we turned. There were some nonsensical things that are nothing." He took a beat. "Oh, I see what you're saying."

Caesar yawned. "I don't. Somebody fill me in."

"Did this book have any real meaning before someone attributed meaning to it? Like he read it and decided it was real."

He followed exactly what I was thinking. "If other soul mates carry memories that no one talks about, and anyone who would know about coming back with memories has since died—Frederick doesn't have one, so he doesn't know that..."

"We're literally at war over something that doesn't matter."

Rowan paced to the window to stare bleakly outside. "Maybe that's true of most wars. Maybe most things are nonsense if you take the time to really look at them."

"We still have to win the war, even if it is meaningless." I realized as I spoke the words that I absolutely meant them. "He has to be stopped. We'll complete the prophecy by ushering in a new non-Frederick- led generation of vampires who can hopefully do better."

Griffin set down the book on the table. "Look, our girl is an optimist."

I couldn't stop eyeing him, and it wasn't going to get any better. I'd sent Ace out on a mission, which meant I had enough time to thank Griffin for getting the book, personally.

"Hey, Griff," I said as I shot a smile at him. "Want to talk about sex? With me? Right now?"

He opened and closed his mouth. "Sure. Absolutely. Right here? In the room with all of them?"

"No, although I would be open minded about discussing that on another night. For tonight, how about you and I go talk about sex in another bedroom?"

His monster rose to the surface to regard me. It was such an unusual moment for Griffin, because he kept his beast so tightly leashed most of the time, I hardly ever saw him. But there he was, smiling back at me. Griffin sometimes forgot how physical of a creature he was. The cerebral was great, but Griff needed to remember to let his monster come out and play.

"Actually," I took his hand and brought it to my mouth, "you can have me...*if* you can catch me."

I didn't give him the chance to answer. I stalked Tanner, but Griffin would have to find me. Caesar and Rowan would hate me running off, because they didn't want me out of sight for safety, but I didn't care right then. My need for Griffin got to win over their need to suppress my wildness.

I took off running, pleased as the muscles bunched and stretched in my legs. I got a chance to get to know the layout of the area when we battled Fredrick's goons, so I ran everywhere I could think of, not stopping for even a second. Griffin was faster than me, but I could out dodge him. We ran for at least a half an hour before I spun around a corner and he tackled me to the ground. Before I would have impacted, he rolled beneath me to take the brunt of the force and then rolled us both over so he was on top. His fangs were elongated, and his eyes were red. Oh yes, I'd awoken the monster inside of Griffin.

And it was *so* hot.

"You're not scared of me when I'm like this, and it makes me hot. It makes me want you even more, and I always wanted you. When I was human and now, there is nothing I want more than you all of the time." He bit down on my neck. I cried out for him, clutching to keep him close. I had no warning before he struck, and that was fine by me. Let him take what he wanted from me, because I would give him everything.

We stripped each other quickly, having no use for barriers between us. We rolled around, desperate for each other's pleasure and greedily seeking more and more. I was on top and then he was. He reached down, finding my clit deftly and stroking it. I rubbed against his hand, seeking more, and he moaned.

"Griffin, you can't break me. Fuck me as hard as you want for as long as you want right here on the ground."

He kissed my cheeks. "Yes. Right now."

He pushed himself inside of me roughly. We ended up against a tree, the bark digging into my back. It cut me, probably leaving wounds on my back. I fucking loved it.

Griffin lost control as if the scent of my blood on the night air drove him wild, and I held on for the ride. Waves of pleasure arched through me over and over again. I cried out, moaning, thrashing against him until I finally found my release. I held onto his neck, trembling in aftershocks, and he ground into me. Yes, we'd needed this. Tears rushed from my eyes, and I let them fall. *What an amazing release.*

We were vampires.

Sometimes we just needed to fuck each other, particularly when there was danger coming and we were in love.

I blinked at the thought. *We are, aren't we?*

Lifting my head, I stared at him as he panted above me. "Do you love me?"

Griffin's vampire retreated, going back where he held him at bay most of the time. "I do. I've never been warm, not in any manifestation, but I love you, Maci, with everything in me that can love."

I kissed his cheek. "Griff, you can't possibly think you're cold, not after you just broke that tree fucking me against it."

His smile was huge. "I did, didn't I?"

Yes, he had.

12

Ace wasn't okay. He'd been gone too long, and his distress ached in my bones. As a human, I knew if they were not all right. It hadn't traveled exactly over with me, but some of it was coming back. I sent him to meet his mother, so it was my fault if things went terribly wrong.

With Caesar by my side, I spotted the situation from a distance. His father stood with Ace's mother. He had been such a complete mystery to me, and although I had some answers about why that was—he fell in love with Ace's mother, and they were soul mates. He'd lied and tricked Frederick for her—I still wasn't clear on all of his motives. Neither was Ace, and the stress pulsating off my love wasn't good.

Ace tended to let his fury out in fiery explosions.

"Hi," I said as I slid my arm around Ace's waist. Caesar nodded to me from his other side. If the others knew he was in bad shape, they would've shown up, too. It was an hour until daytime, so he should've returned to us a long time ago, if he'd just been visiting his mother to ask about past life visions.

However, his father's presence changed things drastically. There was a whole hill of pain from his human days there, and maybe some since he was a vampire, too.

They all turned to look at me, and his mother tried to force her lips into the semblance of a smile. Ace shot daggers at his father, but he said, "You're here just in time to hear about why he did the things he did. He's been away, but now that he thinks we're about to go to war, he's come out of hiding. Great timing, right?"

Ace's father glared back at him. "Don't presume to know what I have and haven't been doing. I lived with those monsters for years. I did it to stay with you and to protect your mother." The couple looked at each other, gentleness hitting his gaze for the first time. "And I've stayed away, because if they're looking for me, and they are, I didn't want them to find your mother. At this point, you can handle yourself, maybe even better than I can, since you're awake in daylight while you should still be passing out early every night."

"I can do a lot more than just stay up." For a second, a dangerous glint lit his gaze, but then he shook his head. "Never mind. What I can and can't do is none of your business, but you're going to have to excuse it if I hold onto some judgment of you. I've recently learned from Griffin how you impregnated women and then had them killed because Frederick ordered it, so you don't have any moral high ground to stand on with me."

Ace's father looked down, unhappiness clear on his face. "I am deeply ashamed of those years. They were confusing. I had worries about Frederick, but he was powerful, and all the elders were dead. We followed him, everyone followed.

He seemed right, and we were getting more and more powerful. Towns full of people did what we wanted, but there was part of me that remained uneasy. I did those terrible things. I did. Then I met your mother, and it was like I woke up. She was mine, my soul mate, my everything. I wouldn't let anyone hurt her or take our baby, no matter what Frederick thought. As soon as you were born, when he ordered the women killed, I hid your mother away. I gave him the body of a random woman who had died from using drugs. He never noticed, since they were all the same to him. I brought your mother here, and we changed her. Warren agreed to keep her safe so long as I played ball and kept you safe once you were born, so that's what I did. Go ahead and judge once you've been a vampire for more than two seconds." He pointed at Ace. "*You* were the most perfect vampire I'd ever met. You did everything they tasked you to do and then some. I wasn't about to spill my guts to a person who was basically responsible for destroying anyone that pissed Rowan off for months. Don't act holier than thou, Ace. You won't like how you come off in that argument."

"Okay." I put my hand on Ace's arm. "I appreciate that you never fed from me. I'll say thank you for that, but Ace had a fucked-up childhood. He has lots of reasons to feel the way he does, and it isn't fair for you to belittle or disregard his experiences. He is entitled to his anger about your behavior as well. He's one of the best people I know. Whatever you think you know about him, you don't, but right now, I don't care about any of it. Whether you're all bad people, bad vampires, mean, rude or whatever is not my concern. What I want to know is whether or not you two see past lives. Do you?"

They stared at each other, and his mother visibly swallowed. "No. Is that something you can do? Is that something that *actually* happened to all of you?"

"Thank you." I wasn't in the mood to answer her questions.

Ace and Caesar followed me as I walked away. *When this is over, I'm done with almost everyone else.* We could live somewhere by ourselves doing our own things and everyone else could live with their decisions and what they did and didn't do. I had my own regrets, lifetimes of them. I was tired of carrying around the burden of everyone else's mistakes.

"Maci," Rowan said as he ran out the door. "That feeling I got last time? I have it again. They're coming."

With almost no time left before the sunrise, they were coming. They'd have a full complement of vampires with them, and then the sun would come out. It would thin us out, because more of them could stay awake than we could. We'd be overrun—it was actually really good strategy.

My mind pinged. They had to be stopped before they arrived. The constant fighting in the fields hadn't worked, and fighting here was fruitless. They just had so many more people than we did. It would be a bloodbath, and we'd be the ones drowning instead of reveling in it.

I turned back to Caesar. "Get everyone out of here. Everyone who lives here, I want them lined up away from here in that field. You know, over where you fought them when you were hiding me when I was a human."

He scowled at me. "I'm not going to leave you, Maci."

"No, you're not. Absolutely, you're not. But I need you to get my father and everyone else out. After you've done that, come back to me. We have things to do here."

He nodded. "Okay. That I can do."

Ace was next.

I said to him, "He burned that woman to death. The one

whose memory I carry? He burned her like she was noth-ing." I chewed on my lip, determination stiffening my spine. "He isn't going to get the chance to do that to anyone here. I don't know what we're going to do yet, but as long as we have this large group hanging around, I am going to be responsible for them. Get them away, Ace. His battle can't be with them."

His battle was with me.

~

Ace

THE CONVERSATION with my father had thrown me. I'd been prepared for my mother but not my father. *Fuck him.* He was bad, even by vampire standards, and I'd be happy to be rid of him. How dare he judge me? I'd gone out of my way to control my bad nature. I even lied when it was supposed to be impossible. My father was the nightmare.

End of story.

But Maci gave me something to do, so I was going to do it. Whatever she wanted or needed, she would have it. I stopped in front of Warren's place.

I hated the man. With a vengeance.

When we'd first arrived, it had been hell to deal with him.

I hardly let myself think about that night anymore, but right then, my memories flooded me, whether I wanted them to or not.

We'd followed my father's directions, leaving our car miles away and walking the rest of the way. Warren must have known we were coming, because he stood outside with a female vampire. They both silently regarded us, and I must have looked like I'd been dragged from the pits of hell, because even though they checked out all of us, they couldn't take their eyes off me. I challenge them to know how great they looked if Maci had died on their watch.

She was my...I didn't even know how to phrase it.

"You've had a bad night," Warren said in a low voice. "I can understand. You didn't know she was being dosed with my blood. You thought she was gone permanently, which would be a blow, since you love her." He put his arm around the female next to him. I'd never seen a female vampire before, but she just looked normal, just like us, really. Not quite human, something other, and more like one of us than any human woman did.

Would Maci look like that?

"If we didn't know that she was going to return, we would've been wrecked, too."

Fury rose inside me like electricity I couldn't turn off. "How *dare* you act parental? Whatever you are, you aren't a father. Not a real one." Were all vampire parents that fucked up? "She barely survived her childhood. Whatever game this is you've been playing, you're disgusting."

Rowan cleared his throat then said, "My friend is exhausted. He's been up for over twenty-four hours. At this moment, he has no tact, and I'm grateful for it. You are all those things he said. Why are we here? I don't want anything to do with you. Just give me her location so I can wait there until she returns."

"If I knew it, I'd give it to you. I've never been privy to Frederick's dumping grounds. Funny, he calls himself that now. For years it was Edwin, his middle name. I guess he's comfortable going back to the original name now. After he did some things, he changed it to Edwin." He shook his head. "You love her. Come inside. We'll get you set up in a house where you can be comfortable. When she rises, one way or another, you'll find her or she'll find you. Maci is not lost to time. She will return to you."

"Love?" It was Caesar who spoke. "Vampires don't love."

Warren sighed. "Yes, we do. We don't just love, we love eternally. Soul mates. Some of us have more than one, as is the case with all of you. You love her completely. Instantly. Both as humans and now, so strongly I can see it. How can you not? You must feel it. The all-consuming-ness of her. You don't even need to feed from humans anymore. You can feed just from each other."

Griffin visibly swallowed. "This wasn't what we were taught."

"Well...they lied to you. Constantly. My poor daughter. Did she not know she was loved?"

That was the hit that broke me that day. I'd been up too long, and Warren was right—much as I hated him. Maci never knew how much I loved her. My knees gave way, and I would have fallen if Caesar and Rowan hadn't caught me.

Her father stared at me. "How are you even awake during the daytime? You shouldn't be able to do it for years to come."

That was always the million-dollar question, not that we ever had answers. I just fucking could.

Maci

"I want to be here when he arrives. I want the rest of you to be hidden away, just me." I sighed.

Rowan shook his head. "You don't actually think we're going to let you do that, do you?"

"I'm not saying actually leave, so you don't have to go far enough away to let me out of your sight. Just don't be visible. Let me talk to him alone. If he has a crowd around him, even better. Anyway, after that, while he thinks he's going to hurt all of us, the rest of the group will take over his home base."

It took a second, but Rowan's smile was huge. "Oust them from their home? Take it over. That's right. Let's see what happens when they're the ones not comfortable anymore."

Caesar shook his head. "They'll just stay here."

"Not easily. Burn what you can; destroy the rest. They can't stay easily if we remove their ability to shield from the day." I looked at Rowan. "Can you do that for me?"

He kissed me quickly. "I can. Whatever you want."

No way was I being separated from Caesar. I'd be lucky if he stayed out of sight like I asked him. I squeezed his hand as Rowan left. Where were Griffin and Tanner?

As though I'd conjured him, Tanner appeared. "What can I do?"

A good question, since it would take more than Rowan to trash the place. "Help Rowan destroy everything. Leave nothing where they can sleep well here. They'll have to hide in closets, crawl in corners like rats. After you're done, you and Ace go take back their homes for us. That'll mean you can't be here, so I'm counting on you, okay?"

If I hoped to get them to go, I needed them to believe it was worth it. And it was. If we had any chance of pulling off the plan, everything had to go right. So far, nothing we'd done particularly went the way we intended.

"It'll happen. I'll stay awake through the day until it's done. I can do it."

Rowan grabbed my arm. "We'll all make it. You can count on us, Maci. You can."

We could talk later about how it didn't make them less than anyone else because they were unable to stay awake, but I didn't have the time for it in the moment.

Griffin ran out of our house and into my vision as Rowan left with Tanner to do what I'd asked. "I found something. I swear whatever we just did by the tree woke up my brain, but I knew what book to look through." He held it up. "I think we should talk about this."

I wanted to hear what he found, but I wasn't sure we had time for reading hour. "Griff, we're about to go to battle. Is what you found relevant? I really want to know, but maybe later, after, unless it will help or hurt now?"

I hated saying no to him. Griffin was different from my other loves. He wasn't a fighter, although he could fight. He shook his head, grabbing my arm. "If fighting is coming, I want to get you out of here. I know the others." He shot Caesar a look. "And they think you can lead us. I know you can, and I'm not a coward, but we lost you. For nine fucking months, you were dead. We knew you'd be coming back, but, no, I don't want you to fight." He took a deep breath. "Okay. I've spoken my piece. None of you will care or agree with me on this subject, so I'll get on board. No, this book won't matter just now. But afterward, we really, really need to talk about it. How can I help?"

My heart turned over. I really fucking loved Griffin. Part of me wished I could be the girl who would run away. Even among vampires, we were different. Ace's mother hid away for years. How could she stand that? It would kill me. My own mother, who I still hadn't laid eyes on, abandoned me to some kind of plan by my father. What sort of person was she? It didn't matter. I was a fighter. I'd been born—reborn —that way.

I cupped his cheek. "Do you remember the test you gave me? The one about the standard miners?"

"Yes, and you asked me after I was reborn how I would handle it now. I told you. I'd kill the miner who was sick. It's the only sensible way to solve the problem. You had said the leader should kill themselves to save the rest."

That was exactly right. "Now? Since I've been reborn? My opinion has changed. If the leader got them stuck in there, then she or he deserves to kill themselves for the error because they were in charge. If I'm in charge, I'm going to see to it that we don't get stuck. If you want to help me, help Tanner and Ace get where we're headed set up. I'm counting on you. Yes, absolutely, afterward you will tell me about that book. I can't wait to hear about it."

He leaned over and kissed me. "I'd burn the world to the ground for you. I'm not some kind of vampire pacifist. I just want us. I don't care about everyone else. I know that it's not possible, but I would take you and keep you from them, if I could. That would be my preference."

"The goal is to just to make our family survive. I might get lost in doing this. Don't let me, okay?"

He kissed me again. "I won't, Maci. Make no mistake, I'll be right there next to you. Just do me a favor? Don't forget the house that we loved. When you were human, you loved that house. It was ours. We deserve the right to live when this is over. Not to take over for Frederick." He pointed at the book. "And that actually relates to this."

I couldn't wait to hear more.

13

The guys did as I asked. It was still dark when I stood with Caesar on top of a roof, staring down at the scene below. The other vampires were coming, so I hoped my guys were okay with the upcoming sun. A quick glance showed me Caesar was still upright, but for how long?

I didn't dare bring it up, not when I was doing such a good job of pretending to look bored.

I was absolutely not filled with ennui right then. Just the opposite, in fact. I'd never been so completely focused in my life.

Or my death.

Or since whatever it was at this point.

"Do you need to feed?" Caesar asked, nudging my shoulder with his own.

I nodded. "I'd love to feed, but now is definitely not the time. That's just for you and me, when it happens. I don't want to add it onto our night of the vampire damned or whatever we want to call it. Does that sound like a good movie title for this?"

He smirked. "I'd love to watch a movie sometime. I didn't mean me, actually. As much as it would pain me, I thought maybe you should feed from a human. Just enough to get you fed if not full, so to speak."

I'd fed from a human since my guys found me again. The buzzing noise in my head that signified their approach was too loud, too present. I touched a hand to my temple and said, "I think it's too late."

I spotted the vampires, and my spine stiffened. Frederick was in the back, following the other elders who fed from me constantly when I'd been their servant. They all made my human-self miserable, but they'd fathered all of my loves. Well, not Ace. His father was his own version of problematic, which was neither here nor there at the moment.

Fredrick snarled as he spotted me. The whole group moved like they were going to pound on the house, a sea of power and strength. I lifted my hand in the universal gesture for stop, and surprisingly, they all obeyed. *How interesting.* These vampires liked to take orders, but why shouldn't they? They'd only taken order after order since rising.

None of them understood how we were supposed to live, or how farcical they looked compared to what they could be. "Hi. My name is Maci," I began. I smiled like I was sweet. I was absolutely not sweet, but they didn't know that. Maybe I'd risen as Maci the friendly vampire? I couldn't help it. My nerves had my thoughts spinning in ridiculous directions. I cleared my throat and tried again.

"Some of you probably remember me from when I was human and you fed from me. I should have died then, but I didn't." I nodded toward Frederick. "I died when he killed me, instead. I don't actually remember it, but he clonked me over the head. Maybe I died then? Maybe it was later. Doesn't matter." I spun in a circle. "As you can see, I rose."

"What are you all doing?" Frederick snarled to his group. "Get her."

"They can try, but in a little bit." I shrugged. "The thing is I think you should hear some things before you do it. Just a few things, then by all means, come and get me."

Caesar made a noise. He didn't like me basically taunting them. That was okay. I didn't care for it much, either, but I had a plan, and so far it had played out just the way I wanted.

"He didn't want me reborn, because he didn't want me to know what I know. He didn't want me to have the capacity or knowledge to tell you how he burned a female vampire to death after she wouldn't have sex with him. How he altered the lives of all vampires everywhere because she said no to him." I shook my head. "He doesn't have a great sense of how vampires should live, not the least idea about it. But what Frederick knows is how he burned her to death. Afterward, he took all the women away from you. The Betrayer, as you call him? He fathered the human that was me and he lives with my mother, who he loves. Ace's father Vincent lives with the woman he loves. I live with the men I love."

There, I said my piece. Almost. "Oh, and Frederick, I know how much you like to burn people and things, so I thought I'd make you feel right at home. We're taking your home right now, while you stand here messing with me."

Caesar lit the large match he carried and dropped it straight onto the ground on top of the gasoline he'd put there minutes before. It wouldn't burn the place down, but it made them all dart back in terror. We all hated fire, a natural vampire instinct since it could destroy us.

For a second, I was frozen, staring into the blue heart of the flame, utterly transfixed. She burned and screamed in terror, the greedy flames gobbling her up one crackle at a time. The sound of her voice still reverberated in my ears as she screamed and screamed. I shook my head.

"Let's get out of here." I nodded at Caesar. Hopefully I'd wasted enough time for my guys to have accomplished the rest of the plan. The sun was going to be out, golden light scouring the earth soon.

He squeezed my hand, and we jumped down the other side of the house. "Remind me never to piss you off, Maci."

I grinned at him as we ran. "I'm scary, that's for sure."

He rolled his eyes. "Agreed, but I knew that before today. I'm just glad they all know it now, too."

So was I.

THEY TOOK the town with no issue whatsoever. The remaining vampires ran when they arrived, and most of the servants vanished, too. Only a few still lingered, and they weren't people I recognized. I didn't know if I should feel good or bad because the ones who were my friends were long gone. Were they dead, run off earlier, or had they preferred to stay with Frederick? I shook my head. I'd love to tell them straight out how the only ones who might ever make them vampires were with us.

But it didn't matter.

My father ran to me, grabbing my arms. "This was such a good idea. We should have done this years ago. They can't stay together today in comfort. Brilliant. This is why we needed you."

I shook my head. "This was one of my ideas. We need others, but not today. They're going to be pissed at rising, really mad, I can promise you that. We need to have the daywalkers patrol all day and the nightwalkers to take over at rising."

"On it." He nodded. "It'll be done."

I had to find my guys. I turned toward Caesar. "Hanging in?"

"You can count on me. I told you, stop worrying about me. It's my job to worry about you."

A sweet thought, but it didn't mean he wasn't suffering. I rounded the corner and headed straight for what had been Frederick's office. Since all of his books remained, I at least knew where Griffin would be.

I heard them before I saw them. All of them were in there.

"Hey," they cheered as I walked through the door. "It worked. It all worked."

Ace opened his arms, and I stepped into them. He kissed the top of my head. "Well done."

"It worked for now. It's not going to go away this easily. We've taken their stronghold, but we have to keep it, and then we have to kill them." I closed my eyes. "And all of you need to go to bed."

"You do, too." Rowan shook his head and took me from Ace. "Just because you can doesn't mean that you absolutely should stay awake. You had a long day. Go to bed. Wake in rising. There'll be plenty of battle waiting for you then."

I sighed. "You are actually the one with the battle memories. They wanted you for that, remember. You don't have to lead but what about the plan?"

He made a face. "That's part of what is so strange. I'm not that much of a battle genius. Never have been. I'm defunct that way."

I groaned. It was really awful when they doubted themselves, when they were critical of who they were. It was like pain when they criticized themselves.

I shook my head. "Who knows what you'd be able to do if you were allowed to be new vampires and not immediately sent into the game like you'd been drinking blood for years." I held up my hand. "We can discuss this another time. We need to go to bed. Feed. The whole nine yards. The good news is they need to do that too."

With various nods, they all started spreading out around Frederick's home. We were familiar with it. It was remarkably like his last home, which I cleaned many times. He was clearly the kind of person who liked things the way that he liked them. The guys spread out in Frederick's bedroom. He had fresh sheets on the bed and the couches covered in sheets too. The servants must have been preparing for bed before they'd taken off running, and the guys had probably spread the sheets themselves. I walked to the window and drew the curtains so we were in the dark.

Maybe I should stay up and be part of the daywalking guards? I just wouldn't tell my guys, so they wouldn't worry.

"Maci." Ace put out his hand. "You always feed us to sleep. We're going to do that for you today. You're not going out there, despite what you're thinking.

Damn it. Ace really was as devious as me. Two vampires who could lie when so few could, and we were together. The whole world was going to be constantly suspicious of us, and they probably should be.

I scowled at him. "I think maybe I..."

He shook his head. "I think if you don't sleep, you can't battle tomorrow."

Griffin rubbed at his eyes. "And we have to talk about what I found."

Fair enough. I did need to be something other than a total zombie the next day. I didn't want to risk being so exhausted I slept through the entire rising. I crawled into the bed and Ace threw himself down on one side of me while Griffin took the other. Tanner leaned over Ace to kiss me once, then twice. His lips were soft, and I smiled against him.

"I have the couch by the window. Caesar is patrolling the house once more, and then he'll take the place by the door. Rowan is in the corner over there. Being you, you can probably rise mid-day, so I wanted you to know how we're set up in case you wake up confused or not sure where you are."

That was sweet. "I'm going to try to make it to rising."

"Great." He nodded at me. "I know you like all the information you can get. You might sleep better knowing."

He squeezed my foot as he stepped away and Rowan entered the room. "I hate this place. It reminds me too much of my human childhood. He always hated home. Must be residual pain. Never mind. Griffin and Ace, you two were sneaky getting next to her tonight. I get it tomorrow, sending me off on that errand to check the locks. I was halfway there before I realized it."

Rowan didn't sound actually annoyed. If I wasn't mistaken, I could hear amusement in his voice as he threw himself down on the couch. It was a cute idea to feed me to sleep for a change, but I wasn't the one who usually had trouble knocking out. Caesar entered and, with unsteady movements, took his place on the couch.

"Love you," he called out before he squirmed around.

They were all in pain. Well, maybe not Ace, but the others. I patted Ace on the knee. "Tell you what? Let me feed all of them and then you feed me. That'll be a change but I want to try it. Or we feed each other, how about that?"

"Probably a good idea."

Griffin groaned. "We'll all get there, Mr. Daywalker.

Don't act all high and mighty because you're so used to it now."

I laughed. "It wasn't so long ago that this caused him pain, too. Actually, no, it was quite a bit ago? That's a human memory, so I guess it's been...almost a year?"

Time got funny in my head when I really stopped to consider how long ago things happened. Before death and after were complicated ideas.

Ace leaned back against the headboard. "I haven't struggled with it since that night. It surged me forward in my abilities. I might be able to go days."

"Fuck. Shut up before I break your nose." Griffin was in no mood for the conversation, and I tried not to find it amusing. Grumpy Griffin was really amusing to me.

I stared toward Caesar. He was really hurting. I could feel it in my bones, a distant pulse of pain like it was my own ache echoing through me. Why did I have this gift? Would we ever know? I sat next to him and then leaned down so he could reach my neck. He didn't even grumble, opening his mouth to bite down on me.

I closed my eyes. "Thank you for being there today even when it was hard."

He sighed, his whole body relaxing on the couch. In seconds, he was out cold. I lifted my head. Blood still trickled down my neck. It would have bothered me as a human; I could remember that it made her feel a general sense of yuckiness. My biggest concern currently was the idea I might waste it. The guys could smell it, the awake ones all shifted to watch me, like they couldn't wait for their turn to lick at the red liquid I knew they all craved.

I walked over to Rowan. He didn't like sharing blood in front of others, although he'd made no such indication when I'd first come back to life. "Do you want to do this someplace else?"

He shook his head. "Normally, yes, but I want to wake up in this room. So, no, here will do. Thank you for thinking of it. Maybe I can afford to be picky when this whole scenario is done. It's very human of me, I think. Vampires don't care about such matters."

"There are a lot of things about me that are very human, too." I extended my neck.

"Yes," Griffin said from the bed. "I'm aware. It's part of what we're going to talk about tomorrow. Neither of you are insane. None of us are. Try not to worry about it for the moment."

Rowan bit my neck, and I closed my eyes. If I let myself, I could fall asleep right there on top of him then spend the whole night sprawled over him like a limp doll.

But I wasn't done, so I forced my lids open. There wouldn't be rest until I finished. This was a change in how I did things but this needed to work. We had to be reciprocal and I was glad to see it could work that way too. Also, I needed to stay up and so I was glad to see I could.

Ace leaned back on his elbows. "You okay?"

I was and Rowan was out. But maybe I wasn't as tough as I pretended to be? I couldn't go endlessly without a feeding or sleep, much as I might like to think I could.

I left Rowan and went to Tanner, who reached for me, drawing me down next to him on his couch. "Think I could keep you right here? I'd love to cuddle all night. I could feed off you and you could pass out right here. Just give in."

"Hey," Griffin threw a pillow at him. "She sleeps on the bed. You lost out on it, so don't cheat now."

Tanner smirked. "But I'm a vampire. We're monsters. We cheat by nature." His mouth came down onto my already open wound and he sucked, hard. I moaned, pleasure flooding me. There really was a difference in how they fed and the effect it had on me. Caesar and Rowan hadn't elicited the same reaction with the few sips they'd stolen. It was about intent. Tanner meant to do what he did.

But it didn't last long. He was as exhausted as the rest of us, and none of us could follow through on what he started. I lifted my head. When we had time, he would pay for that little episode. Maybe I'd make him wait for it after I got him going sexually? We'd see. I had a hard time saying no to any of them, even for pretend.

And I didn't like to wait.

I rose and walked over to the bed.

Griffin shook his head. "You don't think we were going to let him turn you on and then leave you like that, did you?"

I climbed between them. "Seems like you might be a little bit tired for what he started." I smiled at Griffin.

He grinned at me, a goofy one for him, and not his usual smile. "Ace isn't stronger than me, despite what he might think. I'm the only one who really understands us now. I'm just about as tired as you are, my love." He kissed my chin. "Which means I have plenty of energy to give you what you need."

I shook my head. "How do you know how tired I am, Griffin?"

"I can feel it like you can feel it in me. We can all tell how you are most of the time. It would be annoying, if I didn't love you so much."

That word again. "You guys love slinging that about. She's not here to hear it. I love you guys too, but no matter how many times you say it, you can't make the human you didn't say it to hear what you should've said."

Griffin shook his head before he flipped me beneath

him. Ace rolled to his side, scooting close from the other side.

He winked at me as he spoke to Griffin. "I don't think she appreciates our dedication to making her come yet."

Ace bit me as Griffin pulled down my pants, giving him access to my underwear. I caught my breath, surprised. With a smooth move, Griff pushed my panties away and slipped his finger inside of me.

"Maci," his voice was in my ear, "I don't need you to feed me to sleep. I can go down any time I want to today. Feeding from you is not what I want right now. But I think—and Ace thinks—that we need to remind you that things can feel fantastic just because they can." He kissed my cheek, ever so gently. "Not to mention, as vampires, we can feel things more acutely than humans. So, this? It must just be rushing through your body."

He stroked my clit, and I drove myself against his hand. If they wanted to do this then I was game. As he fed from me from behind, Ace was hard.

"You don't pay attention to Ace feeding. He's just doing that, just feeding a little bit, because it enhances things for you. Sex and blood. Sometimes I want to separate the two, but that's really foolish because it either comes down to sex, blood or power with vampires. You hold all the power. So we can give you sex and we can play with blood, just like you can."

I always loved to hear Griffin speak. In every lifetime, I'd loved it. This wasn't different.

He pressed a second finger inside of me. I moaned. Yes, it was just what I needed. He was right. I craved the interaction, his touch. There was so much fucking pain all the time. There had to be pleasure.

"As for whether or not I can tell that girl I love her

despite the fact she's gone—you're still her, Maci, deep inside. You know it, and I know it, too."

Griffin bit down on me then. He wasn't gentle, not with his teeth or his fingers, which drove me wild. Every stroke brought me closer but not quite where I needed to be. *Fuck.* If they were going to drain me dry, so that I passed out, I wanted to come first. I knew they wanted my orgasm, too. Ace lifted his head, licking my wound closed.

"She's fighting it. Why would you do that, baby, when we know how badly you need to come? That's what we want to give to you. Come on his fingers, come screaming for us. You're so pretty when you give in."

His softly growled words were so fucking hot, but I didn't know what to do, because I did want to come. Badly. Right then. A surge of pleasure hit me, and I exploded around Griff's fingers, pressing against Ace as I did. Colors crossed over my vision, and I cried out, a hoarse sound I'd never heard myself make before. My body shook and Ace wrapped his arms around me, holding me tight. Griffin licked his bite mark closed.

"Good girl," Griff said as he peppered kisses over my cheeks. "Rest now, Maci. You need it more than anyone I know." He licked his lips. "Ace is going to give you just what you need and everything will get settled in the morning."

I could barely form words, but I managed, "You guys both need release."

Griff flipped me over so I faced Ace. "We're both fine. It feels good to be hard like this, pressed up against you. It makes me feel wanting, and I like it."

Ace extended his neck. "Feed, Maci. You haven't taken one break, not one, since you rose the first time. We thought we'd still be locked in the basement feeding you. We should have been, but we're out here and you're leading a war.

You're so hungry, you don't even know it anymore and now —whatever is happening—we can feed it. So take what you need, because it's ours to give you."

It was hard to argue with him when he made sense. I bit down on his neck, and I drank him in. They were right. I needed this, and them. Body and soul.

THE SUN SET and with it came the tug pulling at me to wake. I was pretty out of it, still happily unaware of my surroundings when the sounds of my guys talking finally made me lift my lids.

"She's pretty out of it." Rowan said as he ran his hands through my hair. "She needed to sleep. I'm glad you did whatever it was that the two of you did."

Ace sat down on the bed, despite the fact I'd never felt him leave it. "I'll always take care of Maci."

"Same for me." Griffin was across the room. "She's ours. We all managed to stay up yesterday, so that'll get easier and easier. Hopefully, there will come a day in the not too distant future when we can sleep at sunrise and rise at sun down without worrying about getting our asses kicked. In the meantime, I'm glad we have some protection. I think she's awake."

I raised my head. "Hard to sleep in with you guys talking over my bed."

"We missed you." Caesar walked over and kissed my cheek. "I wish we could leave you alone to rest, but I think you know we're very much at risk today. Soon, you'll get to lounge around if you want."

I didn't think that was exactly my nature, but I liked the thought just the same.

14

Griffin waited for me in one of the father s' offices. I didn't know which one; I just knew it wasn't Frederick's. Crossing the room and circling around the desk, I placed myself comfortably in his lap. "Okay. Tell me about your book."

He kissed my neck, his lips lingering. For a second, I thought he was going to bite down on me. Maybe he considered it, because his breath continued to stir the hairs at my nape for long after he placed the kiss, but at last he lifted his head.

"I love how you smell," he said, his warm eyes full of soft feelings for me.

I tugged his arms further around me, snuggling into his embrace. "I love how you smell, too, but if you want me to look at your prophecy book, it might be better if you didn't distract me."

"Right. Of course, you're the one who sat on my lap, which essentially means you're the one being the distraction, and you knew it."

He had always been the one to say things just as they

were, even when we'd both been humans. I blinked. He'd challenged me. And he played sports. I turned to look at him. "Sorry, strange memory to have. What did you ask me?"

"Was it something about you being human or humanity or something?"

He hit that one correctly on the first guess. "How did you know?"

Griffin held up and wiggled the book. "See? It's going to turn out my skill set does not make me completely useless to you."

I leaned back against him. "Were you under the impression that I thought you were useless? You're not. You're my Griffin. You're essential to me, and probably the smartest person I know."

"Thank you." He kissed my neck again. "This book is about vampire women. There aren't that many around, just you, Ace's mom. Your mom. Some others, but really not a lot. And I get the feeling the other women, maybe because they lived so long on the run, terrified, I feel like they haven't come into their own in the way that you are."

Was I? "Is that a compliment or do you really think that?"

"I really think it. I'm a vampire. We don't do compliments, just truth."

I shook my head. "You and I both know that's not true."

"I do, actually." He held up the book. "Because I read this. As I was saying, this book is about female vampires and the things you're able to do. It's fascinating. The thing you can do where you can see back into those other people's pasts? That is your vampire gift. We all have them. I can see far..."

I interrupted him. "Right. Caesar can smell ovulation."

"That's weird, right? Yes. He can do that." He laughed. "Anyway, yours is that you can see people's pasts. It's not some weird thing that happened because we're reincarnated or whatever. That's just bullshit. It read as bullshit to me when they told us about it, but then we all could see that past life?"

I nodded. "It doesn't make sense if it's just my gift. You saw the burning. You saw the whole thing, too." In fact, he'd been the first one to see it.

Griffin held up the book. "It's because we're your soul mates. There's more. Do you remember that your human-self used to have those dreams? The ones where you would sleepwalk?"

"Yes, but that was my dad feeding me. I didn't understand or remember then, but I do now."

He shook his head. "I don't mean that."

Griffin was so excited he pushed me off his lap, and I got up. He needed to pace. It was adorable, but he wouldn't like to hear that right that second.

"Yes, your dad did that, but you used to dream. We pulled you out of the woods once. Sorry, the humans did." He patted his head. "That slip will make sense in a second. The humans we were pulled you out of the woods."

I blinked. Yes, I had that memory. "Okay?"

"You can't tell me that was some kind of memory of that woman who died. It wasn't. It was someone else. You were moon seeking. It was sort of beautiful. The one who died in a fire? I've seen her whole life with the one whose memory I saw. She didn't do that."

My stomach clenched. "Who is it then and why do I have their memory?"

"It doesn't matter, sweetheart. The point is that you can encounter memories and we're so connected to you we can see them with you, sometimes. It's your vampire gift." He held up the book. "Very rare among females but lots of reference to them. Powerful vampires. I don't think Frederick or the fathers know anything about this. Yours doesn't. They all think it's about those people you saw. People we saw. And I think we only saw them because they told us we would. Because we read about them and told your humanself about them." Griffin sat back down and patted his knee. Did he want me to get back on his lap?

I walked back over and sat down on him. "Okay. So I could...what? Channel all the dead vampires?"

"Maybe if you tried hard enough."

I was absolutely not doing that. "Griffin, I don't want to carry around the memories of..."

"I don't think you need to worry about that. It seems that people with your gifts, they are also able to better access their past human lives. Again, through our connection to you, we can do that too, more than we should be able to."

Now it was my turn to get up. "Am I making us weaker? The humanity I can access? Is it hurting us?"

"No. I don't think so. I wouldn't want anything else. The way that I love you? The way that I know that they do? Maybe it's enhanced by the fact that our human selves did too. I can feel my love for you—intense, soul mate—and also gentle and easy. That was my human side. I get all of it."

I sat on the corner of the bed where I could regard him properly. "This is wonderfully interesting and I love it—in both the human and vampire way—but can it help us with this or is it just sort of good to know?"

"Oh, it'll help." He took my hand in his and kissed it. "He's never going to see you coming."

❧

ROWAN LEANED against the wall in the hallway when we came out. "You guys okay?"

"Yes. I think we may have just worked out a plan." I kissed his cheek. "Do you think we could round up some humans who want to be vampires and maybe get the process started?"

He blinked. "I don't know that we have the time to wait for an army to rise from the ground."

"No, we don't. What about just giving some of my blood?" I chewed on my bottom lip. "The humans will die, but we'll make them vampires. They want that. Can we do that?"

He nodded and then looked at Griffin. "Someone want to let me in on this plan or am I just rounding up servants from wherever they've fled? Do I get to know what we're doing?"

"You get to know." Was he feeling threatened, since he was the plan maker? "Griffin can fill you guys all in, and I'll go find the servants. I was one of them once, so maybe seeing me as a vampire will inspire them." I held up my hand. "I'll tell Caesar when we go. He won't want to be separated from me."

"None of us much care for the feeling." Rowan grabbed me and pinned me to the wall. His vampire was close to the surface, and my monster rose to greet him. I was used to seeing Tanner this way, not Rowan.

I stroked my finger over his bottom lip. "So now that we've said hello this way, I'll ask if everything's okay?"

"I'm struggling with my beast today. Some days it's a battle. Just a vampire thing. Maybe you haven't faced it yet, but mine is riding me. I miss the woman I love. Maybe Caesar could stay here, and I could go along as your protection tonight?"

I nodded. "Okay. Let's do that. Griffin, tell the others. I'll tell Rowan about the plan. I have to go find some servants."

Griffin tugged me against him. "I don't struggle with my vampire. We understand each other perfectly."

I rolled my eyes. "Liar."

"See? Human thing."

I EXPLAINED my plan to Rowan as we drove to a local motel to search for the servants. Without much money, if they weren't staying there, they were probably on the streets. Rowan drummed his fingers on the steering wheel in the parking space where we paused for a second, considering his options.

"It's a good plan, but it doesn't let me kill enough people." He closed his eyes. "Bad rising, probably because I stayed up yesterday."

I stroked my hand through his hair. "Should we see if Griffin's right?"

"What do you mean?"

I closed my eyes and thought about Rowan as a human. It was always a little bit like pushing through fog but at least I could do it, unlike others, it would seem. He'd looked at my human-self like she spun the world, and he'd worried about her, and the others, all the way to the end of his life. I pictured him smiling.

Rowan audibly caught his breath. "I can feel my human-self like he's here with me. For just a second, like I was both of us." He leaned back in his seat and blinked rapidly. "I feel calmer."

That was what I hoped would happen. "Griffin thought I could do that. Bring our humans to the surface. And you would get that from me because of our connection. Our soul mate connection."

He stared at me a long moment. "Our soul mate connection, that we formed as humans. Because we just did. Because you were going to be a vampire too, and the vampire I was going to be recognized the vampire in you. Not because we're long dead people. But because we're these people."

I nodded. "It feels right to me. Doesn't it feel right to you?"

"It does." He kissed my lips, gently. "Thank you for reminding me of who he was. I lose him sometimes, and he was a nice kid."

"He was."

I felt them before I saw them. My other guys were all there. Caesar tapped on my window, and a second later, I rolled it down. "None of us want to wait at home. All of us are perfectly capable of defending you as easily as Rowan here is." He glared at Rowan. "Maybe some of us would be better at it."

He'd always find me, that was what Caesar promised, and he had proven that over and over.

Rowan shook his head. He was calm but I was sure he could be angry again in a hot second. If that happened, I'd leave them to it. I had many problems in life but solving their macho shit was not one of them.

"If you need a reminder of my power, Caesar, I'd be happy to demonstrate it."

I got out of the car. They could sort it out. They'd been pretty much brothers since birth. I walked toward the motel. "Which one of you can cause trances and mind erasure the best?"

It wasn't something we'd done since I rose. Maybe I was

the best, but I'd never done it and it was not the time I felt like practicing. Tanner was quickly on my left, Ace on my right.

Tanner grinned at me. "They don't really think they're stronger than me, right?"

"You're all dwarfed by me." Ace shrugged. "But I don't feel like showing it off all the time."

Griffin laughed, catching up. "Okay. I'd never suggest that I could beat any of you in a physical fight, but I'm smarter than the rest of you. This is my plan we're enacting. Go ahead and beat each other. I win in the end."

"Did I miss the part where you all woke up this ridiculous today? I'm stronger than the rest of you." I might not be, but I'd lead with that.

Tanner through his arm around me. "You absolutely are. My vampire thinks your vampire could kick our collective asses. He's been waiting for you since the change. The second we met you as humans we were connected. I think it was that vampire blood speaking to each other."

I cupped his cheek. "Then I guess it's a good thing our fathers believed in prophecies."

Right then, I believed we could pull off Griffin's plan, but it was going to take finding some women who wanted to be vampires. In the end, I would make them vamps, if that was what they still wanted.

"Hi," said a voice I hadn't expected to hear. I recognized it, though, instantly from a different world. "I see you have finally found us."

Wanda. She saved me because Ace's father asked her to do it. I knew why he asked her, but I wasn't sure why she'd done it on her end. Once, Wanda had been a servant, but she was one of the few to get out. She owned a bar they all hung out in, near where my human-self grew up. She kept the human alive when she almost died, even giving her a place to live for a time.

I hadn't seen her since, but now she was there.

"Wanda," I walked toward her, hands outstretched. "I didn't expect you to be here."

She waved her hand. "I'm thinking about leaving, but I hoped to see you again. I don't know how they think they're going to beat you, with you being fated or whatever."

I didn't know if I should correct her assumption or not. I wasn't fated, I was talented, but maybe we'd leave them with some misinformation. I didn't want to have the whole argument about whether or not I was fated, so it might be better if she thought I was.

"I'm glad to see that you're fine. I should thank you for the kindness you showed the human I used to be." Even if I didn't know why she offered it, which was going to bother me until I got answers. "Was it because you knew I was fated?"

She nodded. "I was close with Ace's mother. Have they met yet?"

"Badly." I shrugged, then I touched Ace's arm. "And not something we're going to discuss. Ever." I nodded to her. "Did you want to be a vampire?"

She took a step toward the door of her hotel room. "When I was young and beautiful, maybe. When I could have spent eternity looking like all of you, I likely would have said yes. Who would want to be eternally like this?"

I thought Wanda was beautiful. Actually, I'd never given it any thought since my rebirth, and it wasn't something I'd have dwelled on presently, either. What did I care about physical looks? There was blood, sex, and power. The rest of it was nothing, at least for the moment.

But my human-self thought she was beautiful. She lived

a long, hard life, and the map of that time was written on her face. When I looked at Wanda, I could see all the things that happened in my human life. Wanda lived and she would die—in her human cycle, if we didn't interfere with it.

"We don't actually care about such things. There are other factors that make us attractive as vampires, like power." I stepped back. "But you've certainly earned the right to change your mind, if that is what you want. Thank you, again. I don't know what would have happened to me, if you hadn't intervened."

Griffin stared at me, adding logic. "You'd have died and risen. Your father had been feeding you for some time."

"Well, then, we wouldn't have had the time we had together, not with me as a human basically being your paramour and you guys as vampires not at all sure what to do with that little human. Is there anything we can do for you, Wanda?"

She sighed. "Don't die. I like hanging out with the vampire crowds the way that I do. I'm sick in the head. And I hate Frederick. I'd rather things go forward with you all in charge."

I didn't want to be in charge. When we were done, we intended to go back to how it had been in the past. Vampires would make families and not be dictated to by insane leaders who had no business leading anything at all.

"If it were me, Wanda, I'd get away from the vampires. Far, far away." That was the absolute truth. "If you need anything from me, ever, I'm here for you. Anything at all you need."

She stared at me, and I hugged her. It wasn't natural for me, but I did it anyway. "I mean it. Anything."

"Wanda," Caesar said from behind me. I guessed he and Rowan either sorted out their shit or paused it. "You kept her alive until I could find her. Thank you. If she had been reborn before then, I'm not sure we would be where we are now. Rowan sent her away with no help."

I knew the roaring response was going to come before it ever did. "Because I was not informed about her situation. If I had known human-Maci needed help, she would have gotten help. Or she would have stayed with us. I'm not a monster." He lowered his voice. "None of us are, despite what they told us."

So much pain resonated in his voice, I had to pause. The servants could wait a second. I turned toward him. "She wasn't upset with you when she died. Not even a little bit."

They didn't get closure with that Maci. She'd been basically out of it when she died, and when I showed up, I hadn't wanted or needed what she had emotionally from them. I loved them, they loved me—that part was easy, and there was no doubt of it, but they still lived with the pain of what hadn't been done for that version of me.

I thought about how much she loved each of them. Not just as humans, but she'd loved them as vampires, too. The way it had felt when Caesar showed up—she'd equally hated and loved him until quickly that hate vanished. He was like a gift presented to her from the universe. The way he had cared about her, it changed his whole life for her. She hadn't experienced anything else like it in her whole life or any of her other remembered lives.

And then Griffin had come. *Brilliant, smart and confusing.* He'd hurt her, but then he fixed it. Griffin never let her down. He stayed with her, talked to her, made such an effort that she felt the way he loved her even when he never said it. He mended her heart.

Tanner sought her out when he couldn't even speak. He treasured her immediately, as though no time passed between them. Instantly, they'd been back in love. She wanted to wrap herself up in him and never let go. What was more, he might have let her if she tried it.

Ace had been so wounded and frightened, but he'd switched immediately to protection. He'd amazed her, enthralled her, and made her believe there might be a future for them despite the odds. He battled for her every step of the way until she died. She felt his devotion in her cells, in her heart, in her soul.

Rowan returned to her last, but it had been no less intense of a reunion. He'd challenged her, and they clawed at each other like animals, angry and desperate for each other. But he was willing to destroy everything for her, and she knew that he loved her. He was desperate for her love and attention, and she wanted to give him the world of love, if he would accept it.

I sent the thoughts to the surface of my brain, hoping my men would feel it. One of them made a sound like a gasp and then silence. They all felt it; she loved them with everything inside of her. They needed to know, so they could experience that love the way she would have wished it.

No more questions. No more doubts.

I stepped back. "Okay?"

"Maci." It was Caesar who finally spoke, his voice rough. "You just had to know."

I turned my back on them. If they needed time to digest what I showed them, that was fine, I'd understand. But I would finish what I needed to while I still could. They didn't leave me to do it alone. Instead, I was instantly surrounded. I planned on bothering the front desk clerk, but instead I turned to Wanda, who stared at us with confusion evident on her features. Yes, she would have no idea what just transpired.

And I preferred it that way.

"Where are the servants?"

She pointed behind her. "Three rooms, fifty-two, fifty-three, and fifty-four."

They had to all be sharing, but it still meant a lot of them to be sharing just three rooms.

I knocked on fifty-two. After a moment, the door swung open. Five women stared wide-eyed at me. I probably looked pretty scary to them, not only as a vampire, but who knew what Frederick told them about me.

Or maybe they'd known me as a servant, and who knew what they'd think about me then.

I didn't specifically recognize any of the servants, but that was fine. "Hello, I'm Maci. I want to talk to you guys about moving forward with some things."

It was stupid of me not to realize they might want to kill me. Frederick did, and they were loyal to him—stupidly so, but loyal just the same.

The woman at the front of the crowd firmed up her lips then launched herself at me like she could take off my head. She'd never be able to hurt me, but it didn't matter. I wasn't prepared for her, and she would have at least knocked me over, and who knew what she would attempt next?

But she never got the chance. Instead, she landed with a crash against the wall, pinned to it on the other side of the room. She screamed out in pain, and I whirled around to see Rowan standing with his arms crossed over his chest.

"No one is going to fuck with Maci. I don't know what you've been told or what you believe, and I don't even particularly care. You're going to listen to Maci. If you don't want to do what she says, fine, you don't have to, but you'll make no moves to hurt her. Never again. Do I make myself clear?"

The others nodded their heads fast, and one of them

spoke, "I don't know why Kristen did that. The rest of us would never hurt Maci. You're all vampires. You're gods." She seemed to regard me for a second. "And goddesses."

I got to my feet and stared where Kristen flailed against the wall, an angry moth with claws. *Well, that isn't going to be helpful.*

"Rowan?"

He shook his head. "She's going to stay there for a long while. I'm deciding whether or not I'll kill her. Don't give her any more attention in the meantime, Maci. She's handled."

Okay. I would leave that alone for the moment. I didn't know Kristen, and I didn't appreciate being attacked. Maybe spending time against the wall would be good for her.

"Let's start again. I'm Maci , and I know some of you want to be vampires. All of you probably. Why else would you be doing what you're doing?" I smiled. "Maybe I can make you one."

15

Tanner turned out to be the best at putting humans in a trance. Hilarious, considering he couldn't talk without me, but he was so good at it, he could actually make them go blurry without words.

"Okay, little human," Tanner said to one girl, sounding amused. "You aren't going to remember any of this, but when I say go, you are going to drink Maci's blood. It won't taste good to you at first, but trust me, it's delicious. An acquired taste. When I say stop, you'll stop and go straight back to your hotel room. Tomorrow, you will find Frederick and those vampires. They will feed on you, but you won't remember *any* of this."

They might kill her, but lucky for her, she would get what she thought she wanted. For that reason, my guilt for her and the others could be minimized. Besides, if the guilt really started to bother me, I could just let my monster take control and I could feel nothing about it at all.

So interesting to be a vampire who could control that. And my past human-self.

All of it was very loud in my head all the time.

"Yes," she said and nodded.

I elbowed Tanner. "*Little human*?"

"I don't remember her name," he explained with a shrug. Neither did I. Maybe my monster was already nice and close after all.

"Would you?" I lifted my wrist toward him and his eyes flared red. Without answering aloud, he took a long, hard bite. When he lifted his head, my blood dripped down his mouth. I grinned at him. He was ridiculously cute.

Instead of focusing on my men, I dug into the task at hand. I let that nameless human and so many other of her friends feed from me. The night spun on, feeling endless to me.

By the time the last one finished, I was past ready to be done. Although I gained no pleasure in them feeding from me, my guys seemed to have a vastly different experience. Perhaps because all of the servants had been women, and they watched me embrace each one? Whatever the reason, their reaction seemed akin to them watching porn.

Caesar held me from behind, his cock pressed against my ass firmly. His boldness and his breath near my ear said that if I just gave him permission, he'd fuck me from behind right then and there.

It wasn't happening. Rowan's phone dinged and he nodded, trying to focus past his reaction. "Your dad says everything is good back at their location. His spies say Frederick's people are in chaos right now. They had a terrible rising and are still trying to get things fixed before the sun comes up again. You scared him with the flames. He knows you remembered."

I closed my eyes, not wanting to think of my death in flames again. Of course, him admitting that meant he thought I was some sort of chosen one. Which I wasn't, but we could play on his fears when I brought them to their knees at the next rising. I'd be there, and they wouldn't even know it. From that moment onward, I'd be inside of all of them just waiting for the right moment to show them what I could do.

We got back in the car and made our way home, leaving the servants to sleep. Likely, they'd be feeling pretty confused the next day. Wanda wouldn't say anything, I knew. She was trustworthy, but I was pretty sure Caesar gave her a little vampire suggestion just to be sure she kept quiet while we'd been busy.

It was quiet in the car, but the overall mood remained light. We might not have won yet, but we found hope.

"Maci!" a woman greeted me as I got out of the car. It took me a second to realize it was my mother. *Well, I made Ace deal with his. My turn.*

Ace reached for me then cupped my cheek. His meaning was clear: *You aren't alone.* I stared at my mother with his warmth surrounding me like a cape for a second then stepped out of his embrace.

"Want to take a walk?" I asked her.

She nodded. "Very much."

"Good. Come." I left my guys behind. The sun would be out soon and there was no way they would let me get far away, but maybe they'd give me some privacy for this particular conversation. She wasn't likely to hurt me.

We walked for a few minutes, the breeze cool against my face, before I asked, "How close to rising can you stay up?"

Her smile was fast. "I can stay up for days. Where do you think you get it from? Your father took years to get where I was in months. You're even faster, from what I understand."

Well, that was interesting. I hadn't considered vampire

genetics, and I didn't have the time to deal with them in the moment.

My voice broke a little, but I got out the words. "You left me with a drug addict. Well, you left *her*. The previous me." I might as well get the truth out there fast, while I had the chance to say the words I held like wounds in my chest from her life. "And she wasn't kind. She would leave Maci, and sometimes she even tried to force men on her."

We were already pretty pale as vampires, but her face went chalky. "I didn't know. Your father...he never told me. I asked about her regularly, and he always said she was okay. I would have come. I always wanted to come, to check on her for myself, but he told me not to ever go near you." Tears leaked from her eyes. "He said we had to stay away for your own good. You're the one who was prophesied."

I almost dropped the bad news. *No prophecy mattered more than your own kid.* But she looked at me with such disastrous pain in her eyes, I couldn't say it. Maybe we'd both been the victims of things beyond our control. The politics of vampires just fucked with us all.

"Look..." I realized I didn't need to keep poking at her. If she hadn't known, she did now. There would be problems with my father because he lied to her, and maybe that was between them. The human I was had died. I could feel that version of Maci, but no amount of yelling at my mother would bring her back. "I'm okay. Obviously, I'm a vampire now. Whatever happened when I was a human, I can't change it. When this is over, let's see if we can get to know each other. Maybe we can be friends."

She wiped at her eyes, her lip trembling. "He always said I could have my daughter back when she was reborn. I should have known it would never be that simple. I just wanted it to be because it was so hard to give over the baby.

To hand her over like she was a tool and not just a beautiful human baby that I'd birthed. They killed me the day that you were born. When I woke up, you were all I could think about. No one would even tell me where they took you for almost a year. I didn't even know where they'd sent you." She took my hand in hers. "I'm sorry. If friends is what I can have, then I'll look forward to that. Maybe I could even meet the guys who are following us around like I might try to stake you."

"I'm very lucky in my soul mates." I touched her arms, staring into eyes like my own, but nothing like my own at the same time. "There's a fight coming. I don't know if it'll be big or small, but it will be tomorrow."

Her eyes flared red, the warrior in her grin familiar. "I wouldn't miss it."

I ROSE the next day knowing our wait was over. Around me, the guys all still slept, their even breathing sounding like home. I could hardly remember our going to bed. The joyful sexiness of the night before hadn't happened, as I'd been lost in my thoughts. *Humans and vampires. Babies and decisions. Soul mates and prophecies.*

My men seemed equally lost in ruminations. We were soul mates but also individuals, and none of us really had time to process any of it as it happened. I could bring on their humans, I could influence their powers, but I couldn't be in their heads all the time. That was probably a good thing, as it wouldn't be fair to never give them time to be alone.

Why was I up before sunrise, then? I didn't know. The feeling I got before a battle wasn't there, no buzzing in my brain. We weren't about to be under attack. I slept between Tanner and Caesar last night, and their warmth cocooned me still. Neither had roused. I got out of bed, carefully rolling free of their limbs, then walked to the other side of the house to look out the window.

It was the middle of the day.

I knew what I had to do. The certainty of it filled me with motivation. I couldn't stand still a moment longer. I got dressed quickly then took a brief second to pause. It was time to play my role, but I didn't know if I had to wake the guys. They'd find me when they roused. They always would, and it might be cruel not to wake them. I shook my head. Why was I worrying about it? I knew what to do. The guys would want to be awake. End of story.

I crawled back onto the bed. "Caesar," I whispered, but he didn't wake. I had to try, so I turned toward Tanner and tugged his arm, calling his name.

I saved Ace for last. He was the best with the daytime waking, yet even he didn't stir right away. Finally, his eyes opened. He blinked at me, his monster right on the surface of his gaze. I smiled at him. "Awake?"

He blinked. "Sure. What's wrong?"

"We have to go there now. I can't explain it, but I have to be there now. I can't wake the others, although I tried. I thought about just leaving, but I worried you guys would never forgive me." My voice shook. "I need you to come, Ace. Please. I have to go now."

He took my cheeks in his hands, comfort in his touch. "You didn't feed before you went to bed, Maci. I'll tell you what? I want you to feed right now. If you still want to go after you feed, we'll go. I'll figure out how to wake the others then we'll go. Okay?"

His words sounded reasonable. *Yes, I'll be calmer after I*

feed. He extended his neck and I bit down on him, his familiar flavor rushing over my tongue, tasting like mine. Warm and solid. His power rushed through me. I closed my eyes.

A HAND STROKED MY HAIR. "She was hysterical, didn't seem like herself. I think her anxiety was through the roof, very nearly to the point of being frantic," Ace whispered. "I'm not waking her a second before she rouses on her own."

Caesar kissed my cheek. "She's up. Slowly, baby. You did the right thing. No way did anything have to happen at noon, but what the fuck is the matter with me that I didn't wake up? I can't have my girl needing me and not even budge."

"We're baby vampires," Griffin said, looking disgusted with himself as he sighed. "Whatever we're pretending, we're still young. After today, maybe we can rest on a more regular schedule."

I lifted my head. "Thank you, Ace. I was obviously...off."

"It's always going to be my pleasure to take care of you."

I kissed his chin before I moved over to feed Tanner. When I would have given him my neck, he offered his instead. *Really?* I bit down and drank from him without thinking about it too much. I didn't want to drain him, just to give him his voice back. Still, I took a longer minute than I usually would.

When I pulled back and closed the wound, he kissed me on my chin, and then trailed the kiss up to my lips when they were free. "I'm sorry I didn't wake. Next time, just feed from me while I'm asleep. I give you permission, eternal consent."

"I didn't know I needed to feed until Ace told me to do it. Then I suddenly knew, but I still didn't realize how out of it I was."

Tanner smiled at me. "You had to have been starving. We need to know that you have to feed even if you think you don't before bed. Every night. You *have* to feed."

"I think you're right, but for now, I need to go kill the psychos holding up our life. And I feel smart and ready to do it."

"Good." He kissed the end of my nose. "Thank you, Ace," he prompted.

"Yes, thank you, Ace." Rowan hugged him. "My weakness continues to plague me. Daytime is such a problem."

I shook my head. "It turned out I was the one who was off. I don't even know at this point what woke me, but we need to see if our plan is working out. The servants should be heading over there shortly."

"Right." Griffin got off the bed where he had lounged, looking far too gorgeous. He threw me a playful wink. "The next time you wake up in a state, just feed off me. It's fine."

That was absolutely not going to happen. "That just doesn't feel consensual, even with prior permission."

I was pretty sure that if I ever woke up in that state again, I might obey his order anyway. If Ace couldn't help me or couldn't wake up...the whole situation seemed weird, and I didn't like not knowing why it happened.

The drive to check on whether our plan was working took very little time. My father, mother and Ace's father were already there, binoculars trained on the scene below. "Remind me why we sent them in there to let them feed on them again?" My father turned to me. "Oh, and if you intend to throw me under the bus with your mother, a warning in advance would be nice.

"Are we setting up a parental relationship I'm unaware of?" I shrugged, giving him an eye roll. "You dug that hole. Vampires don't lie, but you did for *years*. At least I know where I got that little ability from, too."

Ace's dad laughed. "You realize she's exactly like you."

"I'm starting to," my father answered, his expression torn between amusement and annoyance.

Caesar slid close, his arms wrapping around me from behind as he addressed my father. "Don't ever criticize anything she does. I mean, *ever*. If you do, we're going to have a problem."

I had to bite my lip to resist laughing. His threat was, of course, ridiculous but I loved that he felt that way. Everyone should have someone who thought they were basically perfect in their life to love them. I snuggled further into his embrace. *If only we could just stay like this for a while.*

But there were the servants, and my entire plan, left to consider. "I'm not going to explain any details until things are done. Then I'll fill you in, I promise." I finally answered my father's question. "If you don't like my plan, you're welcome to use your own."

Griff stroked a finger down my cheek. "Ready for what's next?"

I guessed we would see. I had no idea if I was ready, since I'd either be able to do what Griffin told me I could or I wouldn't. In either case, I really preferred our plan over one where I was a prophesied super vampire who came to save them all. I wasn't the scarred-forehead wizard of vampires. Abruptly, I remembered those books, surprised to find a human memory that didn't make me feel horrified for the Maci before. *She really liked to read.*

"Maybe I am ready for what's next." I kept my gaze on the servants. Sure enough, the vampires were feeding. They looked hungry. They'd been kept nice and cushy by Frederick, so it had been a long time since their food didn't just appear in front of them. They had to be so relieved to see their servants arrive.

"About what percentage of them have fed?" I asked, shooting a look at my father. "Hazard a guess."

"Eighty to ninety percent."

That was better than I thought we'd get. The servants should be passing out from blood loss. If I hadn't fed them, they would be. It was a good thing that my father had done that for me for years or I wouldn't have made it through my human years with the feeding I did.

"Okay. I'm going down." An alarm jangled inside of me, telling me it was time. Time to end Frederick and his top followers, then we'd see if there was anything left to save in the others. They'd all been deceived for a long time. If they could get with the new program, they didn't have to die. I wouldn't even be the one making the decision. I'd leave that to the Betrayer, who happened to be my father. He'd been fighting them—albeit for his own reasons—a lot longer than me, after all.

A hand grabbed my arm—my mother. "I told you I'd be here. Even if *someone* tried to fool me about the timing and I almost missed it." She shot my father a disgusted look, and he glared back at her. I could feel the tension of their ongoing fight, and knew it had to be about me and what he had and hadn't done for years. I figured they would work it out one day. It was a soul mate thing; we forgave each other. Even as a baby vampire, I knew that much.

"Thank you," I told my mother. "I'm glad to have you. More than glad. I...I appreciate that you got here despite obstacles as large as the ones my father must have thrown at you."

Her smile was a little wobbly, and I squeezed her finger-tips. We had a lot of work to do to mend our relationship, or maybe build one.

But I had things to say to my guys. Things that I should have said before we left the house. I turned away from her, surprised at the urgency when I didn't even realize I needed to talk to them until that moment.

"Guys, could we talk for a second, please? Follow me over here."

I think my distress must have been in my tone, because they all joined me. Still out of sight from our enemies, I ensured our privacy before I started to speak. "I don't know if this is going to work, and I don't know if they're going to kill me if it fails."

"They won't." Rowan's eyes flared red. "I won't allow it."

He still thought he held some control over the universe. I loved that about him, even if I couldn't believe in it myself. "Okay. Let's hope it doesn't come to that, but if it does, and there is some kind of reincarnation afterward, some sort of choice in all of this...I will always find you. Okay? I will always be yours. This was the best bit of luck in the universe that I found you, and I want to let you know I will always find you."

Ace shot Griffin a look but the other didn't respond. I didn't know what it meant, but I figured they could explain later.

"Don't worry about what you can't control in this," Tanner took my hand. "Just do what you can. We believe you can do this."

My love who could sometimes not find his voice's words still rang in my ears as I walked toward the group forming around Frederick. Vampires were supposed to be so fearless, but I didn't feel brave right then. Instead, I was a girl in way over my head trying to pull off a plan we just threw together. I tried living my life as a human, and they didn't let me. I wasn't asking permission this time. Now I just had to take control and get this man out of my way.

He pushed forward, fury in his eyes. "You."

Well...that was articulate. I could say something but that wasn't the point. It was better to show everyone what I knew they needed to see. It was hard to deny the evidence in front of their eyes. The vampires who couldn't change their minds about him were too far lost. We'd know soon.

My blood beat inside their veins, each and every one of them, even if they didn't know it yet. I'd given it to them. Those I shared my blood with could be manipulated to be affected by my power. I lifted my head to the sky, and I let them in. All of them. The presences I ignored, the ones that sometimes woke me from sleep, both as a human and now as a vampire. I hadn't even realized until that moment what the voices were.

But Griffin had known.

He'd always known.

We carried our ghosts around with us. All of us did. Maci the human lived with them constantly. Fear was her ghost. Loneliness. Uncertainty. As a vampire, I'd always have those, too. Maci the human was one of my ghosts. The memories of those who came before me would also always live in my mind. I could feel all of them. Frederick couldn't feel his, but I could.

I let them *all* in.

Rowan touched my back. It was the last thing I noted before I released them all, freeing them like butterflies hatched from the cocoon of my chest. The memories of all the people Frederick and betrayed and killed, one by one, they flew out of me. I started with the women—most of these men would forever live half-lives because they believed a man who cheerfully killed all the women who could have been their soul mates. He'd done that, and they'd let him. The women who had been killed for carrying girl babies, each life snuffing out and taking love and possibility with them. The women he'd killed because it was funny to him. The women who wanted to be vampires but never would because he'd lied to them.

It wasn't just the women because I also released the memories of the men. Of his followers, who he simply rid himself of because he could. The ones who dared to question him, the ones who got in his way—over and over, I let them see. They thought they were *safe* with him? How foolish! He might have hidden that side of himself, but he couldn't hide it anymore. As I showed the others, he could see himself, too. Every memory wanted to greet him, but they said hello to me instead. I let them have their say with everyone.

The last thing I shared was myself. I showed them my death, the meaningless death of a nothing human. One he tormented and beat until the life was pounded out of her. It wasn't how vampires used to live, nor how they had to live going forward. Those memories I'd been forced to endure came next. The ones of how it could be, when they lived a good life. Powerless in the end, but I wasn't. Didn't the vampires in our time want a chance at something like that? I let them see how Frederick wanted to rape her, how all of it happened because he had been denied by a woman who didn't want to have sex with him.

Finally, I let it go. I panted, sweat beading across my face and neck. I burned a lot of energy, and it wasn't something I ever tried to do before, especially not to that degree. Touches of it, while sharing memories with my guys over the last weeks. "As a human, I was asked to consider a scenario about depleting oxygen. About who deserved to live and who deserved to die. If anyone." That had been another time Griffin knew things. "I don't have room anymore for anyone who thinks this is okay. We're vampires. We love our monsters. We don't let them control the world." I looked at Tanner. He would understand the difference. "The strongest of us know to shut it down if it's too much. Maybe you forgot that, Frederick, but I didn't."

I didn't need matches to set him on fire. I had Rowan and Caesar. Frederick never even saw them coming. Ace lifted him in the air, and Rowan flung him backward. *Why bother with flames outside when I have it inside of me?* The power that I needed welled up.

"You burned her to death. I'll be kinder to you."

As he'd done with the vampire who wanted to kill me when I'd been a human, Griffin staked him. One second Frederick was there, and the next, he was gone.

I turned my head. "All of them."

Rowan grinned at me. "Like your boss?"

"Like my boss." Rowan showed he could do it to a human, so I had no doubt he could handle it with the vampires, too.

There they all were. All the fathers. The ones who tortured my men as children. I wasn't putting up with them anymore.

One by one, they went down. They didn't even try to resist. The memories I sent out changed them all. Struck them, but for some people, it was too late for redemption. It was time they all remembered their humans.

Another gift I can give them.

I closed my eyes. I'd probably be spent afterward, but it

would be worth it. *That's just fucking fine. If I fall, Caesar will catch me. He always does.*

"Maci..." Griffin called my name, and I lifted my eyelids.

"Did I faint?" We were in the back of the car, clearly heading away from the scene I'd just made.

He nodded. "More like collapsed, but it's fine. What you did was impressive as hell. More than I could've imagined, and I gotta confess something to you."

"*Now* he has to confess?" Tanner laughed. "What's the point now?"

"What's that?" I asked and sat up. All the guys were in the car with me.

Griffin admitted, "I lied."

He lied? "Well, we all do. It's okay. The whole *vampires don't lie* thing is nonsense."

"I mean, I lied when I said you weren't prophesized. Of course you were. I made up the rest. You didn't like being destined. The second I told you that you weren't, you did what you were destined to do."

I stared at him. "Griffin."

"I know."

I started to laugh. It was a beautiful night outside, the moon hanging large and orange in the sky. "Stop the car."

"Did you break her?" Caesar asked as we got out of the car, me still clutching my sides in humor. "I don't think she should be laughing about this."

Rowan and Ace were next to me, and Ace rubbed my back. It was the latter who spoke first. "What are we doing out here, Maci?"

A field in front of us swayed heavy with corn, so I walked

toward it. "We're going to be vampires. We won't worry about prophecy right now. I'm hungry, so catch me and let me feed."

With that, I ran like my life depended on it, because it did. The rest of my life. It was Tanner who caught me in seconds, but he threw me to Rowan. Tanner wanted to be his monster for a while yet, which I understood. So did I. And, if Rowan's red glinting gaze was any indication, so did he. I'd deal with Griff's lies some other time. I wasn't a destiny.

I was a vampire named Maci, and I just won.

It was time for blood. *My trials are over.*

ABOUT THE AUTHOR

As a teenager, I would hide in my room to read my favorite romance novels when I was supposed to be doing my homework.

I am the mother of three adorable boys and I am fortunate to be married to my best friend. I live in Austin Texas where I am determined to eat all the barbecue in town.

I am in love with science fiction, fantasy, and the paranormal and try to use all of these elements in my writing. I've been told I'm a little bloodthirsty so I hope that when you read my work you'll enjoy the action packed ride that always ends in romance. I love to write series because I love to see characters develop over time and it always makes me happy to see my favorite characters make guest appearances in other books.

In my world anything is possible, anything can happen, and you should suspect that it will.

I'd love to hear from you! Please visit my website at www.rebeccaroyce.com to sign up for my newsletter and learn about my books!

Here's where you can find me online:

Rebecca's Randomness Reading Group https://www.facebook.com/groups/RebeccasRandomness/

https://www.rebeccaroyce.com

https://www.facebook.com/authorrebeccaroyce/

www.twitter.com/rebeccaroyce

Instagram: rebeccaroyce79
Cheers!!
Rebecca

OTHER BOOKS BY REBECCA ROYCE...

Contemporary Romance

Redheads:

Redhead on the Run

Redheaded Redemption

Real Men Love Redheads (coming soon)

Reverse Harem Story (completed series)

Unconventional

Unexpected

Undeniable

Kiss Her Goodbye (completed series)

Hard Truths

Dark Truths

Deadly Truths

Stupid Boys (writing with C.R. Jane)

Stupid Boys

Dumb Girl

Crazy Love (coming soon)

Science Fiction Romance:

Wings of Artemis (completed series)

Kidnapped By Her Husbands

Rescued by Their Wife

Crashing Into Destiny

Meeting Them

Reclaiming Their Love

Loving Them

Ship Called Malice

Saving Them

Dark Demise

Light Unfolding

Still Waters

Rising Tides

Lost Star

Pointed Arrow

Super Soldiers

Uncivilized (coming soon)

Illicit Minds

Illicit Senses

Illicit Connections

Illicit Alliance (coming soon)

Shifter World

Planet Bear

Planet Cat

Planet Wolf (coming soon)

Heart of the Nebula (writing with Heather Long)

Queenmaker

Endless

Wards and Wands (completed series)

Hexed and Vexed

Curse Reversed

Meow, Baby (novella, co-written with Ripley Proserpina)

Tragic Magic

Why Yes, There are Witches (novella)

Safe Haven

Everywhere and Nowhere

Dimension X (coming soon)

More coming soon....

Soul Bound

Prisoner of the Dragons

More coming soon....

Shadow Promised

Strange Days

Weird Nights

Bizarre Years

More coming soon...

The Westervelt Wolves (completed series)

Her Wolf

Summer's Wolf

Wolf Reborn

Wolf's Valentine

Wolf's Magic

Alpha Wolf

Angel's Wolf

Darkest Wolf

Lone Wolf

Fallen Alpha

Alpha Rising

Alpha's Strength

Alpha's Sacrifice

Alpha's Truth

Alpha Enticing

Hidden Alpha (coming soon)

Cascade (completed series)

Haunted Redemption

Phoenix Everlasting

Fragility Unearthed

Persuasion Enraptured

The Swamp Princess (completed series)

Hidden

Pursued

Caught

The Coveted (writing with Ripley Proserpina)

Eyes in the Darkness

Voices in the Darkness

Return to the Darkness

Prison Princess (part of the Prison Princess world, writing with CoraLee June)

Young Adult/New Adult Urban Fantasy/Post-Apocalyptic:

The Warrior (completed series)

Initiation

Driven

Subversive

Redemption

Justice

Warrior World (spin off of The Warrior, completed series)

Deacon

Micah

Jason

Fantasy Romance:

Life of the Chosen

The Ritual (coming soon)

The Storm (writing with Ripley Proserpina) **completed series.**

Lightning Strikes

Thunder Rolling

The Deluge

Addalee Ackers

The Hunted (coming soon)

Stand Alone Titles